P9-BZR-054

Reluctant Runaway

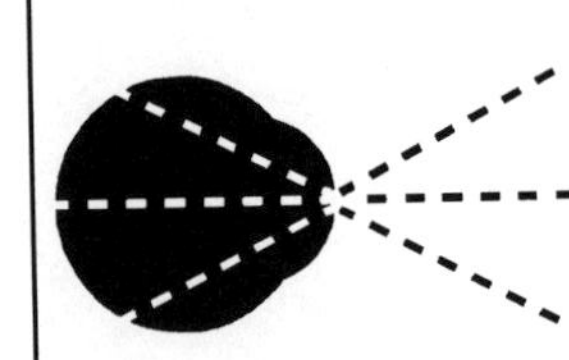

This Large Print Book carries the
Seal of Approval of N.A.V.H.

TO CATCH A THIEF, BOOK TWO

RELUCTANT RUNAWAY

JILL ELIZABETH NELSON

THORNDIKE PRESS
A part of Gale, Cengage Learning

Detroit • New York • San Francisco • New Haven, Conn • Waterville, Maine • London

GALE
CENGAGE Learning™

Thorndike Press, a part of Gale, Cengage Learning.

Thorndike Press® Large Print Christian Fiction.
The text of this Large Print edition is unabridged.
Other aspects of the book may vary from the original edition.
Set in 16 pt. Plantin.
Printed on permanent paper.

LIBRARY OF CONGRESS CATALOGING-IN-PUBLICATION DATA

Nelson, Jill Elizabeth.
Reluctant runaway / by Jill Elizabeth Nelson.
p. cm. — (To catch a thief series ; bk. 2) (Thorndike Press large print Christian fiction)
ISBN-13: 978-1-4104-2127-2 (alk. paper)
ISBN-10: 1-4104-2127-9 (alk. paper)
1. Missing persons—Fiction. 2. Art thieves—Fiction. 3. Large type books. I. Title.
PS3614.E44585R457 2010
813'.6—dc22 2009041241

Published in 2010 by arrangement with Multnomah Books, an imprint of Crown Publishing Group, a division of Random House, Inc.

Printed in Mexico
1 2 3 4 5 6 7 14 13 12 11 10

To all the runaways out there.
Please come home.
The porch light's on,
and the door's always open
at God's house.

ACKNOWLEDGMENTS

No author is an island. It takes a community to make a book. This one is no exception. Many thanks go out to my supportive family and friends who took my occasional neglect of them in stride and cheered me on as I hunched over my laptop, engrossed in Desi and Tony's world. Of course my faithful critique buddies get kudos. What would I do without you, Linda Wichman, Donita K. Paul, Sharon Hinck, and Virginia Smith? You bless my world! Humble gratitude to Brian Kendig, Buddy McLemore, and Chris Wilson for offering their expertise in computer security to an inquisitive writer — and to my police procedure expert, Madison Police Chief Stan Ross. Any errors are mine, not theirs. Much appreciation to the friendly citizens of Albuquerque for welcoming me during my visit to their beautiful and fascinating community. And thank you, thank you, thank you to Julee Schwarzburg and Karen Ball, a pair of the finest editors on the planet. You illuminated my path and set my feet on solid ground. To all the kind and dedicated staff at Multnomah, I consider myself privileged to work with you. And thanks be to my Lord Jesus Christ, the author and finisher of my faith — and my dream to become a published novelist.

AUTHOR'S NOTE

While I am aware that security companies do not normally make a business practice of staging thefts, it is a possible scenario and makes for fun fiction. The Tate Art Gallery of Washington DC is fictitious. The New Mexico Museum of Art and Anthropology is a composite of what is available in charming Albuquerque, but the Georgia O'Keeffe Museum is an actual place in Santa Fe. The O'Keeffe painting that draws Desi's attention is fictional — don't look for it anywhere. Cannibalism among the ancient Anasazi is a debated possibility. For an excellent article on the controversy, see http://news.nationalgeographic.com/news/2001/06/0601_wireanasazi.html.

This is how you can recognize the Spirit of God: Every spirit that acknowledges that Jesus Christ has come in the flesh is from God, but every spirit that does not acknowledge Jesus is not from God. This is the spirit of the antichrist, which you have heard is coming and even now is already in the world. You, dear children, are from God and have overcome them, because the one who is in you is greater than the one who is in the world.

1 JOHN 4:2–4

Many deceivers, who do not acknowledge Jesus Christ as coming in the flesh, have gone out into the world. Any such person is the deceiver and the antichrist.

2 JOHN 1:7

Prologue

The young mother bent over the crib rail, and her tear fell onto her sleeping son's cheek. The scents of formula, baby powder, and newborn filled her nostrils. Pain seared her heart.

She straightened and stared down at the child. Her tiny son whiffled a sigh. The sound spoke of contentment. Of trust.

A sob broke from the mother's throat.

I can't do this to my baby. My husband. I can't!

You must!

The woman jerked a step back from the crib. Of course, she must.

But they'll never understand, she whined to that dark, driving voice within.

No answer. Just the dull dread that had clouded her days for so long that she couldn't remember when she was last happy. Free.

Free? Who was ever free?

She thought she'd found a miracle — a new beginning. But she'd messed up again, and now she had to fix the problem.

Her hands fisted, nails chewing her palms. She took one more look at her sleeping child and absorbed the sight into the deepest part of her being. A cry rose in her throat, but she stifled the sound. Feeling sorry for herself had never earned her better than a kick when she was down. Well, this time she wouldn't stay down.

And people would pay.

The woman left the room and strode up the hallway into the tiny foyer. From an entry table, she picked up her scuffed purse and hugged it close. The hard lump inside the bag pressed into her stomach. Her pulse fluttered. How far was she willing to go to take what she needed? She'd never done anything like this before. She set the purse down and stared at it as if the bag harbored a tarantula.

Swallowing a lump, she opened the door and stepped out onto the weed-tufted lawn. The Albuquerque sunshine touched her skin, but she felt no warmth. The dry breeze carried the scent of chilies cooking in neighbors' houses. A dear, ordinary world.

A place she didn't belong anymore.

Several blocks down, a lone car turned

onto the quiet street. The breath snagged in the woman's lungs. She knew that vehicle.

Fighting fear, the woman staggered back inside and reached for her weapon.

One

September night pressed in on Desiree Jacobs like an urgent warning. She shrugged the unease away. Flexing rubber-soled feet, she fixed her gaze on the brick wall half a dozen yards ahead. Under her Mylar jumpsuit, sweat trickled down her ribs.

E-e-easy. This little jaunt was no different than a trip across the balance beam at the gym, a move she'd practiced for twenty-two of her thirty years. Except no thick mat waited a few feet away to soften a fall. Only ten stories of empty air. A single misstep off the steel girder and she'd make a nice Impressionist splat on the pavement of the alley below.

Then Max can attend *another* funeral.

Desi sighed. *All right, girlfriend, you win. Bungee cord it is.* She took a step backward onto the roof behind her. Amazing how easy it had been to get into this co-op apartment building next to the exclusive Tate Art Gallery of Washington DC. Delivering pizzas opened doors fast. Must be the hypnotic smell of sausage and pepperoni.

Desi knelt beside her discarded delivery uniform. She stripped off her backpack, then pulled out the bungee cord and clipped an end to the harness around her torso. The other end went around a pipe sticking out of the roof.

Lifting her arms, Desi stepped back onto the beam. Just *try* to keep her away from that American artist collection. She took a step, then one more, toes outward, heel to instep. *And this step is for the Cassatt.* She moved forward. *And this one for the Savage. And this one for Grandma Moses.* She hopped and switched foot positions. *Expect me soon, Andy Warhol.*

At midbeam she stopped and looked up at the sky. One plump star winked at her. If Tony could see her, he'd have a cow. She winked back at the star. What an overprotective FBI agent boyfriend didn't know couldn't hurt him.

Desi adjusted the backpack straps around her shoulders. She quick-stepped forward, one step back, then a trio of toe-steps forward. And those were for the three Georgia O'Keeffe's. *I'm coming, darlings.*

The tenth-story ledge of the Tate Gallery

building loomed close. She smelled the brick cooling from the heat of the Indian summer day.

Almost there. Almost . . . *Yesss!*

Her breath came strong and even. She knelt on the two-foot ledge and glanced back at the wide-open space she'd conquered. The girder formed the only remaining connection between buildings that once shared a roof support system. A handy choice of approach under cover of night.

She shrugged out of her pack and unhooked the bungee cord. Good riddance.

By feel, Desi located her narrow-beam flashlight and trained the glow on the window in front of her. The pane was an unimpressive standard thickness, and the wood frame showed weather wear. Desi kneaded gloved fingers together.

Where were the booby traps?

Her gaze stopped on a slim white sensor strip across the inside of the sash. Even a trained eye could miss that one. Any tampering with the frame, and alarms would shriek loud enough to startle a poor unsuspecting burglar right off the ledge.

Desi gulped and peered downward. The ground was there, in the blank darkness, hard and unforgiving. Cold sparks skittered up her spine.

She stiffened her jaw. No way was that a premonition. She pursed her lips at the window. What about cutting the pane? Nope. A web of hair-fine wire covered the glass, not obstructing the view of the drab roof opposite, but any slice would end in handcuffs for the window surgeon. Nuh-uh! She didn't need *those* bracelets.

Time to find another way in. And in a hurry. Tony would snort and paw if she wasn't ready on time for the White House Midnight Masquerade. Besides, she couldn't afford to give him explanations.

Rising, she hefted the pack in her right hand and pressed the left side of her body against the building. She swept the flashlight beam ahead of her on the ledge. All clear. She lifted her foot and then halted midmotion. Indrawn breath hissed between her teeth.

Idiot!

Planting her foot back where it started, she panned the light up the wall. Sure enough. Stubby plastic-coated sensor rods stuck out from the brick at irregular intervals — no slipping around, between, or under these babies. A broken rod or an attempt to remove one from its socket released an ultrasonic frequency that tripped an alarm, and voilà, one bagged burglar.

So where did that leave her? She frowned. With a sackful of goodies and no place to go, except . . .

She looked down and smiled.

Chuckling, Desi set a grappling hook in the chink between the ledge and the window and then clipped the end of the rope to her torso harness. Lying on her stomach, she turned and flipped her feet into open space. She balanced on the rim of the ledge, abdomen muscles and extended arms bearing her weight as if she were about to start a routine on the uneven bars. The bottoms of her feet sought and found the wall below.

Blood pumping, she pushed away from the ledge. The tether flowed with steady friction through her gloved fists. Piece of cake. Just a few smooth hops and —

Cra-a-ack!

Desi's line jerked. Bits of debris bounced off her head and shoulders. Her feet lost purchase. In free swing, her body rammed the wall, spurting a grunt from her throat. Pain shot through her shoulders and hips. She dug her fingers and toes into the chinks between the bricks and went still — except for her heart, which threatened to backflip right out of her chest.

Below, muted smacks taunted her ears — cement chunks bursting against pavement.

Her imagination went into overdrive, picturing the landing should her body take a similar dive.

Stop it! Think. You can beat this.

A portion of the ledge above had given way. The stress of the hook and her weight must have been too much for the aged cement. Thank goodness the ledge hadn't crumbled beneath her while she knelt by the window.

Now, any wrong movement . . .

She sucked in a breath. She needed a better hold on the brick. Reluctant to disturb so much as an air molecule, she slid a finger over . . . another . . . another. *Oops!*

A toe slipped. Her weight shifted. She jammed the foot back in tight, gritting her teeth against a yelp. Her big toe had felt better after a collision with the bedpost in the dark.

Snap! Scra-a-a-ape . . .

The tether line went limp. Desi held her breath.

The grappling hook remained aloft, but the sounds from above indicated that it must have pulled free and now rested, without anchor, on what was left of the crumbling ledge. If the hook plunged downward, the weight would pull Desi from her precarious hold on the brick.

Great! Where's an angel when you need one?

Rotten cement on the ledges hadn't figured into her calculations. That was the two-edged sword when owners insisted on locating art galleries in charming but antiquated facilities, which left them vulnerable to intruders but created unintended death traps for thieves.

Trust.

Okay, that thought hadn't come from *her* mind, but it was right. Time to stop relying on her own resources. Hadn't the past months taught her a thing?

All right, I'm busted, Lord. Again. What's our next move?

No angelic chorus answered her plea with divine instructions. Desi sighed. Her breath fanned the brick in shaky drafts. Her cheek stung, pressed against the rough surface. Her fingers started to cramp, and her leg muscles ached. She couldn't hang on much longer.

Should she try to climb up toward a ledge that she knew was brittle and crumbling or risk moving down toward the lip at the next floor, its condition an unknown quantity? The latter option could pull the grappling hook off the ledge above before she reached the doubtful security of the next level, and she'd join the smashed pieces on the ground.

Let go.

Of all the kooky ideas . . . Wait . . . maybe . . .

Desi licked her lips, mouth as dry as the cement flakes that powdered her shoulder.

All right, what if she let go and performed a calculated fall onto the next ledge? She would need to hit leaning into the building. The impact might breach the cement if its condition was as unstable as the ledge above. Then again, the lip might hold her, and she'd be in a firm position when — not if — the grappling hook tumbled from above. Was the lower ledge strong enough to withstand the impact of her falling body? God knew.

Okay, Lord, I have to trust Your wisdom. Here goes!

Desi released her hold and left her stomach behind. Terror clawed up her throat and came out in a strangled gurgle.

The impact shuddered through her bones. She folded her knees forward, throwing her body sideways. Air woofed from her lungs. Cement fragments pelted her from overhead just as the grappling hook plummeted toward her then past into the darkness. Her harness jerked, tugging her toward the edge of her perch. She came to a halt with one shoulder hovering over thin air.

Clink . . . clink . . . clink . . . clink . . . clink . . .

The sound of the metal hook bouncing off the building ticked off seconds. Desi's brain fought to regain focus. *Thank You, Abba Father!* She lay where she had landed and enjoyed each breath. A giddy laugh bubbled from her throat.

Next move? Get her scraped and sore self inside, alarm or no alarm. Well, better *without* the alarm. Now that she'd risked this much, she ought to taste the victory, even if she *was* starring in this little caper as a bad guy who ought to lose.

Desi sat up. A few feet away a window beckoned, and really, she couldn't have fallen more than a few feet. Things often weren't as terrible as they looked. Then again, sometimes they were worse — like with Max's situation.

Max's husband, Dean Webb, was cooling his heels in jail while his two small children were left bewildered by their daddy's sudden disappearance from their lives. How would Max ever be able to help them understand what their father had done for greed?

Fury clotted in Desi's stomach. Too bad they quit clapping criminals into public stocks. Give her a dump truck full of rotten vegetables to fling and —

Whoa! She'd promised herself and God to work on her forgiveness skills.

Better concentrate on encouraging Max. Maybe she should let her best friend and treasured employee win this one.

Yeah. Right. Lip curled, Desi imitated Maxine Webb's West Texas drawl. "In a pig's eye!"

Her flame-haired friend would skin her alive with a dull knife if she suspected that Desi hadn't done her best to beat Max's precautions. They had an internal audit on their work. If Desi could navigate through the safeguards the same way a thief would — no cheating — they'd keep working on the plan until it was Desi-proof. No exceptions. Their bread and butter came from keeping HJ Securities Company the best in the business of art and antiquities protection.

Of course, the timing for this caper could have been better. If the gallery hadn't insisted on moving their grand opening up to the day after tomorrow, she wouldn't be stuck on a crumbling ledge on the same night she was due at a White House party.

Desi climbed to her knees, pulled the grappling hook up, and secured it in her pack. Scoping out the window, she found it booby trap–free. She dug out her cutting tool and made a neat hole in the glass. A specialty hook probed inside, and the interior lock clicked open.

The slither between lintel and sash tested every scrape and bruise on her body, but at last Desi stood on cushy carpet inside some executive's office. She took a few steps on wobbly knees, nerves still doing the boogie-woogie. A fat leather office chair beckoned. She collapsed into it, leaned back, and perched her feet on the desk. Her right big toe throbbed.

Small price to pay.

She dug a water bottle out of the pack on her lap and took a long pull. As she lowered the bottle, her gaze met the lighted face of the desk clock. Her feet thumped to the floor. Scrambling through her bag of tricks, she found her walkie-talkie.

"Max, do you read me? I'm in, and I'm in a hurry."

The instrument crackled. "You're in where? In trouble? That I can believe." Male hoots sounded in the background. "You have a little more than an hour to get ready for that society shindig with Tony. Now tell me where you're stuck, and I'll send the cavalry after you."

More background guffaws.

Wouldn't the night guards love to brag to their buddies about how they rescued the high-toned security woman from a pickle? Well, not tonight, boys. "I'm sitting in a ninth-floor office, looking at the clock."

"Get outta here! No *way* you breached that window security."

"Way! But take heart, no one else will be loony enough to follow in my footsteps."

"Do I even want to know?"

Desi laughed. "I'll explain later. Right now, I do have to get outta here pronto. Tomorrow night we can pick up where we left off, and you'll have your chance to nab me in the gallery showrooms."

Low-voiced grumbles answered her, foreground and background.

Grinning, Desi switched off the walkie-talkie and loped — er, *limped* for the elevator.

If Supervisory Special Agent Anthony Lucano of the Boston office of the Federal Bureau of Investigation wanted to walk into the White House ballroom with her on his arm, she didn't intend to disappoint him. And she sure didn't want him to catch a whiff of her derring-do tonight. That would be asking for trouble in paradise.

■ ■ ■ ■

Clad in nothing but her shower towel, Desi brushed a final stroke of genuine Egyptian kohl onto her left eyelid. An awkward activity with one hand, but Max had the other trapped on the bathroom vanity counter, doing a warp-speed job on Desi's fingernails.

Good thing her shoulder-length hairstyle was wash-and-go. All she needed with her costume was the gemstone-studded headdress. The attached set of false bangs matched her sable-brown hair. She lifted the piece from the hotel bathroom vanity and held it to her head. The bangles dripping from the sides swayed and sparkled, highlighting the shades of green and gold in her hazel eyes.

Ooooh, Tony was gonna love this.

Max glanced up from her bent-over position. "Give me a sec, and I'll pin that on."

Desi set the headdress down and picked up one of a set of amber hairpins that had belonged to the mother she'd lost to a car accident when she was a baby. Her father, world-renowned security expert Hiram Jacobs, gave the pins and other jewelry heirlooms to Desi shortly before his murder four months and two days ago.

Daddy, did you already know you were a target?

Her vision darkened. To lose a parent in an accident hurt, even though she'd been too young to remember. To have one stolen by a killer . . .

Hot pain seared through her insides.

"Hey! Hold still." Max clicked her tongue. "What have you done to your fingertips? Looks like you lost a fight with a blackboard."

"A brick wall. And I won."

"Ai-yi-yi!" Max screwed the top on the polish bottle. "Let's get you into that neck-snappin' dress. One look at the Queen of Sheba and the guy'll need a brain transplant to think straight."

Desiree laughed. If only she could cheer Max up so easily. "Better not distract him too much. The poor man wants his gray matter working. The director of the FBI will be there, and Tony's got a sweat on to make a good impression for his office. Budget time and all that."

Max lifted a corner of her mouth. "He could stand on his head and whistle Dixie. He's got to be flavor of the year after haulin' in a top al Qaeda operative, alive and kickin'."

"You'd be surprised how fast such things are forgotten in Washington. But it's significant that his office chose an agent who's only thirty-five and just climbing into supervisory level to attend such a highbrow function. He's getting favorable notice, all right."

In a flurry of fabric, Desi let Max help her into the shimmering emerald gown of watered silk. The high-waisted style copied Anne Baxter's costume when she played Nefretiri in Cecille B. DeMille's tour de force *The Ten Commandments.*

"Sit down by the table, and we'll add the crownin' touch." Max waved the headdress.

Desi saluted and took a seat. Fingers played in her hair, not once jabbing her scalp with a fastener.

"A fine piece of work if I do say so myself." Max stepped back. Then she knelt and picked up the shoes that matched Desi's gown.

"Hey, you don't have to treat me like Cinderella. I can put those on myself." Desi snatched at the footwear.

Max avoided her and grabbed Desi's right heel. "As I thought. You've got a big toe turnin' black-and-blue."

"I swear I'll tell all when we've got time." Desi bent the digit and winced. "At least I chose to wear the Persian slippers instead of the strappy sandals."

Max sniffed. "You'll have to throw in a funky hip sway to convince anyone that your limp is a fashion statement."

"Call me Forrest Gump."

"Run, Forrest, run!" Max chuckled like her old self.

Desi would take ten jammed toes to get another reaction like that.

Feet encased in the slippers, she rose and Betty Boop–wiggled across the room. She glanced over her shoulder. Max lay on the floor, clutching her sides and wheezing.

Man, she's lost weight. Max used to fit the cliché *pleasingly plump.* Now . . .

They'd talk about it later. "How's that?" She batted the false eyelashes that made her lids feel sultry.

"Works . . . for me . . . You'll just have to . . . fool Tony."

Not going to happen. The man was born with an extra set of eyes and trained to use them. She'd have to fess up sooner or later. Later would be fine. He hated when she walked into danger. Ironic. Considering his occupation, she's the one who should lecture about risks.

"I wish you were going along tonight." She helped Max up.

“Why? So I can distract the big boy from your bad deeds?”

Desi stuck out her tongue. “No, so you can get out of this hotel for something besides work. We’re in the capital of the U.S. of A. for crying out loud.”

“Like we’ve never been here before?”

A chill breathed over the room. Their eyes met. Too true. They’d shared the same glass of fear and loathing on the trail of Hiram Jacobs’s murderer.

Max began to pick up discarded clothes. “I need to call home and find out how Mom’s doin’ with the kids. When I called this mornin’, she told me Grandpa Steve was comin’ over to take them out to a matinee.”

She bracketed the words “Grandpa Steve” with two pairs of finger swipes. They grinned at each other.

“The Lord has a colossal sense of humor.” Desi laughed. “Who’d have thought Tony’s Godzilla of an ex-partner would take a shine to a pair of little kids? Even kids as cute as yours. That bullet in the chest must have been a wake-up call for the Man with the Iron Heart.”

Max shook her head. “He’s been a miracle for us, steppin’ in when . . .” She cleared her throat and went back to housekeeping.

A rap sounded at the door.

"Showtime!" Max opened the door with a flourish.

Tony's tall frame filled the entrance. Desi's breath quivered in her throat. *Oh, mercy!* King Solomon never looked so fine.

Who would have guessed she'd swoon over her twenty-first-century agent-man in a beard and Middle Eastern robes? The Hebrew amulet that hung from a chain around his neck matched the color scheme of her headdress. Max must have advised him on that. An understated gold circlet framed wavy black hair cut too short to be period perfect. But who cared?

Desi stepped forward. A white smile split the dark beard. His brown eyes widened into a stare that set a pedestal under her feet and turned her limbs to warm taffy so she could tumble off her exalted perch straight into his arms.

Max smirked, and Desi could almost hear her thought — *Neck-snappin', oh yeah!*

Tony stepped over the threshold, his thoughts also clear. By sheer willpower, Desi put a hand on his chest and stopped him.

"Rain check." Her voice came out husky. "My lipstick looks better on me for now."

His muscled ribs expanded under her palm, then relaxed. Tony smiled and offered his arm. Desi curled a hand around his elbow, and they paraded past a grinning Max into the hall.

"Have fun, kiddies."

Tony lifted a hand in a backward wave.

Desi glanced at her friend. *Thank you,* she mouthed. Then she looked up at the man beside her. Way up. The top of her head broke even with his square shoulder. The sharp planes of his profile made him more a rough-hewn Marlon Brando than a refined Robert Redford. She inhaled a deep breath of her date's sandalwood scent.

Tony chuckled as they neared the elevator. "I intend to collect on that rain check."

"And I intend to let you."

His gaze darted toward the floor and then back to her face. "Are you hurt?"

Drat, the man was sharp. "Close encounter with a wall in the dark."

Tony's sideways glance promised more than a heated embrace. She knew that set to his jaw. He meant to worm the facts out of her or eat his badge.

Let the battle of wits begin. Desi grinned on the inside. When she was with him, even if she lost she won. If they weren't both committed to respecting each other and God, they'd be deep into a torrid, steamy affair by now. Maybe someday they could have a torrid, steamy marriage.

Desi's cheeks heated, and she turned her face as they entered the empty elevator. There she went, thinking the *M* word again. Mere months ago, she and Tony had been adversaries. Then they became allies. Now much more. But she couldn't assume he wanted a permanent commitment. Besides, she still knew little about him — except that she adored him. The guy was an expert at avoiding personal topics, about himself, that is. For sure, they had things to work on.

The *M* word could wait.

Tony's arm circled her waist, and he lifted her chin, a knowing crook to his mouth. She narrowed her eyes. Should she slap away the smirk or yank off his crown and muss his hair?

He nuzzled the tender skin under her left ear. "A little something to tide me over."

His false beard tickled, and the air in Desi's lungs turned to helium.

"You smell great." Tony lifted his head, dark gaze intense. He rubbed the side of her jaw with his thumb. "You know you drive me nuts figuring out what crazy business you've been up to."

So he'd guessed she'd done a caper tonight. Too bad she couldn't promise never again to take chances. He'd have to accept her for who she was and what she did for a living, or they wouldn't make it as a couple.

He smiled, laugh lines creasing his tanned face. "You couldn't shake me off your trail before, my queen. And you won't succeed now."

Desi stood a few feet away and studied Tony as he visited with Director Richard Harcourt of the FBI and a senior presidential aide. The director made a formidable Roman Emperor Constantine and the aide a dapper George Washington.

"They're grooming him," said a voice in her ear.

Desi turned to meet the amused hazel eyes of a blunt-mannered man she'd met at the hors d'oeuvres table. His massive build and shiny moon face fit a Jabba the Hutt impersonation better than the Darth Vader costume.

"Hamilton Gordon?"

The man nodded double chins. "Very good, my dear. Almost as skilled as a federal agent at matching faces and names. The talent will serve you well if you're going to stick with him all the way to the top." He inclined his blond head toward Tony's group. "I own a corporation, and I know the signs when the powers-that-be have plans for someone." He winked.

Desi's gaze darted to the group of men. Did the director have an acquisitive gleam in his eye? Constantine put a hand on Solomon's shoulder, and the king leaned toward the emperor. Director Harcourt stood inches shorter, but no observer with a grain of sense could misinterpret the picture of a superior showing interest in his subordinate — except someone too distracted by the flutters of her heart. She'd missed the obvious.

What did this development mean? To her? To Tony? Her roots, not to mention the headquarters of her business, were in Boston. Comprehension sent gooseflesh up her bare arms. An FBI agent didn't control his destiny. Tony could be transferred to the Washington office, the most coveted post in the Bureau, in a heartbeat. But the professional coup would mean a long-distance romance for them. The odds of such a romance lasting were dismal, especially when half of the couple thought communication was a one-way street.

Her stomach clenched.

As if sensing her turmoil, Tony whirled, but his stare went past her shoulder. Desi looked around. Hamilton Gordon was gone. A red-eyed Max staggered toward them, face pale, freckles standing out like pepper in porridge.

"Max!"

"T-trouble," her friend croaked and crumpled forward.

Two

Tony dashed past Desi's open-mouthed stare just as Max went down. For a second he thought he was too late, but he managed to catch Desi's friend before she hit the floor.

Desi knelt beside him. "Oh, Max!"

"Bring the woman this way."

Tony looked up to find the White House aide standing over them. "George Whitcomb as George Washington," the guy had said when he introduced himself. Tony hefted Max and stood up. He took two steps, and a fist slammed his shoulder. He looked down.

Max's face glowed like a fire engine. "Put me down, you lummox! People are starin'."

"They're staring because you fainted."

"Texans don't faint."

"Then you did a world-class imitation." He set her on her feet.

"Tony-y-y, how can you be so cold?" Desi

scooted by, glaring.

"Hey, I'm the one who caught —"

She skewered him with her eyes, then turned her back on him and hugged her friend. The women buried their faces on each other's shoulders.

Desi and Max whispered together. Something was off here. Not because one wore the kind of dress over the sort of figure that made a man forget his name and the other crashed the party in a sweatshirt, blue jeans, and furry bedroom slippers. Get a load of those!

But no, that wasn't the issue. It'd take total chaos to send down-to-earth Maxine Webb into hysterics and do-or-die Desi into shock.

Tony stepped forward, but Whitcomb/Washington swooped in and herded the women toward a door. The ladies went without argument. Tony followed, invited or not. The aide took them to a small room furnished with a sofa and a couple of stuffed chairs.

The white-wigged aide waved toward the furniture. "Shall we all sit?" He might be a pompous little housefly, but he had a way with social crises.

Desi settled Max onto the sofa. The redhead doubled over and rocked back and forth. Bits of phrases reached Tony's ears.

"I can't handle this . . . not again . . . family curse . . ."

The Queen of Sheba beamed at the pseudo first president of the United States. "May we have a moment? We have a few things to sort out here."

"Yes, of course. Not a problem." The aide cast a glance at Tony. He frowned back. King Solomon was *not* about to budge.

Desi nodded in Tony's direction. "He can stay."

Nice of her.

"Very good." Whitcomb/Washington dipped his head and went to the door. A Secret Service agent Tony hadn't noticed before stepped from the shadows.

The aide leaned toward him. ". . . breach of security. Find out how . . ." The men slipped away.

Sooner or later, pointed questions would come. Wild-eyed women in street clothes didn't barge into a White House bash without knocking the pins out from under everyone.

Max sat huddled, silent now. Desi stared at her with a helpless expression.

Desiree Jacobs helpless? Anger spurted. Whatever caused the problem wasn't acceptable. He'd have to fix it.

She looked up at him. "In the ballroom, Max told me she got some bad news tonight. A loss in her family —"

Ice bit his gut. "Not one of the kids!"

"No, but it involves a —"

"I'll tell." Max sat up, tears streaking her face. "I acted like a nut coming here, but I couldn't think . . ." She shook her head. "I didn't know who else I could trust. Just you two."

That trust sat heavy. Max had been through a lot. Enough to cure most people of trusting anybody.

The Texan pressed her hands to her cheeks. "I kept sayin' to myself, 'If I can get to Desi and Tony, everything will be all right.' But that was silly." Her green eyes dulled. "No one can fix this. It's a family curse. I thought I'd ducked the disaster, but it got me. And now my niece has run off, leavin' a baby . . ." Max's voice broke. "Her four-month-old son is without a mama, and her husband has no clue where his wife is."

Tony frowned. Nice wad of information. But that "family curse" thing?

"Curse!" Desi plopped down beside Max. "What kind of hoodoo are you talking?"

"Oh, not some horror flick stuff." The redhead slumped. "This thing is a bitter joke with us. We call our track record with marriage 'the family curse.' "

Tony narrowed his eyes. "The rate of failed marriages is around 50 percent. How far off is your family?"

"With my niece's disappearance? Try 100 percent. Dean and I used to be an exception, but now I don't have a marriage except in name. Everyone else is widowed or divorced, sometimes more than once. Same song, second verse, for generations."

Tony whistled. If he were hot on a case, he'd call that consistency a strong chain of evidence. But evidence of what? He sat in a chair by the sofa. "Start from the beginning, and give us —"

"— the facts, ma'am, nothing but the facts."

Tony shot her a look. Guys had a few "looks" in their arsenal, too. Desi clamped her mouth shut; Max gave a husky chuckle. The mood in the room lightened. Probably Desi's intention. Smart lady.

The smile faded from Max's face. "Here's the scoop then." She folded her hands on her lap like a witness on the stand. "I was in bed, and the phone rang around midnight. No problem. I wasn't asleep. Not unusual these days." Her gaze lowered. "But I wondered who'd call at that hour. Thought maybe it was you or Des, but it was my sister Jo from Albuquerque, bawlin' her eyes out." Max moaned. "I hurt so ba-a-ad for her."

Okay, derail the tears and get back on track. "So Jo's daughter is gone?"

"Right. Her name is Karen, Jo's only child. I've prayed hard over that girl. She used to run with a rough crowd, an outlaw motorcycle gang. Then she met Brent Webb. He coaxed her to visit his church singles group. She found a new bunch of friends, broke away from the gang, put her life in the Lord's hands, married Brent, and —"

"Wait just a New York second!" Desi sounded as confused as he felt. "Is this Dean's brother Brent Webb?"

Max nodded.

"Your niece is married to your husband's brother?" Desi's voice rose a notch.

"It's not illegal or immoral." Max glared.

Desi shook her head. "No, but a tad on the odd side. How come you never told me?"

Max's stiffness melted. "I meant to. You were out of the country on that Madrid job when this whirlwind romance grafted the family trees. By the time you got home, the elopement wasn't at the top of my mind anymore. Then things got crazy with the FBI castin' suspicions on HJ Securities about art theft and . . ." Max shrugged.

Tony rubbed his chin. "You say your niece ran off, but you've also termed it a disappearance. Did your niece leave of her own accord, or is foul play suspected?"

"The police don't know *what* to think. Karen's purse is gone, but all her clothes are hangin' in the closet. Their clunker of a second car is missin', but the baby was still in his crib. How could any mother run off and leave her newborn alone in the house?"

No answer he cared to share on that one. He'd seen too much of the seamy side. "If she left on her own, why would she have done it? Do you blame yourself?"

Desi stared at him like he'd lost his mind, but tears flowed down Max's face.

"You think the scandal about Dean wrecked your niece's marriage." He made his words a conclusion, not a question.

Max hugged herself. "I don't know. Maybe our mess gave someone . . . ideas." Her voice came out muddy. "I can't take this again." She dropped her arms to her sides. "Maybe Dean's family has a curse, too. Native American artifacts were stolen from the New Mexico Museum of Art and Anthropology, and a guard is in the hospital. Karen and Brent are suspects. She's a receptionist, and he's an archaeology graduate student interning at the museum. Her running off seems suspicious to the police. And if she didn't run . . . if she was taken . . . it still looks as if she knew —"

A movement caught Tony's eye, and shock jolted through him. He cut Max off with a lift of the hand and leaped to his feet. "President Curtis."

Dressed as King Arthur, the lean, shrewd-eyed president of the United States stepped toward them. George Washington trailed at his heels, and Emperor Constantine strode behind. Flat-faced Secret Service agents took up posts by the door.

Max's mouth hung open, and Desi's eyes went huge. The women rose in slow motion.

"Agent Lucano. Miss Jacobs. Mrs. Webb." The president's gaze halted on Max, who looked like she'd be happy to melt into the upholstery.

Tony stuck out his hand. "Mr. President. It's an honor." Whatever salvo the commander in chief meant to fire, he'd take the first hit.

President Curtis returned a firm grip. "The honor is mine. Your quick thinking last June saved countless lives. Rick has breaking news about what al Khayr meant to try. He can take you aside and tell you."

He glanced at the FBI director and then at the women. "But now, I crave an audience with these fair ladies." A weathered cheek creased into his trademark one-sided smile.

Max's face went as bright as her hair. Desi flushed, but held out her hand, palm down. President Curtis chuckled and bowed over it.

Desi laughed. "Your costume wears you well, Mr. President."

"Likewise, Ms. Jacobs." Both sides of the president's mouth lifted, a look not often seen in media appearances.

Tony's chest filled. His Desi could charm the stripes off a zebra.

President Curtis studied her face. "So this is the woman who KO'd one of the most dangerous men in the world."

Desi went as pink as Max.

"My Secret Service detail talked about little else for days." The president leaned closer. "They think I don't know what interests them beyond guarding me." He shot a glance at the agents by the door. The barest ripple betrayed a reaction.

"And Maxine Webb." The president took one of her hands and patted it. "I received a detailed report of the matter. You were wounded for your country. If I had an award to give for your valor and pain, you'd have it. Will you accept the thanks of a grateful nation?"

Max blinked like she was waking up. "Mr. President, I'm overwhelmed. Truly. My shoulder doesn't hurt a speck. Honest." She rolled it back and forth. "But how can you say — I mean, you shouldn't be *thankin'* me. My hus—"

"I'm aware of your circumstances, Mrs. Webb. Like I said, you sustained loss in service to your country, and we're indebted to your honesty and courage."

As if a lifeline of oxygen flowed from the president's grip, Max seemed to inflate. What was that change on her face?

Tony's voting stance for the next election did a 180. He might not agree with some of this president's positions, but only a great leader would take the time to return an ordinary citizen her self-respect on a silver platter.

"Now suppose you tell me what brought you here tonight." The president spoke in that tone of warm command familiar from public broadcasts.

This should be good. Tony moved closer.

Max and Desi started to talk at once. They stopped, glanced at each other, and laughed.

From the corner of his eye, Tony caught a motion from Director Harcourt. Blast! He followed the director to a corner away from the women and the president.

"A major attack on this country has been stopped." Harcourt kept his voice low. "Sarin gas was to have been released in the Manhattan subway system, with a simultaneous bombing at the Statue of Liberty. The attack would have happened last spring if you hadn't caught Abu al Khayr."

"I had a little help." Tony jerked his chin toward Desi.

Harcourt smiled. "A resourceful helper." His face sobered. "Al Khayr's people are also resourceful. They regrouped and were poised to strike again. Fortunately, the delay gave us time to figure out their intentions and make arrests. The whole cell is now in custody."

"Congratulations, Mr. Director."

"You and I know it's the street agents with their ears to the ground who make these things possible. I want you to sit on a panel to reorganize the Terrorist Activities Task Force. You'll be sifting through personnel jackets, interviewing candidates, and evaluating operational procedures and communications interfaces. I need street agent input."

Tony stared. A double-edged opportunity if he ever heard one.

Stuffed-shirt committees tended to find his ideas too off the wall. But could he pass up the chance to influence the way things were done in the Bureau? What about his current position as Squad Supervisor? No way did he want to be cooped up in a meeting room when he could direct operations in the field. And did this assignment mean he needed to leave Boston?

He glanced at Desi, half a room away. Could he stand to lose her because he'd been reassigned two states away? Would he kill his career to stay near the woman he loved?

Tony met Harcourt's gaze. "What's the time commitment? And will I need to relocate?"

"The panel convenes in two weeks. You meet here in Washington twice a month for six months, usually for a few days at a time, once in a while for a week straight. In between, you'll receive material to study at your local office. There's a cash bonus, but it'll come out of your hide in effort outside your regular duties. Travel expenses provided. No one is required to relocate for this temporary assignment."

He grinned at his superior. "Count me in."

"I already did." The man held out his

hand. "Welcome aboard." They shook.

A feminine laugh drew Tony's eyes. He glanced over to see Desi chatting with the president of the United States. If she was nervous, it didn't show. Must come from running a business that served kings and billionaires on a daily basis.

Harcourt tipped his head in her direction. "Delightful woman. I enjoyed meeting her. Our nation's capital is a great place to live and work. Excellent atmosphere for business if she were to consider relocating . . ." He paused and smiled. "Down the road, of course."

Tony's mouth opened, but no sound came out. He watched the man return to the group near the president.

Desi leave Boston? Why would she . . . ?

Oh! Heat crept up his neck. No promises, but a dangled carrot. Washington *would* be his dream post, but no, he didn't want to move away from Desi. If it came to a choice, though, would she leave her home for *him?*

Tony's hands fumbled for pockets but didn't find any. Blasted robes. How did those Bible guys wear these things? He readjusted his braided cloth belt and joined the others.

Desi touched his arm when he came up beside her. Her eyes shone too bright.

Something he wouldn't like was going on in that head of hers. He hadn't forgotten Max's tidbit of information about the antiquities theft in Albuquerque. Irresistible bait for a Jacobs.

"Your family has my sympathies in the disappearance of your niece." President Curtis narrowed his gaze at Max. "But I do have a rather fussy question. How exactly did you get into the White House this evening?"

The Texan colored. "I suppose it comes from hangin' around Desi."

Desi shot her friend a don't-blame-*me*-for-this glare.

Max smirked. "Well, it did. What do you always say? Keep it simple and seize the moment. Those watchin' for the devious will often miss the obvious. You taught me those things, and you got 'em from your father."

Desi lifted her hands. "Guilty as charged."

Tony grinned. He could vouch for *that* confession.

Max's freckled face turned serious. "I needed to see Desi and Tony. Thought maybe someone would radio inside and have my friends come out. But before I could get to the gate, a group of teenagers charged up the walk. One of them was the granddaughter you're raisin', Mr. President.

She let me in . . . sort of."

The president's head jerked back. "Avery?"

"She didn't know she did it, sir." Max rushed on. "You know how a bunch of teen girls can act like a herd of green broke mustangs? They were laughin' and jabberin' and millin' around until I'm half-dizzy watchin'. The gate opens, and they head for it. Avery grabs my shirtsleeve and pulls me along without givin' me much of a look-see. She pokes this ID badge at me and says, 'If they have to stick me with a Secret Service escort *and* a chaperone for a walk to the convenience store, the least you can do is keep up and not drop your belongings.' I took the badge and didn't argue. It was dark, and I trailed on the fringes, huggin' the shadows away from the security detail. They were watchin' for threats from the outside anyway. Keepin' order with the girls was supposed to be my job — er, the chaperone's job."

President Curtis shook his head and grimaced. "Sounds like my granddaughter. She was upset that we wouldn't allow her to attend the masquerade, so we let her have friends over instead." He cocked a silver brow at Max. "And how did you get into the ballroom? That's as much of a feat as entering the building."

"Piece of cake actually." She grinned; Whitcomb/Washington frowned. "We came into the White House through the kitchen, and when those girls saw all those goodies for the party, their eyes lit and they scattered like spooked quail, security detail scurryin' to keep up. Nobody cared a hoot about me. I grabbed a server's coat off a hook, clipped the badge to it, found a loaded cart, and played caboose at the end of a train headed for the ballroom. Didn't catch a second glance from anybody. They must not have noticed my slippers." She waggled a fuzzy foot. "Another Jacobs maxim — if you act like you know what you're doin', people will think you do and leave you alone."

President Curtis snorted a laugh. Desi clapped a hand over her mouth. Director Harcourt chuckled and stared at the floor. The aide went bug-eyed. Tony battled down a guffaw. Desi was a matchless original, but her best friend was the flip side of that rare coin. Look out planet earth!

"I do feel kinda bad about something." Max looked down. "That other poofy-haired redhead must be stuck outside the gate, and your granddaughter is minus a chaperone."

The president turned toward his aide.

Whitcomb/Washington nodded. "Mrs. Webb's story checks out. Ms. Parkins lost her pass during the impromptu excursion. Her story wasn't believed when she presented herself at the gate, so no alarm was raised about an imposter chaperone. I've vouched for her now, and she's been reunited with her charges."

The lines in the president's face relaxed. "Then I believe this incident can be put behind us. Please consider yourself invited to stay, Mrs. Webb, and enjoy the hospitality of my home."

"Call me Max, Mr. President. And I'm honored by the invitation, but —"

"Max and I have a job to finish tonight."

Tony frowned at Desi's interruption.

"We need to be on a plane to Albuquerque in the morning. Her sister needs her." Desi nodded at Max.

His gut did a dive. Sure, Max needed to go to her sister, but why did Desi have to go along? If she thought she was going to interfere in a missing persons investigation, or more likely, throw herself onto the trail of thieves who had already put someone in the hospital —

He tried to catch her eye, but she didn't spare him a glance.

President Curtis nodded. "Understandable." He turned to the aide. "Order one of the limousines. Tell the driver to take his passengers wherever they want to go."

"I'll escort them to their hotel," Tony said through a rigid jaw.

The dismal truth hit him.

Unless he and Desi worked out a healthy balance between his need to keep her safe and her compulsion to take risks for a cause, it wouldn't matter where he was assigned. They wouldn't be together.

THREE

Might as well be a hearse, not a limousine. Desi breathed in the scent of fine leather and looked around the darkened vehicle. On the opposite passenger bench, her back to the driver, Max brooded in silence. Tony shared Desi's seat, but occupied the far end of the bench. She studied his wooden profile.

Something was eating him, but as usual, he was Mr. Sphinx. "You didn't have to leave the party because Max and I needed to go."

"That's not it." Tony turned toward her, face oddly pale under the passing streetlights. "Max should go take care of her sister, but why you? There's more to this story."

"Don't look at me like I'm a suspect in a crime."

Max jerked as if startled. "He's right, Des. You're up to your neck at the office. You don't need to babysit me."

"He's wrong, and it's not babysitting to support a friend in a crisis. I'm happy to avoid my paperwork for another couple of days, and Tony'll be glad for the time to catch up on his own work."

Tony leaned forward. "I'm right here, ladies. Talk *to* me not about me."

Desi glared at him. "It so happens you're right. I do have a secondary reason for going to Albuquerque." She turned to her friend. "But you're the priority."

Max gasped. "Oh dear, I forgot! HJ Securities provides the protection for the New Mexico Museum. And my niece and nephew are suspects in the robbery. Des, I'm so sorry. This puts the company in a bad spot."

Desi shrugged. "Don't worry about it. I'm sure I'll get there and find out that the Denver branch has everything under control. They're primaries on this. I'm just the meddling boss coming to breathe down their necks."

Tony stared at Desi under lowered brows. "I thought HJ Securities was in business to prevent theft, not investigate it."

She lifted her chin. "When did I mention conducting an investigation?"

His gaze bored into her. "Are you saying

you wouldn't fight Goliath with one hand tied behind your back to protect HJ Securities and help Max? I can't see you sitting this one out."

"You're making assumptions I don't appreciate, Tony."

"So tell me I'm wrong. Tell me you're not going to Albuquerque with sleuthing on your mind."

"I don't owe you promises or explanations."

A muscle jerked in his jaw. "I'm not asking because you owe. I'm asking because I care."

"But you don't trust me not to do something foolish. That's insulting."

Tony frowned and shook his head. "I know you, Des —"

"And I *don't* know you. I'm supposed to live in a glass house and tell you my every move, my every thought, but you don't let me past your outer layer. Sure, I know you're a Red Sox fan, and you jog every day. Your barber could know that much. But your mother had to tell me you're in the Big Brother program and mentoring an inner-city teen."

"Mom mentioned that?"

"Why wouldn't she? Why didn't you? Don't you think I might have enjoyed knowing something so important to your life?" Her fists knotted. "Or maybe you didn't feel the need to share because *I'm* not so important to your life."

Tony looked at her like he might tell the driver to head for the nearest asylum. "Where did this come from? I thought we were talking about your trip to Albuquerque."

"Yeah, Des. A little off topic there."

Desi stared at Max, but her friend wasn't playing favorites.

Max turned toward Tony. "And what's up with you not telling her about that kid you mentor?"

Desi forced her hands to unclench. Where *had* that come from? A picture flashed in front of her mind's eye — Tony leaning forward to hear Director Harcourt speak in his ear, the man's hand resting on his shoulder. For all she knew, she could lose Tony to a coveted promotion tomorrow. Maybe he held himself back to keep from getting too involved with her so the break wouldn't be painful.

For him, anyway.

Cold wrapped around her insides. The thought made awful sense.

Someone jabbed her arm, and she looked at Max. "What?"

"Did you hear that?"
"Hear what?"
"Great. When he starts tellin' you about the kid, you're not listenin'."
Tony barked a laugh.
Desi glared at both of them. "Don't expect a few dribbles of belated information to thrill me." She zeroed in on Tony. "My best friend's niece is missing."
Max moaned and slumped against the seat.
"And my security business may see repercussions from a theft we didn't prevent," Desi continued.
Max put her head in her hands.
Desi patted her friend's knee, but kept her gaze on Tony. "I'm going to Albuquerque as a bosom buddy and a business professional. If you can't trust me to conduct myself properly in both capacities, this discussion is over."
Tony opened his mouth, closed it, and then stared at her with that hard, assessing look she'd thought she'd never see again. He shook his head and looked out the window.
Silence fell like a rock through sullen water.

Seated before the computer in the Tate Gallery's workroom, Desi tapped the screen displaying Max's fresh set of schematics for cameras and laser detectors. "I can't beat this."

Desi had studied the 3-D layout from every angle and come up with zilch for an approach. A thief would have to be Rubber Woman or Elastic Man to navigate without tripping the alarm. And *kablam!* Steel doors would trap the burglar inside the display room with loot worth millions but no way to make off with a Dresden thimble.

Yawning, she glanced at her watch. Five a.m., and her sore toe hadn't hindered her from stealing an O'Keeffe and the Grandma Moses. Smooth jobs fueled by the steam pouring out her ears. Where did Tony get off presuming she'd head for Albuquerque for any reason except legitimate business and moral support for Max? But at this hour of a sleepless night, the anger edge had begun to wear off. She stifled another yawn behind a gloved hand.

Max yawned instead and crossed her arms. "You have to try anyway. That's the deal."

"Slave driver." She took a good look at her friend. Red streaked the whites of her eye, and her lips were pinched and colorless. "Let's call it good." Desi rose from the desk chair. "I shouldn't have kept you up all night."

"We always finish a job." She delivered a flat stare.

Desi knew when to drop a subject. Max was steamed, too — about the mess in her family. The woman meant to get to Albuquerque or bust, and this assignment was an obstacle on the route. One bright spot — better to see her friend angry than defeated and hopeless.

"Let's get to it then."

Desi went into the gilded reception area and took her starting position outside the double-wide entrance of the main gallery. The lights went out. She stood in darkness relieved by the dim glow of a nearby *Exit* sign.

"Ready. Go." Max's muffled voice floated from the equipment room.

Desi pulled her infrared goggles over her eyes, and the lasers popped into view. She spotted a narrow hole in the grid, bent a knee up to her chest, and then straightened it through the opening. Folding herself almost double, she flowed after the limb with her torso and head, followed by her other leg. Her toe complained, but she ignored the griping.

Several moves later, she worked herself to

a dead end. Oh well, she could turn around and find an alternate route. Her pulse throbbed in her neck, and she pulled in deep, even breaths. Pivoting on the balls of her feet, she faced the direction she'd come.

Hey, what?

The configuration of the laser beams had changed. No body-sized opening existed. Desi tried toward the left. Same result. To the right. Again, no way.

"Max, you're a genius! You've got the lasers rigged to change configuration on a timer."

Her friend's chuckle came from outside the doorway behind her. "Yep, the program is run by a client-unique algorithm the NSA would have fun decrypting. Even power failure can't shut it down. There's battery backup."

"Congra—" Desi turned.

Wa-a-a-ah! Wa-a-a-ah! Wa-a-a-ah!

She charged for the exit, adrenaline spiked to the moon. Before she covered half the distance, the metal doors snicked shut. She halted, breath spurting between her lips. Max had won this round, and Desi should be delighted. So why did frustration gnaw her insides?

Because she hated to lose, that's why. No wonder few professional art thieves retired.

The game was addicting. They loved to play, they played to win, and they even loved the art they stole. One day, a pro would find the Tate Gallery an irresistible challenge and lose their freedom. Desi would hear and rejoice, even as she felt a pang of sympathy in her secret heart.

The lights burst on. "Hey!" Desi squeezed her eyes shut. A heavy tread entered the room, and she peeped through half-open lids. "Tony!" Her eyes popped wide. "No way, buster. I'm mad enough at you as it is. Don't you dare!" She backed away. "I'm going to Albuquerque with Max, and you can't stop me."

Tony came on, jaw set in stone. He caught her right wrist and snapped a handcuff onto it. Desi winced. The metal sent a chill through tender flesh. The cuffs snapped again. She gaped at the sight of Tony's left wrist connected to hers by a short length of chain. He folded their shackled hands together. The warmth of his clasp chased away the cold.

"I can't let you leave with those words in the limo between us."

"What words? *You* never say any—"

He caressed her knuckles with his lips.

Shockwaves coursed down her spine. The low-down, sneaky — and very clever — rat!

"If you think you're going to get to me with this backward romancing, you're . . ." Her protest fizzled into a splutter as he tugged her forward, and her stupid feet cooperated.

"Let's take another drive. This time without so much ice between us that Jet Li couldn't bust through with a flying heel kick."

"Jet Li?" It was as if her brains had sprung a leak en route to the elevator. Elevator? They were in the elevator already? This man was sooo bad for her good sense.

"Not familiar with Jet Li?" He grinned down at her while the car descended. "Chuck Norris then. Is that better?"

Desi didn't answer. Thoughts spun. Last night — a few hours ago, really — came back to her in detail. Was she fooling herself that there was any hope for them?

He squeezed her hand. Maybe. A girl's got to hang on to hope.

Stepping out of the Tate Gallery into the cool dawn of a new day, Desi breathed in early commuter smells. She sneaked a peak under her lashes at her crafty captor. Better to be cuffed to the annoying man than sitting with a wall of silence between them.

A pair of cabs idled at the curb. Tony took her to the one in the lead. He motioned toward the other one. "For Max, as soon as she closes up shop here."

Desi looked away. She couldn't let him see evidence of thaw. If the guy wasn't so thoughtful, it would be a lot easier to stay mad. But if he never trusted her with his inner self or had faith in her ability to make good judgment calls . . .

Tony helped her into the vehicle — an awkward maneuver with their arms linked. The driver pulled out without comment. No doubt a cabbie in DC saw lots of strange things.

"Given these —" Desi held up their jail jewelry — "I'm surprised you didn't stuff me into the back of a Bucar or patrol special."

Tony lifted her arm and unbuckled her wrist and then did the same with his own. "I wouldn't put a stray dog in the backseat of any vehicle that hauls suspects. You have no idea what lowlifes do in those after they're arrested." He tucked the cuffs into his jacket pocket.

Desi glimpsed his shoulder-holstered gun. "Don't talk to me about staying out of danger when you strap on one of those at the same time as you stuff your wallet into your pocket."

"I'm trained for what I do."

"So am I."

They locked stares.

"Are you trained to walk across steel girders ten stories in the air?" Quiet intensity gave Tony's question the force of a shout. "I saw your planning notes in the Gallery workroom. I doubt aerial gymnastics is in the HJ Securities job description — even for the boss."

"Is that what's got your tie on too tight?" Nuts! She knew he'd ferret out her activities of the night before, but he must not have checked out the roof and noticed the broken ledge. She'd have gotten more than this mild rebuke.

Tony shook his head. "No, but it's an example of the wild risks you take."

Desi frowned. "Supervisory Special Agent Anthony Lucano, your background investigation on me missed a juicy tidbit."

"Oh, boy, I'm in trouble. Women never use your full name unless you're about to get your ear twisted. My mother taught me that much. Ouch!" He rubbed the side of his head.

Not going to charm her that easily. "As a junior in college, I was offered a tryout for the U.S. Olympic team in floor exercise, uneven bars, and — guess what? — balance beam. I never tried out — too focused on finishing school and heading home to help with the business. Gym time is a firm date with me three times a week — minimum. I haven't fallen off a beam on a straight walk-across in . . . well . . . forever." She shrugged. "Besides, Max made me wear a bungee cord. I'll bet you didn't know that, now did you? It wasn't in the notes."

A tint of red crept out of Tony's collar.

"See?" She settled back. "You don't know the whole story, Mr. Jump-to-Conclusions. And yes, I still ran the risk of injury, but not any more out of reason than for you to chase some crook through a back alley. We do what we do."

Tony pulled her close. "Okay. I'll grant I didn't know about the bungee cord or your shot at competing in the Olympics. Impressive. But I'm still not 100 percent with a balance beam act between skyscrapers. I need you safe."

Desi leaned her head against his shoulder. The smooth weave of his suit jacket welcomed her cheek. "I'd trust you with my life. Now you have to trust me. And when you can't, you'll have to trust the Lord to take care of me."

She felt as much as heard his chuckle.

"How did I find such a wise woman?"

Desi sat up and smoothed her hair. "All right, oh trustworthy male, now you owe your wise woman a piece of juicy trivia about *you.* We still have a lot to find out about each other."

"What would you like to know?"

Desi tapped her upper lip. "How about this? Fair is fair. Max has exposed the shady side of her family tree — their rotten record at wedded bliss. And you already know my tree is more like a stick. Few relatives and none close." She laughed, but a lump rose and cut off the sound. She swallowed the haunting loneliness. "Maybe that's why I'm so impressed with your abundant family, branches shooting out all over the place to hear your mom talk. So who is the most disreputable member on your particular bough and why?"

Tony lowered his eyes, brows sucked together. If she didn't know better, she'd think the fingers tapping his knee signaled nerves.

His hand stilled. "Those marriage statistics in Max's extended family bug me. So far out of normal range. There's got to be a reason."

"Have you figured it out?"

He shook his head. "Not enough data to be specific, but I do have a thought. This isn't science, more like an observation. I investigate a lot of people, and I've noticed that a bad choice at a critical moment by one family member can set off a chain reaction that destroys generations." His lips settled into a thin line.

"You mean like the tendency to alcoholism being in the gene pool?"

"Not exactly, though it's a related issue. More like the day Esau decided it was more important to have a bowl of stew than his inheritance. So Jacob, the sneaky younger son, got the inheritance, and Esau, the elder, cut himself and his descendants out of the lineage of Jesus."

"But Esau's problem went a lot deeper than one bad decision. It was a whole mindset of immediate gratification — the Bible version of the fast-food mentality. Literally."

Tony laughed. "Bingo, babe. A mindset leads to a certain result. If Max digs deep enough into her history, she might find out where this marital self-destruct sequence originated."

Desi shook her head. "That doesn't explain all the widows and widowers in her family. Max's dad passed away from cancer a few years ago, so her mom is single, but not a divorcée."

"Maybe we haven't gone far enough with the theory yet." He shifted in his seat. "Lots of times I've wished I could put this stuff in an investigative report, but there's only room on those for what can be observed and quantified." He shook his head. "Not many years ago, I would've laughed anyone out of the office for thinking something like this."

"Okay, spit it out. I won't laugh. I promise."

Tony met her gaze. "By taking the attitude that marriage is temporary — a throwaway option — the members of Max's family may have attracted spiritual forces that make sure their 'curse' happens one way or another."

Desi let out a long breath. "Yikes! That's scary."

"Tell me about it."

She stiffened with sudden realization, then glared in his face. "No, *you* tell *me* about it. You've dazzled me again with what a deep man you are, but you still haven't shared that juicy tidbit off your family tree."

"Rain check." He echoed her words about the kiss they didn't share the night before. "We're at the airport."

"Airport!" Desi looked around. She'd assumed they were headed back to the hotel.

"Yep, your all-purpose FBI agent not only packed your belongings — er, paid hotel staff to do it — but he booked you and Max on the earliest flight to Albuquerque."

"You didn't show up this morning to talk me out of going?"

"I don't want to control your life, Des."

They got out of the taxi. Bustle and noise surrounded them as the driver lifted luggage out of the trunk. Desi recognized one of the bags as Tony's. He must be returning to Boston. Or maybe . . . no, he wouldn't . . . Would he?

"No, I'm not going to Albuquerque," he whispered in her ear. "I'm headed back to Boston."

"Are my thoughts that obvious?"

"Sometimes. You can't help your expressive face."

His grin raised her hackles sky-high. Someone please inform her when she had made up her mind whether to kick this guy or kiss —

"Jabba the Hutt!" The name burst out before she thought better.

"What?" Tony whirled in the direction of her stare, and his face went hard.

An enormous man in a sports jacket and chinos flowed up the sidewalk toward them.

"Ms. Jacobs." Hamilton Gordon stretched a puffy hand toward Desi. "Pleasure to run into you again."

Her fingers slid in and out of his dry grip.

Not Jabbalike at all. She'd expected a mauling or at least a little dampness. Tony edged a shoulder between them, smooth and irritating at the same time. Gordon's smile widened to include Tony, though he didn't offer a handshake. Just as well. Her agent-man didn't look receptive.

He jerked a nod at Gordon. "Tony Lucano. You were dressed as Darth Vader last night."

"What did I say about powers of observation?" Gordon angled an amused look in Desi's direction. "Hamilton Gordon. Meat packing's my game, so folks call me Ham." He ho-hoed, mottled skin flushing.

Desi dredged up a smile. The subject of their conversation at the party hit her afresh. Tony was being groomed for more than what Boston could offer.

"I take it you're returning to Santa Fe this morning," Tony said. "A booming interstate business can't do without its CEO for long."

His tone prickled the hairs on the back of Desi's neck. What was going on here? She glanced at Gordon.

The man frowned. "I was acquitted of those RICO charges. You weren't even an agent on the case."

"A buddy of mine was, and you were guilty."

The men glared at each other. Then Gordon's shoulders lowered, and he spread massive hands. "The Lord had mercy. I'm not the same man I was then."

"Yeah, I heard you got religion."

"No, I found the Lamb of God. The body and blood cleansed me of sin. The Lamb will do the same for anyone. Even an FBI agent." A smile wrinkled folds around his eyes.

Desi laughed. The curdled-cream look on Tony's face was too rich. She hooked his tense arm with one of hers. "Tony and I are believers, Mr. Gordon."

"Ham." He nodded. "One of you may be a believer, but the other seems to be a judge."

Desi braced for eruption, but Tony's muscles relaxed under her fingers.

"I'm all for getting right with God, Mr. Gordon. Provided your faith is real, but I'm the kind of guy that requires proof."

Gordon inclined his head, though Desi noticed Tony wasn't invited to call him *Ham.* "Perhaps if you watch my pastor on his television broadcast, you'll be assured of the soundness of my conversion. Reverend Archer Romlin has a powerful ministry. Here's his card."

Gordon produced a rectangle of stiff

paper from his jacket's inner pocket. Desi took the card. "We don't want to keep you from your flight, Mr. Gor— Ham."

"I leave in my corporate jet in an hour. I came to the public terminal hoping to speak to you, but I see that now is not the moment to bring up —" He paused and a grimace that approximated a smile passed over his lips. "Let me just say I'd like to discuss mutual history that may offer business opportunities to both of us." His gaze bored into her. "Perhaps we might connect during your stay in Albuquerque." He nodded to her, measured Tony with a look, and walked away.

"That was . . . interesting." Desi stared after him. "You could have been nicer to a new Christian."

He snorted. "Jabba the Hutt. You made a good call."

"People can change."

He frowned.

"They can! Jesus changed both of *us*."

Tony's expression softened, and he touched her cheek. "Hey, you're cold. Let's get inside. For now, believe me, I'm neither paranoid nor overprotective where this guy is concerned. I'll tell you what little I can when we get to your departure gate." He handed her an e-ticket. "Meet you at the security checkpoint. My flight is with a different airline."

Desi watched him head for an outdoor baggage kiosk. The wind picked up strands of hair and teased her cold cheeks with them. She headed for the indoor check-in desk.

While she waited her turn, she kept an eye on the doors. As she reached the counter, Max came puffing inside. *Wonder if I look as disheveled as she does?* Desi glanced down at her fieldwork jumpsuit. Not her usual travel attire. No doubt her hair was still goofy from all the pins and the headdress from the party. Oh, well.

Max was waiting for her when she finished checking her bag.

"I did mine outside. C'mon." Max jerked her head toward the security line.

Tony joined them and pulled out his credentials for a quick hustle through the checkpoint. He walked with them to their gate. The attendants were already boarding passengers. Max headed for the entrance ramp like she'd bowl over the first fool who got in her way.

Desi gazed up at Tony. "I appreciate you doing this against your better judgment."

He smiled, but unease showed through narrowed eyes. "Please stay away from

Hamilton Gordon. He operates out of Santa Fe, and that's barely a skip and a jump from Albuquerque."

"You said you'd tell me about him."

Tony shoved his hands into his pockets. "I can't say much, just what's public record. You'll have to listen more to what I don't say." He met her eyes. "Three years ago, Gordon was acquitted of RICO charges involving the transportation of stolen livestock across state lines, money laundering, and other financial offenses. The case against him was solid until a couple of key witnesses disappeared." One hand popped from his pocket and chopped the air. "The setback hasn't taken the Bureau's eyes off him. We're good at patiently waiting in the weeds."

Tony's gaze softened, and he tucked a strand of hair behind her ear. The brush of his fingers tingled her skin. This man could kill as easily as caress with his touch. The hand slipped back into his pocket. He rocked on his heels, frowning.

"And now?"

"Can't go there." He shook his head. "But isn't it strange that this man knew where and when to find you this morning, including where you're headed? I'm tempted to ditch my job and hop on this plane with you, or else throw you over my shoulder and drag you back to Boston. Promise me, darling, that you'll call me right away if Gordon approaches you."

Emotions swirled through Desi. Dismay. Yes, it was weird that some stranger knew her last-minute movements. Delight. He'd give up his job for her! Well, almost. Disgust. *Uh, Mr. Caveman, I've got two feet.* She'd smack him for sure if he hadn't called her *darling.*

"Last call for Flight 859 to Phoenix," the loudspeaker blared.

"I've got to board. I'll do my best to avoid trouble. And, yes, if Ham — uh, Mr. Gordon — contacts me, I'll let you know."

"Good." Tony moved toward her. "Now, what do you say I collect a down payment on that rain check?"

She let him pull her close. Hey, if he wanted to kiss a messy-haired woman in a Mylar jumpsuit, who was she to stop him? And the man could kiss.

A few minutes later, lips still warm and happy, Desi boarded the plane and spotted her first-class seat beside Max. The redhead was asleep, or at least imitating slumber as well as she'd done a faint. A rush of tenderness filled her. For her friend. For Tony. He was a first-class man. He'd made a big dent in his credit card to provide them with a comfortable ride. She'd find a way to pay him back later.

Right now, she was going to fall into that butter-soft chair and shut her eyes. Soon enough, she'd be thrust back into the madness of a missing niece, an enormous criminal with a mysterious agenda, and a boyfriend who was so good at his job that he could get transferred right out of her life. And let's not forget the museum theft.

She yawned as she dropped into the seat. What was taken? If she knew that, she might be able to — Her head hit the backrest, and exhaustion snuffed out thought.

Desi left the plane in Albuquerque after two o'clock that afternoon, Max beside her. She wasn't rested. Sleep lasted the three hours until their layover in Phoenix. But the Arizona stop allowed her to clean up in the bathroom, brush her hair and her teeth, and put on the change of clothing from her carry-on. Oh, and call the office to inform them of her unscheduled detour. Max had cleaned up the same way, after she called her sister to tell her when they would arrive.

As they hustled toward baggage claim, a large poster of Georgia O'Keeffe grinning from the passenger seat of a motorcycle caught Desi's eye. Too bad she wasn't here for pleasure. A stop at the Georgia O'Keeffe Museum in Santa Fe would top the sight-seeing list.

At the baggage claim, they found their carousel still empty, but lots of people milled around. Max pursed her lips and craned her neck. "Where is she?"

"If Jo were here, she'd just have to stand and wait for the plane to cough up our bags."

"You're right." Max fidgeted with a button on her blouse. "But she should've been here by now."

She said the words again after they'd collected the luggage. Then in another fifteen minutes, while they sat and watched others get bags from different flights and trot merrily off. Max got on her cell phone again, anxiety lines punctuating the space between her brows.

Max flipped the phone shut. "Still the answerin' service. Something must have come up. I hope . . ." Her voice trailed off.

A uniformed police officer approached, gaze fixed on them, and he didn't look happy. Maybe Max had reason to worry. They both stood.

The young officer stopped in front of

them. He looked at Max. "Are you Maxine Webb?"

"That's me." Her fingers fluttered to her throat.

The officer frowned.

Desi held onto Max. *Please, God, no more bad news.*

Four

"We need to ask you some questions," the officer said. "I'd like you to accompany me to the station, Mrs. Webb."

"Thank God!" Max collapsed to her knees.

Desi went down with her. "Breathe deep now, slow and calm."

Max's hyperventilating eased. Desi looked up at the officer, whose name bar read *Gillis*.

The young man's brow furrowed. "Are you all right, Mrs. Webb?"

Desi stood up. "Max thought you'd come to tell her something happened to her sister Jo Cheama."

Gillis's face smoothed. "Mrs. Cheama is down at the station. She was fine when I left."

Max leaped to her feet. "Why didn't you *say* so? You have no business scarin' people out of half a lifetime." She snatched up her carry-on, grabbed the handle of her Pullman, and marched toward the doors. "Where are you parked? Let's blow this joint."

Desi followed, leaving Gillis to catch up or get lost. Bother! Was this about the theft investigation? The disappearance? Just what they needed: involvement with the authorities right off the bat. At least Tony wouldn't think they'd done this on purpose. And what did they want with Max? The woman hadn't been in Albuquerque since Christmas.

Something smelled funky. The wait with no Jo because she was down at the police station the whole time. Then the officer showing up right when tension got high, finessing a yo-yo of emotions. And now Max was all relieved and eager to go wherever she was told and answer anything they asked.

Desi stepped through the automatic doors onto the sidewalk. Hot, dry air wrapped around her. Stark contrast from the cool of Washington and the air-conditioned airport building.

A patrol car idled at the curb with a jowly older man at the wheel. Gillis's partner? He shot her and Max a narrow look, but didn't bother to step out. The bad cop to baby-face Gillis's good cop. The young officer darted past them and opened the back door.

Desi grabbed Max's arm. "Someone warned me about the backseats of law enforcement vehicles." She looked at Gillis, then scowled at the officer behind the wheel. Letting someone mess with Max was *not* on her to-do list today. "We'll take a taxi." She ignored Gillis's openmouthed stare and glanced around for a cab.

The driver's door of the patrol car thunked wide, and the partner stepped out. He stood with an arm draped over the roof. Swamp-gray eyes studied her up and down. He must have considered his stare intimating.

Too bad. She'd been hazed by tougher than this character.

A Yellow Cab pulled into the curb ahead of the patrol car. "Here we go, Max. Our chariot awaits."

But an older couple slid into the cab's rear seat, and the car pulled away.

Swamp Eyes rapped his knuckles on the roof of his vehicle. " 'Round here you have to call for a taxi ride. They don't just show up looking for fares. This ain't New York." His lips curled back. "Take whatever transportation you want, Ms. Whoever-You-Are." An alligator grin said where he thought she should end up. "We'll give Mrs. Webb a ride."

Desi out-grinned him. "This is your lucky day, Officer. You get a two-for-one deal. Where Max goes, I go. Plus a whole pack of HJ Securities Company lawyers, hollering 'don't answer that.' " She folded her arms across her chest. "You want to question Max, which means you're fishing for information. But as my Texas friend might put it, the water hole is gonna dry up and blow away if this is the best welcome Albuquerque's finest has to offer."

"You're Desiree Jacobs!" Officer Gillis's outburst earned stares from passersby. "I thought you looked familiar." He glanced at his partner. "She was all over the news a while back. Clobbered that terrorist dude —"

"I know." The older officer's glare said "get back to the academy."

A squeak came from Max. Her pressed-together lips quivered, and her cheeks sucked in like she was about to swallow her tongue. Desi didn't dare meet her friend's eye, or they'd both be rolling on the pavement. She kept her gaze on the officers. "I'll call for transportation. No doubt any cabbie knows the way to the station. Or, if you prefer, you can follow us there . . . just to be sure we desperate criminals don't make a run for it."

Desi looked from one to the other. Hard to tell which one's face glowed brighter. Jowl Face was bust-his-buttons furious. The younger officer seemed undecided whether to fall out on the side of sheepish or thrilled to meet a celebrity.

A second patrol car slid up behind the first, but this one had a different insignia. Two Native American officers burst out the doors and strode toward the first patrol car.

"Sergeant Seciwa." The one in the lead, a muscular, middle-aged man, held out a hand to Desi, who shook it. Then to Max, who did the same. "And this is Officer Chimoni." He waved at the lanky man behind him, then turned toward the city cops. "You're interfering in our investigation. We have property jurisdiction to talk to Mrs. Webb, and we'll share whatever information we gather."

Gillis's partner slammed his door and barreled onto the sidewalk. "We've got the lead on the break-in investigation."

Big and Brawny stood as impassive as a granite cliff. Swamp Eyes thrust his jaw out far enough to halt traffic.

"Call me dog bone," Max whispered into Desi's ear.

Desi's blood heated. Things were way out of hand, and no one seemed inclined to tell them why.

"Neither of you needs to speak to Mrs. Webb." A feminine voice spoke from the direction of the terminal.

Everyone turned like a whip had cracked.

A brown-haired woman of medium height and sturdy build stood several feet away. She wore a dark pantsuit and a confident smile. She flipped open a black leather case to display FBI credentials. "Rosa Ortiz of the Albuquerque Field Office. The lead on the museum theft case is now ours. We would be grateful for cooperation."

"So now I need to go with *you?*" Max flopped her arms.

"No, Mrs. Webb. You and Ms. Jacobs are free to leave. Welcome to Albuquerque."

Finally, someone with manners.

The agent looked toward the four policemen. "Our office has determined that Mrs. Webb could not have been a factor in the theft of the Indian artifacts."

Max stepped forward. "What's being done to find Karen?"

The agent's expression hardened. "Believe me, we intend to locate her."

Max moaned. "She's in trouble, but everyone wants to believe the worst about her."

"Let's go find the number for cab service, Max." Desi tugged her friend's carry-on. "We can't accomplish anything standing out here."

A small sedan pulled up to the curb, and an auburn-haired woman got out.

"Jo!" Max charged her sister.

They embraced like they hadn't seen each other in years. From inside the sedan, a baby wailed.

Desi's heart turned over. Poor little tyke. Max might be reunited with her sister, but would this child ever have a happy reunion with his mother? The odds didn't look good.

Desi bounced a cooing baby Adam on her knee in the kitchen of Jo Cheama's neat little adobe home. The baby's pudgy cheeks dimpled with smiles now that he'd been changed and fed. After a hot shower and a couple stout cups of coffee, Desi felt more human herself. She'd even put in a call to the museum administrator, but he'd left for the day, and she'd spoken to the manager of HJ Securities' Denver office. He reported that the museum administrator had a bad case of pass-the-buck-itis. A common illness when disaster struck.

The afternoon was waning, and Jo had something bubbling in the Crock-Pot that smelled like enchiladas. Desi's mouth watered.

"I can't believe they made you come down to the station to answer questions when you were babysitting Adam." Max stared at her sister seated across from her at the table.

Jo lifted one shoulder. "He was the pet of the break room while I spoke with the officers. They didn't get much out of me, because there wasn't much to get. Frankly, I went down there hopin' for answers. I came away feelin' like they don't know much more than I do."

The woman's lined face was life-worn, her auburn hair streaked with gray and not bouncy like her sister's. She wore a beaded headband and a turquoise squash blossom necklace and looked good in them, but not natural born. She'd been married to a full-blooded Zuni. Divorced now. So where was little Adam's grandpa now that crisis had struck? Probably better out of the picture from what Max had told her about Pete Cheama.

Jo glanced toward the clock over the sink. "Brent has a part-time job as a hotel desk clerk, but he'll be here soon to get Adam. I've asked him to stay for supper. You'll need to hear from both of us to give you a solid start." She smiled at Desi, hope a dim spark in her eyes. "When I heard you were comin' with Max, I said to myself, 'Any woman who can handle a terrorist should have no trouble with the hairy unwashed down at that bar on old Route 66.' "

She headed for the stack of corn tortillas on the counter. "That ringleader, Snake Bonney, had somethin' to do with Karen's disappearance. He hated losin' his hold on her."

What was the woman talking about? Max and she should act like private detectives? Desi looked at her friend.

Max gave an elaborate shrug. "Um, sis, I —"

"We can't wait for the city cops, the Native police, and the feds to settle their turf wars." She formed enchiladas and plopped them into a glass casserole dish. "They think Karen ran away, that she's guilty and hidin'. I know better. My Inner Witness is screamin' that Karen's in trouble and needs help. Now!"

Inner witness? Desi bounced the baby and studied Jo's back. Was that some new term for mother's intuition?

Jo whirled, wiping her hands on a dishrag. She pinned Max with a look. "You were always the smart one in the family. If you can't figure this out, I don't know . . ." She turned away and gripped the edge of the counter.

Max put her arms around her sister. "I believe Karen's innocent, too. And you know I'd do anything to help her, but —"

"Oh, thank you!" Jo collapsed on Max's shoulder, weeping.

The baby stiffened and howled. Desi stood up, bouncing the child. She met Max's eyes. *Bewildered and frustrated? Yeah, me, too.*

Desi left the room, baby still squealing. Max needed space to deal with her sister. Firmly. They were *not* getting involved in the investigation.

Any woman who can handle a terrorist? She could do without that kind of notoriety. People had the wrong idea if they thought a desperate act of self-preservation meant she flew into town, minus airplane, dressed in a blue bodysuit with a red *S* on the chest.

"Sh-sh-sh." Desi paced the living room, patting Adam's back.

A real superwoman would be able to get a hysterical infant to stop crying.

"He's colicky."

Desi turned at the male voice.

A young man stood on the braided rug inside the front door. Lean and on the tall side with light brown hair, longish and a bit shaggy. Stealthy sort — walked in without a sound. Or maybe not. Hard to hear anything with a baby wailing in your ear.

The man smiled. "Desiree Jacobs. It's been a while. Mama Jo said you were coming with Aunt Max. How was your flight?" He brushed a strand of hair away from blue eyes.

Now the family resemblance became clear. "Brent Webb! You were a gangly teenager when you visited Boston that time. You've grown into a —"

"Married man with a baby. Let me take him."

"Gladly." Desi handed Adam off.

Brent held the baby facing away from him, dangling over one arm. Adam's wails tapered off into hiccups and whimpers.

Desi studied them. "What are you doing? Squeezing the air out of him?"

Brent laughed. "He's got a tummy ache. Sometimes pressure on the stomach eases the pain. It'll pass, but maybe later rather than sooner."

"I'll leave it to your expertise." Desi held up her hands. "He's a cute little fellow, but I don't have the credentials. Single woman. Never babysat a day in my life."

"Don't worry about it." Brent settled into a wooden rocker. "When you become a parent, you pick up on stuff. As one of my profs says about an archaeology dig, 'you become invested in the project.' "

Adam screamed and went stick straight.

Brent got up. "Guess I can't sit yet." He took up pacing where Desi left off.

She flopped onto the sofa. "Let me get my second wind. No wonder parenting is a two-person job."

Brent paled and fixed his eyes on the tile floor.

Desi smacked herself in the forehead. "That was a dumb thing to say. I'm sorry. My brain isn't in this time zone yet. We've got to trust that Karen is going to turn up unharmed."

The young man frowned. "I don't believe she ran away. She wouldn't do that to us!" He stared at Desi, daring her to challenge his statement.

She kept silent. The baby was quiet, too.

"And if she didn't leave on her own, that means —" a muscle in Brent's cheek jumped — "she was taken. Do you know how horrible the statistics are for recovering someone alive after they've been gone for two days?"

Desi sat forward. "Two days! I thought she disappeared last night."

Brent sighed. He put the baby on his

shoulder and sat in the rocking chair again. Adam lay against his father, sucking his thumb, eyelids drooping.

"That's the first Mama Jo knew about it. I didn't want to worry her. Thought I could find Karen myself. When I didn't, I notified the cops, but they didn't give the matter high priority." The rocker picked up speed. "Someone's unhappy wife packs a bag and runs? No biggie. But then they figured out she was a receptionist from the museum where those Anasazi artifacts were stolen, and all of a sudden they're hot to locate her."

"Did the theft happen on the same day Karen disappeared?" She picked up a magazine from the coffee table and fanned herself.

"The night before."

"Don't the police think it's strange that she'd take off *after* the theft?"

"Yeah, they think it's real weird." The rocker creaked into overdrive. "I'm a prime suspect as the thief, and maybe I did away with my wife because she found out."

"That's bogus! You're no murderer. One look at you with that baby over your shoulder and . . ." Desi's breath hitched. She quit fanning.

Brent's brother had looked like a dedicated family man, and he turned out to be —

"You're thinking about Dean." The rocker stopped, and his eyes darkened. "I love him, but I don't understand what he did. We're not at all alike."

"Yes, you are." Desi nodded. "He's not a killer, and neither are you."

"Thanks. I think. But you didn't say I'm not a thief."

Desi shrugged. "You could be, but that feels too much like lightning striking twice."

"To the police, it looks like bad seed related to bad seed."

"The cops are paid to have suspicious minds. You reported your wife missing. Real dumb if you wanted to get away with murder and burglary."

"Not so dumb if I wanted to make myself look innocent."

Desi groaned. "Do I ever know how you feel! I've had the long finger of the law pointed my direction."

"But you came out of it great." Adam stirred. Brent sighed, and the rocker started in. "If they don't find out who took those things, this is going to ruin my career. Who'll want to hire an archaeologist suspected of stealing artifacts in grad school? I've already been barred from my internship at the museum. Temporarily, they say." Brent's nostrils flared. "But who cares? I just want my wife back. And Adam needs his mommy."

Desi eyed the sleeping baby. Brent's reactions rang true. It was Jo who seemed off. But that was a subject to take up with Max. She met Brent's gaze. "You see me now, after my mess has been sorted out. When I was in the middle of it, I didn't know how I'd come out alive. But by the grace of God, here I am. We can trust Him now, too."

Brent shook his head. "He's seemed pretty far away these past months."

"Months?" Desi sat forward.

"Yeah. Karen's pregnancy was rough, and she missed a lot of work. Good thing she had an understanding supervisor. Then after the baby came, she took a leave of absence. Depression set in, and she . . . changed. Wouldn't go to church. Wouldn't even step out of the house. At least not until the day of the robbery, when she went in to work for a few hours. She came home wiped out and slept the clock around."

"I suppose her returning to work the same day as the robbery looks suspicious to the police."

"Sure, and exhibiting symptoms of mental

instability doesn't help."

Desi frowned. "Postpartum depression isn't uncommon. You'd think people, especially professionals, would be aware of that these days. Did you get help for her?"

"Sure. The doc put her on medication. That meant she couldn't nurse, so she felt like a failure as a mother on top of everything else."

Desi got up and stretched out a kink in her back. She tossed the magazine onto the table and took a chair next to Brent. "Max said Karen had some issues before coming to the Lord. Maybe that's a nosy comment, but . . ."

"No offense. When we first met, she was messed up, but then she fell in love with Jesus. Got out of a dangerous relationship. Turned her life around. I was so proud of her. Proud to be her husband. Then, a few months ago it was like her faith got — well — twisted. She turned into some brittle person I didn't even know."

"Still conflicted about her heritage."

Brent looked up as Jo walked into the room, Max close behind. "How long have you been listening?"

"Long enough to know you've missed an important piece of the puzzle. Not meanin' to, of course, because you see Karen for herself and not as a half-breed."

Jo turned her gaze on Desi. "Even in the twenty-first century, marriages between Native Americans and whites aren't well received, especially if it's an Indian man with a white wife. My marriage couldn't survive the strain. Pete found comfort in meth. I chose divorce to protect Karen from the drugs, but I couldn't guard her from everything. She grew up torn between two cultures and not accepted by either. The motorcycle gang accepted her. The church accepted her . . . to a point."

Brent surged to his feet. The baby startled and fussed. "What does *that* mean?"

Jo shook her head. "Not a good presupper subject. Max and I had an interestin' conversation, but I think we should save more serious talk until after supper."

Brent jerked a nod. "I'll put Adam in his crib."

"Great." Jo's smile didn't reach her eyes. "The food'll be ready in about twenty minutes. Time for me to run to the store for milk. I know that's what you like with your meal."

Desi looked from one to the other. *The thought's kind, but the tone's subzero. What's between these two?*

"Des and I'll get the milk." Max stepped

between her sister and Brent. "I know the way."

Jo shrugged. "The car keys are hangin' on the hook inside the door. I'll set the table." She walked away.

Max's gaze followed her sister from the room and then locked onto Desi. "Off we go, then. Bye, Brent."

He nodded and headed toward the back bedroom.

"Bring that along." Max pointed at the glossy periodical Desi had used as a fan.

Desi picked it up and opened her mouth.

Max held up a hand. "Don't ask. Yet." She led the way into the warm New Mexico dusk. They climbed into Jo's beat-up car and pulled out of the driveway.

Max let out a long breath. "Under control, she says? Not hardly. What my sister calls an interestin' conversation, I call downright spooky."

"Spooky how?"

Max tapped the magazine in Desi's hand. "Like that."

Desi looked at the title on the cover. "*The Inner Witness*? Jo used that phrase in the kitchen. Sounds like something to do with Jehovah's Witnesses." She wrinkled her nose. "Is your sister getting hooked in with them? I can see why you're nervous."

"Beyond nervous. Jehovah's Witness stuff I have an answer for, but I don't know *what* to do with the Reverend Archer Romlin."

"Romlin? I've heard that name recently."

"Maybe you caught his TV show sometime."

"No, but I met this large fellow at that White House party. Tony says Hamilton's a crook, but Ham claims to have come to the Lord under this Reverend Romlin's ministry. Says his life's turned around. I don't know the whole story, but if it's legit, that's a pretty cool testimony."

"Big 'if' there. Jo talks about this Romlin every time I call these days. I tuned into the show a few times out of curiosity. I've got to admit that the man sounds and looks great." Max cast Desi a sideways glance.

"But?"

"He *feels* wrong. When he talks about Jesus, he calls Him the Lamb of God."

"That's scriptural."

"Yeah, but they've got this ritual Feast of the Lamb thing goin', kind of a cross between the Jewish Passover and Christian Communion. Romlin promises miracles to those who daily consume the body and blood."

Desi looked down at the magazine. "I'm all for regular Communion. I've received answers to prayer when the bread and wine reminded me of the price Jesus paid to redeem me." She flipped the pages and stopped on one displaying a full color photo of the Lord with His pierced hands outstretched. *Our Communion is with Him through the precious blood,* the caption read. She tapped her upper lip. "On the surface, this stuff looks great. But you're right. It feels wrong."

"That's the spooky part. The lingo is ambiguous enough to question and yet close enough not to condemn. Jo says Romlin teaches his followers to listen to their Inner Witness. She's convinced hers is sayin' we're the ones to get to the bottom of what happened to Karen."

Desi groaned. "Is Inner Witness another term for the leading of the Holy Spirit, or does it refer to another kind of spirit — a dangerous fake?"

"Exactly!" Max turned the vehicle into the grocery store lot. "I love my sister, but she goes from one faddy spirituality to the next."

"Yeah, you've told me about a few of her faith experiments. 'Always learning, but never coming to knowledge of the truth.' One of the toughest kinds of people to reach."

Max parked the car. "My opinion? A lot of Karen's identity problems came from all the screwed up philosophies Jo's tried. I had high hopes when Karen met Brent and started goin' to his church. Thought maybe she'd help her mom find the way, but I think the opposite happened. Jo and this Inner Witness Ministries pulled Karen into something that's . . . off. And did it before she had a chance to get her feet on solid ground with the Lord."

"Could the Inner Witness have anything to do with Karen's disappearance?"

"Wouldn't a cult be a better explanation than bein' a thief or a murder victim?"

Desi shook her head. "I've heard how hard it is to get people free of cult ideology, but it's an avenue to explore that won't put us afoul of a legal investigation. The magazine says the ministry headquarters is in Santa Fe. Too convenient to ignore. We should look into this."

"Deal." Max held up her hand.

Desi smacked it. She laid the magazine on the seat. "Just a PO box listed. Think you can dig the street address off the Internet tonight?"

Max shot her a look.

Desi laughed. "Sorry I asked."

They went into the store, bought the milk,

and drove back to the house. A big pickup with dual rear wheels was parked at the curb. The rays of the lowering sun sparkled off the chrome on the roll bar.

"Oh, man, Jo's ex is here. He'd better not be high. With that baby in there . . ." Max got out and slammed the door.

Desi followed at a hustle. Raised voices came from inside the house. Max broke into a run; Desi followed. When a woman screamed, Desi pulled her cell phone from her purse. A man bellowed as she punched in nine. Glass smashed. She punched in one.

All went still.

Max stopped with one foot on the porch step. Desi crept up behind her, finger poised over that last button.

A bird called from the branches of a tree.

Max jumped and let out a little laugh. Desi breathed again.

A gun blast shattered the air.

Five

"No, Max!" Desi tackled her friend from behind, and they tumbled together up the single step onto the porch.

Max struggled. "Let go of me! That's my *sister* in there!"

"And that's a gun in there. Hold your horses, and let me scoot up to the window and take a peek inside. You finish calling 9-1-1." Desi handed Max the phone and scrambled on all fours to the living room window.

Desi raised her head and peeked over the sash. The great room was empty. No, wait! A man with a long black ponytail and shiny cowboy boots backed in from the kitchen, hands raised. Jo followed with a shotgun pointed at Shiny Boots's middle.

"Go on. Git now!" Jo's voice blasted almost as loud as the gun.

"You'll wish you'd let me take him." The man rushed for the door.

Desi turned toward her friend. "Look out!"

Max jumped up as Shiny Boots charged outside. The man dodged around Max and hopped off the porch. Long, jeans-clad legs ate up the distance to the pickup. Shiny Boots leaped in, gunned the motor, and peeled out, leaving black streaks on the road.

Desi stood up on unsteady legs. "Your sister is the gun-toter, not the guy who left a layer of rubber behind."

Max groaned. "Jo inherited the lion's share of the temper in our Irish. Pete must have done somethin' to provoke her. No one can do that like her ex."

The front door banged open, and Jo came out. No gun, but her eyes spat fire. "Would you believe that crackhead came here to get Adam? Said he needed to take him to a safe place."

A siren's wail approached. Jo's gaze targeted Max and the cell phone. "You didn't call the police!"

Max planted her hands on her hips. "We heard gunfire. What were we supposed to do? Twiddle our thumbs?"

"Point taken." Jo stepped across the lawn as the cruiser pulled up to the curb.

A pair of officers got out. Thankfully,

not the ones who'd tried to haul Max in for questioning. Desi stood beside her friend. "I wonder if they get called here often. Those uniforms don't look too alarmed."

Max's shoulders slumped. "I work for you to get a little peace and quiet. My family's always been chock-full of drama."

"I didn't know you found our brand of adventure relaxing."

Jo came back across the lawn, and the police cruiser pulled away. "Guess we got that straightened out. No law against a woman accidentally discharging a firearm in her home."

"What did you shoot?" Max stared at her sister. "Pete didn't have holes in him."

"Oh, I'd've peppered him with buckshot. He knew that for sure when I emptied a barrel into my wall tiles. Let's go eat. And don't forget the milk." She went into the house.

Desi got the carton out of the car. "Wonder where Brent and Adam were when the OK Corral went down?"

Max took the milk. "Good question."

"Right here." Brent stepped around the side of the house, carrying a bright-eyed baby. "Jo shooed us out the back door as soon as she saw who drove up. We took a walk to the park. Was that a gunshot I heard?"

"It wasn't a truck backfiring." Max marched toward the house. "Which you'd know —" she tossed over her shoulder — "if you'd stuck around to help my sister."

Desi fell into step with Brent.

The young man gave her a lopsided grin. "My mother-in-law is one lady who can take care of herself, even against a kachina dancer."

"Kachina dancer?"

"Zuni medicine man. That's what Karen's father is. Or was until he married white and got strung out on drugs." Brent stopped beside the porch.

Desi looked into the young man's solemn eyes. "I sense more to the story."

Brent disentangled his son's fist from his hair. The baby chortled and grabbed another wad. "After he and Jo split, Pete went back to the old ways. He can't stand me. Says I lured his daughter from her heritage with this Jesus talk. He'd like to get his hands on Adam and make sure none of us ever sees him again. Just disappear into the desert."

Desi frowned. "That's pretty hard to believe with our sophisticated search methods."

"Tell that to the families of the kids on the cartons." He jerked his head in the direction Max had gone with the milk.

"You've got me there. So Cheama is using Karen's disappearance as an excuse to say Adam's in danger?"

"It's more complicated than that. He claims the spirits have told him that Adam is the focus of battle in the unseen realm and will be destroyed unless protected by the ancient arts of the Zuni shaman. He believes it, too."

Desi looked at the ground. "He might be a little right."

"Ouch!" Brent pulled his son's fist out of his hair and kissed the dimpled knuckles. "What do you mean? I thought you were a Christian."

"I'm not saying Adam needs a shaman's protection, but he should be taken out of harm's way. If something's up that Pete knows about, Karen might have known it, too. If she left on her own, her love for you and the baby may have been her motive. I know what a parent will do if he thinks his child is in danger. Not many months ago, my father died doing what he thought was best to protect me."

Brent's brows lifted. "But what could be so scary that a mother would leave her child?"

"I have no idea, but it's as likely as any of the other unproven theories floating around."

Max poked her head out the door. "Are you ever comin' to the table? I'm starved."

Desi laughed. "Good to hear those words out of you, woman. You're too skinny. Enjoy your sister's cooking tonight, because tomorrow you fly back to Boston with Adam. Your kids need you, and your mom will be tickled silly to get her hands on another baby."

Max stepped outside. "No way, Jose! My sister needs me."

Brent handed Adam up to her. "Jo needs you to look after Karen's baby. *I* need you to do that. If the police hadn't told me not to leave town, I'd take Adam myself."

The infant went after Max's hair, toothless grin on his face. Max disengaged his fingers and looked from Brent to Desi. "What about our plans to drop in on the ministry headquarters?"

"I'll do it. In fact, if it'll help your family and tie off a loose end, I'll even figure out a way to talk to this Snake Bonney without diving into some biker den."

"You're kidding, right?" Brent stared at her like she'd lost every marble in her head.

Max laughed. "Desiree Jacobs never kids about helpin' people she cares about. I'd say the hairy unwashed better watch out. She'll have 'em shaved and bathed before she's through." She headed inside.

"Thanks for the vote of confidence. I think." Desi followed Max into the house.

"Anytime, lady."

Making up the rear, Brent gave a tentative chuckle. "Oh, I see. You two *are* kidding."

"Nope." Desi clamped her lips shut. *Me and my big mouth.* How was she supposed to keep her word to Tony? And she needed to talk to Pete Cheama, too. Her beloved FBI agent would have a fit. Still, she really only promised to stay away from Hamilton Gordon. Not a word about Reverend Romlin or anyone else.

Too bad she made that promise about Gordon. She was aching to know what the man meant by "shared history." On second thought, he was an unconvicted criminal entrenched in a pseudo-Christian cult. What could be good about sharing history with him?

Desi took her place at the kitchen table and smiled as the enchiladas were passed around. She glanced at Max eating like she'd never seen food before. Good for her.

Many enchiladas later, Max yawned and

pushed her plate away. "Early to bed tonight."

"Me, too." Desi got up. "Let's get these dishes done."

Jo smiled. "Not you two. Shoo! Brent and I have it covered. I'll even waive the serious discussion until tomorrow."

Desi didn't argue, and Max trailed behind her to the great room. Desi got her laptop out. "No shut-eye until I download the report from the Denver office on the museum theft."

"I'll get you that street address for Inner Witness Ministries." Max's laptop appeared.

They both logged in using Jo's wireless connection. The room fell silent except for the clinking of dishes from the kitchen.

"That's funny." Max looked up from her screen.

Desi tore her attention from the report that was anything but amusing. "What's funny?"

"No problem findin' a fancy website for the ministry, complete with street address, but I can't find a home address for Reverend Romlin — and I know tricks to get that information."

Desi chuckled. "The man's homeless?"

"I doubt it, but he knows how to keep his private information off the web, and that takes doin'. I did find this." Max turned her screen toward Desi.

The page was crude and colorless, like a prototype site. No graphics or photos, a little bare-bones text about the ministry, but nothing they didn't already know.

"Look here." Max pointed. "A different address than on the other site. I checked to see if Inner Witness still owns this property, and they do."

"Give me both addresses, but I'm more interested in visiting the less public place."

"You got it." Max stifled a yawn.

"Hit the hay, girl. But tomorrow do me a favor and scrounge around for a connection between HJ Securities and Gordon Corp. I'd like to know how I drew Gordon's attention."

"I'm on it." Max grinned and handed Desi a slip of paper with the addresses. She wandered toward the bedroom. "You comin'? You've got to be as wiped out as I am."

"In a few minutes." Desi went back to the report from the Denver office.

Her heart beat an angry tattoo. Whoever robbed the museum had outstanding computer skills — and inside help. The security system hadn't merely been shut down, but fried to a crisp by a malicious virus that could only have been introduced to the control computer via an infected disk from inside the secure room. The night guard didn't have access. He prowled hallways, peered in the windows of locked display room doors, and probably snoozed in the lobby with his feet up on the receptionist's counter. But someone who worked in the museum during the day could have collected the necessary thumbprint and voice activation code.

Desi read on. Ah, a thief got careless with glass in the display area, and left blood near the artifact case. Should be a good clue for the authorities. She scanned the document further and gasped. No wonder the police suspected Brent and/or Karen of complicity in the theft!

In addition to the digital print reader, the computer control room was also secured by voice recognition software. Brent spent most of the day before the break-in recording interviews with museum staff for his thesis, including the curator and the administrator — the two voices that opened the door if the right words were spoken. But how would Brent know the code words to splice together? No doubt that was the unanswered question that kept him from being arrested.

Was the young man as dishonest as his brother? Desi hadn't thought so this afternoon, but now? She shook her head. She wasn't ready to convict him on circumstantial evidence.

Karen also worked for a few hours the day prior to the theft. Her supervisor said she gave the young woman the new punch code to get in the front door so she could open up the next day. But the museum never opened. The theft was discovered in the early morning when a patrol car stopped by on regular rounds and couldn't raise the guard. Unless the guard was tricked into opening the door, the thieves would have needed the front door code before they could get to the computer room. If Karen played a part in the theft, was she an accomplice, or was she snatched and forced to reveal the code and then murdered?

Brent's fears for his wife were well-founded. Unless, of course, Karen ran away to serve a cult. Not an attractive alternative, but better than being dead. Heart heavy, Desi shut down her laptop. Tomorrow might be a good day for answers. And she wouldn't even ruffle Tony's feathers.

How much trouble could she get into just checking out a ministry hole-in-the-wall?

■ ■ ■ ■

Desi drifted awake. Light showed around the edges of lavender curtains. Morning, finally.

She'd awakened at 2 a.m. and 4 a.m. from dreams of Jabba the Hutt with a Darth Vader voice chasing her through a room full of blue-eyed babies. Each time she woke up, Jabba was about to catch her because the babies floated all over the place like they were weightless, crying and grabbing her hair.

Stupid dream. Symptom of an overtired brain.

Desi's gaze traveled around the room. So this was the bedroom Karen had as a girl. Jo must not have changed much since her daughter moved out.

A desk sat near the window with a shelf over it. A dream catcher hung from a corner of the shelf, and a couple of odd-looking wooden dolls gazed down at Desi. Max said they were kachinas, representing spirits honored in tribal ceremonies. Strange critters with distorted faces. Other than that, the room was pretty much teen-rebel stock decor — heavy metal band posters, a dusty lava lamp on the dresser, and a jarring color scheme of red, black, and shock me purple.

Desi rolled onto her back and stretched. The big toe on her right foot gave a twinge. Someone stirred and sighed, and Desi turned her head. Tousled red curls covered the pillow of the twin bed next to hers.

Max was going home today. Without her! What had she been thinking?

Okay, so it was a good idea for Max to take Adam and do a Houdini. But Desi's synapses hadn't been firing on all cylinders when she volunteered to visit with a media minister and a motorcycle thug on her own. Talk about opposite walks of life.

She closed her eyes. Another round with Jabba the Hutt didn't sound too bad.

"Psst! You awake?"

Desi looked over at Max, who propped herself up on one elbow.

"Go home with me. You don't have to interview people about some cockamamie spin-off on Christianity. And you sure don't need to talk to some dude named Snake." Max wrinkled her nose. "If we can dig into Ham Gordon from the Internet, we can research this Inner Witness thing the same way . . . from Boston."

Desi laughed. "Thanks, Max. You clarified my need to stick around. We don't rely on Internet research when we work with a client. We do personal interviews."

"You're not working for a client."

"Sure am. You and your family. But I'm not requiring a contract or a fee."

Max put her bare feet on the braided rug. "Stubborn woman." She stretched.

Desi rolled out of bed. "I've had to learn to stand my ground against a certain smart-mouthed Texan."

"Oh, hardy-har-har." Max chucked her pillow.

Desi grabbed the soft mound and flung it back.

Max lunged to her feet. "Pillow fight!"

Laughing, Desi put her arm up, and a pillow whomped her shoulder.

"Hey! You two are having way too much fun in my house." Jo stood in the doorway, smiling. "I've got breakfast ready. And we need to talk over these plans of yours."

Desi changed out of her pajamas into business-casual pants and top and then ran a brush through her hair. Max threw on jeans and a T-shirt.

"On to the grub." She led the way into the great room.

Desi ran a stockinged foot across the cool floor. "Your sister has beautiful tile work. And these mosaics on the walls." She touched a star made out of tile chips that repeated itself at hip height around the perimeter of the room. "Gorgeous. Mexican influence."

"Anything Hispanic is common in Albuquerque, but Jo did the mosaics. She's quite the artist. Commissioned work, nothing commercial."

"Really! Maybe she'll do a piece for me."

Max laughed. "Always on the lookout for choice art."

"You got it. I had no idea you had an artist in the family." Desi sniffed. "Jo could make a living as a cook, too. Let me guess. Tex-Mex omelets like you make."

"Yeah. But Jo's may have more zing than you're used to."

"My taste buds are revving up already."

They sat at the trestle table, and Desi watched Jo slide omelets onto plates at the counter. The woman glanced up, but said nothing. Still looking peaked. But then, her daughter was still missing.

Desi's gaze strayed to the black pockmarks that peppered a mosaic on the far wall. No wonder Pete knew Jo meant business.

His stated purpose for coming after the baby had a noble ring, but was he serious about Adam being in danger or just taking advantage of circumstances for his personal agenda? Why did he think Adam might be a target? Easy to claim "the spirits told me." More likely he had indications from natural sources.

Did that mean he knew what led to Karen's disappearance? If so, why didn't he give the information to the authorities? Or maybe he had Karen and was trying to get his hands on his grandson, too. But if he took Karen, why didn't he grab Adam at the same time? Mother and child were alone in the house at the time of the disappearance.

Way too many unanswered questions, and only one way to get answers: Ask!

"Earth to Desi." Max's fingers snapped in front of her face.

Desi looked up. "Just thinking."

Jo set plates of steaming eggs laced with ham, cheese, and peppers before them. "Want to share those thoughts?" She sat down.

"I need to ask questions about all these interesting characters that keep popping up in this mess — your ex-husband, this Snake fellow, and the Reverend Archer Romlin."

Jo frowned. "Reverend Romlin doesn't belong in the same group as those other two."

Defensive reaction. Interesting. Desi

smiled and picked up her fork. "Everything's on hold until after I eat this." Her stomach growled. "Pass the salsa."

Fifteen minutes later, she laid her fork on the empty plate. "Okay, Q & A time. Are you up for it, Jo?"

The woman wiped her mouth with her napkin. "I've changed my mind. I don't think you or Max should get involved." She glanced at her sister. "I mean, it's enough that you're willing to take Adam for a while." She turned toward Desi. "You should go with her. I do want my daughter back, but I don't want anyone else to get hurt."

Desi laughed. "Max said sort of the same thing this morning. Is this a reverse psychology ploy? Because the more you try to talk me out of it, the more I think I need to chat with some people. Maybe find out things they wouldn't tell a cop."

Jo shook her head. "You haven't heard then? It was on the news last night."

Max sat forward. "We went to bed before the news came on. What happened?"

"The guard that was injured in the robbery went into convulsions and died."

Desi rocked back, breath leaving her lungs. "That's awful."

"Head wounds can be that way sometimes." Max shook her head.

Desi looked from one woman to the other. "The death escalates the seriousness of the museum theft. Anyone involved could be looking at murder charges."

Jo's face quivered. "I know, but I don't want to think about it. Karen can't be a part of this. She wouldn't!"

Desi glanced away. A few months ago, she would have sworn that her father would never be mixed up in a theft ring, yet he was. But for reasons no one would have guessed in a gazillion years. Maybe Karen had good reasons, too. Or maybe her disappearance was unconnected to the theft. No one had proven anything. Maybe it was time someone did.

Was she supposed to be that someone?

Tony would pull an ogre face. Max and Jo thought so one minute, then wanted to hang back the next. She'd put the brakes on, too, but the more she learned about Karen, the more something tugged at her to find the girl. Overwrought emotions or a prompting from the Holy Spirit? Whatever the Reverend Romlin taught on the subject — and she intended to look into that — God *did* often lead by an inner witness. A red-light/green-light knowing in the heart.

She'd take a few cautious steps and trust

that He'd show her if she was on the right track.

"You're stayin'.' " Max wrinkled her nose. "I see the decision on your face."

"And you're going."

Max sighed. "I guess that's the way things have to be."

"I'll get these dishes cleared up." Jo stood. "And take Max and Adam to the airport. The flight leaves in a couple of hours."

"Will you go by where Brent and Karen live?" Desi stood up with her dirty plate. "I'd like to ride along. I need to ask Brent a few more questions."

"Sorry." Jo followed Desi to the sink. "Brent's dropping Adam off on the way to work." She set a fistful of silverware in the sink and looked at her watch. "Should be here any minute."

"How about I ride to the airport with you anyway? You can tell me about Inner Witness and if Karen —"

The cordless phone on the counter shrilled. Jo snatched it up and turned her back on Desi.

"It's for you." Jo thrust the phone at her.

Desi took it, questioning the woman with her eyes. Jo shrugged and stepped away to join Max, who was rinsing dishes. Must have stomped a sore toe asking about the

Inner Witness and Karen in the same breath.

"Hello?"

"Is this Desiree Jacobs?"

"Speaking."

"I'm Ivan Spellman, administrator at the New Mexico Museum of Art and Anthropology. You called here yesterday?"

"Yes, Mr. Spellman, but this isn't the number I left with your secretary."

"Yes, I know. Unfortunately, she mislaid that one. But the police told me you were coming to Albuquerque and where you'd be staying."

"Would that be Officer Gillis and his partner who filled you in?" *Foul play, gentlemen.* They overstepped professional bounds giving out that information.

Spellman cleared his throat. Maybe he guessed he'd said more than he should about loose lips in his local PD. "Well, it doesn't really matter. Why did you call me, Ms. Jacobs?"

"As the head of HJ Securities, I wanted to let you know that I'm here if you have any questions or concerns about your loss." Desi walked over to the kitchen window and looked out onto a cement patio. A large shed occupied most of the yard beyond that. Not a garage. What was it? She pulled her mind back to the phone conversation.

"I'm up to my neck in questions and concerns," the administrator said, "but the police are handling the investigation. Or they were until the FBI decided an Indian artifacts case needed to be theirs." The man sounded like his breakfast didn't agree with him.

"I'm aware that the authorities have the case in hand." Try nearly being hog-tied by a bullheaded boyfriend determined to make that point. "We're happy to let them do their job, but we're also committed to making our expertise available to you and to them."

Spellman snorted. "Your *expertise* should have stopped this nightmare from happening. As of today, I want your staff to stay clear of museum property. We're going to look for a new security service."

She took a deep breath. *Daddy, I could do with a dose of your patience.* "I'm sure you're aware that there are circumstances no security company can guard against."

"Like treacherous employees? I keep hearing that song and dance, but a faithful employee died defending this museum."

"A terrible thing, Mr. Spellman. Do you know if he had family?"

"Well, ah . . . er, no. But I'll find out. In the meantime, unless someone can offer me ironclad proof that one of my people is a thief, I don't want to hear the suggestion again."

"Is that why you suspended Brent Webb from his duties?"

Indrawn breath. "Webb is a student, not an employee."

"And his missing wife?"

"You tell me. You're staying at her mother's house."

"But you wouldn't object to her being guilty?" Why was she pushing this man? The soul of diplomacy she wasn't today.

Heavy pause. "Mrs. Webb was a part-time receptionist with a poor work record over the past eight months. Her supervisor has been reprimanded for keeping her on. Whether that means she's an accomplice in the theft, I'm not prepared to guess."

She turned and grimaced at Max, who was staring at her with a dirty dish in hand. Jo scrubbed at a frying pan, lips pursed. Good thing the woman couldn't hear the administrator's side of the conversation, or he might wind up with a load of buckshot in *his* tail.

Desi switched the phone to her other ear. "Mr. Spellman, we both want the culprits to be caught. Just as no security company can guard against every eventuality, no employer can guarantee his employees' honesty. We need to continue working together, especially since we know little yet. Maybe I could drop in and see you in person later today."

The man on the other end cleared his throat. "That might be all right. I'd be interested to hear why you're staying at the childhood home of one of the suspects."

Desi forced a laugh. "That's an easy one. Other answers may be harder to come by. Does two-thirty work for you?"

"Make it at least three."

"I'll see you at three, Mr. Spellman." Desi put the phone back in its stand and whirled toward Max and Jo. "Aagh! Mr. Concerned Administrator hasn't bothered to find out if his dead employee was a family man, but he's sure busy hunting a scapegoat for the theft — as long as it's not someone on his payroll."

Jo shook her head as she put the pan into the dishwasher. "One of those tooth-grindin' conversations."

Max crossed her arms and leaned a hip against the counter. "Tough customer, eh? At least you got in to see him. Maybe you can check out the theft scene while you're at it."

"I'll take a look, but after multiple law

enforcement agencies and the experts from our Denver office have swept through there, I don't expect to find anything new." Desi looked at Jo, who was wiping her hands on a towel. "I'm no private detective. If I uncover anything that might help find Karen, even if it's incriminating, I'm going to head straight for Agent Ortiz."

"Understood." Jo nodded.

"And stop stonewalling me when I ask questions that make you uncomfortable."

Jo's chin came up. "I'm not uncomfortable talkin' to a genuine seeker about the Reverend Romlin. Karen was helped by his broadcasts and the ministry team that visited after Adam was born. That church of Brent's didn't offer much personal attention."

So there was the bone of contention between Brent and Jo. Interesting to know what Brent's side of the story was. "This is no witch hunt. I'm trying to understand what Karen might have been thinking when she disappeared."

Jo tossed the towel onto the counter. "Ask what you want on the way to the airport. But if you try to smear the Reverend, you'll have me to answer to." The woman stalked out.

"Whew!" Max shook her head. "You mash

her buttons almost as well as her ex. She should be kissin' your feet for helpin', and she acts like you're a threat."

"Maybe I should get a hotel room." Desi scratched her head.

"A cell phone's playin' somethin' majestic from Karen's room!" Jo's voice carried from the other end of the house.

"That'll be mine." Desi headed for the bedroom. Brent came through the front door with Adam in his car seat as she hurried past. She waved at him. "Tiptoe in with sock feet."

"Jo's on the warpath, eh?" His laugh followed her.

Desi got to her phone right when it stopped playing *Agnus Dei.* She checked her missed calls record and groaned.

Max came in and started tossing things into her wheelie. "Bad news?"

"Paris office. If it's not coming from one direction, it's another."

"More of that wranglin' over contract language with the Louvre?"

"No doubt. Chances are I won't be going with you to the airport. Jo isn't really open to talking to me anyway. When I'm done with Paris, I'll rent a car and skedaddle for Santa Fe."

Max laid a hand on Desi's arm. "Stay in

touch. Okay? And call Tony with an update."

Desi sighed. "Only because I miss the big lug, but I know he'll give me a lecture."

"Hey, at least he cares." Max went back to packing. "He could be a good source of information. Get him to sniff around after our good Reverend. He's got resources we couldn't even dream about."

"Maxie-girl, you're a gem. Just when I think this whole morning's a bust, you hand me a nugget." Desi picked up a framed photograph from the dresser. "This must be Karen. How old was she in this picture?"

Max looked over her shoulder. "Seventeen. That was her senior picture."

A husky young woman stood framed in an adobe archway. She wore jeans and a light-colored buckskin jacket with fringes around the shoulders. Her features were pleasant and regular, skin tanned or naturally bronzed. One hand rested against the arch; the fingertips of the other touched the squash blossom necklace at her throat — either the same necklace or a copy of the one her mother wore.

Karen's elbow-length dark hair flowed long and loose with a hint of the curl from Jo and Max's side of the family. But the attractive widow's peak on her forehead was a unique feature. Full, rouged lips curved into a smile that imitated sultry but didn't quite pull it off. Too pinched at the edges. And the eyes —

Desi's heart wrenched.

Poster child for a lonely generation in the midst of a crowded world.

A feminine scream sounded from the other room, followed by a male shout. The baby wailed.

Desi locked gazes with Max, and they both charged for the great room.

SIX

"She's alive! She's alive!" Jo had Brent in a bear hug, and they whirled around the room.

They stopped when Desi and Max skidded to a halt in front of them. Wearing a goofy grin, Jo stepped away from Brent. The baby howled from his car seat in the middle of the floor.

"Karen's alive!" Brent blurted, face flushed.

Max stared from one to the other. "What in the world —"

"My car is gone." Jo grasped her sister's arms. "And Karen's the only one with an extra set of keys. Mine are still hangin' in the foyer."

Brent knelt to unbuckle his son from the seat. His hands shook.

Desi let out a gust of breath. "I hate to be the killjoy, but anyone who knows how to hot-wire a car could have stolen it."

Jo shook her head so hard the beads on her necklace rattled. "It's Karen. I know . . . in here." She tapped her chest.

"Your inner witness?" Way to antagonize the woman, but this situation kept going from nuts to bonkers.

"A mom's knowing. But you can't relate to that."

Touché, lady. Desi looked down.

Max touched Desi's shoulder. "Jo, my friend is tryin' to help . . . at your request."

"Okay, so I'm touchy. But now that I've found somethin' real, my sister and her friend are still passin' judgment on my beliefs. I'm tired of it, and I . . . Oh, never mind." Jo looked toward Desi. "I'm sorry. I'll try to be more cooperative."

"Forget it." Desi waved a hand. "So back to the car theft. Why did it have to be Karen?"

"Yeah." Max tilted her head. "Pete was plenty mad at you when he left here —"

"I doubt it was Pete." Brent stood up, holding Adam.

Jo nodded. "Not Pete's style. He's more likely to get wasted and wreck the vehicle with a crowbar, not sneak off with it in the night."

Brent switched Adam from one arm to the other. "When Karen disappeared, so did our rattletrap of a second car. If it died on her, this is the logical place she'd come for fresh wheels."

"Fair enough." Desi pointed at Jo. "You're going to call the FBI, and that's what you're going to tell them."

"Got it!" She smiled and years fell away from her face. "So when they find my car, they find my daughter." She bounded toward the kitchen.

Brent looked at his watch. "I'm going to be late for work. Maybe I should call in —"

"No," Max said. "You need to be where Karen would expect to find you if she's lookin'."

"Good thinking." Desi nodded to Max.

"And *you* need to call Paris, remember?"

"I haven't forgotten, but first I'm going to call a cab. You and Adam have a flight to catch. And I'm going along to make sure you're safe —"

"Nix that. You stay and see what the feds say about the disappearance of Jo's car."

"But Pete Cheama's out there."

"So?" Max took Adam from Brent. "Me and Little Bit'll be fine. What do you think the dude can do in the middle of a crowded airport with me screamin' my head off and scratchin' his eyes out?"

Desi laughed. "I almost forgot you're

Texas Irish like your sister."

"You got that right. Let's hop to it."

The room emptied in a flurry. Desi held Adam while Max finished packing. Then they waited on the porch for the cab. Agent Ortiz would descend on the house soon.

Desi nudged Max. "If Karen was here last night, don't you think it's strange she didn't try to speak to her mother? At least reassure her that she's okay?"

Strain lines appeared around Max's mouth. "Nothin' has added up right yet."

The cab arrived, and Desi helped the driver load the bags into the trunk while Max installed Adam's car seat. A few minutes later, Desi watched the cab and its precious cargo pull away. Then she walked back toward Jo's house.

How maddening to think the missing girl might have been so close, and they missed her. *Father God, keep Karen safe wherever she is.*

Behind her, a vehicle pulled up. She turned to see the Hispanic agent climb out of the passenger seat of a dark blue sedan. Ortiz wore a crisp brown A-line skirt, a cream-colored blouse, and a blazer that matched the skirt. Her walk was confident, face tight and eager. Delighted about the new lead, but not, Desi bet, for the same reason as Jo.

Desi didn't want to be the one to point out the obvious to Max's sister: If Karen was desperate enough to steal her own mother's car and not say boo to her loved ones, she was more than a runaway. She must be in trouble up to her cute little widow's peak. The possibility of a murder charge due to that guard's death fit the bill.

Agent Ortiz nodded at Desi. "Good morning. Thank you for notifying us. Do you know where the vehicle was parked?"

"Jo called it in. I think the car was in the port next to the house."

"That's right." Jo came up to them. "I'll show you."

The agent lifted a hand. "No, let me check out the area. Wait here, please."

"You need a hand, Orty?" A voice called from the direction of the sedan. A slender man in a rumpled suit leaned against the front bumper. He took something out of his pocket, a crack sounded, pieces sprinkled on the ground, and then he popped an item into his mouth.

A peanut?

Desi looked toward Ortiz, who curled her lip toward her partner

"Hang tight, Stuey." The name was dipped in sarcasm. "I'll let you know."

The man nodded and pulled another peanut from his pocket.

Ortiz headed for the carport.

Jo's fingers closed around Desi's upper arm. "I want them to find Karen . . . and yet I'm scared for it to happen. Can you understand that?"

Desi laid her hand over Jo's. "I may not have children, but I know what it's like to be afraid for a loved one."

"Thanks. I'm sorry about that remark earlier." Jo took a deep breath. "I feel like shell corn on a hot skillet. Sometimes the heat gets too much, and I pop off." She tried a smile, but her eyes stayed dark and sad.

"Rhoades!" Ortiz's shout came from the carport. "Get the lab on the horn and tell them to trot out here. We've got what looks like blood here."

"Blood?" Jo's fingers turned to claws around Desi's arm. "Oh no! My baby's hurt." The woman turned, wild-eyed, and raced toward the carport.

Tony's rigid thumb ruffled a stack of papers on his desk. He pushed stiff fingers through his hair. Might feel great to jerk some of it out about now.

He stared at the map in front of him.

Three red circles glared back. The little eyes marked trucking companies in Boston that had branch offices in Hollywood, California, a hotspot for pirates of copyrighted property.

This case was the most massive and organized bootlegging operation Tony had ever seen. The public had no idea the amount of money that exchanged hands over pirated music and videos, and they usually skipped past that pesky FBI warning on DVDs. They'd probably start a grassroots uprising if they realized how much pirates cost honest folks in higher prices.

So while the FBI in L.A. hunted for the copying center, he'd been handed the job of cornering the distributor. Perfect sideline for a legitimate national freight company? You bet! Tony smacked the map with an open palm. Problem was no judge would give them a search warrant for all three trucking companies. And since the black marketeer they arrested with the goods last night had zipped his lips, they didn't have enough cause to go after the most likely suspect: Gordon Trucking.

Tony's fingers rummaged through his hair again. Why was he doing that?

Desi. She liked his hair a mess, and she was never far from his mind. What was that lovely lady doing today? Sleeping in? Not likely. One o'clock in Boston, but 10 a.m. in Albuquerque. She'd no doubt been up for hours — and up to who knew what.

His little crusader wouldn't be able to resist helping Max's family. He knew it better than she did. Scary thought, for him. Too bad she hadn't figured out how dangerous the tendency to ride to the rescue could be in this nasty world.

Would you have her any other way?

He shook his head. Too deep a subject for a quick answer. Better see if any of the other squad members had uncovered anything to give this dead end fresh direction. He looked out the glassed-in enclosure of the private office he rated as squad supervisor.

What little he could see of the bullpen showed few agents at their stations. The rest of the squad was out chasing leads. Or more likely, chasing their tails, the way this case was going.

In their seats, Tony counted Ben Erickson, Valerie Polanski, and Matt Slidell. Ben was on the phone, Valerie filling out paperwork, and Matt glued to his computer screen. What else was new? The wunderkind wouldn't miss a slipped decimal point in the stockholder's reports of "Ham" Gordon's corporation, but it would take a nuclear explosion to get him on another task until he finished. Talk about a one-track mind.

Tony stood, tugged his cell phone from his belt pouch, and checked the charge. Good. Desi had called him last night to let him know she and Max had arrived at the Cheama home. If she called again, he'd be available.

He took a step toward his office door, and the desk phone rang. He went back to his chair but didn't sit. He'd done too much of that today. How did the professional paper pushers stand it?

Pun intended.

"Lucano here." He heard the sound of heavy breathing, like someone puffing from a long run or maybe pain.

"You Desiree . . . Jacobs's boyfriend?" The voice was male.

Tony stiffened. "Who wants to know?"

"Please I —" the man sucked in a breath — "know her face. From the news. Same place . . . I got your name."

"What do you want with Ms. Jacobs?" Tony pressed a button on his phone. *This call will be recorded to insure quality crook control.* He waved like a demented cheerleader at his team members outside the glass walls.

"Nothing," the strained voice said. "It's you."

Erickson caught his wave and trotted to the door. Tony scribbled *start trace* on a piece of paper. The Minnesotan read the note and dove back into the bullpen.

"You're looking for me?" Tony watched Erickson grab a phone receiver. *Pedal to the metal, you big Norskie!* "It's no secret where I can be found." Polanski darted over and hovered in his doorway.

The caller chuckled, and then hitched his breath.

Pain then. Back when his ex-partner was recovering from a bullet wound in the chest, Tony heard the sound often enough to recognize it now.

The man let out a soft grunt. "But it's not . . . common knowledge . . . you're looking for . . . people who haul . . . pirated discs."

Tony's heart jerked. "What do you know about that?"

Erickson flashed him a thumb's-up. *Way to go, Minnesota!*

"Don't ask for . . . explanations. This is . . . all I can give you. A trucker named Elvis. He can . . . lead you to the new Waco."

"Wait a minute! Is this some kind of joke?" This guy was going to get his chops busted if he was a prankster playing off that not-long-enough-ago cult tragedy in Waco, Texas.

"No joke." A breath rasped. "It's a puzzle. Connect the dots. You'll . . . figure it out. Gotta go."

"Wait! You sound like you're hurt. We can —"

Click.

Tony slammed the receiver down. He strode into the bullpen. "Sorry people. He hung up on me."

Erickson shook his head. "I put switchboard on it, but there wasn't enough time to complete a trace."

"The informant knew about our pirating investigation. He said to look for a trucker named Elvis, who would lead us to the 'new Waco.' " He bracketed the last two words with fingers in the air. "Legit or a crank? What do you think?"

Erickson scowled. "Sounds like the guy's using."

Polanski shrugged. "You got me. I'll have the lab get the recording off the system and analyze it. Maybe they can find some clues to location from background noise."

"Do it." Tony turned toward the big blond agent. "Erickson, you get on the Elvis thing."

"Elvis? Did I hear someone mention The King?"

Tony looked down to find Slidell blinking up at him.

What do you know? Something besides equations gets his attention. "We just had an anonymous call. The man said we should look for a trucker named Elvis."

"I gathered that much." Slidell tapped his lip.

Desi does that, too. Stop thinking about her! But that heavy-breathing guy mentioned her first thing. That means something. Was it a threat?

"CB handle." Slidell's expression flattened. "It's not unusual for road rangers to presume on a famous name."

"So this could be a legitimate lead. If we find a driver with a CB handle of Elvis working for Gordon Trucking, we might have a break in the case."

The computer guru smiled. "You're passably bright." He turned to stare at his screen.

Off in the ozone again. And not one to kiss up to the boss. Wouldn't occur to him. At least he could like that much about the guy.

Tony shook his head. But Slidell was wrong about one thing — Tony was dim, going on dimmer. Sure, he would have figured out the CB handle thing in a minute or two. Way too slow, because his thoughts kept straying to Desiree. But what could he do with an innuendo about her from an unidentified subject? A big fat nada, that's what.

He was in Boston. She was in Albuquerque. He couldn't protect her from herself, much less somebody with evil intent.

And that knowledge might send him straight to the funny farm.

It *was* blood. The lab person determined that much in two seconds flat. But whose? The answer would take a while.

From a shady spot under a tree, Desi watched the lab agent leave. Standing beside her, Jo hugged herself. The stocky Ortiz had had to restrain Jo from charging all over the scene of the investigation. Now the agent and her peanut-eating partner walked up to them.

Mr. Peanut wore a smug grin. Desi's jaw clenched. The guy was eating up the new leads like a fresh bag of nuts.

"We'll test the DNA," Ortiz said. "See if it matches Karen's."

The partner nodded. "We'll let you know if it's hers."

"That would be good," Desi said. At least the man wasn't a complete toad.

Jo clasped her hands together. "Please do."

Ortiz angled her head toward her partner. "This is Agent Stuart Rhoades. One of us will be in touch, or you can call us at the office."

"Do you have a cell number?"

Ortiz pulled a card from her jacket pocket, scribbled on the back, and handed it to Desi.

"Thanks."

"Welcome." Ortiz smiled. "Where's Maxine Webb this morning?"

"She went back to Boston with Brent and Karen's baby."

Rhoades's eyes narrowed.

Ortiz nodded. "Good idea. The baby's in capable hands, and Ms. Webb is distanced from the investigation." She looked at Jo. "I see Pete Cheama paid a visit."

Jo's chin came up. "Who told you that?"

Ortiz grinned. "Dually tire marks in front of your house? The ex drives a pickup with dual rear tires? It doesn't take a rocket scientist. I thought you had a restraining order on him."

"I handled it." Jo's face closed in.

"We heard." Rhoades chuckled. "The Albuquerque PD aren't rocket scientists either, but they know two plus two when they're called to a domestic disturbance involving a shotgun." He pulled out a peanut. "You do know your ex is in over his head with some bad folks, don't you?"

Jo said a foul word. "I didn't, but it doesn't surprise me. Hey!" Her eyes widened. "Maybe Karen's disappearance is connected with his problems, not the museum robbery. Ever think of that?"

"We've thought of it, Mrs. Cheama." Ortiz nodded. "We're looking into all possibilities."

"Have you talked to Snake Bonney?" She poked a finger at the agents. "That motorcycle bum called her a couple of times before she disappeared. I told you about that."

The peanut flipped in the air. "Bonney says he hasn't seen Karen since she left him."

Jo snorted. "He's lyin'. Karen told me they ran into each other at the mall a month ago. Then he started callin' her again. Don't tell me you trust some lowlife called Snake."

Rhoades's chest puffed out, and his cheeks expanded.

Desi blinked. Maybe he is a toad. She touched Jo's arm. "I doubt they took Snake's word. I'm close friends with an FBI agent, and he'd do a background check on a holy angel."

Ortiz smiled. "Lucano, right?"

A bug-under-glass feeling prickled across Desi's skin. "Do you know him?"

"I've spoken to him on the phone a few times."

She'd boil Tony in oil if he was keeping tabs on her through Bureau channels. She forced her jaw to relax. "I'm going to be at the museum this afternoon. Is there anything I should know about the robbery that would help us do our job better?"

"Sure —" the peanut-eater snorted — "keep out of our way and let us do *our* job."

"I wouldn't dream of stepping on your toes, Agent Rhoades. But the more thorough we are on the security end, the less likely you'll need to investigate a robbery there again. Good deal for everyone concerned. Yes?"

"Si." Ortiz laughed. "I like your confidence."

"Confidence based on experience."

The female agent nodded. "I like that even better. Let me tell you this, then. You'll figure it out when you get there anyway. The robbery wasn't motivated by gain. Someone wanted specific Native American artifacts."

Desi's heart rate quickened. "So if you

find out why the looters grabbed those particular pieces, you might know who took them."

"Exactly," Ortiz said. "And *looters* is a good term. The entrance was slick and pro, but the snatch was messy. Lots of broken glass, as I'm sure your branch office reported. HJ Securities was on-site almost as fast as we were. If it means anything, we found their input helpful on the security breach. They determined right away that inside help was needed to get into the control room. They even told us how the alarm system was sabotaged."

Desi smiled. "We try to be efficient. Observant, too. The team's report says you collected blood evidence not related to the bludgeoned guard."

Rhoades's eyes widened, and Ortiz's lips puckered.

Jo looked from one to the other. "Someone was hurt? Someone who might need to steal a car?" Her forehead wrinkled. "But why would the thief wait so long to grab transportation? And this person wouldn't still be bleeding." She shook her head. "No, the thefts can't be related. I could see Karen needing my car, but stealing artifacts priceless to her heritage? Forget it!"

Rhoades stuck a peanut in his mouth.

"Blood doesn't lie." His *'s'* came out mangled from the bulge in his cheek. "We'll know pretty soon if there's any connection."

"Talk to you later." Ortiz dipped her chin.

As the two agents walked away, Ortiz glowered at Rhoades. "Don't even *think* about tossing that shell into the backseat."

He chuckled. "Why not? It'll be right at home with the rest . . ." Their voices faded.

Jo stared at the ground, clenching and unclenching her fists. "Life shouldn't be so hard, you know." She turned and plodded into the house.

Desi sat on the porch step. She needed to call Paris, but who cared about business? Max's niece could be out there hurt.

It might be better to find out the bleeder from the carport wasn't Jo's daughter. But if the droplets weren't hers, that didn't prove she hadn't helped hijack the car along with a wounded person. Or maybe the blood belonged to Karen's kidnapper, and she'd been forced to assist with the car theft. If daughter was like mother, she could have inflicted bodily harm on anyone trying to control her. Maybe not enough to escape, but sufficient to leave a trace behind.

All speculation might fade into insignificance if the blood found here was Karen's, and it matched the blood from the museum.

If solid evidence tied the missing woman to the fatal robbery, Jo . . . Brent . . . Max . . .

None of them had even begun to taste heartache.

"Good news." Polanski walked into Tony's office. "Elvis is in the building."

"Meaning?" Tony laid down the report that graphed the spike in pirated discs showing up nationwide over the past twelve months.

"I chatted up the secretary who's been cooperating with us over at Gordon Trucking. She told me the name on Elvis's employment record is Bill Winston. A check on him came up negative. I mean, the guy exists — birth record, social security number, driver's license, yada-yada — but he was clean. Too squeaky. How many people have never had a parking ticket?"

Tony leaned back. "Winston's got a better record than I do."

"Me, too. Anyway, the guy came into Boston two days ago with a shipment from . . . guess where?"

"The Sante Fe headquarters of Gordon Corp."

Polanski made a buzzer sound. "No points on that one." She tapped the graph on Tony's desk. "Los Angeles, California. Also, conveniently, home to a manufacturing and distribution center for Gordon Corp's bone meal products."

"Well, there's a couple of dots connected."

"Right. Now let me challenge you again."

"All right. I'll play."

"Guess where the dude is right now?"

Tony grinned. "You said Elvis is in the building, so he must still be in Boston."

"Dingdingding. That is keeeerect. And I'll do one better. He's at Gordon Trucking as we speak, getting ready to leave for a run to — ta-da! — Sante Fe. What do you want to bet he'll be hauling a bundle of hidden cash from the black-market sale of pirated goods?"

Tony stood, heart rate kicking up a notch. "Then we'd better hustle if we want an audience with the King." He strode out of his office, Polanski dogging him. "Erickson! Join us for a drive over to Gordon Trucking."

The Minnesotan hopped up. "Count me in."

They headed up the hall toward the elevator. The door folded open, and Katsuo Hajimoto, another squad member, stepped out. His flat features brightened. "I dug up some goodies on the relationship between Gordon and this Reverend Archer Romlin.

Gordon's pouring a river of dough into this Inner Witness Ministries. And the more I look at Romlin, the less I think he's who he says he is. Tax deductible contributions to a tax exempt ministry would be a slick way to launder dirty money."

"Good work, Haj." As much as he hated scandal that caused people to sneer at the church, he hated ministries that dishonored the Gospel worse. People were left with no one and nothing to trust. "Write up what you've got and go after anything else you can find. When everyone comes in, tell them to work on their reports. We'll meet to compare notes before the end of the day. The three of us should be back in a couple of hours."

"Got it." Hajimoto hustled toward the bullpen.

Tony's group went to the parking garage, where they climbed into a tan SUV. Erickson drove, Tony rode shotgun, and Polanski settled in the back.

"I love these new wheels of yours, bossman." She sniffed. "Even smells new."

"Yeah, sure. Pretty nice." Erickson ran a hand over the seat. "If I can't be wide open in the saddle of my Harley Super Glide, this'll do."

Tony laughed. "Hard to haul the team

around on a motorcycle. Enjoy this ride while you may. It'll get broke in soon enough."

Erickson chuckled while he wove through downtown Boston traffic. "Y'betcha. Maybe we'll catch a fine fish to take home today."

Tony grinned but shook his head. "I'm looking more to startle the fish and see which way it darts."

Polanski laughed. "I like the way you think."

"Here's the plan. I'll approach the guy, let him know he's been fingered as someone transporting stolen goods across state lines. You two wander around his truck. Don't go where you're not invited, but act like you might."

"Ah, the fish'll start to jump." The Minnesotan hooted. "That's always fun."

"We'll either get a quick reaction, or if he's a cool one, he'll react after he thinks we've left. But there's no way he'll take off with that cash still in his truck."

"If he knows it's there," Polanski said. "He could be a blind mule."

"Doubtful." Tony glanced back at her. "But even if he's ignorant, the noise he'll make about being rousted by the feds will get someone's attention. We'll see action."

Polanski smacked her hands together.

"Without a doubt."

"Absitively posolutely." Erickson jerked a nod.

Tony chuckled. "The important thing is we don't let Elvis leave the building without him either trying to ditch the goods or us putting a tail so close on his mud flaps he feels our breath on his neck. Polanski, fill Erickson in on what we know about Winston."

She outlined her criminal background check results, and added, "According to his birth certificate, he was born William Winston, no middle name. He's forty-four now. I didn't find record of a marriage license and no children with him listed as the father."

Erickson frowned. "So he's Joe Citizen with no life but his eighteen wheels? Feels like a fake identity. Bill Winston — B.W. Can't put my finger on it, but that rings a bell."

"Ding, ding." Polanski laughed. "Something for you to figure out after we put on our dog and pony show."

"Here we go people." Tony studied the Gordon Trucking building — basic cement block with a brick facade and sheet metal roof. "Your source in there gave you Winston's truck number?" He lifted a brow at

Polanski.

"Eighteen. Should be painted on the doors."

Tony made a circling motion. "Swing to the rear where the trucks are." He turned toward the backseat. "How sure are you that the secretary hasn't told our guy we're interested?"

"As sure as she wants to keep her job."

"Good enough." A paved lot four times the size as the front one came into view. Half a dozen semis were backed up to loading docks. "One of these'll be our guy. Cruise slow."

"There's eighteen." Erickson pointed.

"And Mr. Winston, no doubt, standing by the driver door checking his manifest." Tony studied the man. Dark, bushy sideburns stuck on out both sides of his face. The eyes were hidden under sunglasses. He dressed trucker generic in faded jeans, long-sleeved flannel shirt, and stuffed vest.

Erickson stopped the SUV in front of their subject. The man looked up but didn't move.

"Polanski, go around the truck and approach from behind," Tony said. "Minnesota and I will move in from the front. Sandwiched between us and these semis, he won't go anywhere until we're done talking to him."

Tony got out, the vehicle between him and the subject. The other agents stepped out and slammed their doors. Polanski walked with controlled haste toward the far side of the truck. The subject's head turned to follow her, but the rest of him stood as if staked to the ground.

"William Winston," Tony called. "FBI. We'd like a word with you."

The man released his clipboard and a hand dove inside his vest.

Tony went for his weapon. "Get down, Erickson!"

Instead, the Minnesotan lunged between him and Winston, hand inside his jacket. Tony freed his gun as his legs moved apart, knees flexed. "Minnesota! Get —"

Blam!

The blast reverberated, followed by another. An angry word left Tony's lips as his gun swung into position. Erickson fell out of his view, leaving him looking up the barrel of the subject's weapon.

Tony pulled the trigger, and Winston staggered backward, gun discharging.

A bullet whined past Tony's head. He fired again, then again. Winston flopped to the ground.

Fists squeezed Tony's lungs. "Erickson!

Minnesota!"
Silence answered.

Seven

Eyes on the downed trucker, Tony raced around the front of the SUV. Polanski quick-stepped into view from the far end of the semi, gun pointed at the subject on the ground. Tony knelt beside Erickson, sprawled by the driver door. So much blood. He laid two fingers on the pulse point at the throat.

"This one's finished," Polanski said. "How's Erickson?"

The Minnesotan's chest was a mess; his face peaceful as a child's. The spirit was gone — not in the building. *Why, God?* Tony looked at Polanski and shook his head.

She said something sharp in Polish. "How could this happen?" She shoved her pistol into its holster like she was punching someone. "We knew we'd get a reaction from Winston. But taking on three FBI agents in an open gun battle? Off the charts insane! Was he on something?"

Numb calm blanked Tony's insides. "Testing for drivers is strict. One offense and they lose their license. Besides this guy's record — or lack of one — showed no indicators for drug use." He looked down at the body of the man he'd grown to like and respect. An ache radiated from his marrow. His shoes crunched on glass from the shattered driver's side window as he stepped around Erickson. He opened the blood-spattered door and got on the radio.

Within twenty minutes, the crime scene was cordoned off and Evidence Recovery Technicians trolled the area. A pair of ambulances sat nearby, lights lazily turning. EMTs lounged on the bumpers while the coroner finished with the bodies. No rush on this call-out.

At least nobody indulged the usual morbid humor that helped them cope with an overload of gruesome. The death of an agent rated reverent concentration.

Tony swallowed the bile in his throat and continued his phone conversation with the Assistant Special Agent in Charge, Bernard Cooke. "Winston's truck is now fair game for a search, but it'd be better if we could get a warrant for the whole property."

"I'll see what I can do." Cooke's voice held a trace of gravel. Everyone came a little unglued when one of their own went down. "Break that truck down to the bare chassis if you have to." The ASAC cleared his throat. "With an agent-involved shooting, there'll be an internal investigation. Henderson from the OPR is on the way."

Great. The Office of Professional Responsibility. Tony bit out a laugh. "Correction. He's getting out of his car. I'll follow up with you later." He broke the connection.

Half-Pint Henderson walked up to Tony, his stare dark and flat. "I have to take your gun."

"I expected that." He handed it over.

"Polanski fire hers?"

"Nope."

Henderson nodded. "I'll verify with her and check her gun."

"You do that. Better not take my word for it." Did that flare-up come out of his mouth?

The short man's eyes slitted. "I'm just doing my job, Lucano. And you, more than anybody else, need me to do it right."

Tony shoved his hands in his pants pockets. "I know." He squeezed a coin until it hurt his palm. "But I need to rip something up, and you're handy."

"I hear you."

"What do you want to know?"

"Nothing right now." The OPR agent's

gaze wandered the scene. "I'll wait for the initial reports from the coroner and the ERTs. Then we'll sit down at the office in a recorded session and go over the details from your perspective."

"All right. Then I'm free to go about my business?"

Henderson nodded. "For the moment."

Tony took his hands from his pockets. "I'm going to tear a truck apart."

"Find something while you're at it." The OPR agent walked away.

A gurney carrying a white-sheeted body rattled past.

Less than an hour ago, Minnesota was breathing the same air he was. Where was the big Norske now? Why had they never talked about anything that mattered forever?

Tony stared at the pavement. Absorbed in his work. Distracted by his personal life. A slow burn spread across his skin. He stood naked before God, and a few fig leaves of excuses couldn't begin to cover him.

The rich browns and ochers of desert landscape swept past as Desi drove Interstate 25 toward Santa Fe. With her cell phone set on speaker and fitted into the dash holder of the rental car, she took care of business with the HJ Securities office in

France. Keeping her eyes on the road and her hands on the wheel was no problem, but keeping her mind on the conversation with Paris? Forget it!

Business lasted until she neared La Cienega, too close to Santa Fe for a call to Tony. *Sorry. Later, hon.*

Inside the city limits, she stopped at a gas station to exercise her feminine right to ask directions. Fifteen minutes later, Desi parked across the street from a clapboard building sandwiched between a liquor store and a bakery. A painted sign over the door said Inner Witness Ministries. Then in smaller letters beneath, Washed in the Blood. Desi winced. Scriptural, but a little off-putting for anyone who didn't speak Christianese.

She watched pedestrians and vehicle traffic. Traffic was fair at the bakery and good to brisk at the liquor store, but no one went in or out of the ministry entrance. Gray drapes covered the display window. She'd have to go in to see if anyone was there.

Desi crossed the street between spurts of traffic. Bakery smells brought a tummy rumble. Past lunchtime and she hadn't eaten anything since Jo's Tex-Mex omelet. Desi warned her stomach to cease and desist and opened the door to the ministry headquarters. Canned worship music and the cloying scent of potpourri greeted her. After the bright sunshine outside, the florescent lights pulled her into a dim, secretive world.

In front of her sat a hardwood desk with a flat PC screen, but no receptionist. Behind the desk, a pair of portable partitions blocked the view of the rest of the office. A narrow opening between them led into an unlit rear area — black and forbidding as a cave. Dank cold flowed toward her, and Desi shivered. Silly impression. She shook her head and turned away.

To her left, three stuffed chairs were arranged around an oval coffee table with ministry magazines scattered across the top. Five pictures hung over the sitting area, the center one a huge version of the painting of Jesus she'd seen on the magazine at Jo's house. His arms stretched toward her. Was he saying "Come to Me" or "Get Me out of here"?

"Anybody home?" No answer.

The glow of the PC screen beckoned, and Desi walked behind the desk. The screen saver was on. She jiggled the mouse, and a spreadsheet of revenue figures appeared. The details were lost on her, but the bottom line trumpeted that this ministry could afford a better facility than this stark storefront or the cheap warehouse-type building at the other location. What were they doing with their money? Donating it to the poor?

Yeah, right.

She left the computer and stepped toward the pictures. The top one to the left of the portrait of Jesus was a photograph of a short, slender man standing behind a podium, Bible open in one hand, the other arm raised with the pointer finger stabbed heavenward. The Reverend Archer Romlin. Hair as thick and gray as wool, eyes pale and compelling. One could almost see lightning shoot from their silver depths. The next photograph showed Romlin in a TV studio in front of cameras, the same dynamic energy radiating from his face and posture.

Desi moved to the photographs on the other side of the portrait. One was of Romlin praying with a large group gathered at the front of an auditorium, and the other . . .

Goose bumps chased up her arms. Hamilton Gordon. The massive man filled the right half of the picture. He posed sideways, dressed like an executive on the golf course — but he stood in the desert without a green in sight. His bulbous face was turned toward the camera, but his hand clasped the man's on the other side of the photo, Reverend Romlin.

Desi laughed out loud. Talk about David shaking hands with Goliath. And what were the two of them doing out in the middle of nowhere?

She peered closer. There! Behind the men — turned earth and a pair of shovels. They were breaking ground. For what? A new ministry facility? That would explain where the donations were going, but it didn't give her a clue why they were building so far from civilization. The only structure in sight was a crumbling cliff dwelling in the far background. You don't find those near any well-traveled road.

"Oh, you're here already. Ham said not to expect you until after one o'clock."

At the sound of the breathy voice, Desi turned to see a young woman coming in the door. Her fresh face and bouncy ponytail didn't put her too far out of her teen years. The snug clothes over a generous figure emphasized her youth rather than adding maturity.

The woman looked back at the entrance. "How did you get in? Wasn't it locked?"

Expecting someone from Ham Gordon's office? Maybe she should explain . . . in a minute. "No, sorry. I walked right in."

The woman's cheeks reddened. "I stepped out for lunch. Can't have been gone ten minutes. I was sure I locked up after myself."

"No harm done." Ten minutes? Not hardly. She'd watched the door for longer than that. "I amused myself, looking at the photos."

"Terrific, aren't they?" Ponytail gave a tight smile and hurried to her desk, where she deposited her purse.

Prada? Someone gets paid well for long lunches and unlocked doors.

"Those pictures show how far Reverend Romlin has come in the past three years." The woman's eyes lit like she was a fan swooning over a pop star. "Prime-time television. Speaking engagements nationwide. Got to get the word out! And now Sanctuary. Those of us in the Inner Circle are so excited we could just about bust."

Sanctuary? The thing they're building? "Tell me more about Sanctuary."

The woman smiled like she'd been offered a special treat. "Come on back, and I'll show you the model for the Holy City." She pointed toward the blackened rear area.

Holy City? Yikes!

"It's even got the prayer kiva at the center. One of Ham's best ideas — incorporate native culture into the total worship experience. He saw the model last time he dropped in, but I'll bet he'd like his administrative assistant to have a gander, too." She flicked a light switch on the wall, and the area behind the partitions lit up.

Should she or shouldn't she? Little Girl Friday seemed to think Desi was the administrative assistant who worked for Hamilton Gordon — an unknown quantity who could walk through the door at any moment. Besides, it didn't feel right to keep letting this airhead believe the wrong thing. Oh, well. Desi's conscience might have misgivings, but the rest of her was following the young woman into the back room.

They stepped into a long room dominated by print shop equipment. Rather run-down machines for a ministry with money.

"Never mind that stuff." Her hostess waved a hand. "We're donating it to the local Salvation Army. Over at the new warehouse, they're busy as bees with the new equipment. Books, CDs, the magazine. Orders are pouring in. Got to get the word out!" She laughed. "But I said that already. Listen to me go on. This is what you need to see." She led the way to a square table and pulled back a maroon velvet cloth, beaming at the revealed miniature structure like she was looking into heaven itself.

The model consisted of three concentric oval walls made of adobe, each two stories high. The insides of the walls were lined with apartments like rings of condos. A low, hump-roofed building filled the central courtyard. This structure had no door, but a ladder led up to a large hatch in the middle of the hump. The prayer kiva? Much of it must be underground or no one could stand up inside.

"Impressive." Desi closed her mouth on the hordes of questions that fought to escape. She was supposed to be someone in the know.

Ponytail let out a moony sigh. "And to think I get to be one of the first to move in."

Move into a religious commune in the middle of the desert? Worser and worser. Maybe a teensy question wouldn't hurt. "You're a member of the Inner Circle? Does that mean you get to live in one of these?" She pointed to the central wall of apartments.

"Oh, no, no, no." The hair whipped back and forth. "That's for people like the Reverend and Ham, the ones adept at hearing the Witness. I'll be happy to share a room with other novices on the outer wall." She stepped closer to Desi. "I've attended the Reverend's meetings since he started out in ministry, but I was surprised when he invited me to apply for initiation into the Inner Circle. Few of his followers are even allowed to know there is one." She giggled. "But he says I have a pure heart, the kind that can have a direct pipeline to God if trained properly." The ponytail bobbed up and down.

No doubt the good Reverend intended to train her himself. "When's the grand opening?"

Her hostess let out an adolescent squeal. "Only six months!" She sobered. "But you'd know better than I do how well construction is coming. Ham told me you keep a finger on the pulse of everything to do with his business. That's why he wanted me to give you hard copies of those financials for your files."

Fess-up time. Desi opened her mouth.

The woman clapped a hand to her cheek. "I knew I forgot to do something before I went to lunch. I pulled them up but didn't print them out. Just give me a sec."

Desi followed her into the front room. "I'm not here for the ministry's financial records."

Her hostess paused with her hand on the

mouse. "You're not? But Ham said —"

"I'm not who you think I am. I don't work for Hamilton Gordon. I'm here to see what I can find out about a missing woman."

"Missing woman? I don't understand. Ham is missing someone?"

"No, I said I don't work for —"

The door thrust open, and a beanpole of a man strutted in. Thick glasses magnified cold brown eyes. His head swiveled from Desi to her companion and back again. "Which of you is Hope? I'm Chris Mayburn, here on behalf of Hamilton Gordon."

Mouth ajar, Ponytail lifted an arm and waggled her fingers.

Desi laid a hand on the young woman's arm. "I'm a drop-in interested in the ministry." She smiled at the newcomer. He frowned back.

The man turned his attention to Hope. "The papers? And a disk, if you don't mind."

"You're Chris." The young woman squeaked a laugh. "When Ham called I thought the Chris he mentioned was a woman."

Mayburn's frown bowed to meet his lifted chin. "As you can see, you were mistaken." He rested a frigid gaze on Desi. "I trust no other mistakes have been made."

Desi smiled. "Hope's been the perfect promoter for Reverend Romlin's ministry."

The woman coughed. Desi didn't look at her. A laser printer whirred.

"Indeed." Mayburn tilted his head. "Where have I seen you before? You look familiar."

"I don't care to guess." All that positive publicity for HJ Securities a few months ago had its downside, and she was looking at it in this man's flat stare.

"Ah, the Jacobs woman." His tone implied that she might carry something contagious. "What brings you to Inner Witness Ministries?"

"The sister of a friend speaks well of the Reverend Romlin. I was in the area . . ." She shrugged.

"But how did you find this office?"

She widened her eyes à la Hope. "Isn't this where inquirers are supposed to come?"

"The public office is two miles from here. Reverend Romlin uses this one to confer in private with . . . ah . . . substantial investors."

Yeah, the ones who like to build secret cities.

"Are you interested in making such an investment?" The glasses glinted as Mayburn's lips stretched into a smile the width and warmth of an elastic band.

"I'm interested in everything about this ministry. Your boss and I met at that White House bash. He was the first one to tell me about Reverend Romlin."

"See?" Hope chuckled. "Everything's cool." She stood up and held out a manila envelope. "The hard copy and a CD just like you asked."

Mayburn took the packet. "Well, then, I'll get back to the office." He nodded to Desi. "Why don't you drop by Gordon Corp while you're in town? No doubt Mr. Gordon would love to renew your acquaintance."

"I'm afraid I won't have time today. I have a business appointment in Albuquerque."

"Another day perhaps. And you're staying where?"

"If Mr. Gordon wishes to meet with me, he'll find me."

"He will? But I —" Mayburn clamped his jaw shut and went as red as the tomatoes in Desi's morning omelet.

She smiled. "Ham knows all, sees all. At least, a great deal more than he ought."

"It's the Inner Witness." Hope's whisper was worthy of a séance.

More like illicit access to people's private information. How did Gordon know to find her at the DC airport yesterday? Was he tracking her moves now? He was sure to find out about her visit to this office. Did she care? What was his interest in her? Icy fingers stroked her insides. Tony was right. These people were trouble with a capital T.

Mayburn tucked the envelope in the crook of his arm. "Nice meeting you, Ms. Jacobs." His arctic gaze contradicted his words.

"Are you a believer, Mr. Mayburn?" Little Miss Ponytail stared at him with gentle eyes.

The administrative assistant stiffened. "I work for Mr. Gordon."

"One more thing." Desi lifted a hand.

"Ye-e-es?"

"Your boss wanted to discuss a matter of mutual interest with me, but he never got around to it. Do you have any idea what that might be?"

"It wouldn't be my place to say . . . even if I did." The man flung the door open and left.

"Poor thing." Hope sighed. "No faith to anchor his soul."

Desi studied the young woman's earnest face. "Faith is a wonderful thing when it's invested in the right Person. I'm a believer in Jesus Christ as the Way, the Truth, and the Life."

Hope nodded. "We're saved by the body

and blood."

The fine words came out as lifeless as stone. Why did she get the feeling they weren't in the same book, much less on the same page? "Maybe you can help me."

"I'll do my best."

"The niece of a woman I care about has gone missing from her home, leaving a husband and baby behind. Before her disappearance, she was into the Inner Witness message. The girl's mother said people from this ministry visited her often —"

"You're talking about Karen."

Desi stepped toward the younger woman. "Do you know her? Do you have any idea where she might be?"

Hope frowned and dropped her gaze. "I went to her house with the visitation committee, but we didn't connect. You know how it is sometimes." She sniffed. "Then I heard she'd run off, maybe stole some stuff from a museum."

"Could Karen be out at this Sanctuary you're building?"

The woman's ample bosom filled. "No one's out there yet. Except the workers, of course. I'm going to be in the first group. I have to be, or I'll just die!"

Enough teenage drama. "But maybe she sneaked out there. Maybe she's helping build —"

"No way! I don't even know where the Holy City is. Just the Reverend and Ham know."

"But there must be a contractor."

"I don't know about that." Her mouth drooped. "You're not a real seeker, are you?"

"I'm seeking a young woman who may be hurt, whose life may be in danger. Her family is worried sick about her. Don't you have family worrying about you?"

Hope shifted from one foot to the other. "They don't need to fuss. I've found what I need. They don't understand . . ." She bit her lip.

Desi pulled an HJ Securities card from her handbag. "If you think of anything that might help Karen, call the number on this card. They'll put you in touch with me."

Hope nodded.

Was that a shimmer of tears in the woman's eyes? Desi's heart lifted. There was hope for Hope yet. "Call me." She touched the young lady's hand and then left the ministry office.

Desi pushed the speed limit on I-25 south toward Albuquerque. Okay, so she'd be late to the museum. A little embarrassment was minor compared to the bizarre information she'd uncovered. Too late to make a good impression on that buck-passing administrator anyway. The man had lawsuit on his mind. She'd seen the type before.

But she'd give her left arm to find directions to the desert compound. If Tony was investigating Gordon, he needed to know that the man was funding a handy-dandy getaway villa.

She punched in Tony's number on her cell. The phone rang until his voice mail came on. Rats! "Call me when you're free, sweetheart. I need to lay a load on your broad shoulders."

What was the handsome lug doing? It had to be pretty intense to keep him from answering her call.

EIGHT

Tony yanked the crowbar. Metal shrieked, and his nerve endings danced. He yanked again, and the wheel cover sprang loose from its housing. He stood back and filled his lungs.

He was alive. The bee-buzz of the bullet almost kissing his head played again in his ears. *As long as I've got breath, Minnesota, somebody will be on the trail of the people behind what happened today.*

Around him, his squad worked with fevered efficiency. Even Slidell was there, laptop in hand, figuring dimensions and possible hiding places.

Tony's cell phone sounded. He grabbed it and checked the caller ID. The ASAC. He'd better have good news. "Lucano here."

"It's a no-go on the warrant for the Gordon Trucking building." Cooke spat a few colorful words. "The judge feels we don't have proof that Winston wasn't acting on his own."

Tony resisted an urge to throw his cell across the parking lot. "Thanks for trying." A sour laugh left his throat. "If we can't catch a break when we lose an agent and the big guns shoot for a warrant, I don't know what it's going to take to bring these people down."

"Pavement pounding, elbow grease, and gray cells. Keep at it." The ASAC broke the connection.

And prayer. Tony let out a breath. Can't forget the most important ingredient. *Sorry, Lord. Help me stay focused. Guide us all. We need Your help.*

He looked down at the phone. The display said he'd missed a call. He checked his messages, and Desi's voice warmed a few degrees of chill off his insides. Sure, she sounded like she'd welcome a little heart-to-heart — it had to be rough trying to support Max and her sister through a missing persons case — but her tone was vibrant, confident. His Desi.

Now *would* be a good time for a strong shoulder. Hers supporting him. She'd like that. He punched in numbers and then stopped with his finger over the last digit.

What was he thinking? *"Hi, honey, I lost one of my squad today. Good-bye. Call you back later."* What kind of a jerk did that just to get a little weight off his chest? Tony canceled the call and flipped the phone shut.

"We've got something!"

Slidell's shrill cry drew Tony at a lope.

Desi tapped in Max's cell number. *C'mon, pick up!*

"Hey, Des, how's it goin'?"

"Great to hear a sane and friendly voice."

"You've been hearin' some crazy, unfriendly ones?" Concern flowed over the line.

"I'll tell you in a minute. First, where are you?"

"Home and A-OK. I'm in the kitchen, but I'll hold the phone toward the living room. Listen." Children's laughter and garbled little voices. "My live wires are havin' a blast with their baby cousin. Adam just lays there and kicks, but they think every wiggle is a hoot."

"No sign of Pete Cheama?"

"Not hide, nor hair. Now give, woman. What've you been up to?"

"I'm almost back to Albuquerque from my little jaunt to Santa Fe, and what's going on with Inner Witness Ministries is going to blow your mind." Desi gave Max the quick version of her encounters with perky

Ponytail and Prune Face from Ham Gordon's office. "Mayburn recognized me, so Gordon is going to be aware I'm sniffing around the ministry. But they won't know I know about the Holy City unless Hope tells someone she let the cat out of the bag — which I doubt she'll do. She cares too much about being accepted by these people."

Max gave a low growl. "Do you think Karen might've found out about this place? Maybe they grabbed her to keep her quiet."

"Or maybe she's as sucked in as Hope, and she's out there because she wants to be."

Silence on the other end, followed by a sigh. "Then her mind is captive, not her body. Tough to get a person free if they don't want to be."

"First step is to discover her physical location. We can deal with her mental and spiritual condition after that." The countryside began to give way to businesses and homes. "I need to concentrate on driving now so I can find my way to the museum. But we need to locate this desert hideaway. That's a project you can sink your teeth into. Phone calls. Internet searches."

"You got it! Construction materials don't just poof into existence. They're buying them somewhere and transporting them somehow."

"I like how you think, lady. A community like that is going to need plumbing in particular. I so cannot see Ham Gordon using an outhouse."

Max snickered. "You've brought Tony up to speed on this?"

"I'm trying. I've got a call in to him. Waiting to hear back."

"Then at least you've got *your* bases covered."

"Uh-oh, do I detect an issue?"

A soft groan. "Same old. Nothing you can do anything about, so forget it."

"Ma-a-ax?"

"WhatamIgonnado?" The voice lowered to a run-together whisper. "Dean called again as soon as I got home. He wants to see the kids on the next family visitation day. But, Des, I can't bring them to a prison. It's hard enough for me to go in there."

"You know how I feel, Max. You don't owe the man a thing. He should be grateful you haven't filed for divorce. Yet. Send him pictures."

Heavy breathing. "It's not that simple. They're his kids, too, and he is still my husband. You don't understand, because you're not —"

"Married. Yes, I know."

"Don't be hard, Des. I didn't mean anything by the comment."

"Well, you're right. I don't understand, but that doesn't mean I won't support you in whatever you decide to do."

A trill of laughter. "That's just it. I can't decide."

"And it doesn't do any good to ask me . . . oh, crumb!"

"What?"

"I missed my turn."

"Guess that's my cue to get off the line. Call me back if you find out anything interesting at the museum."

Desi promised and closed the connection. *Lord, I'm sure not the one who can advise Max about that louse — er, her husband. I'll leave the issue in Your hands.*

Good idea.

Desi's hair stood on end. Her Daddy didn't raise no dummy. She took a deep breath and sat up straighter. *Yes, Sir, leaving a problem to You is a very good idea 100 percent of the time. But I suspect You're going to have to help me remember that.*

"See here?" Slidell showed Tony figures on his computer screen. "The gas tank is

10.378 square inches too big. Haj is checking now." The math whiz nodded at a pair of feet — one blue sock, one brown sock inside black loafers — sticking out from under the truck.

"Waaahoooo!" The wild rebel yell burst from below. The stocky Japanese man rolled into the open and hopped up, suit covered in grit and dust. "There's a piece welded onto the tank. Good weld. Same shape and size as the tank. Hard to detect."

Polanski pumped her fist. "Anybody got a giant can opener?"

Slidell sniffed. "Common sense would indicate that the access point is inside the cab, requiring a key or a code."

Polanski rolled her eyes. "It was a joke, Dell."

"Oh." Slidell fixed her with a blank stare.

A tight band around Tony's chest throbbed. His gaze assessed the core of his squad — a color-blind Japanese guy, a humorless genius, and a wisecracking Pole. So why did they have to lose the cheerful Norske? The tightness turned to burn. And what were they doing standing around? They had crooks to catch.

Tony smacked his palms together. "Haj, Polanski, find the door to this gas tank safe."

One glance at his face and the pair hopped

into the cab without a word.

Circling to the rear of Winston's trailer, he found squad members at work on the cement loading dock. They were well into the job of removing the contents of the semi — nasty grunt work requiring manual forklifts to haul out pallets of canned meat products.

Tony waved one of the men over. "Any sign that the pirated discs were stashed in there on Winston's California to Boston route? Busted jewel case, anything?"

The man shook his head. "Not yet, but we've got our eyes peeled."

"Crawl on your hands and knees with magnifying glasses if you have to."

The agent's nostrils flared. "We're not going to miss anything." The look was cold, angry. A reflection of his own.

Tony walked up the side of the truck. The ruddy patch on the ground beside the driver's door caught his eye. Winston's blood. If only a much larger stain didn't match it farther up the pavement. Tony slammed the side of his fist against the trailer.

A throat cleared behind him. He whirled and found Slidell staring up at him. The guy had been on his tail the entire time. His senses had known it, but his brain refused to acknowledge the information. *You're losing it, Lucano.* "What!"

Slidell's brows climbed. "I completed my analysis of Gordon Corp's financial records. There were indicators that the company is not doing well."

Tony squinted at the setting sun. "Maybe that's why Gordon needs the extra money from transporting bootlegged property."

The agent shook his head. "My analysis shows that cash is being siphoned out of the company, not artificially injected into it."

"You mean Ham Gordon is slitting the throat of his own corporation?" Tony rocked on his heels.

Slidell pursed his lips. "Someone is diverting funds, but who's doing it and for what purpose I can't tell from the data. However, no bootlegging money is shoring up the bottom line. Mr. Gordon could lose his company within a few years . . . or even months if the cash hemorrhage accelerates."

"Whoa! This is bombshell stuff and could go public soon. If you can pick the inconsistencies out from the stockholders report, others can."

Slidell shrugged. "Anyone with a similar IQ." He met Tony's gaze without a blink.

"The true financial condition could stay

under wraps until the company goes belly up?"

"Quite possibly."

"A lot of people could lose a pile of money if we don't get our finger in the dike — and fast!" The investors in Gordon Corp had no idea what was about to hit them.

At five minutes after three, Desi parked the car in the museum lot and hurried through the New Mexico heat into the cool foyer. A receptionist sat behind a marble-topped counter, the spot Karen must have occupied when she was on duty. Desi approached and stated her business.

The woman called for a guide, who escorted her past exhibits and through a door marked *Private.* At the end of a scalding white hallway, they came to the administrator's suite. A middle-aged woman looked up from her desk. Her hairdo and the shape of her face bore an unfortunate resemblance to a Russian wolfhound. Tearstained, blotchy skin and bloodshot eyes didn't enhance the picture. The guard's death must have hit staff hard.

Desi introduced herself, and the secretary offered a weak smile. "Please have a seat." She waved toward a pair of guest chairs by the wall. "Mr. Spellman is on the phone.

When he gets off, I'll notify him you're here."

Desi acknowledged the instructions with a nod and took the offered seat. The secretary turned to the side, donned a pair of dictation headphones, and began pecking at a computer keyboard. Every so often, she stopped typing and dabbed at her eyes with a tissue. Fifteen minutes later, Desi had the room decor memorized and a hole glared through the closed door marked *Administrator.*

She rose and went to the desk. The name on the plate said Hannah Grant. She tapped the secretary on the shoulder. "Ms. Grant."

"What? Ohhh." The woman swung toward her, hand over her heart. She yanked off the headphones. "I forgot . . . Er, I mean, I'll see if Mr. Spellman is free." She leaped up and hustled into the next office without knocking.

A moment later, she came out, followed by a medium-sized man with medium-brown hair — the soul of average, except for a large Roman nose. "Ms. Jacobs." Spellman held out his hand. Desi shook it. A tad clammy. Nerves?

"My apologies for being late." She glanced at the flushed secretary, who ducked her head and returned to her desk. "My business in Santa Fe took longer than expected."

Spellman grunted. "I'm a busy man. Let's get our cards on the table." He led the way into his office. They settled into guest chairs by a round table in the corner.

"One thing puzzles me, Mr. Spellman —"

"A great many things puzzle *me* about this situation." He scowled.

"Why do you consider us your adversary? We're here to serve — especially in the wake of a break-in."

Spellman leaned toward her. "You must not understand what a disaster this theft is for us. All of our Native American artifacts are on loan from the tribes. A tribal lawsuit and all the negative publicity . . ." The man's Adam's apple bobbed.

"So someone needs to get the blame."

He sat back. "You do see my position. Nothing personal. I'm sure you have insurance."

"As do you."

"But our reputation . . ." He lifted his chin. "We're a stand-alone facility, Ms. Jacobs, dependent on donations and grants to survive. We don't have an international presence to carry us over the bumps. This can't be the first successful theft in a facility protected by HJ Securities. You'll recover. We might not. Particularly with a death."

"I appreciate your candor, Mr. Spellman. Let me also be clear. I have no intention of allowing HJ Securities to become a scapegoat in this tragedy. No fault has yet been determined. And, like you, I support my staff. That's why I'm staying at Jo Cheama's house. My main electronics expert is her sister."

The administrator sniffed through that large nose. "And related to two of the prime suspects. I have it on good authority that this Maxine Webb will be thoroughly questioned."

Desi's blood heated. The Rookie and Swamp Eyes of the APD again. "The FBI cleared Max Webb of suspicion."

"Oh." Spellman blinked. "But I thought . . . The police were positive she had to supply the thieves with privileged information about our alarm system. Much of it is her brainchild."

"The police officers' assumptions were based on inadequate information. While Maxine Webb did design the security template around which your individual system was built, she had no access to the facility-specific safeguards on the computer control room."

Spellman went stiff. "Are you accusing *me* now?"

"That makes as much sense as accusing Max. No motive. Why do you think neither you nor your curator is high on the suspect list, even though you had access? Motive is a prime factor that law enforcement must have in making an arrest."

The administrator pursed his lips and glanced down. "But she is related to —"

"A pair of young people whose guilt has yet to be proved."

Spellman stared her in the eye. "But she is married to —"

"A man she helped bring to justice."

The administrator deflated. "So we're left with a mystery."

"We are indeed."

Spellman spread his hands. "My position hasn't changed. The board will discuss the engagement of a different security service at the meeting tonight."

"I'm sorry to hear it, but that's your prerogative." Desi rose. "May I at least walk through your museum before I leave? I'd like to see the theft site."

Spellman stood. He puffed out his cheeks and then expelled a breath. "Very well. But after you go, tell your staff that they're no longer welcome here."

Desi inclined her head and went to the door. She turned with her hand on the knob. "Since you brought up my company's record, you might be interested in a statistic. In the past decade, none of our clients has sustained loss due to either systems or operations failure. In every case, human error or human tampering was at fault. I believe this event will prove no exception."

Desi left the administrator with his mouth open, nodded to the red-eyed secretary, and made her way back into the public area. A sign said she was in an exhibition of Western American artists — as if she couldn't guess from the vivid Joseph Henry Sharp on the wall.

Commanding her knotted muscles to relax, Desi stopped to examine a Frederic Remington sculpture and gather her thoughts. She took deep breaths and let patrons flow around her. The way the robbery had happened bothered her.

She wandered over to an Albert Bierstadt painting, but her mind was too far away to appreciate it. The thieves' methodology was schizophrenic. Finessing entrance to the museum took brains and elegant planning, but once inside the building, they acted like thugs — bludgeoning the guard and leaving him sprawled in the lobby, then smashing the display case. Whoever masterminded the theft employed nasty people to do the hands-on work.

Shaking her head, Desi passed a George Catlin display and stepped into a hallway. She checked her cell phone. On and charged, but still no call from Tony. She looked around. Where was the Native American exhibit?

She found a museum directory. A whole section devoted to Southwestern artist Georgia O'Keeffe? *Temptation, get thee behind me!* Desi looked at her watch. The museum closed in thirty minutes. Not enough time to pay proper respect to Georgia and scope out the theft site.

On to the Native American exhibit. Oh, no! Danger! The route to the theft site took her through the O'Keeffe exhibit. She'd have to ignore the display. Desi forged ahead. O'Keeffes flowed by left and right. Stunning floral studies. Delicate shells. Multihued landscapes.

Feet? What are you doing?

Desi stopped in front of a landscape. Every brushstroke proved Georgia's love of her New Mexico desert, the place where she could see forever — her "faraway." The painting that drew Desi showed a rust brown and tan butte. Evenly spaced black arches in the cliff face betrayed the touch of ancient man. Georgia's flowing strokes and delicate mix of hues beckoned the viewer with a promise — *Life is simple here.*

If only that were so.

Georgia had created a brilliant artistic illusion. Life wasn't any simpler for those cliff dwellers than for people today. More elemental, fewer choices, but human nature wasn't any different then than now. And she was in the same boat as Ham Gordon on one thing — she couldn't see herself using an outhouse on a regular basis. Or worse, a handy creosote bush.

Desi stepped into the Native American history exhibit and came to a case of Mesa Verde black on white pottery, examples of a firing technique lost today. A decent find of these could make a dirt-grubbing pothunter rich overnight. Why weren't these taken?

She turned and found an empty rectangular case minus a glass cover standing in the middle of the floor. The theft site. No sign of the break-in remained except for the bare display pedestals. What was missing? She looked at the labels on the pedestals — a hooked-bone gutting knife, a curved flaying knife, and a black on white bowl. Good value to the pieces, but not as much as items sitting a few feet away.

Desi studied the label on the side of the case.

Anasazi Religious Artifacts. Chaco Canyon. Circa AD 1130

Below the label was a set of small headphones and a button to push for recorded information about the exhibit. Did it still work? She put on the headphones and pressed the button. A mellow female voice filled her ears.

"Anasazi is a term coined early in the twentieth century to describe the ancestors of today's Pueblo Indians, such as the Zuni and the Hopi. The word Anasazi *is Navajo for 'ancestral enemies' and is not a term embraced by modern Pueblos. The Hopi call their ancient ancestors Hisatsinom, or 'the Old Ones.'*

"These Old Ones were an agrarian people who inhabited portions of Utah, Colorado, Arizona, and New Mexico until around 1300 AD, when their settlements were abandoned. The reason for the disappearance of the Anasazi is an unsolved archaeological mystery. Modern-day Pueblos maintain that the Anasazi haven't disappeared, for they are them. But the fact remains that impressive settlements such as Cliff Palace and Pueblo Bonito were abruptly left empty.

"What enemy did the Old Ones flee? Or what natural disaster overtook them? The answer remains shrouded by the mists of time.

"Likewise, the purpose of the implements displayed here is not known, but their discovery inside a sacred kiva suggests that they were used in rituals of worship. Dark rumors of cannibalism among these ancients persist. Some archaeologists maintain that the evidence is strong that the Anasazi, like the Aztecs, partook of a sacred meal of sacrificed human flesh mixed with corn. The nature of these implements suggests their use in rituals that involved blood sacrifice."

Blood sacrifice? The words hit Desi between the eyes. Her head whirled, and her knees weakened. She staggered backward.

What did Agent Ortiz say about the theft? That someone wanted certain artifacts. Desi's heart slammed against her ribs. What did she say back to the agent? *If you find out why the looters grabbed those particular pieces, you might know who took them.*

Tiny millipede legs crawled across her skin. She knew a religious group with a twisted obsession about salvation through body and blood. They were building a commune, complete with Anasazi kiva, somewhere in the desert.

Desi shook her head. No! She was thinking crazy. Who could conceive an act of cannibalism, much less carry it out? Her flesh crawled. The Anasazi may have done it, the

Aztecs did, other tribes and peoples throughout the world — all in the name of worship. But not here in the heart of the good old U.S. of A.!

Why not? Didn't she say it to herself a few minutes ago? Human nature hasn't changed.

Acid flavored Desi's tongue. She swallowed. Hard.

Karen, have you already become a human sacrifice?

Nine

Thoughts whirling, Desi left the museum. Perspiration coated her skin — and not from the heat. Inside the rental car, she cranked up the air-conditioning with a trembling hand.

Should she try calling Tony again? No, if he were free to talk, he would have called. With his job, he could be in a situation that didn't bear interrupting.

Like this wasn't a priority situation?

She reached to press the autodial and then drew back. There was someone else she could contact. Desi scrambled in her purse and found the card Agent Ortiz had given her with the cell phone number on the back. She placed the call.

"Ortiz." The agent's voice came through crisp and clear.

"Oh, thank goodness, you answered your phone."

"Desiree Jacobs? Are you all right? You

seem —"

"Ready for a white jacket?" Desi laughed, the sound about an octave too high.

"Where are you?"

"Sitting outside the museum."

"Oh, yes, you said you'd scheduled a visit with the administrator. So what's up? There hasn't been another theft . . ." The woman's voice took on an edge.

"Nothing like that. It's just . . ." Desi bit her lip. How did a person share something so bizarre over the telephone? They didn't. "I've run across information that may shed new light on your case. Can I speak to you about it in person?" At last she sounded like she had some wits about her.

"Sure. I'm at the office. Need directions?"

"Please." Desi scribbled on the back of the card.

She drove, stomach churning. Despite the air-conditioning, her hands were clammy.

Was she running off half-cocked with this Anasazi ritual notion? Did two and two add up to four like she thought, or had she worked herself up into making two and two equal five? But she had to report her findings, didn't she? And if she couldn't talk to Tony, she needed to talk to somebody who could do something. But how could even the FBI help? That was one big desert out there, and with no location for this Holy City, her suspicions were speculation. Except she'd had an eyewitness gander at plans for a desert compound. She wasn't speculating about that.

Desi turned into the guest parking lot. She studied the soaring fortress surrounded by a high iron fence. Would Ortiz listen to her appalling deduction about the use of the stolen artifacts? Or would the agent laugh her out of the office?

Desi squared her shoulders, wiped her palms on her pants, and marched up to the guardhouse. She stated her business and showed her ID, and the guard pressed the button to admit her beyond the fence. She went up the walk between a trio of flagpoles and entered a walled-in foyer. Another guard behind a desk stood up, ready to run her through the metal detector. Desi detoured to the reception cubicle behind bulletproof glass, where a dark-haired man sat.

"Excuse me. I'm here to see Agent Ortiz."

The man came to the window. "You'd be Ms. Jacobs?"

Desi nodded.

"Ortiz had to go out on a call, but she'll get back to you as soon as she can."

Desi's heart flopped to her toes. "This can't wait! A woman's life is at stake."

He snatched a pen. "Give us the situation and the location, and we'll get someone there."

She blew out a breath. *How about I just bang my head against this counter?* "I hoped the FBI would be able to find the location if I gave the situation. Is the peanut-eater around?"

His lips twitched. "Agent Rhoades is with Agent Ortiz, ma'am."

Oh, so now she was ma'am. Pigeonholed somewhere between a crank caller and a harmless hysteric. She gave him a thin smile. "As an agent at Boston HQ would be happy to testify, I'm a miserable failure at waiting when it's time to act. Every minute wasted may mean a wife and mother will never be reunited with her family."

The receptionist scratched behind his ear. "We can't respond to an emergency at an unidentified location."

Desi deflated. "I know . . . and I apologize for overreacting. Frustration'll do that."

"Maybe this will take the edge off." He sent a white envelope through a slot in the bottom of the window. "Ortiz left it for you."

She took the envelope. "Thank you. And you may tell Agent Ortiz that I've gone back to Jo Cheama's. Let me give you my cell phone number."

"Not necessary."

"Of course not. You're the FBI."

"That's right, ma'am."

She gave him a look under lowered brows.

He cleared his throat. "Miss?"

"Miss or Ms. Jacobs, or even Desiree, will do. Anything but the way I address my friend's ninety-year-old grandmother."

The man laughed. Even the guard snickered.

"You're a long way from being anybody's grandmother," the receptionist said.

She smiled and headed for the door. Back in her car, Desi ripped open the envelope from Ortiz and pulled out a single sheet of paper.

> Thought I should clue you in since it'll be on the news tonight. The wreckage of Pete Cheama's truck was found at the bottom of a ravine. No sign of Cheama. We need to find him ASAP. Tell Jo.

Desi stared at the words. Tell Jo? How many more shocks could Max's sister absorb?

"Good work, everybody." Tony surveyed his sweaty squad assembled near the semi cab. "Get home and grab some shut-eye while the lab processes what we've got. Come back in the morning ready to hit the ground running."

With nods and waves, the crew dispersed. No smiles, no jokes, but a lighter step as they walked away. The vise around Tony's heart eased the smallest bit.

For a day full of shocks, they'd been due a couple of pleasant surprises. The crew emptying the trailer hadn't found a mere scrap of a jewel case but a whole DVD crushed in a corner. And the money, wads of it in the extra tank under the truck chassis.

Tony headed for the car Slidell had driven to the scene. His own vehicle had been towed away. What had he said? *It'll get broken in soon enough.* Famous last words.

Slidell took the driver's seat. Minnesota's spot. They were going to find out why he'd never be in it again, and someone was going to pay. Tony got in beside the computer expert. Haj and Polanski took the backseat. On the way back to the office, Tony had Slidell tell the others his findings in the Gordon Corp stockholders report.

When Slidell finished, he angled a look at Tony. "So who do you think is gutting Gordon's company?"

Polanski snorted. "Not much to figure

out. Gordon's gotten heat from us for years, so he siphons cash out of his company, runs a big moneymaker with pirated property —"

"— and now he's about to do a powder." Haj nodded. "We need to let Albuquerque HQ know to double the surveillance on this pug-ugly."

Tony nodded. "Done. As soon as I hit the office."

Slidell cleared his throat. "One minor quibble. We're assuming that the same person is bleeding the company and running the bootlegging operation."

"Two crooks in the same corporation running dirty deals?" Polanski frowned. "C'mon, Dell, the odds aren't with that at all."

Slidell held up a hand. "Just saying."

"Point noted." Tony dipped his chin at the math whiz. "We won't close our minds to a more complicated picture, but right now Ham Gordon is our biggest target. Literally."

Haj snickered. Polanski chuckled. Slidell gave no reaction as he guided the car onto the freeway. They continued to bat ideas around until they reached the office.

Tony climbed out in the parking area. "Go home. I'll see you tomorrow."

Polanski got out and stretched. "I'm going

to give my family extra hugs tonight."

Haj stepped out beside her. "Ditto."

Slidell pulled away with a wave.

Polanski took a couple of steps then turned. "You're the best squad leader I've ever worked with. It wasn't your fault about Ben today, just dumb rotten luck."

Tony's throat tightened. "I appreciate that."

Polanski nodded and walked away.

Rotten luck? More like not enough information about the guy they went out to interview. What more could they have done to be prepared?

Hands in his pockets, Tony watched his people drive away. If only Des were in town. He needed to see her. Firming his jaw, he went up to his office. He had messages on his phone from ASAC Cooke and Henderson from OPR. He called Albuquerque HQ and left a message for Agent Ortiz about increasing surveillance on Gordon, and then he punched in Cooke's extension. The man picked up on the third ring.

"It's Lucano. I'm back in the office."

"Good. What did you find?"

Tony updated him.

"You've accomplished a lot for today."

"Just getting started."

"Right, but give it a rest for the night. Take

some downtime."

Sure, go eat ravioli with his mom and make small talk. Like she wouldn't throw an Italian fuss and then pray him half-bald. Prayer was good, but . . . "I think I'd rather keep busy, sir."

"Lucano, I'm going to stay here until Henderson's done taking your statement. If you don't get your hind end out of here right afterward, I'll put you on report."

Tony swallowed a sharp answer. He was getting the same advice from a superior that he had given his team. "Can you tell me one thing?"

"Go ahead."

"Erickson's family. Who let them know?" He cleared his throat. "I should have been the one."

"It's done. He came from a small town, the kind of place where everyone knows everyone. I made the call to their local PD. They sent a couple of uniforms over. Known faces. More personal that way. The parents are getting a telegram from Director Harcourt, too."

Tony pinched the bridge of his nose. "I want to go to the funeral, and the only thing that'll stop me is if I'm putting the cuffs to Ham Gordon at that very moment."

A pause on the line. "You've got time off

coming. Take some. Hand the case over —"

"Respectfully speaking, sir, but you're off your rocker if you think I'll let anyone else get their hands on this case."

"Then get some distance and perspective. I'm ordering you to have a chat with the in-house psychiatrist tomorrow, make sure your head's on straight."

Tony's lungs went hollow. "Haven't I done all right so far?"

"We want to keep it that way. Plus, we need to make sure the Bureau has crossed every *t* and dotted every *i* when it comes time to make arrests. We don't need to give any fancy defense lawyers ammunition to use against the people we had on the case."

"I can buy that. I'll make an appointment."

"No need. You're set up for the first slot in the morning."

"I'll be there."

"Good. Now get done with Henderson so I can go home, too."

Tony walked down to the Office of Professional Responsibility department. Henderson looked up from his desk. The OPR agent pointed toward the door of a small conference room.

They went in and took seats at a small table. Without preamble, the OPR agent punched the record button on a portable machine. They went through the usual spiel. Yes, Tony acknowledged his awareness that the session was recorded. Of course, he would give the facts with veracity. Blah. Blah.

Henderson folded his hands on top of a manila folder he'd brought in with him. There'd be initial feedback from the coroner, early lab results. Tony's fingers itched to snatch the folder out from under the smug little OPR's hands. Instead, he balled his fists under the table.

"All right, Agent Lucano —" Henderson nodded to him — "tell me what happened that led up to the shooting incident."

Incident? An agent was dead! That was no incident. It was a senseless tragedy.

Tony walked Henderson through the anonymous phone call and checking up on Bill Winston, aka Elvis. Henderson stared at a spot in the corner of the ceiling. Tony's skin warmed. *Look at me, you —*

The OPR agent fixed Tony with an unreadable gaze. "So after you did due diligence on verifying Bill Winston's identity, you went to Gordon Trucking to see him in person."

"The next logical step."

"But you already suspected that his real

name might not be Bill Winston."

"Correct. We hoped a little fishing expedition might get us more to go on about his identity and, more importantly, point us to the next guy up on the food chain."

Henderson pursed his lips. "Give me the sequence of events after you and your squad members arrived at Gordon Trucking and confronted the trucker."

Every muscle rigid, Tony laid out the bare facts — Winston standing with his manifest, the three agents getting out of the SUV, Polanski heading toward the rear of the trailer, the trucker going for his gun, the shouts, the shots.

"Stop there." Henderson held up a finger. "You yelled for Erickson to get down as soon as you saw Winston reach into his jacket? And he didn't respond to the command?"

Tony rubbed his palms down his pants. "He might not have heard me. Sometimes when the fight-or-flight instinct kicks in, auditory input doesn't register from a source other than the danger point."

"I'm aware of that, but —"

"Evidently, Ben's reaction to danger was fight. He went for his gun. If he'd been a bit faster, he'd be alive. If he'd ducked like I told him, I'd be the one cooling on a slab."

The OPR agent blinked. That place in the corner of the ceiling again claimed his attention. "Why did you say that?"

"Winston was more than handy with a gun. I wouldn't have beaten him to the draw. As it was, the trucker missed plugging me in the head by a literal hair after he shot Ben. Without those extra seconds to get my weapon free . . ." Tony shrugged. "There's no doubt in my mind that Agent Erickson saved my life at the cost of his own."

Henderson nodded. "That's good information, Lucano. I'll keep that in mind when I write the report."

"Thank you." Who would've thought he'd feel grateful to an OPR guy?

Henderson pulled a sheet from the file. "It's not surprising that you found Bill Winston a bigger challenge than you expected." He laid the paper in front of Tony.

"An outdated Most Wanted sheet? This top-ten perp is dead."

"He is now."

A shaft of ice speared up Tony's spine. "I shot a dead man? A felon with a rap sheet a mile and a half long?"

"Bernard Walker faked his death." Henderson nodded. "Not hard to do with an accident at sea. But apparently he couldn't bear to leave behind his devotion to Elvis and his penchant for aliases with the initials B. W."

"B. W.?" The letters pulsed in Tony's head.

The OPR agent picked up the sheet. "Brian Wilkins, Bob Warren, Bruce Webber, the list goes on until we get to the one that's not on here — Bill Winston."

Tony leaped up. "It's my fault. I didn't listen."

Henderson rose. "What are you talking about?"

Tony leaned on his knuckles toward the OPR agent. "On the way over to Gordon Trucking, Ben remarked that the initials B. W. bothered him. I passed the observation off. He was going to look into it after we had our chat with Winston."

"Are you saying you were negligent?"

"I should have put the brakes on and checked out the hunch. But I didn't, and now my agent's dead. It's my fault."

From the expression on Henderson's face, he was looking at a dead career, too. Big deal! He didn't deserve the badge in his pocket. Might as well leave it on the table and walk.

Ten

"Sit down, Lucano."

In this context, the OPR agent was the boss. Tony sat, palms flat on the table.

Henderson put the flier back into the folder. "Had you known Bill Winston's true identity, what would you have done differently?"

"A ton more backup, flak jackets, and bust out of the vehicle with our guns drawn."

Henderson nodded, gaze shuttered. "Did you have time to stop and run Erickson's mental blip through the computer before Winston took off in his truck?"

Tony shook his head.

"Verbally, please."

"No, but that doesn't mean we couldn't have pulled him off the road later or taken him at a truck stop along his route."

"Possible scenarios, but not without increased risk. More civilians around." The OPR agent leaned forward. "How often would you say agents walk into situations where not all factors are known?"

"Most of the time, but we do what we can to minimize surprises."

Henderson tapped the folder. "If you had run a search on the computer for B. W., what do you think you would have found?"

Tony shrugged. "Maybe nothing. Maybe a hit on a dead man. Or just a long list of crooks with the initials B. W."

"I see, and that information would have told you what about Bill Winston?"

Tony lifted his hands. "Enough. I get the point." So how come he didn't feel any better?

The OPR agent smiled and managed to look halfway human. "Your willingness to take responsibility is admirable, but a bit exaggerated. I'll let the psychiatrist make that call." He stood and tucked the folder under his arm. "I think we're done."

Tony rose. "Do I get my gun back and a copy of what's in the file?"

"Tomorrow — after you're cleared by the shrink. For now, Cooke wants you out of here."

Tony walked to the door. "About the time I think I could like you, you irritate me worse than a bad shave."

He chuckled. "Just doing my job, Lucano."

Tony drove to his condo on autopilot. *Why did a good man die today, Lord? I know You're not going to answer me. You never answer that kind of question, but it's burning in me.*

It's not your business.

Tony gulped. Did he just hear that? His throat tightened. What had he read to Max's son last weekend from C. S. Lewis's Narnia series? — *I tell no one any story but his own.*

Okay, Lord. I don't like it, but I'll give that one a rest. But just so You know — I'm still steamed about it.

The guard at the booth of his gated community waved him through. So he lost a good agent and killed a man in a split second on a sunny afternoon. At least his badge got him a cheap rate in an exclusive community. Hurray for the perks!

Tony slid the Chrysler 300 into his attached garage and let himself in the side door. Air-conditioned silence greeted him as he slipped off his shoes. Home sweet home. He left the lights off and opened the curtains on his picture window. The deepening twilight cloaked his living room in shadows. He went into the kitchen and got a glass of water. Then he plopped into his old recliner, put up his feet, laid the chair back, and stared out the window.

He should call Desi. But he didn't move.

■ ■ ■ ■

She should try calling Tony again. Desi sat in the car in front of Brent and Karen's house. She should have gone back to Jo's like she told the guy at the FBI office.

She couldn't do it. Couldn't face Jo and try to sort out what she should and shouldn't tell this worried mother about what she'd discovered today. She couldn't blurt out her deduction about the Anasazi artifacts. That was for people like the FBI — people who'd seen things and could cope. The news about Pete Cheama was a footnote in comparison. Jo would hear it on the news soon enough, and Agent Ortiz could reach Desi on her cell phone no matter where she was.

So she'd driven around Albuquerque until she decided to find the home where Karen was last seen. Desi studied the little gold house. A cracker box in a neighborhood of cracker boxes on the fringe of the city. But then a graduate student with a part-time job, a wife, and a new baby couldn't afford much. A strike against Brent as far as motive for stealing valuable artifacts. He should be off work by now. Not that she could unload her horrors on him either, but she had questions he might be able to answer.

Desi shut off the car and shifted her feet. Something crackled on the floorboard. The message from Ortiz. She bent toward it. "Ow!" She pressed the heel of her hand to her cheek where she'd rammed it against the steering wheel. Nice bruise tomorrow.

She set the crinkled note in the driver's seat and got out. The flowers in the bed of hardy perennials under the front window were drooping and bedraggled. No doubt Brent didn't think to water them. She climbed a cracked front stoop and knocked on the door.

A minute later, the young man pulled the door open. Despite the tired slope to his shoulders, his eyes brightened when he saw her. "Hey, come in!" He pushed the door wide.

Desi stepped into a narrow hallway scented with Oriental takeout. "You look pretty wiped. Rough day at work?"

"No worse than usual. Riding a hotel check-in desk can get interesting sometimes. People, you know."

"I do know."

"I'm just bummed." He shrugged. "Not even Adam to come home to."

"Then I guess I don't need to ask if you have a few minutes to talk to me."

"I can do better than talk. I've got plenty of takeout for two." He headed up the hallway.

Desi followed. "I'm not hungry, but . . ." Her mouth watered at the scent of Chinese. Well, maybe she was a little hungry. She couldn't help anyone by starving herself.

Brent got out another plate and fork and set it on the laminate-topped table in the sliver of a kitchen. Desi took a seat and looked around. "Did you decorate in here or did Karen?"

"Karen did this herself."

The mature Karen had cheerful taste, not like the bizarre decor in her childhood bedroom. Sheer yellow curtains hung at the small window that looked into the backyard. A bright floral border trimmed the top edges of walls sponge-painted a delicate blue.

"A lot of hope went into this room."

"Yeah." Brent sat down across from her and stared at his half-eaten food. "Can't figure out where it all went."

"It's not gone, Brent. You've got to hang on to it for her." What was she doing giving this young man a pep talk when she had such hideous suspicions about — ?

Stop it! She wasn't going to let her overactive brain cells go there. Not here, not now.

Karen was okay. She had to be.

"Aren't you going to eat?" Brent waved his fork at her.

She stuffed a bite of sweet-and-sour pork into her mouth. "This is good." After a second helping, she pushed her plate away. "Tell me about the taped interviews you were doing the day before the robbery."

"You know about that?" He shrugged. "The cops made a big deal, but I gave them the tape, and whatever they were looking for they didn't find. Something about 'not the right code words.' I didn't understand, but I didn't ask since they were willing to let the subject drop."

Relief loosened Desi's muscles. "I'm glad you're in the clear on that. So what about your church? What are they doing to support you through this time?"

Brent scrunched up his nose. "I think we got to be a bit much for them. Too needy. They threw us a shower for the baby, brought food when Karen was on bed rest before Adam was born. And afterward, too. But then this depression thing hit her. It was like they didn't know how to deal with it. One little ray of sunshine used to come over and tell Karen she needed to repent for her negative feelings — that she was dishonoring God."

"Oh, dear."

"You said it." Brent went to the sink with their dishes. "Karen didn't tell me about the problem until after she stopped opening the door for anyone from Central Christian and started opening it for that bunch her mom sent over from Inner Witness."

"No wonder Jo has hard feelings toward your church. They dropped the ball big-time and left Karen vulnerable to a cult. Not that Jo sees her group that way."

"She doesn't, but I sure can't use mine as an example of a better alternative." He ran water in the sink.

Desi stepped up beside him. "There are great fellowships out there, dripping with compassion. You just need to find the right one for your family."

"I know that, but Karen was too young in the Lord to see it." Brent scrubbed at a plate like he wanted to wear through the ceramic.

Desi tugged a dish towel from a hook. "Are you looking for a new church?"

Brent stopped scrubbing. "That hasn't been high on my priority list right now."

"Maybe it should be. When she comes home, you're all going to need lots of loving arms around you." She took the dish from Brent, rinsed it, and wiped it dry.

Brent looked at her with a wry curl to his

mouth. “I’m barred from the museum. Church hunting would give me something to do in my free time.”

Desi looked at her watch. After 6 p.m. No contact from Agent Ortiz. No call from Tony. It’d be after eight in Boston. *Tony, you’re all right, aren’t you?* Tiny moth wings fluttered in her stomach. “I should get going. Jo probably fixed supper for me, and I’m already full.”

“Jo won’t care. If you leave right now, you’ll make her place about the time Reverend Romlin comes on television. She won’t give you a second glance.”

“All the more reason to move along. I want to hear this fellow’s spiel.”

Brent followed Desi toward the door. “Hey, you haven’t told me if you found out anything interesting in Santa Fe.”

She turned in the dinky foyer. “Enough to confirm that Inner Witness Ministries is about as genuine as a three-dollar bill. But we already knew that. I didn’t find out anything about Karen, if that’s what you mean.”

Desi waved and headed for her car. She was too good at giving out selective information. She ought to be ashamed of herself. But she wasn’t. Until the right people could investigate, Karen’s loved ones didn’t need a load of her unconfirmed suspicions — and that included Max.

What was with the FBI today that they couldn't keep appointments or return phone calls? Didn't they realize she was dancing on a bed of hot coals?

A knock on the front door brought Tony out of a fog where Elvis oldies kept playing through his mind. The knock came louder. *Go away!* Tony held his eyes closed and gripped the arms of his chair. Another chorus of "Blue Suede Shoes" had more appeal than talking to someone.

"Lucano! Open up in there!"

Tony's eyes popped wide. No!

"It's Steve, and I'm gonna bust down the door if you don't open it."

Tony slid out of his chair, growling under his breath. His gorilla of an ex-partner would carry out his threat. What was Steve Crane doing here? Crane wasn't one for social calls, except when it came to Max's two kids. And the guy was retired from the Bureau. No way he could've heard about what happened this afternoon. The administration would've kept the name of the dead agent out of the early news to give the family time to get acquainted with their loss.

Releasing the chain lock, Tony opened the

door wide enough for his body to fill the gap. The smell of pepperoni greeted him from the box Crane held in one arm. The other arm shoved the door wide, and Steve was in his living room just like that.

Tony's hands fisted. If he wasn't so groggy . . . "Stevo, which of my nerves are you trying to get on, because you just tripped over my last one. Can't you tell I was sleeping?"

"Yeah, right!" The lights snapped on. "That's better."

Tony rubbed his face. "I'm holding the door open. Why don't you take a hint?"

Crane plunked the pizza box on the peninsula between the living room and kitchen. "Is that any way to greet an old friend who cut short a hot date to come sit with a pal in his hour of need?"

The words were lighthearted, but something in the tone knocked Tony off balance. Was the guy serious? Some misguided altruistic impulse brought him here? Nah, not Stevo. Okay, he'd play along for a few minutes. Maybe he'd get rid of him faster. "You? On a hot date?"

"One hundred percent straight up, pard." Crane opened the box and popped a stray piece of cheese into his mouth. "We were on dessert at a great Italian place — you should take Desi there sometime — and I get this phone call." He started opening and closing cupboard doors. "Where do you keep the plates? I'm hungry."

"I thought you already ate."

Crane grinned as he pulled two plates out of a cupboard. "Quick, ain't ya? You know me — I can always eat, and the smell of that pepperoni is driving me wild. I get the half with anchovies." He dug into the box. "Don't bother fighting me over it 'cuz the way you look right now, I'd wipe the floor with you."

Tony snorted. "Don't worry. I hate anchovies, and I'm not hungry." He crossed his arms, and a rumble sounded. Tony looked down. Was that *his* stomach?

Crane let out his smoke-hoarsened laugh. "Here. Fill up the Grand Canyon before the neighborhood thinks we're about to have a thunderstorm." He held out a plate.

Tony stared at melted cheese, puffy crust, and pepperoni glistening with grease. "Fine! I'll eat some." He snatched the plate and returned to his recliner.

"You got a brewski in here?" Steve's voice followed him.

"If you count root beer."

"Ah, the hard stuff." The refrigerator door suctioned open. "My favorite." Crane came back into the living room.

Tony took the can his ex-partner handed him.

Crane settled on the sofa and pointed a half-eaten wedge at Tony. "Here's the plan. We do ordinary stuff. Pig out, watch the Sox on TV — there should be about half a game left. Then you can unload whatever you got to say. Even take a swing at me if it makes you feel better."

"Okay, so you heard about Ben," Tony said with his mouth full. "How?"

Crane fried him with a look. "Why is it you always underestimate the retired agent grapevine? You should know better after the way they helped us out with that art theft case."

"You guys continue to amaze me."

"I'll accept that answer." Crane clicked the television on. "Sox are playing Seattle tonight. Should be a good game."

Boston was behind. Bad game; great therapy. After an inning, Tony stretched and found that his muscles had begun to loosen up.

With a commercial blaring from the set, Crane went to the kitchen. "I'm going to get another soda. You want one?"

"After all that pizza? My mouth is like the Sahara."

Steve returned with the cans.

Tony took his and popped it open. "Who did you have out on a date?"

"That's for me to know and you to find out."

Tony groaned. "That comeback was old when I was a kid."

"Well, it was fresh in my day. Besides, you wouldn't believe me if I told you."

"Try me."

"That comeback's stale, too." He took a sip of his root beer. "Lana, Max Webb's mom."

Tony choked and lowered his can. "You're —" *cough* — "kidding."

"See? I told you."

"Don't get me wrong." Tony cleared his throat. "I'm just . . . surprised."

"Surprised that a pretty lady would go out with an old dog like me?" The muscles in Crane's neck stood out.

Whoa! Stevo had it bad. This was good. "Lady was all right for the Tramp."

"Sounds like you spend as much time as me watching Disney movies with Max's kids." His ex-partner looked at him sideways. "I was pretty sure you'd be torqued about me and Lana."

"Why would I be? And what do I have to say about it anyway?"

Crane dodged Tony's gaze. "Not a thing, so drop the subject."

Tony grinned. What do you know? The tough guy cared what he thought. Kind of nice in a scary sort of way. Almost as scary as what Max's take on the relationship might be, or what Desi was going to say when she found out.

Tony sat up rigid. "Oh no, Desi! I haven't called her."

Crane stared at him. "Oh man, you idjit on a half shell, you haven't told her?"

Tony crushed his can in his fist and stood. "She's dealing with enough without my problems." In the background, the crowd on television went wild over some play neither of them had seen. He snatched up all the empty cans, then stalked through the kitchen and out to the recycling bin in the garage. So he should have called Desi by now. He'd fix the mistake as soon as he threw his uninvited guest out. Tony tossed the cans into the bin and turned to find his ex-partner leaning against the doorjamb.

"You'd better get on the horn, pronto. I guarantee she's not going to thank you for sparing her feelings. And you'll be chump change if she hears the news from Max first."

Tony's insides froze. Crane got the call

from his buddy in a restaurant while eating with Max's mother. Steve would have explained why he needed to run out on her, and Max's mom had been home for at least an hour with no reason to keep the breaking news to herself. That horse was out of the barn and long gone in a puff of dust.

"Coming through!" Tony charged past Steve into the kitchen and snatched up the cordless from the counter. He pressed in the autodial number and held his breath.

At the sound of Desi's voice, Tony's heart leaped then plummeted. Her recorded greeting. Her phone was in use. She was talking to someone else.

Sweat oozed from his pores.

"Hi, Max." Not Tony. Rats! "What's up? Results already on our searches?"

On the sofa next to her, Jo gave her a second dirty look, identical to the one she dished out when Desi's phone went off a few seconds ago. Desi got up and walked to the corner of the room, where her low-voiced conversation wouldn't interrupt Jo's fixation on the program. She kept an eye on the TV screen where Reverend Romlin preached his little heart out.

Max huffed. "It's frustrating. There doesn't seem to be any connection between

Gordon Corp and HJ Securities. No business reason for the man to seek you out. I'm still tryin' to find evidence of the construction project. But I didn't call about that. I —"

"Listen to this!" Desi held the phone toward the TV set.

"The Bible says, 'Give and it will be given to you, pressed down, shaken together, and running over.' Are you a giver?" The Reverend pointed his finger at the camera, those silvery eyes glittering. *"Do you lead a lifestyle of giving? This verse isn't for the Sunday penny-pincher. The one who needs to have his fingers pried off his check when the offering plate comes around. This is a promise for the cheerful giver. Do you belie-e-e-eve that Gawd has a special place in his heart for the generous spirit?"*

Desi put the phone back to her ear. "What's wrong so far?"

"Not a thing. I had the urge to say, 'Amen, brother, preach it.' If he could bottle that voice, he'd make a mint . . . What am I *sayin'?* He's already makin' a bundle off it!"

"Now, that's a big amen. Remember? I caught a peek at his financial records. Okay, here we go. I think we're getting to the punch line — or, rather, the bottom line."

Desi turned the phone toward the television again.

". . . expand your vision, brothers and sisters. Get out beyond that local group that confines you to a specific place and time. Don't be temporal; be spiritual. Here at Inner Witness Ministries, we're all about taking you to the next level of development in your walk with Gawd. But to accomplish our mission, we need your help. Here's your chance to show Gawd your giving heart. Make your generous checks out to —"

Desi turned toward the wall. "Oh, gag me with a spoon." She made an obnoxious noise.

Max laughed then quieted. "It's not funny. My heart hurts for the people deceived by this shyster. Any ministry that exalts itself above the role of the local church . . . Grrr! Huge red flag. What's Jo doin' now?"

Desi looked over her shoulder. "Making out her check as fast as her fingers can fly."

Max groaned. "What's the matter with her? She's not a stupid woman."

"I know, hon, but she'll have to figure this out for herself. Pray that this man's charisma wears thin and she's able to see Jesus as the Savior whose love doesn't need to be bought."

"There are a lot of people like Jo out there

— professional seekers. Easy prey."

"And no telling how many armchair Christians who think they can make it on electronic fellowship alone."

"Don't let's get started, woman. I didn't call to depress myself with a philosophical chat on epidemic church problems."

Desi snickered. "Sounds like a good title for a seminar."

"Ho-ho-ho! I'll leave public speaking to you." Pause. "So, how's Tony doin'?"

"How should I know? He must be up to his ears in a case."

A hitch in Max's breathing. "You mean he hasn't called you yet? Oh dear."

"I don't like the sound of that. What's the matter? He's not hurt, is he?"

"Nothing like that. It's just . . . well . . ."

"Max, if you don't spit it out, I'm going to —"

"Des! Tony's fine. He shot a killer today and —"

"Feels like the scum of the earth." Desi walked into the bedroom. Enough of the Reverend Romlin. "Isn't it ironic that the best agents feel the worst when they do what the situation calls for? I could kick myself for not trying to reach him again today. And I'm sure going to kick him twice for not calling me to unload." She sat on the edge of the bed. "How did you find out? He didn't call you, did he?"

"I got the news from my mom."

"She's on the FBI hotline now?"

"Sort of."

"As Desi Arnaz used to say to Lucille Ball — 'you've gots some 'splainin' to do.' "

"All right. But sit down first and keep your cool."

"I am sitting down, and this is as cool as this cucumber gets when something serious goes down with Tony and he leaves me in the dark. As usual. Oh, don't worry, I won't scalp him until after I hug him. So get back to the mom already."

"Maybe I should let you call him."

"Ma-a-a-ax!"

Heavy sigh. "Steve Crane took Mom out to Carlucci's tonight and —"

Desi gave a thin shriek. "Your mom and Crane?" She flopped backward. "Has the world gone insane? I can't believe —"

"Des!"

"What?"

"Shut! Up!"

"Sorry." What was the matter with her? Pulse jackhammering, brain misfiring, and mouth in hyperdrive. "It's been a rotten, frustrating, horrible day."

"You and Tony must've had the same kind

then. One of Steve's retired agent cronies called him while he and Mom were at the restaurant. Take a few deep breaths, Des." A beat of silence. "It's bad. One of Tony's squad was killed in the shoot-out."

Desi's heart stuttered. She jerked upright, mind reeling. "Who? Hajimoto? Polanski? Erickson?"

"Yeah, that last one."

Desi slumped. "Oh, no, not Ben. He was Tony's driver during that business with al Khayr. Ben helped save my life!" Tears welled from her eyes. "Tony must be beside himself. He liked Ben . . . a lot. Thought he had great potential." A sob jolted her ribs. "And now all that possibility is gone!" She looked up. "God, what's going on here? Where are You?"

"That's it, Des. Get it out." Max's voice came from a distant place. "I'm here. God's here. We've got big shoulders for you right now."

"But where's Tony?" Desi mashed the phone against her ear. "Why didn't he call . . . let *me* be there for *him?*"

"You know these shooting investigations are pretty intense, and with a double on his hands, he may not have had a spare second."

"I'm sure you're right." A hollow ache spread from Desi's core. "If we're going to make this relationship work, I suppose I'd better get used to being an afterthought."

"Des, you know I love you to pieces, so in the spirit of friendship, I'm going to ask you one question."

"Go ahead . . . I think."

"Would you like some cheese with that whine?"

A laugh stumbled over a sob. "Youch! Thanks, I needed that." Desi got up and paced. "I'm going to get off the phone now. Maybe Tony'll be free soon and have a chance to call."

"Better yet, *you* call *him.* He may be too torn up to reach out to anybody."

Desi stopped pacing. "You're telling me he's home?"

Agitated breathing.

Desi squeezed the phone. "How long since he left the office?"

"Couple of hours. Steve dropped my mom off at home mid-date to go sit with him."

"So the ex-partner who drives him up a wall is better company than the woman who thinks he hung the moon?" Desi ate up the floor in hefty strides. "Tony and I needed each other today. He's not the only one with earth-rattling news. I'm sitting on a bombshell that not even you know about, and he couldn't return a phone call. Why? He was too shook up? Oh, no, not Anthony Lucano. I can just hear his reasoning. 'Protect Desiree at all costs. Make sure she never does anything dangerous or has to deal with bad news. After all, I'm her guardian angel.' "

"Des, stop! What bombshell?"

"Forget it, Max. And don't try to call me back tonight. I won't answer, because I can't be responsible for what I might say. If Tony ever does get around to ringing my number, he'll be lucky if I pick up. Bye, Max."

Desi closed the connection and stood staring at a hideous black and purple wall. Tears blurred the colors into a muddy mess. She faded onto the bed and curled into a ball.

What kind of terrible person had she turned into? A fine man was dead, his family devastated, Tony grief-stricken and no doubt finding a million ways to blame himself, and here she was bawling her eyes out because she wasn't in the loop.

She loved Tony with every molecule of her heart and soul, but if he didn't trust her enough to share himself with her, how could they have a relationship worth keeping?

Her ringtone started playing. Desi squinted to focus the caller ID. Her throat closed.

Tony.

Eleven

The phone rang in Tony's ear . . . once . . . twice . . . *Pick up, honey.* On the third ring, he turned away from a scowling Stevo.

The phone clicked. "Hello?"

"Desi, is that you, sweetheart?"

"Ye-e-es." Ragged breath.

Tony's heart tore. "Are you crying?"

"No." Deep breath. "I mean, yes, but I'm trying not to."

"Were you just on the phone with Max?"

"Uh-huh."

He leaned his forehead against the refrigerator. "She beat me to the punch."

"Don't blame her." The edge in Desi's tone could have cut rock.

"You're mad at me, and you have a right to be."

"I'm angry, and I hate myself for feeling that way."

"So I act like a jerk, and you take it out on yourself?" He stuck a hand in his pocket.

"Oh, Tony!" Stifled sniff. "This can't be about me . . . or even about you. Ben's poor family!" The sobs came unglued.

Pain skewered a spot between Tony's eyebrows. He squeezed his eyes shut, and wetness fell onto his cheeks. He could only manage a hoarse whisper out of a strangled windpipe. "Yeah, I know."

Desi's crying gentled. Little sounds intruded on the quiet between them. A ticking clock. A gust of wind rattling the windowpane. The soft click of the front door closing.

Tony pulled in a deep breath. "Des, I'm sorry I didn't call sooner. The job got ahold of me, and I didn't want to stop and think. But then they made me go home, and it was like . . ." His fingers wrapped around a fistful of hair. "I shut down. I don't know how else to explain it."

"Let's not worry about that now. I want to be there for you."

"I wish." He wandered into the living room and plopped into his chair. "I should have called you right back after you left that message this afternoon. I ought to have my head examined for stopping myself."

Slight pause. "You stopped yourself?"

"It wouldn't have been fair to dump on you and then run back to my business when you've already got Max's burden on your shoulders."

"You delayed the inevitable by a few hours, Tony."

"Yeah, but I figured if I waited we could talk as long as we wanted."

"That part's good."

What was off about the tone of this conversation? He called and apologized. She cried . . . well, he did, too, a little. Now they were ready to wrap their arms around each other. It was all good. What had he missed?

"Never mind, darling." Small sigh. "We'll deal with us later. Right now, I'm afraid I have to toss a few of my burdens your way. I've found out some wild things."

"I'm all ears, babe." So that was it. She had information, and he'd blown her off. He should have known that Desi hadn't called this afternoon just to vent.

"The morning started out with quite a jolt — stolen car, blood drops."

"Details, hon." Tony sat forward as she told him about the stolen car, Jo and Brent's frenzied conclusion that Karen must be alive, and the blood in the carport.

"Jo's on pins and needles for the results," she said. "I don't know whether to hope the blood is Karen's or not."

"Tell Jo not to expect a quick answer.

These things don't work as fast in real life as they do on *CSI*." He chuckled. "Turn-around for DNA is at least a couple of weeks in our swamped crime labs — and that's with a rush on it. Average is sixty days. But the Bureau is very good at meticulous, long-term investigations, so the wait doesn't bother us too often."

"The Bureau might have to kick it into high gear on this one . . . like yesterday."

Tony squashed a spurt of irritation. Desi was under a lot of stress, the same as he was. "We're good at that, too. What've you got?"

"Well, I didn't mean to horn in on the missing persons investigation, but just to drop by Reverend Romlin's ministry headquarters in Santa Fe. Talk to people, maybe find out if anyone had seen or spoken to Karen, or at least if anyone could shed light on what she might have been thinking when she disappeared."

"That's horning in on the investigation, hon, but go on."

Desi huffed and seconds ticked past. The old mental ten-count, but he wasn't about to apologize when he could be saying "I told you so."

"All right, then." Her voice was tight. "I didn't go to the main office. Max found an address off the beaten path, and this bouncy coed type mistook me for someone from Gordon Corp. She gushed all over, so excited about moving into the Holy City."

Tony's spine stiffened. "The what?"

"Believe it or not, the good Reverend and his major supporter, Hamilton Gordon, are building themselves a town called Sanctuary at some supersecret spot in the desert."

"The new Waco!" Tony leaped to his feet.

"Yes, I know. It's very wacko."

"No, I said Waco." He paced his living room. "An anonymous phone caller told me to look for the new Waco."

"As in that sect back in the nineties? David Koresh's bunch that holed up in a compound and wouldn't come out?"

"One and the same."

Desi groaned. "Didn't they burn themselves to the ground? Lots of people died, including children."

Tony's blood ran thin and fast. He strode for his kitchen peninsula and snagged a notepad and pen. "Start at the beginning, and tell me every detail." He wrote until his fingers were sore. "This is great stuff, Des. You've always been a top-notch eyewitness."

"Thank you, dear."

"Don't thank me too much." He put down the pen and flexed the ache out of his hand muscles. "A big piece of me would like to lock you up to keep you out of trouble. These people aren't playing patty-cake."

"Tony, I'm not stupid."

He stood and stretched. "No, you're too smart for your own good."

"Believe me when I say that I don't take foolish chances." Exasperation weighted her voice.

"That shoot-out today was part of this same case. My squad is *trained* to handle situations — we thought we had our bases covered — and look what happened."

"Does that mean I'm supposed to walk around afraid to help people?"

Tony sighed. "I'm nuts about you just the way you are, but that's the problem. Call it a guy-thing, but I need to know you're safe even while you're out saving the world."

"You've always made me feel safe. Even when I couldn't stand the sight of you, I knew that any bad guy would have to come through you to get to me. But sometimes, dear heart, you take that protective instinct too far. It builds a wall between us. Like today — you kept me out, when you should have pulled me close."

Tony closed his eyes and rubbed his forehead. The gal knew how to take the wind out of his self-righteous sails. "Yeah, I'm sorry about that. My logic seemed right at the time."

"I do forgive you, but let's keep working on communication, okay?"

"What do you say we get busy on it face-to-face? I'm coming to Albuquerque."

"When?" The question came out breathless.

Aw, sweetheart, I can't wait to hold you, too. "I'd be out the door right now, but I've got this thing I have to do in the morning. I'll catch the earliest flight after that."

"You can leave your squad?"

"Polanski can hold down the fort. Sounds like the action's out west. If my superiors won't send me on the Bureau clock, I'll take time off and be there anyway."

"What about Agent Ortiz? Will she want you horning in on her territory?"

"We've been cooperating in this investigation. We'll get along."

"You're not coming just to keep an eye on me?"

There was that edge to her tone. Tony puckered his brow. Protect her, yeah, but not smother her. Didn't she get the difference? "Honey, looking after you is the job of a legion of angels, not one man." He forced a laugh. "Don't you want me there?"

"You know I do."

"Good. I'll call you when I have an arrival time."

In the background at her end, a phone rang.

"And I'll pick you up with bells on."

The phone rang another time.

"Can't wait. Get some sleep now."

The ringing phone cut off in the middle of the third jangle.

"Hold on!" Desi's voice came low and urgent. "There's another thing about this 'new Waco' that makes the old one look like a kiddie's sandbox."

Tony's insides curdled. "That'd take a lot, babe. Do you have any idea what went on in Koresh's compound?"

"A rough idea. And Sanctuary's got some of the same things going, plus their own wrinkle. But I can't blurt it out over the phone."

"Des! You're going to drive me to the loony bin."

"No, I'm going to drive you wherever you want to go when you get here."

"Amusing that wasn't."

"Nothing about this situation is amusing."

"Des?"

"Yes."

"I love you."

"I love you, too, Tony. You have no idea." Fresh tears ruffled her tone. "Hurry!"

"I will. Hang in there, sweetheart."

"You, too."

"I will. Bye."

Tony shut the phone off, chest tight. *Desi, darlin', what has your nose for trouble led you into now?* He'd lied like a dog a few minutes ago. He thought he meant it when he said looking after her wasn't his top agenda item. But she had no idea what these people might be capable of doing if they caught wind of what she knew. Until she figured out how to act within safe bounds, superglue couldn't stick him any closer to her side.

Sleep well tonight? Not hardly!

Desi sat on the edge of the bed. She needed Tony, but she was going to smack him if he didn't start trusting her to take care of herself better than a first grader.

The bedroom door crashed open. Desi shrieked and jumped up.

Jo filled the doorway, red-faced. "How come you didn't tell me Pete's truck was found wrecked and he's missin'?"

Desi snapped her phone shut. "I thought you wanted me to respect your religion. Seemed to me that television show was church time for you."

"For somethin' like that I would've stopped and listened." Jo's chest heaved.

Says the woman who couldn't peel her eyes off the tube long enough to ask me if I found anything out about her daughter today. Desi stuffed her phone into her pocket. "How'd you hear about Pete?"

"Agent Ortiz called. She's on her way over, pretty annoyed that you didn't give me the message."

"She'd better keep her bee in her bonnet, because mine will have hers for lunch."

"This I gotta see."

"You might want to know that your house is under FBI surveillance."

"What? Where?" Her gaze darted to the bedroom window.

"When I drove up, I spotted the surveillance car. Believe me, I know what one of those looks like."

"They're watchin' for Pete?"

"I assume so."

"They'll have a long wait. If you can spot a fed with your eyes wide open, my ex can do it blindfolded. They develop a sixth sense for cops on the res. By now he should be hiding out with friends in the desert."

"Knowing the FBI, they've checked the reservations already."

Jo shook her head. "Won't do them any good. Indians take care of their own. They don't trust the white man's law, often with good reason."

"I won't argue with you there."

Their gazes met and held.

"You're an interestin' woman, Desiree Jacobs. I can see why my sister likes you. How about I show you my workshop out back?"

"I'd love to see your workshop."

Desi followed her hostess through the house and out the kitchen door onto the poured slab patio in the backyard. The evening air smelled of grill smoke. A stone path led to the small, tile-roofed building she'd noticed earlier today.

Desi looked back at the house. "What about the visitor we're expecting?"

Jo shrugged. "If she's such great shakes as an agent, she'll find us."

Chuckling, Desi stepped into the workshop. A faint odor of glue struck her. She would have expected the smell to be stronger, but she noted fan-operated ventilation ducts. A workbench hugged the far wall, and a rectangular wooden table sat in the middle of the plank floor. Long banks of lights illuminated tools hung on racks or stowed in bins. Different shapes and colors of ceramic tile filled plastic tubs. An unfinished project sat on the table, pieces of unapplied tile scattered about.

She smiled at Jo. "I'll bet you have fun in here."

"I do." The woman touched a button on an electronic wall panel and soft sounds caressed the eardrums — one of those nature sounds CDs.

Jo perched on a stool and shoved tiles around with her fingers. "How did your business at the museum turn out? Anything that would help clear Karen?"

So the woman did have questions; she just wanted to ask them from the vantage point of her inner sanctum. Desi frowned. What could she tell Jo without saying too much? "The administrator's determined to blame HJ Securities for the theft. He doesn't want any of his employees to be guilty. Liability issues."

"Cold-blooded."

"I think it comes with the territory. Anyway, HJ Securities is out of a contract with the Albuquerque museum. I did get the chance to browse around, but the crime scene was cleaned up. Good information about the Anasazi, though."

"Sounds like a bust of a trip."

Desi held her peace.

Jo placed a tile into the design in progress. "Did you have a nice visit at Inner Witness Ministries?"

Now we get to the point. "I was welcomed with open arms."

Jo smiled. "The staff was friendly, huh?"

"Open and forthcoming."

"See?" Her eyes lit. "No secrets. No trickery. No hidden agenda."

Oh, she wouldn't say that. Desi stared at Jo, an iron band tightening around her chest. *For Karen's sake, for Max's, please don't be a part of Sanctuary.* "The representative told me about the Holy City."

"Oh, wow!" Jo leaped up. "You know about that? Isn't it excitin'?"

Desi closed her eyes against a stab of sorrow.

"See, it's right here."

Desi looked up to find Jo standing beside her with an open book in her hands. Not just a book . . . a Bible. Jo stuck the pages under her face and pointed to a passage in Revelation.

" 'I saw the Holy City, the new Jerusalem,' " she read, " 'comin' down out of heaven from God.' I can hardly wait. Reverend Romlin taught a whole month on this passage. Don't you want to be worthy to live there?"

Desi took the Bible and laid it on the table. “I’m not worthy on my own, but I’ve been made worthy through Jesus Christ.”

“Exactly. The body and blood. The more often you partake, the closer you get to qualifyin’ for the kingdom.”

“Partake?” Desi held her breath.

“Sure. Roasted lamb and red wine. They represent the death of the physical body and the shedding of natural blood so that we might rise above the flesh into the new life of the spirit. I take the elements every day during mornin’ meditations.” Jo blinked at her. “No way! You didn’t think we ate raw meat and drank real blood, did you?”

Desi breathed again. “Of course not.” She studied the woman’s face. Pure innocence. Wholehearted faith. Half a bubble off from finding the real thing.

Jo crossed her arms. “You have strange ideas about what we believe. How can you be sure we’re wrong?”

“My belief about the body and blood isn’t about me. It’s about Jesus.”

“Sure. The Lamb.” She settled onto her stool.

“God Himself who walked among us as a man.”

Jo’s face scrunched up. “That’s bonkers. God couldn’t be a man. He’s . . . well, God.

And the best we can do is follow the Lamb's teachings and hope that we're good enough in the end."

"It'll never happen." Desi shook her head. "There is no cosmic scale out there weighing our good deeds against our bad deeds. To a holy God, any evil act, or even an evil thought, merits death. The only way to escape justice is for someone without sin to take the punishment in our place. God couldn't find a qualified human being, so He did it Himself."

Jo stared at her like a dog at a new dish, as Max would say.

Desi plunged on. "Jesus' broken body and His shed blood paid for all the ways I fall short of what I should be. When I take the Communion elements, I'm reminded that without Him I'm nothing but flesh waiting to die, but with Him I'm a redeemed spirit waiting only for my flesh to be reborn."

Tension melted from Jo's face. "The healing thing. Reverend Romlin's started to teach about that. Different kinds of mutton and wine as a focus of faith for different kinds of ailments. The most effective for just about anything is meat from a newborn lamb and deep burgundy wine. The next best is . . . Well, here's a brochure." She grabbed a glossy leaflet from a counter and handed it to Desi. "We've got lots of testimonies about the faithful getting healed of all kinds of diseases after the sacrament."

Desi took the flier, glanced at the familiar picture of Jesus on the cover, and tucked it into her pants pocket. She touched the smooth tiles on the table. Now where to go with this conversation? Plain speaking hadn't made a dent. She picked up a chipped square and put it in the mosaic. "How's that? It's the right color."

Jo tossed the chip into a waste bin. "Doesn't fit. It's a discard anyway."

"How about this one." Desi took a tile from a tub. "It's the perfect shape and size."

"The color is off a shade. Duh!"

"You're a creator." Desi stared into Jo's eyes. "When you start a project, you have a design in mind, and you won't take anything less than perfection in each piece. God's the original Creator, and His plan of salvation is perfect. It's not obscure or difficult. In fact, it's downright simple, but it is precise. A deviation in any of the essentials and the whole thing becomes a discard."

Jo chuckled. "There was a message in there someplace. Let me think about it, okay?"

"For sure. Any questions you want to ask, Max or I are available."

"It's Karen I care about. Did you learn anything that might help us find her?"

Desi leaned a hip against the table. "The person at the ministry office had met Karen, but hadn't seen or heard from her since before her disappearance."

"I told you they had nothin' to do with that, though the mother part of me wishes they knew something. It's Snake Bonney. Get him to tell the truth, and you'll find Karen. Did you talk to him?"

"My dance card was a bit full today."

Jo bit her lip. "Sorry. I'm impatient. No one believes me about that freak show, Bonney. Maybe I should go with you. Maybe . . ." She shook her head. "The jerk would clam up as soon as he saw mean, mad Mama comin', but as long as a pretty young thing smiles at him, he'll jabber like a monkey. Approach him in the mornin' at home. He'll be hungover and movin' slow and none of his gang nearby."

"Very comforting."

Jo laughed. "You'll handle yourself. Competent seems to be your middle name."

"At least someone has confidence in me." Desi scratched the back of her head. "Though I'm not sure how much I have in myself in a confrontation with a motorcycle outlaw."

"He's got no chops without his pack."

"Hellooo! Anybody back here?"

Ortiz's voice sent Jo to the door. "Come on in. We were chatting about art and stuff."

The agent stepped inside. "No sign of Pete?"

"I'd be the last person he'd contact if he was in trouble."

"No if about it."

Jo put her hands on her hips. "You'd better be here to tell me the results of the DNA testing on the blood in my driveway."

The agent shook her head. "Results aren't back yet. The blood type was O positive, though, same as at the museum, and the same as your daughter's. But O positive is the most common blood type, so that doesn't mean much."

Jo flushed. "You're telling me Karen's still a suspect because you people can't get a move on the testing?"

Desi touched Jo's arm. "Tony says DNA results take at least a couple of weeks, and that's lightning speed."

Ortiz lasered Desi with her gaze. "You've been in touch with Lucano recently?"

"Yes, and I suggest you call him right away."

The agent blinked and shifted. "I see."

"He'll be here tomorrow, and then I'd like

to meet with both of you."

"Lucano's coming to Albuquerque?"

Desi sent her a tight smile. "He has important things on his mind."

"Would someone tell me what's goin' on?" Jo glared from one to the other. "I'm not brain-dead. What you're not sayin' is howlin' louder than the words." She narrowed her eyes at Desi. "You know things you haven't told me."

Desi looked away. "Can't tell you."

"*Won't* is what you mean." Jo slammed her fist on the table. Tiles clattered to the floor. "I have a right to know anything that affects my daughter. I can't stand this limbo. Max said I could trust you. What a lie!"

Ortiz stepped forward. "Mrs. Cheama, please calm down —"

"Don't patronize me!" Jo whirled on the agent. "You're no better." She spat a curse. "Usin' my home as a trap for my ex-husband. Tryin' to find Karen so you can put her in jail." She yanked the studio door open. "You're not welcome here, either of you. Get out!"

Sick at heart, Desi stepped into the dusk, Ortiz after her. The door slammed on the sound of weeping. What could she have done differently?

The agent said a disgusted word. "Volatile

woman. Never know whether to expect co-operation or a cussing out."

"Jo flies off, but she'll cool down fast." Desi headed for the house.

Ortiz matched her pace. "So you're not out on your rump?"

"It's time for me to be away from her watchful eye. I'll find a hotel."

They went into the house, and Desi stepped into the bedroom to pack. The agent hovered in the doorway. "What brought you to the office under a full head of steam?"

"I dumped a load on Tony. You and he have a lot to talk about."

Ortiz pursed her lips. "Jo's right. You're holding back. Not a good idea with dangerous people out there."

"Do agents take a class on terrorizing witnesses about what bad guys *might* do to them? I call that belaboring the obvious." She went into the bathroom and tossed personal items into her kit.

"Are you this prickly with your boyfriend? We can help, you know."

Desi put her kit into her bag. "All right. You want to know my theory?" She sat down beside her suitcase. "Did you listen to the museum recording about the things that were stolen?"

"I gave it a quick run-through."

"And it didn't alarm you? Didn't we agree that if we found out what they wanted the items for we'd know who took them?"

The agent laughed. "You mean that bit about human sacrifice and ritual cannibalism? Makes good tourist copy."

"There's nothing to it?"

Ortiz shrugged. "The so-called experts wrangle about it, but the idea's speculative at best. No application to today's Pueblos."

"Not the Indians." She waved a hand. "Inner Witness."

The agent stared at her. "I shouldn't be telling you, but we've got our eye on this bunch and not a whiff of something like that. White-collar fraud is more up their alley."

A weight lifted from Desi's chest. She had gone off the deep end with the Anasazi ritual thing. "That makes me feel better. A little silly, but better. Walk me out to my car."

"You got it."

Desi left her business card with her cell number on it beside the phone in Jo's kitchen. No sign of the upset mother. Maybe doing some therapeutic tile work.

They went to Desi's rental car, and Ortiz helped her load the luggage. Desi turned toward the other woman. "Thanks."

"No problem." Ortiz slammed the trunk.

"Not about the suitcases. Thanks for getting Max off the hook with the city and tribal police forces."

Ortiz shrugged. "They didn't have as much of the picture as we did. As soon as our own experts confirmed your company's findings, we knew Max wasn't involved. Besides, if three law enforcement agencies couldn't dig up a motive for her, there wasn't one." The agent grinned.

Desi dug her keys out of her purse. "Max couldn't steal if her life depended on it. Do you know she once drove an hour one way to pay for a sucker her toddler stuck in her purse? *I'm* the thief." She jabbed a thumb at herself. "Remember that."

Ortiz saluted. "We'll meet tomorrow after I talk to Lucano." She headed toward her car.

Desi got in the rental. Even if her cannibalism theory was out the window, there was still plenty to look into. Sanctuary for one. She backed out of Jo's driveway then put on the brakes as a realization hit her. She sat and stared into the dark. If the FBI hadn't heard about the Holy City, what else didn't they know about Inner Witness?

She shook herself mentally. Not going

there right now. She needed sleep. Gas, too. The gauge read under the quarter mark. She drove to the station a few blocks away.

While the tank filled, she took out the brochure Jo gave her. Sure enough. The meat from sheep in different stages of maturity, paired with certain types of wine, was touted as a "point of faith contact" for receiving healing from various ailments. Unbred ewe for things like skin ailments and age-related problems. Ewe with first lamb at side for fertility. Mature buck for male problems. And the all-purpose cure-all — newborn.

Brent's words about Pete Cheama slithered through her mind. *He claims the spirits have told him that Adam is the focus of battle in the unseen realm . . .*

She crumpled the brochure. No! Suspicions about what might have happened to Karen were ugly enough, but to think anyone would go after a baby for such a purpose — Bile rose in her throat. She swallowed it.

Ridiculous. She was overtired, overwrought, and making too much of a gruesome legend. But thank heaven Max had taken Adam out of town, because even Mr. Just-the-Facts Lucano believed in spiritual forces unleashed by bad choices. Karen had made plenty of those, especially by getting involved with Inner Witness Ministries.

The pump clicked off, and Desi jumped. Hugging herself, she went in and picked up a bottle of water. Her hand trembled as she handed the attendant her money.

Could prospects get any worse for Karen? For all the poor folks duped by a faux-Christian ministry? Who could calculate the outcry against genuine ministries who'd be lumped in with the false when secrets were exposed?

Desi climbed into her car and closed her eyes. She had to be wrong about the reason those artifacts were stolen, because being right was an alternative too awful to imagine.

She started the car and pulled out. An odd thump sounded behind her, and she checked the rearview mirror. Her throat closed around a scream, and she lost her grip on the steering wheel.

From the rear seat, a hideous kachina mask stared at her, with slitted eyes dark and liquid.

Twelve

Desi's car swerved into the wrong lane of traffic. The driver of an oncoming vehicle laid on the horn. Breathing in gasps, she jerked back onto the proper side of the road.

"Take it easy." The deep voice slurred from the backseat. "You'll get us in an accident . . . don't need another one."

"Pete?" Desi's voice came out a thin squeak. "Pete Cheama?" She applied the brakes and drifted toward the parking lane, her heart performing somersaults.

"Keep driving, Ms. Jacobs."

Something hard poked the back of Desi's neck. She gasped and returned to cruising speed. "What do you want?"

"Take the next right. I'll tell you . . . when to turn again."

"You're not high, are you?"

"No more meth. The old ways of my people saved me, but the world of the white man does not want to let me go."

"This isn't the time for riddles, Cheama. Your daughter is mixed up in something horrible."

"This I know."

"You know?" Desi locked gazes with the person staring back at her in the rearview mirror. Streetlights flashed over his face. Not a kachina mask, but bruises and swelling around the eyes and jaw. "Is Karen alive?"

A car honked.

The hard object jabbed Desi's neck. "Eyes on the road!"

"Take it easy. I'm not used to strange men popping up in my backseat." *Miss Cool I'm not with all these cracks in my voice.*

"I don't know if Karen is alive." Cheama's voice was flat, anything but hopeful. "Looking for her put bad people on my trail. I found out things about their business."

"Your accident wasn't an accident?"

"I should be dead."

"What happened? Who — ?"

"A semi forced me off the road."

Didn't a semi driver shoot Ben Erickson? Desi swallowed. "A Gordon Corp truck?"

"Maybe. No logo on the door."

"Ham Gordon needs to be stopped. Don't you want to help?"

The man snickered. "Gordon is a nutcase. He wants certain things, but doesn't want to know how it happens. See no evil. Hear no evil."

"So someone else is pulling the strings?" Sparks danced up her spine. "The Boston FBI is chasing a bootlegging ring with connections here in New Mexico. Your daughter's biker ex-boyfriend shows fresh interest in her before she disappears. Artifacts are stolen from a museum. A cult is operating out of this area. How does all of this tie together?"

"Maybe it doesn't. Maybe you're connecting dots . . . that don't belong together. Or maybe a few are missing."

"What do you know, Cheama?" The hairs on her neck prickled. "You need to turn yourself in. Agent Ortiz'll get you protection and medical care. I can take you —" The hard object rapped the side of her head. "Ouch!"

"I don't want to hurt you, but be silent."

Sweat popped out on Desi's skin. Be silent. Be still — the words of the terrorist Abu al Khayr when her head throbbed from his blows. She couldn't do this again!

She floored the accelerator, and her unwanted passenger yelped and flopped backward. Jamming her foot on the brake, she hung on while tires screeched, and the vehicle did a 180. Cars darted around them, horns blaring. Desi's vehicle came to a rocking halt straddling the centerline. She fumbled for the door latch and her seat belt, fingers thick and clumsy.

A hand closed around her throat and yanked backward. Her head hit the backrest. She sucked for air, but got nothing. Black spots danced before her eyes. She clawed at the hand.

"Stop!" Hot breath blasted into her ear. "You'll be killed."

Desi froze, and the grip on her neck eased. She wheezed in a thread of oxygen.

"Drive me . . . where I want to go, and I'll talk to you . . . not federal agents. Agreed?"

Desi managed the ghost of a nod. The hand left her throat, and she grabbed for air.

Cheama muttered something sharp in another language. "Get going before the cops are on us."

Insides quivering, Desi put the car in gear and swung the vehicle around. She eyed her cell phone in the dash holder. If she could get her mitts on it for a second, she could punch in Tony's autodial, and when she didn't respond to his "hello," he'd know she was in trouble. For the FBI, zeroing in on the phone's GPS chip would be a piece of cake. Great plan — too bad there was no way to act on it.

Her passenger, his breathing labored, kept his weapon to the back of her head.

She glanced in the rearview. "You need to be in a hospital."

"Turn west at the stoplight, and stay on that highway out of town."

Desi pressed her lips together and did as she was told. For miles, the vehicle held no sound but that of spinning tires on blacktop and the rasp of pain-filled breathing. Albuquerque dwindled and the desert grew. Within a few turns, they were on a little-used side road. Desi's heart thudded. Cheama was taking her away from civilization out into emptiness, where he could do anything to her. She looked at the phone again.

"Give it to me." The weapon dug into her skin.

"What?"

"The cell. Hand it over."

Desi snatched the phone and tossed it over her shoulder. Her captor jerked, and an object thunked to the seat beside her. She looked down to see a foot long piece of wood. Some gun!

"You're hijacking me with a stick?" She

checked her rearview mirror, but from the sound of the continuing groans, Cheama was lying down in the backseat.

"It was all . . . I could find."

"I'm turning this car arou—"

"Do you want to know where Sanctuary is?"

Desi caught her breath. "What makes you think that question means anything to me?"

"Funny answer coming from someone who wants me to think . . . she's never heard of the place."

Desi's pulse picked up speed. This guy said *Sanctuary,* not referring to Jo's ephemeral city in the sweet by-and-by, but the desert compound here on earth. "You're an intelligent man, Mr. Cheama, but you're not thinking straight about getting your daughter back. You need to give your information to the people who can do something about it."

"You take me where I want to go . . . I'll tell you everything I know. That simple. Not . . . talking to the feds."

She squeezed the steering wheel. How far should she trust this guy? Keeping his freedom meant as much or more to him than Karen's safety. How did one deal with a person who grew up seeing the government as the enemy? "You could die, Pete.

Let me take you to a hospital."

"My life . . . is not in your hands."

At least he had that pegged. "Where are we going?"

"What's the matter with your voice?"

Desi cleared her bruised throat. "You choked me. Remember?"

"I did?" A snort ended in a gasp. "Lady, I can hardly see. My arms are half numb. I had no idea what I was grabbing. Just get me to this place . . . and you can forget about me."

Forget about him? Not likely. But he wasn't the threat his "stick trick" and her imagination had made him out to be. He'd even meant well in almost throttling her to death. She could have been hurt or killed jumping out into the middle of the road in a panic. "You'll have to stay conscious to direct me."

"You . . . got it." Noises in the back indicated that he was struggling into a sitting position.

"Now start talking."

"When we get there."

Desi let out a frustrated sigh. "At least tell me what sent you to Jo's to get Adam. Why would being with you make him safe? Seems to me you're a trouble magnet."

"You won't believe . . . my explanation."

"That doesn't mean I won't believe that you believe it."

A raspy snort. "It was a dream . . . while I slept one night in the desert. I heard screams."

"Animals?"

"No. I followed the noise . . . into a blind canyon — a place where no man had walked since before a Spaniard or a white man knew of this land. Bleached bones stuck out of the sand. Human bones . . . they were screaming. The sound hurt like a knife. I kicked and stomped . . . to make them stop. Finally, they were quiet . . . and the bones lay in splinters. Then I woke up, my blanket soaked in sweat."

Pale lines on the highway fled past Desi's window. "That's it?" She glanced in the rearview.

Cheama held his head in his hands. "I told this dream in my medicine society. An elder said I shouldn't have crushed the bones, because now my family line will end."

"So taking Adam was supposed to prevent this from happening?"

"The elder said the outcome might change if my grandson was raised Zuni."

"And you expected Jo to hand him over to you?"

"She knows the ancestral ways. She believed in them . . . once. I hoped she would hear me and understand that her grandchild should not be brought up in the cult of the Christian God."

"Your people see Christianity as a cult?"

Cheama looked up. "I was educated in a university, and I married a white woman. Because of those mistakes, my thinking became twisted, and I used drugs to find a false power, but I also learned new ways to see. A cult is a system of religion. The system of the Christians was forced upon my people centuries ago and has made our spirits weak and our minds confused."

Weight settled on Desi's chest, and her limbs went leaden. Air, soggy as a sauna, saturated her lungs. Her heart muscle ached as it struggled to pump blood as thick as pudding.

"Jesus is not an oppressor." The words burst from her lips, and the pressure on her chest eased. She steadied her breathing. This guy might not be physically dangerous, but if what she'd sensed was accurate, he carried hostile spirits around with him.

She glanced again in the rearview. "Misguided acts have been committed in the name of every brand of religion on the planet, not just by those who claim Christ but don't walk in His ways. Rumor has it your ancestors practiced cannibalism."

"This has not been proved." Cheama's breath rattled.

"I think your dream was about the bones of their victims."

"My dream was about the future, not the past."

Desi slowed the vehicle and pulled onto the side of the road. She put the car in park, flicked on the dome light, and turned toward her passenger. He glared at her, clutching his ribs.

"Maybe your dream was about both. You recognize the purpose of those stolen artifacts. You know they're about to be used again. May have already been used."

Cheama's face tightened. "You see? The elder's words are coming true. Karen is gone. Adam alone remains, and those who hunt me may grab him and use him to flush me out."

"The baby isn't in Albuquerque. How far can these people reach?"

Her passenger grunted. "Gordon Corp is nationwide."

Desi's mouth went dry. What had she done? Adam wasn't safe in Albuquerque, but Boston wasn't any better. People like the violent thugs who killed that museum guard and Ben Erickson had reason to go after him. Max and her family might be in danger because of her bright idea to send Adam away.

"What've you got, Ortiz?" Tony sat back and rubbed gritty eyes. He glanced at his living room clock. Midnight here; 10 p.m. in New Mexico. "I've given you Desi's gold mine. You must have something at your end."

"Pete Cheama, Jo's ex, had a bad accident. We found his pickup a mangled wreck in a ravine."

"Did Cheama survive?"

"He wasn't with the vehicle, and we still haven't found him. There was blood at the scene, but not enough to indicate death. We found a significant stash of street-ready methamphetamine under his front seat."

Tony whistled between his teeth. "Guess the DEA doesn't have to keep wondering who's carrying meth into your area."

"Cheama always was high on the suspect list. Unfortunately, we haven't got the whole picture yet. Evidence shows that a second vehicle was involved in the accident."

"So you're left with more questions than answers. I know the feeling. Was this an ordinary hit-and-run, or did someone try to kill the meth mule? Did a disoriented Cheama wander away, or did someone take him? And if someone took him, why didn't they grab the meth, too?"

"You've caught the gist." Ortiz clucked her tongue. "You can look at the evidence file when you get here. We suspect that the man may be lying dead in the desert somewhere. Good luck on us finding him. I've put surveillance on Jo's house to be on the safe side."

"Thanks." Tony yawned. "I appreciate that, especially with Desi staying there."

"She's not there any longer. Jo went ballistic because Desi kept things from her, and she booted us both out. Desi went to a hotel, but she didn't say which one."

"You didn't make her tell you?"

"Lucano, she's not a suspect, so it's not like we need to keep tabs on her every movement."

"Speak for yourself," Tony muttered under his breath.

"What?"

"Nothing. It's okay. I've got her cell number."

Ortiz laughed. "I think you need to get your tail out here before you bust. I can't wait to see you two together. Got to be better than a daytime drama."

"Anyone ever tell you that you've got a strange sense of humor?"

"Hey, I'm proud of my rep. Get some rest. Another big day tomorrow — guaranteed."

Tony bit back a sharp answer to the laughter in her voice.

"And Lucano —" Ortiz' voice sobered — "I'm so sorry to hear about Erickson. I didn't know him, but he was one of ours. You can count on us in Albuquerque to do whatever we can to find everyone responsible."

"Thanks, Ortiz. Speaking for the Boston office, we appreciate the cooperation."

Tony cut the connection. Just two more hurdles. Get the shrink off his back, and persuade Cooke that his little Westward Ho! was the best scenario for everyone.

He punched in Desi's cell number. His call went to voice mail. Blast! She must have shut the phone off so she could sleep. Not that he blamed her. She'd sounded pretty worn out when he talked to her earlier, and she wouldn't have expected him to call again.

He got up, padded to his bedroom, undressed, and crawled between the sheets. Desi was all right, just catching z's in a hotel room. He'd call again in the morning. Nothing to worry about.

So why, then, was every muscle in his body stretched tight as a drum-skin?

■ ■ ■ ■

I'm an idiot!

No other explanation for why she was still chauffeuring this injured fugitive through the desert.

Too late to turn back. Cheama might know where they were headed, but she was lost — and not because it was dark outside. She'd be just as disoriented in broad daylight. No landmarks in this desolate sandscape, much less a road sign, and they'd made so many twists and turns, for all she knew she could be headed for Outer Mongolia.

Desi leaned forward, straining to make out the vehicle track. The headlights made ghostly wisps out of passing clumps of creosote. Here and there, a piñon pine made a brave stand in the barren terrain.

"Oomph!" Her jaw snapped shut as the car bottomed out on a rut for the umpteenth time. Her passenger yelped. "Sorry." What was she apologizing for? She was out here because this guy hijacked her. He'd better keep his promise to tell her where Sanctuary was located. "No wonder you had a dually pickup, Cheama. My rental car isn't meant to travel a road like this. If it gets worse, I can't promise we'll make it to the reservation."

"We've been . . . on the res . . . since leaving Albuquerque."

"So where's the town?"

"Not . . . going to a town."

Oh, happy day! A mystery destination. Desi gritted her teeth and wrestled the wheel to avoid another gouge in the earth. Too late! The rut grabbed her front driver's side tire. The vehicle plunged to the axle with a hideous scrape of sand against metal. Something popped, the front end lurched, and the rear end slewed to the side. The car jerked to a halt.

Desi sat back, rubbing at the pain in her neck. "Okay, now what do we do?"

No answer.

Desi turned on the dome light and looked into the rear seat. Her passenger was slumped onto his side, eyes closed, skin ashen around angry bruises. *Please don't be dead!* Then she saw his chest rise and fall.

Okay, think. Next move.

A little reconnaissance. She opened her door and eased into the desert night. A cedarlike fragrance tickled her nostrils from a juniper bush haloed in the headlights. Shoes crunching on sand, Desi walked to the front of the vehicle and stared down at the trapped wheel. The tire was flat. She leaned close and let out a hiss. The tie rod could be bent, too. Even if she could get the car out of the rut and put on the spare, she might not be able to drive it.

She rubbed her bare arms against the night breeze. Stars gleamed down at her, looking near enough to touch. Over the purr of the car engine, silence echoed. It was like standing in a deep, empty well. Desi closed her eyes. Her heart rate slowed, and the desert filled her ears. Little scurrying noises. The soft cry of an owl. A rustle. Contrary to appearances, life was busy in the wasteland — but not the kind of life that would welcome her. She wouldn't make it long stranded out here.

Should she try to walk for help? Not possible. Outside the range of the headlights, she'd creep along blind. One false step, and she'd have a close encounter with a stand of prickly pear, or a rattlesnake, or who knew what. She suppressed a shudder.

There had to be an alternative. She was at an unknown location in the middle of the desert with an unconscious man who might never wake up. A vision of herself exploded in her mind's eye: Dressed in cactus-shredded rags, staggering across burning sand, fevered from scorpion sting, dehydrated flesh cracked and bleeding.

Pursued by images of reptiles and gargantuan insects, Desi raced around the car to the rear driver's side door and yanked. It didn't budge. The inconsiderate oaf had locked it. She wrenched the driver door open and dove inside. "Cheama, wake up!" She lunged over the seat back and shook the man. An object slid out of his shirt pocket and thumped to the floor.

Her cell phone.

She groped for her connection to civilization. Clutching the cell to her chest, she sank to her haunches facing the rear of the vehicle.

Her mind cleared, and her blood stopped roaring in her ears. All righty, then. All that fuss for no reason. She looked down at her phone. The screen was shattered and the casing crushed. Little wires stuck out of the cracks. Her heart did a flip.

Terror dug frozen fingers into her flesh. "Cheama, you evil creature, you smashed my phone! We have no way to call for help!"

Thirteen

"I what?" said a groggy voice from the backseat.

Desi held the cell up for her blockhead captor to see. "You knew we were headed into no-man's-land, and you pulverized my phone anyway. Did you stop to think we might need it?"

"Relax, Jacobs. Over that rise . . . is a valley with a small spring. A family lives there. Get out . . . and put some of that lung power to good use. Sound . . . carries in the desert. Yell for help. Someone will come . . . eventually — once they decide you're not out witching."

"Witching?"

Cheama gave a weak wave. "Never mind. Do as I said. Call out my name. We'll be in a warm kitchen . . ." He shifted and winced. ". . . before you know it."

Desi shut the car off and climbed out. "Help! Someone — anyone — hear me?"

"You sound like a half-drowned kitten."

Desi scowled. Cheama's little nap must have given him new strength. She poked her head inside. He was sitting up. "If you're feeling so chipper, why don't you help me holler?"

He grinned, but the puffiness distorted the look into a grimace. "Give it another try."

She threw heart and soul into a major yell. Long moments ticked past. She shouted again, gaze fixed on the rise. What had happened to John Wayne and the cavalry? Wait! Wrong movie. She needed the *Indians* to ride to the rescue.

"I'm not a witch!" Try terrified, white female. "Please! I'm here with Pete Cheama."

She stopped, winded, and leaned against the side of the —

Wait. What was that?

She straightened. In the distance, a vehicle engine roared to life. The sound of labored chugging grew closer, and a light glowed over the horizon.

"Thank you, dear Jesus!"

A small pickup came into view, a lumbering shadow behind its headlamps. Desi waved. Behind her, the car door opened, and Cheama emerged, puffing and moaning. The truck stopped beside them, brakes squealing. A rusty door creaked open, and the driver got out.

The bowlegged man stared at Desi without expression. He wore a Western-style flannel shirt, faded jeans, and a headband around raven-black hair. A jagged scar traced a path from under the band to his cheekbone and then to his chin. The man's attention went to her injured captor. He turned and spoke a few words in what sounded like a Native tongue to someone else in the vehicle.

The passenger door groaned open and slammed shut. A younger, unscarred version of the first man walked past Desi without a glance. He went to Cheama and helped him toward the back of the truck. The older man looked at her and jerked his head toward the cab.

Desi swallowed. She was in no position to stick around her disabled vehicle and try to thumb a friendlier ride. "Thank you." She walked on wooden legs to the passenger side.

A glance into the truck box showed large burlap bags, rounded and fat as pillows, lining the bottom. Pete Cheama was stretched out on several of them with a folded blanket under his head. Perched on another bag, the young man returned her gaze with a flat stare.

Desi settled onto the cracked seat. No seat belt. The cab smelled of cigarettes. No air freshener. Without a word, the scar-faced man turned the pickup and headed back the way he had come. Every bump about jolted her teeth out. No shock absorbers. Even lying on those bags, Cheama must be in agony. Glancing at the stone-faced driver, Desi kept complaints to herself.

They headed down into a valley, and the road smoothed out. On her side of the track, they passed several large beehive-shaped structures made of adobe. Traditional Pueblo ovens.

The truck pulled into a dirt yard outside a single-story adobe house. The driver got out. Desi stepped to the ground. Several sagging outbuildings sat on the property, but in the dark, she couldn't tell what they were used for. She heard the soft cluck of hens disturbed on their roosts and smelled the evidence of other livestock.

A pained cry came from the back of the pickup. Desi hurried around to the tailgate. The two men were helping Cheama get down. As his booted feet met earth, his head lolled and his knees buckled. The men lowered him to the ground. Desi grabbed the blanket from the truck bed.

"You can put him on this and carry him."

The older man assessed her with his penetrating gaze and then accepted the blanket. The men put Cheama on the blanket and carried him in a sling toward the house. The front door opened, spilling light onto a low porch of weathered boards. A wide woman filled the opening. She chattered in a language Desi didn't understand. The older man answered with fierce phrases. The woman backed up and let the men pass with their burden.

At the door, Desi stopped and studied the woman. She gazed back with placid mahogany eyes set deep in a fleshy face. Her hair, drawn back and gathered at her nape, had streaks of gray. She motioned Desi to come inside. Desi stepped over the threshold and watched as the men carried Cheama through a curtained doorway to the right.

Would the injured man wake up to keep his promise about Sanctuary? Even if he told her the secret compound's location, how and when would she get the information to those who could help? What did these people plan to do with her? Moths fluttered in Desi's middle.

The Indian woman pointed toward a plank table that stood near the fireplace.

"Thank you." Desi worked up a smile. "I'm glad to be here. You have no idea, I —"

The woman motioned again without a word.

Desi clamped her mouth shut against any more nervous babble. She walked across well-scrubbed but crinkled linoleum and scooted onto a bench. Rubbing her palms up and down on her slacks, she looked around.

A mottled brown dog lying on a homemade hearth rug lifted its head, thumped its tail, and went back to snoozing. Woven baskets dangled from nails over the fireplace. The mantel was cluttered with pliers, magazines, boxed matches and ammunition, framed photographs, and a pair of paint pots. Strips of meat hung drying on a wire stretched across the room — the source of the gamy scent that unsettled her stomach.

In a far corner sat a metal-framed cot with rumpled bedding. The younger man's sleeping accommodations?

The kitchen area had a large porcelain sink next to a crude sideboard. Open cupboards hung overhead, displaying assorted pottery cups and plates, as well as a motley collection of glass jars. The jars contained different colored powders. Spices?

Her hostess rummaged in an ancient refrigerator. Desi glanced at the bare bulb that dangled overhead. The place did have electricity.

She searched for a telephone, but found no sign of one. Her spirits sank. The Indian woman turned from the refrigerator, offered her a shy smile, and moved to an iron cookstove. Her clean, but faded housedress swished around ample calves. She wouldn't get much company out here and not in the wee hours of the night.

"You don't need to fix anything for me." Desi cleared her throat. "Er, that's assuming it's for me. Whatever you need to do for Pete Cheama, don't let me keep you." No reaction from the woman at the stove. "Can I help you with something?"

The woman glanced over her shoulder, brows lifted. She shrugged and went back to what she was doing.

No English? Lovely.

Voices came from the other room. Cheama was awake. Desi headed for the covered doorway. The younger man stepped beyond the curtain and blocked her path. How did he sense her approach? He stood with feet planted apart and arms crossed over a lean chest.

Desi's hands fisted. "Mr. Cheama has

something to tell me. Who knows when I'll get another chance to talk to him?"

The young man shook his head. Cheama's voice went on in English, but Desi couldn't make out more than a word or two. Maybe if she called to him, he'd tell his guard to let her in. Desi opened her mouth. The young man scowled and took a step forward, looming over her. She lifted her chin and marched back to her seat.

A plate of flat bread made from blue cornmeal had appeared on the table, along with a dish of salt crystals, a bowl of scallions, and one of cucumbers. A spicy scent drifted from the cookstove. Desi's stomach rebelled against the suggestion of food. Her hostess laid an empty plate in front of her and a scarred tin fork and knife. Smiling, the woman got a jelly jar of golden brown liquid from the refrigerator and set it by the plate.

Iced tea? While her hostess went back to the stove, Desi dipped a finger in the beverage and tasted. Tea, yes, and with mint. She might not be hungry, but she was thirsty. Would it be polite to take a drink before others joined her? The woman placed an enameled tray of steaming tamales on the table. Then she sat down across from Desi, expectation bright in her eyes.

Desi glanced around. No one was going to eat with her? The young man lingered at the door to the inner room. Instead of English words, a soft, eerie chant drifted from beyond the curtain. The older man must be singing, hopefully not a dirge. Desi returned her gaze to the Indian woman. Her expression had flattened. She'd insulted her. Desi picked up her glass and took a sip of tea. So good going down a parched throat. She took another, then smiled and nodded at her hostess. The woman beamed back.

Desi inhaled the scent of hot food and stared at the juicy tamales. Her hostess could cook. Too bad the guest didn't feel like eating. She picked up a piece of flat bread, ripped off a strip, and took a small bite. Chewing slowly, she smiled at the woman across from her. A grin and head bob answered her.

Forcing the morsel of bread down, Desi moved one of the tamales onto her plate and then helped herself to a scallion. The woman pushed the dish of salt toward her. Desi dipped the vegetable, rolling it around in the unrefined grains. When she could no longer delay the inevitable, she bit into the scallion. Flavor burst in her mouth, a not unpleasant war of hot and salty sensations. Desi chewed slowly, giving her tense stomach time to accept the offering. Finally, she swallowed. Then she took another drink of the tea.

Her hostess continued to bob her head and grin.

Keeping to her methodical procedure, Desi tackled the tamale. A small bite, a sip of tea, then a slice of cucumber. Back to the tamale, followed by a little scallion and a bite of bread. Wash everything down with tea. Warmth began in her middle and radiated outward.

"This is delicious." She ate more tamale. The spicing was superb and unique. Must be something from one of those jars in the cupboard.

Her hostess looked past Desi and spoke to the young man. Pulling up a rickety wooden chair, he sat at the end of the table. He glanced toward the woman, presumably his mother, then toward Desi. Amusement pulled at the corners of his lips. "She says you have good manners."

Desi stopped with a bite halfway to her mouth. "Ah, you speak English."

The man shrugged. "When necessary."

She put the bite in her mouth and took her last sip of tea. Her hostess grabbed the glass. A refill? Wonderful! Desi rested her elbow on the table and leaned her chin on her hand. “Why does she approve of my manners?”

“You don’t gobble your food like most Anglos. It is our way to savor a meal.”

The woman returned with a full glass. Desi accepted with a word of thanks then took a long pull. She closed her eyes and let the liquid trickle down her throat. There was something to be said for this savoring business. Desi opened her eyes and started to set the glass down. Strange, there were two plates in front of her. She shook her head and blinked. There, that was better. One plate. She released the glass, picked up her fork and stabbed at the tamale, missed and stabbed again. Tricky little bugger. A giggle escaped her lips.

She ate a bite, then drank a sip of tea. “Thish is sho yummy!” She looked at her hostess . . . correction, hostesses. Two of them — identical twins.

What was the matter with her?

Desi dropped her fork, brain fuzzy, but lucid enough to know something wasn’t right. She’d been poisoned! She groped for the table, pushed herself up, and slumped back down. If she had a body, she couldn’t feel it. Dense fog crept over her vision. Arms encircled her, lifting, pulling.

“Easy now. That’s it.” The masculine

words came from a place far away. The arms guided her where they wanted her to go.

Fight it, Des! But blackness sucked at her. Too strong. The last vestige of strength fled. She drifted.

From another universe, angry words spat — a man, then another man, and then a woman. They spoke a language she didn't know, but she understood the meaning.

They poisoned her, and now they fought over where to dump the body.

Resistance sparked, but oblivion snuffed it out.

"What did you do last night after you got home?" The psychiatrist brushed his mustache with a knuckle.

Tony folded his hands and peeked at his watch. He'd been here for twenty minutes and handed the guy a blow-by-blow of everything he did or thought yesterday afternoon. Enough, already! History could wait. He had someplace to be.

He met the man's bland gaze — a look about as safe as a knife in a sheath. "I sat in the dark and stared out my window for a while. Blanked my mind. Then my ex-partner came over and did some pretty good pizza-and-baseball therapy."

One eyebrow went up. "Is he a licensed counselor?"

"No, just a friend." He called Stevo a friend? But he wasn't lying. Only a true friend did what Steve Crane had last night, and nobody said friends couldn't irritate you like all get out. "He brought pizza, and we watched baseball. Just the touch of normal I needed."

The shrink nodded and made a note in the file on his knee. "You're in the early stages of the grief process. This matter will hit you again. And again. Sometimes very hard. The trick is to handle the emotions in a healthy way." The mustache brush again. "Let the feelings wash over you; express them when appropriate. Then move on into normalcy without guilt, as you did last night. Do you have anyone else besides your ex-partner to confide in?"

"Desiree Jacobs. I talked to her last night, too. Therapeutic in a different way."

"Ms. Jacobs is a significant other?"

"As significant as they come."

A knuckle brush, no eye contact. "How did you feel when you got up this morning?"

"Tired, wired, and eager to get this chat over with so I can get on with the case."

"No particular thoughts about yesterday's

violence?"

"Sure, that and all the things I need to coordinate to bring the crooks to justice."

"Anger? Plans for revenge?"

A shrug-off answer stalled on Tony's lips. His stomach had that heavy "don't go that way" feeling he got when God was alerting him to a wrong turn. The psychiatrist looked up.

Tony leaned forward, elbows on his knees. "Sure, I'm angry. Thoughts cross my mind about what I'd like to do. But that's like white noise that doesn't deserve my attention. Not just because I'm a trained professional, but because it goes against my convictions."

Knuckle brushes came fast and furious. "So you'd say you have a system of spirituality?"

Tony sat back. "I have faith in God; I attend church; I pray. Called my mom this morning, told her about Ben, and she prayed, too. Put my whole squad on her church's prayer chain. I'd say, 'Look out, bad guys,' when that happens."

The psychiatrist's pen made check marks on a page. "Social support network, family support, inner moral compass." The man nodded and stood up.

Tony rose. The psychiatrist scrutinized

him. Tony's insides tightened.

The shrink brushed twice at his mustache. "I needed to hear those things to give you unqualified clearance. Your competency appears unimpaired by yesterday's events. The shooter is out of the picture, so you have closure there. And in my opinion, continuing to work the case will cause the least amount of additional stress on you and your squad."

Tony nodded, muscles loosening. "Besides, it's better for the Bureau if the agents most familiar with the case continue to pursue it."

The psychiatrist gave a closemouthed smile. "True, but I'd yank your clearance in a minute if I thought you'd shipwreck with it."

"I appreciate your honesty."

"Likewise."

Tony offered his hand and got a firm clasp in return.

"Make an appointment if you'd like to talk again," the psychiatrist said. "But I'm not requiring that in my report to Cooke."

"I need to see the ASAC about something urgent. Could you call him with your findings? Paperwork takes an eternity to move through this building."

The shrink nodded. "I'd planned on it.

He wanted to hear from me on this right away."

Tony left the office and pulled out his cell. He punched in Desi's number and waited. The voice mail message came on, and he jerked the phone away from his ear and glared at it. *C'mon, Des, turn your cell on.*

He punched in the number for Ortiz in New Mexico.

"Ortiz hacienda," a male Hispanic-accented voice answered.

"Agent Rosa Ortiz, please."

"Rosita!" the voice called at a distance from the receiver. "Is for you."

Tony turned his face toward the wall and let traffic move around him.

"This is Agent Ortiz."

Good, she sounded wide-awake. "I need you to do something for me."

"Lucano? Glad you called, I —"

"Check around and see what hotel Desi's registered at. I can't raise her by cell phone."

"Already done. Your concern about her bugged me, so I got up before daylight and started looking. Are you on the plane yet? She's not at any hotel in town, and she's not back at Jo Cheama's. That place has been quiet as a tomb all night."

Tony slapped the wall. "And you didn't phone me?"

"Cool your jets, Lucano. I was about to . . . before I got in the shower even. I've issued a BOLO on her rental. We'll pull out all the stops to find her. Get here as quick as you can."

Pocketing his phone without a good-bye, Tony double-timed for Cooke's office. People scattered out of his way. In the ASAC's outer office, the assistant waved him through with a smile. He didn't smile back.

"Have a seat, Lucano." Cooke pointed to a guest chair.

Tony settled on the edge. "I just got word —"

The ASAC lifted a hand. "Don't say anything until you hear me out."

Tony gritted his teeth. Now what? Give him his gun and that case file on the desk, and he was gone.

Cooke's chair creaked as he sat back. "Thanks to the speed of our internal grapevine, my good news/bad news probably won't surprise you." He steepled his fingers beneath a fleshy chin. "Because of the nature of this incident, everybody put it at the top of their piles, and we accomplished weeks worth of processing in less than twenty-four hours." The man's arms lowered. "I have verbal clearance on you from both the investigating OPR agent and the psychiatrist. However —" he sat forward — "the review committee wants to go over the reports in writing before issuing their determination."

"Determination?" Tony half rose then sank down under Cooke's glare. "My competency? Whether it was a righteous shoot? What?"

"No one doubts that you acted appropriately, but you are the single witness to an event in which two people died — one of them a fellow agent."

"Single witness! Polanski was there."

"She didn't see anything. Just heard shots."

"So you're telling me I'm on suspension?"

"Nothing so drastic. Just restricted duty. You'll run your squad from your office in this building. No street work."

"You're keeping my weapon?"

The ASAC nodded. "But not this." He handed Tony the folder. "Should be more where this came from on your desk from overnight lab work. Let your squad members do the chasing around. Take it easy for several days."

Tony put the file under his arm. "How about I take some time off? I'm going to Albuquerque. Desi's missing."

Cooke spat a foul word. "Just what you needed right now. Isn't the New Mexico office on it? Let them do their jobs." He pointed. "You of all people should know better than to play civilian sleuth. We need you on that bootlegging investigation."

"Same case. She found out things that may have led to her abduction." Or worse. Tony swallowed. He filled his boss in on Sanctuary. "Wouldn't surprise me if a combination of embezzled funds and bootlegging money is funding construction."

Cooke smacked the top of his desk. "Jacobs walks into more situations than a GI Jane. I don't know whether to put her on the payroll or lock her up."

"You and me both. I'm leaning toward locking her up. As soon as I find her." Tony stared his superior in the eye. "You can grant me vacation, put me on suspension, or even fire me, but I'm on my way to Albuquerque."

"Hold the ultimatums, Lucano." The man studied his ceiling.

Tony gripped his chair. Now he knew the answer to the big question: Would he throw away his career for Desi? He just did.

Cooke leveled a hard gaze on him. "Here's what I'm going to do. I'll send you to New Mexico in a consulting capacity. You know this case better than anybody, and you're an expert on Desiree Jacobs. Let the local agents do the legwork, but find Jacobs and this secret compound, stop the pirating network, and nail Ham Gordon's hide to the wall."

"So I'm taking off on the Bureau clock?"

The ASAC rasped a chuckle. "No way are we going to let Albuquerque have all the kudos on this one."

Classic Cooke. Glory for the home team. Hoo-yah! But he'd take it.

The man leaned across his desk. "The review committee won't be happy with my decision, but guess what? I don't like committees." He sat back. "Something like this Sanctuary thing, the SAC'll want to know. He may notify Director Harcourt that we have a situation developing. Now get out of here, and don't let us down."

Or else. Tony heard the add-on loud and clear, but he'd take that, too. What did a career matter without Desi to share his life?

FOURTEEN

What was that smell? A sweetish spice. Sage? Desi opened her eyes. The plant grew in front of her face. She lay on a familiar-looking blanket under the shade of some large object. Raising up on her elbow, she looked around. Ahead of her lay sand and sun-browned plants, to her back an enormous rock.

How had she gotten here? And *where* was here anyway?

She looked again at the blanket. Oh . . . right. The Pueblo men had used it to carry Pete Cheama. Jo's ex hijacked her, and his friends drugged her, and now they put her outside to sleep it off. Some hospitality! She sat up and rubbed her forehead. A small headache lingered.

Desi touched the rock. Cool, relatively speaking. She pushed to her feet, and a wave of dizziness passed over her. She wobbled and steadied herself. Was it the tamales or the tea?

Her head topped the boulder she'd been sleeping beside. Desi scanned the terrain. Dusty-brown vegetation tufted rolling landscape. In the distance the Sandia Mountains raised pale heads. To her left, a ridge blocked her view. The sun was well up, but it was still morning — unless, of course, what she thought was east was west. Unease tingled across her skin. No sign of habitation, human beings, or a scrap of evidence that she wasn't the last person on the planet.

They wouldn't have taken her into the desert and abandoned her to die, would they? She wouldn't believe that. Couldn't.

"Hey, out there! I'm awake now. You can show yourself."

No answer but heat waves from baking sand.

Something moved by her foot. She looked down. A scaly creature looked back and stuck out its tongue.

Desi screamed and backpedaled; the spiny reptile scuttled away across the sand. Desi plunked down onto the blanket. Her breath came in little gasps.

Just a lizard. Get a grip! Might as well stamp City Girl on her forehead.

Well, that's what she was. No apologies. She didn't belong out here. But if someone had wanted to put her in a prison without bars, they'd done a beautiful job.

Lord, I messed up again. Plunged ahead in my Desi-do-gooder style when I should have asked Your advice. So here I am, a little late. How do I get out of this?

The rustle of the sagebrush answered her. A breeze cooled her skin and rattled the dry plant. The sound soothed, and calm arose from a place deep within.

She swallowed against the cotton in her throat. What she wouldn't give for a drink of water, and she was going to get thirstier. The shade narrowed as the sun climbed higher. She scooted back against the boulder and something thumped. She looked down. Oh, hallelujah! A canteen the same color as the rock had fallen over when she bumped it.

Desi grabbed it and took two healthy swallows. Warm, but wet. She screwed the cap on and set the canteen aside. Who knew how long the moisture needed to last her?

Maybe the small consideration was a sign. Maybe they hadn't abandoned her. They could come back. But from the treatment she'd received so far, that might not be a good thing. On the other hand, about now she'd embrace even Hamilton Gordon like a long lost brother.

A harsh cry vibrated above. She looked up, shading her eyes. A large bird wheeled overhead. Great! Another sign, and this one not good. Once her water ran out, she'd be buzzard food.

Desi stood. She wasn't waiting around to become Special of the Day. But where could she go? Any direction might take her deeper into the desert rather than out of it.

The sun baked the top of her skull. Her headache grew. She sank down against the rock, shuddering at another scream from the bird. Tony had to be wild looking for her. Resolve hardened. She *would* get back to him if she had to grow wings and join that scavenger in the sky.

She must be west of Albuquerque, the direction she and Cheama took last night. If the sun was in the east, and she walked away from it toward the Sandia Mountains, she'd be headed for civilization, maybe parallel to a highway. But would the road be to the north or south of her? Likely south, since she'd gone north into the desert after leaving the paved road.

Logical assumptions, but could she hazard her life on speculation? On the other hand, could she stake her life on rescue? No one, including Tony, had a clue where she was — except people who didn't want repercussions for taking in Pete Cheama.

Cheama, that double-crosser! He strung her along with promises, and all she got out of the deal was a headache and a dry mouth. Her rental car was lost. Her suitcase and all her clothes and personal items gone. And what about her purse? Her life was in there, like any other red-blooded female.

The buzzard squawked.

Desi hugged her knees. What was the matter with her? Fussing about a car and clothes and a purse when she might never have cause to use any of it again? Tears prickled the backs of her eyes.

Suck it up, Des. She didn't need to lose any more moisture.

She was already sweating like a construction worker. Not a bad thing. They said when a person stopped sweating, they should worry about dehydration and heatstroke. The longer she spent out here, the closer she came to that point.

Guess that answered what to do next. In a couple of hours, her shade would be gone. No reason to stick close to the rock when that happened. She'd be fried if she left and fried if she stayed.

All right, she'd wait that long for the man in the white hat to ride over the ridge. Then she'd head south and pray she reached the highway — or even a hovel with a telephone — before she became a desiccated corpse in the sand.

"Any word?" Tony greeted Ortiz at airport baggage claim.

The Albuquerque agent shook her head. "Our local PD had a report of reckless driving by a car that matched the description of Jacobs's rental, but by the time they got there, all they found were rubber marks. Since then —" Ortiz shrugged — "nada."

The airplane pretzels turned to lead in Tony's stomach. "Let's get to your office and compare case files. Maybe something in there will jell into a lead."

Ortiz glanced at the baggage carousel. "No luggage?"

"Just my carry-ons." He tugged his wheelie and gripped the strap of the laptop case that hung from his shoulder.

They went out to the car. A fortyish man with a swollen cheek waited by the vehicle.

Ortiz waved toward him. "This is my partner, Stu Rhoades."

"Pleased to meet you, Lucano." Rhoades offered a hand.

Tony shook it. The guy talked like he had his mouth full. Was he sick, or did somebody slug him?

Something in the man's mouth crunched, and he turned his head and spat.

Tony stared. Peanut shells?

Ortiz put Tony's wheelie in the trunk. "Lucano, you've got shotgun. Rhoades, you get the back." She opened the rear door and grinned at her partner. "With your buddies."

Tony peaked over the top of the door. The backseat of the Bucar was littered with shells. Rhoades climbed in without argument. Shells crunched as he settled into the seat. Tony took off his suit jacket, loosened his tie, and got in the front passenger side. And he thought Stevo's gum-chomping was a crime against humanity — or against him, at least.

Ortiz headed the car away from the airport. "I don't know about this Holy City in the desert. Jacobs might be making too much out of an encounter with an enthusiastic little cultie. We can't find evidence of construction materials purchased in the area and hauled into the wilderness. Gordon recently built himself a mansion near Albuquerque, but that project's done."

Tony shook his head. "These people are too smart to buy materials locally if they don't want to raise suspicion. Ham Gordon's got a fleet of trucks. He could haul things in from anywhere in the country. Here a little, there a little. Maybe even stealing the supplies."

Another crunch came from the backseat. "You got a point, Lucano. We background checked the Gordon Corp drivers when we first got this case and found zippo, but now we're digging deeper. Could be more out there like Bill Windsor who'd do anything for a few bucks."

Like kidnap a woman looking into their desert hideaway. Or even kill. The unspoken thought hung in the air.

Ortiz glanced at Tony, brow furrowed. "Windsor slipped by us on our initial check. We can't afford to miss another one."

Tony bit back a snarl. No point in holding a grudge against the New Mexico office for accepting Windsor's clean-looking credentials. They'd done their due diligence and found no reason to investigate further. Now they had a reason, but at a steep price. Too often, that was how law enforcement went. If only agents were issued omniscience along with their badges.

But then, omniscience in flawed humanity could be an even bigger disaster.

At the FBI building, Ortiz took Tony to a small conference room. He got out his laptop and the Boston case file.

Ortiz brought him a copy of the file from the New Mexico end of the bootlegging investigation, a separate file on the museum theft, and a missing persons file. "Starting to look like there's overlap on these cases. But how they connect is murky at best."

The two of them began laying out data, while Rhoades went to check for new results.

Tony picked up the missing persons report on Karen Webb. "Says here the mother swears the ex-boyfriend took her daughter. Any possibility of that?"

Ortiz shrugged. "It's a common scenario, but low on our list. Bonney and his gang are rough and crude and not above dealing drugs on a small-time scale. The APD breaks up fights at that bar where the bikers hang out, and we get complaints that they like to party on the reservations." She laughed. "Bonney's a character all by himself. Claims to be a direct descendent of William Bonney, aka Billy the Kid. Can you believe it?" She shook her head. "But we can't find a motive for him to snatch Karen Webb, except for some vague mumbling from the mother about revenge for her daughter leaving him."

"Bonney has no connection to Hamilton Gordon?"

"None whatsoever. Of that we're positive."

"What about someone else in the biker gang?"

Ortiz paused with a wad of papers in her hand. "We haven't had reason to pursue that angle, but the way things are going nowhere fast, I suppose we'd better."

Tony picked up the missing persons report on Desi and put it on top of Webb's. He stared at Desi's name on the impersonal document. His insides twisted. He cleared his throat and pulled out the accident sheet involving Pete Cheama's pickup and fanned the three out like a hand of cards. "People are disappearing right and left. No way the events aren't connected."

"That's what we think. We've suspected that the Webb disappearance was connected to the museum theft, but given her involvement with Inner Witness, we're willing to revisit the issue. Haven't told Jo Cheama yet, though." Ortiz gave a small chuckle. "Doesn't pay to jump the gun when we're still waiting for critical lab results that could prove the young woman guilty. She was an unhappy gal. Maybe she wanted quick bucks to get out of town. The black-market value on those artifacts is pretty high."

Ortiz's phone sounded. She picked up and listened a few seconds then set the phone on the table and pressed the speaker button. "Say again? I didn't catch all that."

"There is a package for you in the desert." A man's voice came through without inflection. "You will need to pick it up soon, or it may spoil."

Tony went still. A package that could spoil? Did the caller mean a body? He opened his mouth to ask.

Ortiz held up a hand. "You'll have to be more specific."

The voice gave directions to a location west of Albuquerque. Tony snatched up a pen and scribbled.

"Got it." Ortiz nodded at Tony. "Now how did you get my cell number?"

"Found it in a purse. A dead man said to call."

"Who's dead? Tell us where you are, and we'll come get your statement."

The hiss of empty airspace. Tony gripped the back of a chair. Had they lost him?

"Before he died, the man said to tell Desiree he was sorry. He lied to get her help. He doesn't know where to find Sanctuary."

Tony grabbed the phone. "What do you know about Desiree Jacobs? Where is she?"

A soft click left silence behind.

Tony's fingers fisted in his hair. "I can't believe I blew that!"

Ortiz took her phone. "It's okay, Lucano. I'm pretty sure the guy was going to hang up anyway. Did he sound like the one who called you in Boston?"

"Not at all. This caller was calm — controlled. Mine talked in gasps like he was hurt."

"Cheama?"

Tony glanced at the accident report. "Timing fits."

"One mystery solved, a million to go."

"We can discuss this en route. How soon can we get a chopper?"

"We? You're supposed to have your rear pinned to a seat in the office." Ortiz shook her head. "Guess that's not going to happen."

"You guess right."

"Let's go, then." She led the way out of the conference room. "I'll get ground backup on the road, in case we find trouble out there. Rhoades!" She called to her partner coming toward them up the hall. "Call Kirtland Air Force Base and have them start prepping a chopper. Lucano isn't the only one who gets anonymous phone calls about strange locations in the desert."

Rhoades's nostrils flared. "Sanctuary's real?"

"Lucano's hoping for a live Desiree Jacobs. My money's on a dead Cheama."

"We've got more than one dead guy coming back to haunt us." He waved a sheet of paper. "Results on the prints found on the package of meth under Cheama's truck seat. Under a piece of the tape, they found a print from a Florida-based con artist named Harold Duncan who's been listed as dead for two years. Duncan's specialty was romancing older women out of their life savings. The second set was from a thug named Leon Bender, who's also supposed to be six feet under. None of the prints were Cheama's."

Ortiz groaned. "What's going on around here? A deceased felons convention? So either the drugs were planted by ghosts, or Cheama used gloves to handle a package given to him by two dead guys."

Tony started down the hall. "Let's go get what's waiting for us in the desert. We can call the Ghostbusters later. If Desi's alive out there, with the heat she may not be for long."

Time's up, cowboy. You didn't show, so I gotta go. She must be getting light-headed with the heat, making wacky rhymes to herself.

Desi took a sip of tepid water, the first she'd allowed herself since her decision to stay put. She stood up, hung the canteen strap over her shoulder, and focused on the big bush at the top of the ridge. That was south, the direction she needed to go. If she kept picking out landmarks to move toward, she ought to stay on course.

She picked up the blanket and shook it, then stopped. Her purse! It was under the far end of the blanket the whole time. She snatched the bag and rummaged through the contents. Comb, compact, lipstick — no doubt mush inside that metal tube — pen, small notebook, billfold. She opened the billfold. Every credit card and all her cash were intact. The people who dumped her out here might be full of mean tricks, but they weren't thieves.

If they intended to leave her out here to die, why wouldn't they take the cash at least? On the other hand, maybe they wanted her belongings to be found with her body to add credibility to an accidental death ruling. *Aagh!* She could go round and round about someone else's motives and still not hit on the right one.

She moved out, toting the canteen, her purse, and the blanket. The heat buffeted her. This was late September. What must the desert be like in high summer? The blanket dragged on her arm, but she needed it to drape over bushes to make shade when she stopped to rest. Firming her jaw, she trudged up the incline toward the top of the ridge. At least she was wearing comfortable loafers, and her slacks protected her legs.

Desi's breath came in pants by the time she reached the top of the ridge and peered down into the panorama beyond. Some panorama. She'd hoped to catch sight of a road or habitation. She gazed instead into a ruin of ancient civilization, home now to lizards and spiders. Bare traces of human influence on nature remained — part of a wall here, scattered stones there, and in the center, a depression that might have been a kiva. Not enough to fan the flames of interest in an archaeologist's heart, much less in hers. The place offered no shelter, just more cholla and ocotillo to snag her progress.

With a sigh, Desi worked her way down the slope and walked between dissolving lumps of man's handiwork. Strange to think that hers might be the first human feet to tread here in centuries. This place belonged to the coyotes now. An odd sensation raised the hairs on her neck and arms. Unseen eyes followed her.

Nonsense, girl! The heat's addled your brain.

She took a few more steps, and a wall of oppression halted her. She wasn't welcome here. Clammy fingers worked their way up her body. Darkness fell on her mind as visible on the inside as the desert landscape on the outside. Her heart began to race. Fighting the urge to flee, she made herself walk on.

Yea, though I walk through the valley of the shadow of death, I will fear no evil, for Thou art with me. The Twenty-third Psalm played over and over in her head.

She reached the center of the ruin, every limb trembling. Weak-kneed, she sank down onto remains of a wall. The depression in the soil that must have once been a kiva began a stone's throw away. Shiny objects littered the area, but she could make no sense of them.

They didn't belong here. What should she do? Gather them up and take them with her?

Unscrewing the cap from the canteen, she took a long pull, then another, and another. As if rising from a dark pit, her mind cleared and alarm grew. She'd stopped sweating. Her water conservation strategy had backfired. If she was already experiencing symptoms of heatstroke, she'd never make it to a road that wasn't within eyeshot yet.

She lunged to her feet with a cry. Beer cans! Someone used this place as a party pad. Civilization must be nearer than she thought. A laugh burst from her.

She set her burdens down — the blanket, the canteen, the purse — and began to explore the area. Aha! A fire pit. Oh goody, cigarette butts. Large boot prints. Oh, and um . . . skimpy underwear half buried in the sand? A coed party then, but difficult to tell how long ago. The cans showed no sign of rust, but out here oxidation would be a slow process. Could have been months since someone last visited this location — since after the spring rains anyway.

At the outer edge of the ruins, Desi stopped. If her dehydrated body had any tears to shed, they'd be falling now. Tire tracks! Not from four-wheeled vehicles. Whoever came here traveled on two wheels. Motorcycles then. Who cared! She'd take chariots and leap for joy. Well, she'd leap if that didn't use too much energy. The tracks led off at an angle from the direction she'd intended to travel — a sure bet to take her to a paved highway.

Desi whirled and hotfooted, literally, back to her supplies. She took another drink of water. Rations were low. She picked up the blanket then dropped it. This thing slowed her down, yet she'd need shade for her sizzling scalp sooner or later. It could be miles to the highway. She dug her nail clipper out of her purse. A few snips in the fabric and she tore a wide strip off the end of the blanket. Then she ripped a narrower length for a tie and rigged a headdress.

"Just call me Desi of Arabia."

The rest of the blanket she left draped over the wall. Hope encouraged her feet as she followed the tire impressions away from the dead village. One foot in front of another. Her steps slowed. Nothing but wilderness in every direction, and the tread marks had begun to fade.

She glanced at her watch then took a closer look. Couldn't be! Less than two hours had passed since she left her rock. Seemed like she'd been walking for ages, and her body felt ready to give out. So much for her belief that she kept herself in excellent physical condition. Must be the combination of elevation and the desert climate doing a number on her endurance.

"C'mon, Des. You can make it. Can't be far now."

The sound of her own voice helped her stuff worry to the back of her mind. She took another drink, and the moisture in the canteen barely sloshed as she screwed the cap tight.

She staggered on. *Ouch!* Her toe rammed something hard — the same one she'd abused when she hung on that brick wall in DC — and she pitched forward. *Uhn!* The air left her body as she hit the packed earth, arms too weak to cushion her fall. She tasted sand in her mouth, and bitterness like the flavor of despair. Heat pressed up on her from the baked ground and crushed down from above.

This must be what a clay pot felt like in the kiln.

A deep drone teased her ears. She lifted up on her elbows. Now she was hearing things. The drone intensified. She squinted into the distance. Dust! The drone became a rumble of many engines. Desi dragged herself to her feet.

Swaying, she watched motorcycles barrel closer.

In the lead, a big man in black rode a massive chopper. A red headband circled a mop of ruddy hair that streamed behind him, mixed with the hairs of his bushy auburn beard. The chopper skidded to a halt mere feet away.

Clouds of dust whirled around Desi. Coughing, she closed her eyes. Grains pelted her skin. She hugged herself and ducked her head. The thunder grew to a crescendo and then ratcheted down to a steady roar.

Spitting grit, Desi opened her eyes, and her heart shuddered to a standstill.

At least a dozen hairy men on big hogs surrounded her.

FIFTEEN

Tieless and in his shirtsleeves, Tony paced an office at Kirtland Air Force Base. He finished his call to Boston and looked at his watch. Two hours waiting for a helicopter to become available. Unbelievable!

Most of the choppers were out on maneuvers, a few sat in the repair shop, and one was toting some bigwig to a conference. The report of a mysterious *package* in the desert wasn't priority to anyone but him. He could have driven to the location by now, except Ortiz said the directions were vague enough to require air reconnaissance over a significant chunk of ground.

The Hispanic agent hustled into the room. "One of the copters is back from maneuvers. They're refueling. Let's go."

Tony bounded ahead of her. Outside, the rotors were running on the refueled whirlybird. The pilot motioned for them to climb aboard. Ducking against the wind from the blades, Tony complied, followed by Ortiz. They buckled in and put on their headsets. She gave the pilot the general coordinates, and they lifted off.

Tony keyed his headset to talk to Ortiz. "The ground team all set?"

"They've been cooling their heels at Laguna Pueblo. Correction, their heels are quite warm by now, waiting for our instructions. Did you find out anything in your call to Boston?"

"Just that Polanski, my second-in-command, has everything under control, and Hajimoto, who's been digging into Reverend Romlin's background, says there are suspicious circumstances surrounding the man's credentials. He thinks Romlin isn't the preacher's real name. May not even be a licensed minister."

Ortiz chuckled. "And this should surprise us why? Do you think he might be another dead guy come back to life?"

"Why not? Seems to be a trend. Haj is looking into that angle. Interesting twist from the usual trick of a live person taking a dead person's identity. Anything new at your end?"

"Rhoades called. He had more lab results. The unknown vehicle tire marks and bits of chrome we found at the scene of Cheama's accident come from a semi cab — the same model used by Gordon Corp truckers. The semi forced the pickup off the road."

Tony smirked. "Maybe Cheama was getting too close to exposing the bootlegging operation in his hunt for his daughter, and they framed him. The pieces fit if we assume that he was my anonymous caller about Bill Winston."

Ortiz nodded. "At last, a corner of the picture that doesn't look like a Picasso."

"You and Desi should get along great."

"Oh, we do . . . mostly. She wasn't too happy with me for being unavailable yesterday."

"Sounds like her. She's terrible at waiting." His heart contracted. *Des, hang tight. I'm on my way.* Tony looked down and watched the city pass beneath them. "How long until we reach the search perimeter?"

"Twenty minutes or so."

Tony settled back for the longest third of an hour he'd ever endured.

Desi stared into the flat gray eyes of the lead motorcyclist. He wore a black denim shirt with the sleeves ripped off and the seams hanging ragged. His bronzed arms were a rolling terrain of muscle and tattoos. A massive pewter cross dangled from his neck on a leather cord. A sliver of tattoo peeked from his shirt neck.

Was she face-to-face with the infamous Snake Bonney? He wasn't as big as she'd first thought, charging down on her like that. But he was no pip-squeak either. She'd be no match for him by himself, much less with the gang of hard-faced clones around him. She swallowed — or started to, but she couldn't find a drop of saliva.

A hard grin split the leader's reddish beard. "You lost?" His voice resembled his motorcycle's rumble.

"Out for a walk." Her words came out a croak. "Headed back to the road. The way you —" *cough* — "came." She coughed again and then took a quick sip from the canteen. "See?" She held up the water container. "I'm prepared."

He pointed at her headdress. "You're far out."

Desi blinked. Far-out? This guy wasn't old enough to be a seventies reject. Must be some kind of Sonny Barger hero emulation. Of course, the founder of the Hell's Angels was decades older now, like the rest of the world, and probably didn't talk that way anymore either. Not a good time to point that out, but . . . Okay, she was thinking goofy things to keep from panicking.

"I'll be on my way now. Bye." She stepped forward.

The cycles revved, and the leader drove in front of her — close enough that she could feel his breath. His muscular leg, clad in black jeans, brushed against hers. Desi shuddered.

He grinned again. "I said you're too far out to think about walking back. We can give you a lift to town . . . after the party. Beer. Burgers. Weed. And we know how to treat a lady. Don't we, boys?" He laughed, and his gang echoed.

Desi stepped back. "Thanks for the offer, but I don't have time. I'm looking for someone . . . er, someone's looking for me." *Please let that be true.*

"Get on." He jerked his head toward the seat behind him.

What could she say? She was willing to bet that *no* wasn't in this guy's vocabulary. She swept her eyes over the hedge of growling bikes. There had to be an opening. Some direction she could run.

Get real, girl! Outrun motorcycles when she was struggling to walk a minute ago? Desi's heart pounded. Yeah, but she didn't have about a gallon of adrenaline going for her then.

Her gaze locked with the massive biker to

the right of his leader. If Red Beard's muscles were hills, this guy's were mountains. His dead stare seared her. He licked his lips.

The adrenaline leaked out her feet. Her knees went weak, and she buckled forward.

Father, into Thy hands I commend my spirit —

All went dark.

"We're closing in on the area," Ortiz said into Tony's headset. "We'll start at a central point and work outward in concentric circles." She handed him a pair of binoculars.

"Sounds good to me." His gaze devoured the broken and desolate terrain below. Scattered homesteads showed a faint shade of green among the brown. Maybe Desi made it to one of those. The encouraging self-talk fell flat in his mind. She would have called him.

The chopper reached a place where Tony saw no more signs of habitation. They began to circle slow and low. Through the binoculars, Tony spotted plenty of life — lizards and snakes, scurrying rodents. Nothing resembling a person or even an inanimate package.

Des, you're out here. I feel you. Why can't I

find you?

"There!"

Ortiz gasped. "Break my eardrums already."

"Put the bird down."

"You got it. But don't yell again."

The chopper settled on a flat spot near the ruins of an ancient village. Tony hopped out and ran through the dust cloud churned up by the rotor blades. He reached the swatch of unnatural color among the crumbling stones and snatched it up.

"Indian blanket." Ortiz came up behind him. "Could have been left out here any time."

Tony thrust the article at her. "This is fresh. No sign of fading, and look — an end has been clipped then ripped."

"You're right." Ortiz studied the tear. "Recently, too, or we'd see more unraveling." She shook her head. "But it still doesn't mean the blanket has anything to do with Desiree Jacobs."

"But this does." Tony bent and picked up the shiny tube that had been hidden under the blanket. "Desi's favorite shade and brand of lipstick."

"Then where is she?"

"We need to find out — and fast! I have a feeling we're running out of time."

■ ■ ■ ■

Desi choked against the water splashing her face. Some of it went down her throat. She gagged. Not water. Beer. She gasped and sat up. Or tried to. Arms held her. She opened her eyes and stared into a hairy face.

Red Beard! If that Barbary pirate had lived in this age, he would have enjoyed being an outlaw biker. Desi struggled, and the sweaty arms released her. She scooted away, panting.

"Sorry." Red Beard stood up, towering over her. "We don't do water. Beer was all we had to wake you up. This canteen is about empty." He handed it to her.

She grabbed the container and struggled to her feet. He was right. Almost nothing drinkable left, and he said she had a long way yet to reach civilization.

Red Beard remounted his bike. "Climb on. You've been in the sun too long."

Her options had narrowed to one: Do as the man said. She slung her canteen around her neck, hooked her purse around her arm, and swung her leg over the bike. She maintained a few precious inches of distance from the driver. The bike lunged forward. She yelped and grabbed the solid body in front of her. His denims hadn't been washed in recent history, but so what? Beat doing a backflip off a flying motorcycle.

And fly they did. Half the time the wheels were airborne over dips and hollows. The wind tore the scrap of blanket from her head. She lifted her face, and the streaming air washed over her. A sense of buoyant freedom rose inside her. If she closed her eyes, she could pretend she clung to Tony.

Not really. Tony never smelled like this, and he didn't have a beer belly. But at least she could pretend to pretend. If she were with him, the ride would be exhilarating.

She had no idea how long they rode or which direction. Not toward the exposed ruins she'd found earlier. Potential landmarks flew by too fast to make note of them, and her forward vision was obscured by Red Beard's broad back, but she thought a chalky-colored butte drew closer.

After a while, they entered the shade of the tower of rock, and the sun lost some of its power. With the butte soaring over them, they slowed. Dust boiled as they braked to a halt. Desi coughed and squinted.

Where had they taken her?

She slipped off the bike, staggered, and righted herself. This shaded area was about ten degrees cooler than under the baking sun, but still warm. Others had arrived ahead of their group. Some were women clad in everything from ragged T-shirts and holey jeans to crop tops and cutoffs. The men with Red Beard hooted crude suggestions. The women grinned and waggled their hips, but the looks they gave Desi put her in the category of a new species of bug.

Some of the early arrivals had set up camp chairs and folding tables. Cases of assorted booze were stacked on the ground. About a hundred paces away sat a Range Rover and several four-wheelers. Desi's heart quickened. A little *Grand Theft Auto* would be in order.

Red Beard tugged her toward a small adobe hut minus door and windows. The blank holes seemed to gaze out with sorrow on what had become of it in its crumbling old age. They went inside, and the temperature cooled further.

Amidst laughter and coarse joking, bikers set out kegs and plastic glasses on a rickety table in the middle of the room. The table was the lone piece of furniture except for a large chest in the corner. Mountain Man came in with two canvas lawn chairs. These guys traveled with all the comforts of home. Red Beard took one of the chairs and patted the seat of the other one for Desi.

Mountain Man scowled and stomped out.

Must be his chair the leader gave away.

Desi plopped down, too drained to care that she was sitting next to a man who might decide to rape her before the night was out or that she'd made a very large enemy through no fault of her own. She touched her face. Sticky from dried beer and caked with dirt.

"You've got nice hair." Red Beard fingered a strand. "Real soft."

She pulled away. "I don't know what kind of bimbos you're used to dealing with, but if you expect me to fall for your charms because you complimented my hair, you're in for a long wait. In fact, if you try anything out of line, you'll have a fight on your hands."

His eyes widened then he threw his head back and bellowed a laugh. The cross bounced against the hollow of his throat. He patted her knee. "As much fun as that sounds, Kitten, I'm more interested in washing the dust from my throat."

One of his men handed him a foamy cup. The server winked at her and walked away.

Kitten! Red Beard dubbed her with some wimpy pet name that equated with *helpless plaything?* He'd forgotten that kittens grew into cats with sharp claws and the ability to slip away at a moment's notice. If only her energy level exceeded kitten-strength. But a good front never hurt.

Desi rose and stared at the crowd of grinning men crowded into the enclosed space. The smell of sweaty bodies was rank. "My name is not Kitten. You may call me Ms. Jacobs. Now may I have the pleasure of knowing who you are?"

Someone snickered. "Ain't she hoity-toity?"

Red Beard glared at the speaker. He rose beside her. "Now, boys, mind your manners. I said we knew how to treat a lady, and I could see that's what she is, even under that dumb blanket." He turned toward her. "Allow me to do the honors." He made an odd sort of half bow. "This here is . . ." He went through a dizzying list like Crankcase, Badger, Knife, and less repeatable nicknames. Mountain Man was Tank. Appropriate.

"And then there's me." Red Beard's grin widened, and he began unbuttoning his shirt.

Desi backed away, but she ran up against Tank, who'd crept up behind her with the stealth of the cat she prayed to be when the moment came. He leered down at her. Her blood went arctic. Looked like there wasn't going to be a moment for silent exit.

Only teeth and claws.

"There's the rest of the blanket." Tony pointed.

The bird set down, stirring up grit that stung his face as he ran to the crumpled piece of cloth. He grabbed it and held it to his nose. The exotic scent of Desi's hair. As always, his heart beat double-time at the fragrance. If only it was her he held. An ache settled in his chest.

Ortiz wandered away a few yards. "Here's a bunch of motorcycle tire tracks. Looks like she found a ride. Or a ride found her. Not sure that's good — especially if it's Snake Bonney's gang out for a good time."

Tony studied the crisscross of tracks. "Impossible to tell if they were going into the desert or coming out."

Ortiz put her hands on her hips. "Logistics dictate that we follow the trail into the desert and let the team at Laguna check out the highway. I'm thinking they'll hit the jackpot, not us. Hope so, anyway. Hard to sneak up on them in a helicopter, and better odds than you, me, and the pilot taking on a whole motorcycle gang."

"Right now, I'd take on Genghis Khan and the barbarian horde."

Ortiz frowned. "Hold that thought, Lucano. We may need to go for the guts and glory."

Red Beard shrugged out of his shirt and turned one shoulder toward Desi. "See?" He rippled his muscles. What had looked like a tattoo of a fat slinky wrapped around his thick bicep became an undulating snake that crawled up his arm, over his shoulder, and ended by his collarbone in a gaping mouth with dripping fangs. The tip of the creature's nose and a single fang had been all she could see earlier. Now she had the whole picture.

Better yet, the time hadn't come for her to defend her honor. A high-pitched laugh trickled out her throat. "Decent work of art, Snake Bonney."

His face lit. "You've heard of me?"

"You're Karen's ex-boyfriend. I've been meaning to talk to you about her."

"You know Karen? Who are you?" He strode forward, lips pulled back. "Did you take her?"

Desi tried to shrink away, but had nowhere to go with the immovable Tank at her back. "Me?" Her voice squeaked. "I'm a kidnapp*ee,* not a kidnapp*er.*"

"Huh?" Bonney's brow furrowed. "Someone kidnapped you?"

"What else do you call being grabbed and hauled off to someplace unknown by a bunch of men I don't know from Adam?"

"Who's Adam? You mean Karen's kid? Will you talk sense, woman?"

Desi held her breath and slipped out of the biker sandwich the two big men made of her. She walked back to her chair and sat down. Stay cool. Look calm. Offense is the best defense. "You kidnapped me. Did you snatch Karen, too?"

A dark whisper went around the room, and Bonney scowled at her. Tank crossed his arms over his chest like Mr. Clean without the smile. Or the clean.

"We didn't snatch nobody." Bonney glanced around the room and got a murmur of agreement. "Including you. Way I see it, we saved your life, Miss High-and-Mighty."

Desi tapped her upper lip. "You have a point. I was on the crispy side of well done out there. But if you were so concerned about my welfare, why didn't you take me to a town or ranch house so I could get medical help? I could still collapse and die of heatstroke, you know."

Bonney flashed a grin. "You're tongue's too lively to be next door to dead. 'Sides, this was the nearest shade available, and we've got some serious partying to do. We don't take a detour for nobody when it's party time."

His men cheered and raised their glasses. Bonney grabbed his from the cup holder on his chair, and the whole crowd chugged their glasses empty. The snake on Bonney's arm rippled as he wiped his mouth with the back of his hand. He let out a belch and handed his empty glass to someone who filled it.

Then he settled into his chair next to Desi and put his face in hers. Beer breath washed into her nostrils.

"What do you know about Karen?" His stare was cold. "And why do people keep bugging me like I took her? Like I'd want a woman who's turned into a religious fruit loop?" He ground out a foul word.

Desi refused to look away. "Didn't you call her more than once before she disappeared?"

"After I ran into her one day looking all middle-class American, I got curious about what was up with her. She asked me to call, but I quit after a couple of times. She kept spouting all this Inner Witness stuff." A few more colorful words summed up his opinion.

"Who do you think took her then?"

Bonney shrugged. "Maybe nobody. People get into these groups that brainwash you, and they end up doing strange things. I've heard about this stuff. Gotta be careful what kind of a people you hook up with these days." He nodded like the sage of the universe.

Desi looked away. "That's true." Her gaze passed over the party activity. No one was paying attention to her and the gang leader. Except Tank, whose broad back held up the wall by the door. He stared at them with all the warmth of the machine he was named after. The rest were absorbed in their beer or their joints — which explained the sweetish smell in the room. A few had women snuggled up to them. "Do you consider this your family?"

"We're tight, yeah. Like family, we've got each other's backs. Some of these guys are married, you know. Got kids. Their wives are here. And we're not bums. We work. Pay taxes. But we like to cut loose on our bikes and have a good time. No harm in that, but the cops don't always see it that way. Out here we can have privacy to do our thing. No harm. No foul."

Something softened around the area of Desi's heart. She still had no reason to believe that she wasn't slated to be this guy's cuddle of the evening. He maybe figured she owed him that much. But fear couldn't quite compete with a rush of compassion.

These people weren't putting on a front. They already knew they were bottom of the barrel. Outcasts. Misfits. But who was calling the kettle black? In her business, she rubbed shoulders with people who went to church, wore designer clothes, lived in mansions, drove fancy cars, and maintained all they owned by lying, cheating, and backstabbing.

Who was worse off? The go-for-broke sinner or the hypocrite? Jesus ate with sinners and called the hypocrites vipers.

"Bonney?"

"It's Snake."

She held out her hand. "Hello, Snake. I'm Desiree."

He raised bushy brows and shook it.

"Thank you for taking me in when I was lost," she said.

"Don't mention it." He chuckled and sipped his beer. "Want one?" He held his glass up.

"I'll finish my water. I've heard alcohol is dehydrating."

" 'Kay." He nodded, gaze wandering the room.

He didn't act like a guy with one thing on

his mind. Of course, the party had just started, and he wasn't liquored up yet. Wise to say what was on her heart then scoot as soon as possible.

"Karen got off on the wrong track with her faith. Sometimes happens with young believers. She'll get back to the truth eventually."

Snake stared at her. "You think she's alive?"

"I'm not going to think anything else until we have proof otherwise."

"Good." He put his empty glass in the cup holder. "Me, too. But if anyone's messed with her, they'll have to deal with me."

"Why would you care?"

He frowned. "She was one of us once. Fine if she chooses to walk a different road. I don't have to like it to respect it. But lights out to anyone who hurts her on purpose." He punched a fist into his palm.

Whump . . . whump . . . whump . . . whump . . .

"What's that?" Snake sat up rigid in his chair. The party noises faded.

The sound of an approaching helicopter grew louder by the second.

Desi cleared her throat. "No worries." Everyone stared at her. "I forgot to mention I'm special friends with an FBI agent.

That's him looking for me." *Dear heavens, I hope it's true.*

"The feds!" Tank's bellow catapulted everyone into action.

Shouting and cursing, the gang piled out the door, leaving Desi, Snake, and Tank in the hut. Outside, engines revved to life.

Snake shot her a sad-eyed smile. "You'll be fine then." He grabbed his shirt and trotted for the door, but stopped and looked over his shoulder, tattoo wiggling into a new contortion. "They can't catch us all, y'know." He winked and was gone, leaving her with . . .

She stared into the mountain's face.

He bared yellowed teeth. "Guess it's just you and me, girlie." He stepped toward her.

Desi stood up and inched backward, searching with her peripheral vision for an exit. Solid walls. Tank stood between her and egress through windows or door. Helicopter rotors and motorcycle engines split the air with mind-numbing din.

Tank took another step forward.

He was enjoying the stalk and didn't seem too intelligent. Maybe she could keep him busy until Tony charged to the rescue. "You're not going to escape with the others?"

The discolored grin widened. "No need. I

got a secret hidey-hole under everybody's noses. Big enough for you and me until everyone's gone. Then we party."

He lunged for her.

Sixteen

"Look at 'em scatter!" Ortiz bumped Tony's arm as the chopper closed in on the site.

A cluster of vehicles — motorcycles, ATVs, a Range Rover — began to scatter in all directions. Tony glanced at Ortiz. "I don't see Desi." He keyed the pilot on the headset. "Put down as close to that hut as possible."

"You got it." The chopper descended as the last of the cycles scattered — except for one. The big hog sat alone and unattended.

Unless the owner had abandoned his cycle and hitched a ride, someone was still here. Rage gusted through Tony. Wait until he got his hands on whoever took her.

She'd better be all right, or they wouldn't be.

Desi shrieked and dodged Tank's massive hand.

She flung her canteen and got him in the

face. He staggered back, shaking his head, while she darted around him and made for the door. One stride. Her breath rasped in her ears. Two strides. Three —

Whoof!

The floor leaped up to meet her, and the air left her lungs as a mountain landed across her back. Tank wrenched one arm behind her back and hauled her to her feet. Pain shimmered through her body.

Tony! Help! But she couldn't call out. Her lungs strained to recapture air, but an arm mashed across her windpipe. Tank dragged her toward the trunk in the corner. He thrust her to the floor and planted a booted foot in her back while he tore at the latch.

The helicopter sounded right on top of them. *Hurry, Tony! Hurry!*

Darkness swirled through her vision. The foot in her back kept her from taking a full breath.

The lid of the chest swung open, and Tank dug inside. He roared a curse. The boot pressed down, and Desi's back creaked. Her head felt like an overblown balloon. The boot lifted, and blackness receded.

Tank bent over her, snarling obscenities over the din of the helicopter. The biker picked her up with one arm under her waist like she weighed nothing. She glimpsed a gaping maw where the bottom of the chest should be.

Not going down there!

Desi twisted and raked him with her nails. Red lines appeared on his bull neck. He howled and pulled back a fist as big as her face.

Something slammed into her attacker, ripping them apart. Desi staggered, and the backs of her knees hit the side of the chest. Gasping, she windmilled for balance. Still tottering, she flung herself to the side, away from the trunk and the men who battled only feet away.

Tony!

Tank's feet and fists flew. The scruffy thug fought with no style and no rules — pure enraged street brawler. Tony's moves were controlled, fluid. Dodging a fist, he landed an openhanded chop to the side of the biker's neck. Tank staggered, recovered, and closed in again. The biker's foot rammed for Tony's midsection but caught empty air. Off-balance, he went down, rolled, and came up swinging. A huge fist shaved past Tony's ear, and he answered with a sidekick to the solar plexus that slammed the biker against the wall.

Tank wobbled forward, shook himself, and then charged with a bellow. Tony ducked and rammed the biker in the stomach with his shoulder. The mountain of muscle flipped end over end and whammed onto the table flat on his back. The tabletop split, cups flew, and kegs rolled down on top of the gasping biker.

Desi gave a hoarse cheer.

Tank flailed then froze, bug-eyed, with Ortiz's gun almost shoved up his nose. Silence deafened as the helicopter noise faded and died.

A growl came from Tony. "Why don't you step outside for a while, New Mexico. I'm not done *interrogating* this lowlife." He stared down at the blinking thug.

A shiver ran through Desi. The look scared her, and it wasn't even pointed in her direction.

"Cool it, Lucano," Ortiz said. "You're not here, remember?"

Tony rolled his shoulders and took a step backward. "No problem. This is your collar. I'm a ghost."

Ortiz bobbed her chin in Desi's direction. "I think someone else needs your attention."

Desi sat up. Tony's gaze found hers. Emotions chased themselves across his face. Wide-eyed shock — she must look like a rag doll somebody dragged in the dirt — followed by narrow-eyed fury and a glance at the biker now being handcuffed by Ortiz. His gaze returned to hers, and those chiseled features softened. Life-giving warmth flowed through Desi, lifting her to her feet as if she hadn't an ache in her body.

They moved and met and clung. His fierce clasp hurt bruises she didn't know she had. Her hands fisted in the back of his sweat-soaked shirt.

"You smell like a brewery," he murmured into her hair.

"Do you mind?" she said into his shirt pocket.

"Not one bit."

Two hours later, from her bed in a curtained emergency room cubicle, Desi finished giving Tony a sketchy overview of her adventures, minus the off-the-wall notion of cult cannibalism. She'd bring it up when he was less upset with her and after Max and her family were protected from vicious Gordon Corp truckers. "Pete said they might go after the baby to draw him out." She fingered the tape that held the IV line to the back of her hand.

"Quit messing with that." Seated by the bed, Tony took her free hand. "You're lucky to get out of this with only a little dehydration and mild sunburn."

"I know it, honey, and I'm sorry. But did you hear what I said?"

"Cheama's dead. That's what the anonymous caller claimed."

Desi's heart went hollow. "Poor Jo. She and her ex may not have gotten along, but they were close once. That's got to matter. And Karen, when she finds out . . ." A tear wet her cheek.

"Hey, sweetheart." Tony brushed the moisture away with his fingertips. "You're a soft touch, you know. That's what got you into this trouble." His thumb traced a spot on her cheek. "Did that biker hit you?" The hard tone didn't match the caress.

"Hit me?" She blinked at him. "You prevented that catastrophe, remember?"

"You've got a bruise." His thumb moved again.

Desi turned into the touch. "Mmmm. What? Oh, must be from yesterday. I bumped my face against the steering wheel reaching for something on the floor."

Tony's eyes narrowed. "Don't tell me you throttled yourself, too. There are finger marks on your neck."

"Okay, Mr. Observant. Pete Cheama did that, but it was an accident. He —"

"An accident!" Tony went stiff. "You've got to be kidding."

"He was trying to stop me from running into traffic and getting killed, so —"

"Hold it." Tony held up his hand. "Later on we'll go through every insane detail, but right now you need to relax and let that fluid get into your system."

"I want a long shower. That little medical sponge bath on my bumps and bruises wasn't enough. And a big meal, too, as soon as that doc will let me out of here."

"You lie still, and I'll go make a reservation for you at the same place I'm staying." He planted a kiss on her lips. "Don't go anywhere."

"Don't worry. I think I could snooze the clock around." She yawned.

"Go right ahead."

"Can't. There's too much to sort out. Max and her family need someone to keep an eye on them. Does anyone besides the FBI and me know about Cheama's death?"

"All we know is someone says he died, and they had good reason to lie."

"What a mess. Leaves us with no clue what to tell anyone." Desi started to cross her arms, jerked the IV line, and let out a frustrated noise.

Planting his hands on either side of her shoulders, Tony kissed her again then drew away a few inches. Their gazes meshed. Desi's pulse rate soared. Close exposure to an Italian hunk — great for the circulation. Bad for the concentration.

The laugh lines around his eyes crinkled. "You're determined to worry. How about this? I'll call Stevo. He'll leap at the chance to camp out at Max's house."

"And do you know why?" Desi tried to sit up, but Tony pushed her back down. "Can you believe it?" She subsided against the too-firm mattress. "Steve Crane and Lana Burke, Max's dainty mother? That's like the Incredible Hulk and Tinkerbell. Captain Hook and Mary Poppins."

Tony chuckled. "Beauty and the Beast. We know how that one turned out."

Desi scowled. "You're not taking me seriously."

"Should I?"

Desi opened her mouth then shut it.

"Nothing to say?" He arched a brow.

"I hate it when you're right and I'm an idiot."

"You're never an idiot."

Desi smoothed the sheet, a smile tugging at her lips. "But you *are* right. It's none of my business." She touched his arm. "I think I'm scared that the relationship will work out. Since Max is like a sister to me, I'd feel related to Crane." She shuddered. "That would be too weird."

"I sympathize. Max's boy still figures me for his Grandpa Steve's honorary son." Tony grimaced. Their gazes met, and they both laughed.

"You rest." Tony went to the curtain opening. "I'll make a few phone calls and check back in a little while."

He disappeared, and a pang struck Desi's middle. *Don't leave me, Tony.* She rolled onto her side toward the IV pole. Man, she sounded pitiful. A lot of people in the ER were going through more trauma than her. Moans and the brisk voices of medical personnel in other cubicles confirmed her thought, but the empty ache didn't leave. She snuggled the sheet under her chin and sniffed. Acrid disinfectant smells filled her nostrils.

Sure, go make your phone calls, Lucano. She was stuck here attached to this gadget.

He'd call the hotel, Steve Crane, Max probably, and for sure Agent Ortiz for an update on evidence processing out at the bikers' party site. When she and Tony had left in the Army helicopter, the place was swarming with tribal police, DEA, and federal agents — all hunting for their piece of the pie. The natives wanted to nail Snake's gang for illegal use of reservation grounds, the DEA wanted anything connected to drugs, and the feds wanted clues about stolen artifacts and a missing museum receptionist.

Wonder what they found in Tank's hidey-hole? Like Tony would tell her when he got the word.

Mighty grumpy, girl, when the man saved your bacon this afternoon.

Desi flopped over onto her back and stared at the dull white ceiling. She scratched her nose, and the needle in the back of her hand gave a twinge. Huffing, she rolled onto her side again and stared at the pole. *It's my IV, and I'll grump if I want to.*

She yawned and closed her eyes. No way was she going to sleep though. She might be safe, but what about Max and the baby?

Under the shade of a tree outside the hospital, Tony finished his call to Steve Crane. He went inside and threaded between ER traffic to Desi's cubicle. Sticking his head through the curtains, he grinned at the still form under the sheet. *Lights out, sweetheart.* Maybe she'd stay asleep until he checked in with Ortiz.

"Excuse me, sir."

Or maybe not. Tony glanced over his shoulder to find a stocky, gray-haired nurse trying to get by him. He stepped aside, and she whisked into Desi's cubicle.

"IV's all finished," she said as if trying to be heard over a Sunday crowd at a Sox game.

Tony winced. Forty winks cut down to twenty.

"What?" Desi's eyelids fluttered. "Oh, yes, can you get me out of this thing?" Her voice was slurred. Soft sounds followed, like tape coming off, and a rustle of sheets. "Where's Tony?"

He stepped between the curtains. "Right here, babe. I told you I'd hang around."

Her face relaxed.

The nurse scowled. "Sir, you'll have to —"

"Stay!" Desi reached toward him.

Tony took her hand and stood on the other side of the bed while the stone-faced nurse removed the IV needle. He ignored the disapproval and rubbed his thumb across the soft palm he held. She needed him. How many men could say that a woman as strong and independent as Desiree Jacobs felt that way about them? She was a rare find, and this lucky slob had almost lost her.

Lord, I can't do that. Not until we're old and gray. And maybe not even then. I think I'd need to go first. But how could he keep her safe when he loved her the way she was, and the way she was got her in over her head with people like wanted fugitives and outlaw bikers?

"What's the matter?" Desi squeezed his hand. "You look like a man facing the gallows."

Tony squared his shoulders and winked at her. "No, just a lifelong torture rack."

"Huh?"

"Never mind." He shook his head.

"All done." The nurse glared at them both. "You're free to go, Ms. Jacobs. The doctor has released you." With a lift of the nose at Tony, she left the cubicle.

Desi giggled. "At least one woman in this world is immune to your charms, Mr. Lucano. But not this one." She tugged on his hand. "Thanks for waiting for me. I know you're chomping at the bit to get back to headquarters and find out what's going on."

Tony tweaked her sun-reddened chin. "No way, lady. I'm going to escort you to that hotel and make sure you have everything you need. *Then* I'll go to the office and let you rest."

"Hospitals are terrible for that, aren't they?" She laughed, the familiar spark in her eyes. "By the way, darlin', that was a great answer. Nothing warms the cockles of a woman's heart more than knowing she's first place with her man. Now get out of here while I shed this elegant hospital gown and put my grungy clothes back on."

Tony stepped to the other side of the curtain, brows drawn together. Yes, but was he first with *her?*

Her choices never seemed designed to give him peace of mind. And did her remark mean that his job would always have to take a backseat to whatever she wanted? That would never work. An FBI career demanded as much of the agent's family as it did of the agent.

Ridiculous, man! He shook himself. Des wasn't like that — all self-absorbed. If anything, she thought too much about others and not enough about herself. But couldn't that shipwreck their future as much as the other extreme? Fear nibbled at his insides. He couldn't lose her, but could he keep her?

Desi basked in the refreshing shower. The lukewarm droplets babied her tender skin. Starting to feel pruney, she shut off the water, stepped out, and patted herself dry with a soft towel. Then she wiped the moisture from a section of the mirror and examined her face. Oh, crumb! She'd peel — a charming effect with the bruises on her cheek and neck. Ah, well. She was in an air-conditioned hotel room and not nature's oven. Thanks to a phone call by Tony, Jo had sent over clothes that should almost fit her. Plus, her room service meal would be here any second.

Count your blessings, woman! You weren't that far from being a buzzard's dinner.

She put on a sundress that bagged on her and then peeked out the curtains into the fading daylight. Her room was on the sixth floor, and below her the lights of Albuquerque had begun to glow. A lovely city full of strong, diverse cultures that had clashed for centuries — Indian, Hispanic, Anglo. Pete Cheama, Rosa Ortiz, Brent Webb — hard to think of anything the three had in common, except their commitment to this arid but beautiful land.

A knock sounded at the door, and Desi's stomach rumbled. She hurried to open it.

"Tony! What are you doing here?"

He grinned at her from behind the room service cart and wheeled it in, towel draped over his arm like a maître d'. The resemblance ended there, because he was dressed in tan chinos and a green polo shirt. "Not much going on at the office. Ortiz is dog-tired after her big day in the desert. Her partner packed up and went home a while ago. And Tank is in the tank overnight. So I'm at your disposal, milady." He whisked the cover off a chafing dish.

Heavenly smells tormented Desi's nostrils. She clutched her middle and moaned.

Tony shot her a sharp glance. "You all right?"

"Steak! Mushrooms in wine sauce! Baked potatoes! Broccoli smothered in cheese! Get this meal on the table before I drool on the carpet."

He laughed. "Your humble servant, miss."

"My hero." She reached up and kissed his cheek. *What do you know? The guy blushes.*

They laid out the food and condiments double-time. Tony seated her like a gentleman, then bent and nuzzled her neck.

A tingle zapped every synapse. "Wow! That works great even when you're not wearing a beard."

His low chuckle in her ear raised the hairs on her arms. He lifted her chin and pressed his lips to hers. "That was hors d'oeuvres," he murmured. "I'll collect dessert later." His grin was downright wicked as he went to his chair.

Desi uncurled her toes with an effort.

Heavens, the man is lethal! "Hard to believe it was just a few days ago that we were nibbling at a White House buffet. This looks better than anything on the president's table." She spread her napkin in her lap. "Of course, it could seem that way since I'm hungry enough to eat lizard."

"A lot's happened in a short time." Tony nodded and took her hand. He bent his head and asked a blessing on the food.

Desi dived in with gusto. "I don't suppose you could tell me what they found in that hole Tank was about to throw me into."

"I can. Nothing. It would have been just you, him, and the millipedes."

Desi shuddered. "Thank you for that appealing picture."

Tony chuckled. "You're welcome. The DEA took soil samples to see if it had ever been used to store drugs. As per usual, the results will take a while."

She nodded, intent on cleaning her plate. Maybe she'd lick it for good measure. With her broccoli gone, most of her potato and half her steak, she noticed Tony grinning at her. "What?"

"Nothing." He waved his empty fork. "I like seeing a woman enjoy her food."

Desi patted her mouth with her napkin and hid a soft burp. She *had* inhaled the meal in record time. "Usually that saying is the other way around." She studied Tony's untouched steak. "Anything wrong with your meat?"

"No, everything's perfect." He pushed his plate back. "I don't have room for it tonight." He made a halfhearted stab at a broccoli floret.

Desi set her napkin by her plate. "You're thinking about Ben."

Tony frowned. "I should be enjoying your company."

"Oh, honey." She covered his hand with hers. "That's what a relationship means — sharing the bad times as well as the good. You need to feel like you can talk to me about anything."

He pulled his hand away and rammed his fork into the chunk of beef on his plate. "Gordon Corp meat, no doubt."

Desi bit her lip and stared down at the small chunk left on her plate. "Gordon Corp isn't all about a few bad apples in the barrel. There are lots of fine employees and honest investors that are part of the company."

Tony nodded, but the frown stayed on his face. "I know you're right. I also know that what Ham Gordon's doing could cost those employees their jobs and the investors their money. And we don't seem one inch closer to nailing this guy. I feel like I'm letting Ben down."

"Sweetheart." Desi got up and went to him. He welcomed her onto his lap. She snuggled her face into his neck. "I won't bother reminding you that you've been in Albuquerque all of one day. Or how patient the FBI is at long-term investigations. Or how great you are at your job." She rubbed her palm down the side of his face. "Or how much I like that stubble along your jaw. Sends shivers down my spine."

A chuckle rumbled from Tony's chest. "Woman, you are one incredible distraction. Exactly what I need."

She grinned up at him, and he joined their lips. Gentle exploration deepened. She twined one arm around his neck, fingers playing in his springy hair. The other went around his back. His hands caressed her ribs, the side of one leg. A melting sensation flowed through her veins.

He needs me. I need him. Simple as two plus two. He lost someone close to him. I almost died today. His kisses demanded. She reveled in a fierce giving. *It's natural for us to cling to one another. Give comfort. Celebrate life.*

His touch found places no man had gone

before, and she welcomed surrender. Beneath her kneading fingers, his back and shoulder muscles were sleek and firm. Strength perfect for her soft —

Tony pushed her off his lap and lunged to his feet.

"Wha-a-at?" She stared at him.

His hands scrubbed through his hair then found his pockets. He gazed at the floor, breathing hard.

Desi stood frozen, her stomach a yawning pit of disappointment. But disappointment about what? That they'd trespassed beyond the boundaries of their convictions, or that he'd called a halt?

"Des, I —" His voice was hoarse. He cleared his throat. "Sorry. I should never —"

"No, Tony, it was my fault." She reached toward him then dropped her arms. Her skin flushed hot. She'd offered and hadn't wanted to stop. What must he think of her?

He grimaced. "Woman, at the polarity we attract, we need to be careful what situations we let ourselves get into. Right now, me in your hotel room alone with you is more dangerous than an arms bust. I knew better, too. I shouldn't have come. It's just that I . . ." He let his words trail away and shifted from one foot to the other.

Tough for a big, strong agent-man to admit that he was feeling blue and needed company. "Anthony Lucano —" she put her hands on her hips — "you'd rather be out on a bust?"

His mouth tilted up, and he shook his head. "There's nowhere I'd rather be than in your company. But when and if we ever go where we were headed, it needs to be in the right place at the right time after the right vows — with God smiling down on us."

"Amen, hon." She stepped toward him.

"No closer." He tugged at his collar. "The temperature's still a little high in here."

She tilted her head. "Spoken like a man in need of a wife." Oh bother, was that pushy or what? She looked away. He didn't respond. She peered at him from under lowered lashes.

His gaze was on her, steady, sober. "You volunteering for the position?"

Her head snapped up. "There better not be any other volunteers."

He laughed deep and long, shadows gone from his face. "I stopped taking applications when I laid eyes on you, darlin'."

"Good. I'd hate to have to get mean and evil with the competition."

"Speaking of mean and evil." He headed

for the door. "You should call Max. She no doubt thinks I'm the lowest scum on the planet because I haven't made you call her yet. When I talked to her while you were in the hospital, she was big-time upset that you'd been missing and she didn't know it." He stopped with his hand on the doorknob. "Are you ever going to give me that piece of information you withheld from me yesterday?"

"Ask Agent Ortiz. She pooh-poohed my wild conclusion, and I'm glad. Besides, if Max doesn't have any results on an assignment I gave her, any theory will be less than worthless."

"Now I know how you feel when I can't tell you things about an investigation."

"Get out of here, Lucano." She waved.

Tony flashed a smile and left.

Desi got on the phone. A somber-sounding woman answered after the first ring. "Lana, it's me — Desiree. Is Max around?"

"Oh, Desi, dear, I'm so glad you called. Max is beside herself."

"About what? I'm safe and sound. But I do promise to grovel about not calling sooner. Put her on."

Low whimper. "I can't. Steve and I are babysitting. Max went to the prison. Dean jumped from the catwalk of the cell block tonight, and they don't know if he's going to make it. My poor daughter! To have her husband kill himself on top of everything else! How much more can she take?" Lana's voice broke.

Desi's heart echoed the sound. When would the cycle of pain and death end? What terrible consequences bad choices brought, for the innocent as well as the guilty. "Tell Max I'm flying home in the morning. There's nothing more I can do here."

Lana sniffed. "She'll be glad to see you. We all know you did your best out there."

Desi ended the call and sat down on the bed. Her best? She'd accomplished less than nothing. Her crusade had cost crucial man-hours away from the hunt for Karen in order to find and rescue her.

A secret cult hideaway in the desert? Twenty-first-century cannibals? Fantastic tales. Should she believe any of it without more proof?

Tony was right to worry about her. Tomorrow she was turning over a new leaf. No more listening to her own impulses and confusing them with God's guidance.

Nothing and no one could convince her to take matters into her own hands again.

Seventeen

Desi fought herself awake from troubled dreams of desert heat mingled with the sound of a man crying. She blinked at the unfamiliar hotel room, and then awareness rushed in. *Max!* She needed to get back to Boston. She sat straight up.

Rolling out of bed, she stood and stretched, her array of bruises protesting. No decisions to make on wardrobe. Over the underwear she'd washed in the hotel sink and dried with the blow-dryer, she slipped on the sundress Jo had lent her.

She checked the time and did a double take at the clock: 9 a.m. Why didn't the alarm go off? She checked the setting and groaned. She'd set it for 7 *p.m.,* not seven in the morning. She should have woken up earlier anyway. What kind of friend was she?

Desi picked up the hotel phone and dialed Max's house. *Dean, you better not have died on Max. She does not need more guilt-trips to lay on herself.* The phone rang until the answering machine picked up. Desi cut the connection. She hated to dial Max's cell number. What if she was sitting with Dean in his last moments?

Tony. He'd have Steve's cell number. Through the unofficial bodyguard she could at least find out where everyone was.

She punched in Tony's number and then mentally kicked herself when it started to ring. This time of day, he'd be neck-deep in whatever was happening at the office. Oh, never mind. He needed to know she was leaving town anyway.

"Lucano." His clipped tone let her know she was right about him being busy.

"Tony, it's Des. Sorry to bother you."

"No bother, hon." The tone softened, and Desi's insides turned to warm taffy.

At Tony's end, someone in the background called his name.

She laughed. "Liar. You're a popular man."

He answered with a chuckle. "With you, I hope . . . Just a second." That last was said with his mouth away from the receiver. "How are you this morning?" He returned to the mouthpiece. "I almost checked on you before I went in today, but didn't want to wake you up."

Desi sighed. "You should have. I've got to

go back to Boston on the soonest flight out."

"HJ Securities needs you?"

"Max. Dean's in the hospital. Attempted suicide. Didn't sound good last night."

Silence for a beat. "Then Boston's where you need to be. If nothing further breaks at this end, I won't be far behind. I'll —"

"Lucano!" The person in the background had run out of patience.

"Gotta go. Ortiz looks about ready to bust a gasket. Must be something cooking." His voice took on the edge of a hunter catching the scent of a trail.

No fair delaying him a moment longer. "Sure, I'll call you again from Boston."

"I'll call *you.*"

"Sorry, buddy. I'm fresh out of cell phones."

"Get one, and let me know when you have it. Leave the message on my voice mail if you need to . . . What's up, Ortiz?" The connection closed.

Desi frowned. She'd have to chance disturbing her friend at a delicate time. She punched in numbers, and a knock sounded at her door.

"Who is it?" She disconnected the phone without finishing the sequence.

No answer except a louder knock. Someone was way impatient. Seemed to be the morning for it. She went to the door and looked through the peephole. A fleshy face filled her vision. Her heart seized then gave a little jump.

Hamilton Gordon! And he was sweating like he'd jogged up the stairs to her floor. No, that wasn't perspiration on his jowls.

Those were tears.

"We've found one of our corpses come to life!"

Ortiz waved a fingerprint report in Tony's face. "Our prize prisoner is West Coast thug Leon Bender — one of the guys whose prints were on that meth package. He was listed as killed a year ago in a warehouse explosion. But here he is, alive and well, waiting for us in an interrogation cell down at the county lockup. A resurrection story with nothing holy about it. And get this." She leaned in closer. "Bender drives for Gordon Corp when he's not tearing up the desert on his hog."

"No surprise there." Tony took the report. "Someone in that corporation is making lowlifes disappear then hiring them to do his dirty work. And he's been at it for a while. Bill Winston's death was staged five years ago."

Ortiz nodded. "A wealthy, influential

executive like Hamilton Gordon would be in a prime position to help people disappear and reemerge with false identities."

Tony fastened the fingerprint sheet on the bulletin board next to a fresh mug shot of Tank, aka Leon Bender. "For sure a guy like Leon would need someone with brains to help him pull off a death scam." He tapped Bender's picture. "He's not the sharpest tack in the wall. Why else would he try a fool stunt like he did with Desiree? We would've found his hidey-hole in a five-minute ransack."

Ortiz slanted him a look. "I doubt he had a clue that he was dealing with someone who wouldn't leave without his woman. Not the type to believe that someone could care about another person that much."

Tony jingled the change in his pocket. "Point taken. But if we can squeeze Gordon's name out of little Leon, we can start to unravel this whole thing."

"We?" Ortiz laughed. "Yesterday never happened, bucko. You're stuck to the office till the powers-that-be hold some cockamamie committee meeting. Remember? Besides, you've got a personal thing against Leon." She arched a brow at Tony. "Don't worry. Rhoades and I'll go down to the jail and put the guy in a vise." The New Mexico agent headed for the door. "I always enjoy doing interrogations with Rhoades. He can't eat peanuts."

Tony chuckled and waved her away. He turned toward the mishmash of papers and files on the table, the sum of three interlocking, cross-agency cases. The DEA was going to be hot to hop on this Leon Bender meth connection. Looked like Gordon Corp trucks might be hauling drugs as well as pirated discs. And then there was the possible embezzlement of GC funds thrown into the mix. And finally, the FBI, the tribal police, and the local PD wanted Indian artifacts recovered and the thieves caught, which included finding Karen Webb as a possible accomplice. No obvious connection between those cases except . . .

He picked up a file, the one on suspicious activities at Inner Witness Ministries.

Gordon linked the interstate trucking and embezzlement case with the Inner Witness investigation. Webb potentially linked the museum theft and Inner Witness. But what would Ham Gordon or Reverend Romlin want with centuries old artifacts? And how could Karen be involved in the trucking case? Yet the fact remained that Inner Witness permeated the lives of both Webb and Gordon, and that couldn't be a coincidence.

Maybe Hajimoto had found something in his digging into Reverend Romlin. He grabbed a pad and pen and got on the phone to Boston. If something didn't turn up soon, someone was going to get away with murder. His blood heated. *Not* going to happen on his watch.

"Please, Ms. Jacobs, you must go with me to the FBI office. I have vital information."

From the other side of her closed hotel door, Desi listened to the plea for the third time. "Mr. Gordon, I've told you I'm needed elsewhere. You can go to the FBI yourself. I'm certain they'll be happy to hear anything you have to say."

"But I want to speak only to Agent Lucano, and you must be there as an advocate for me. He values your opinion."

What made this guy think she'd be on *his* side? "Mr. Gordon, if you have information about a crime or wish to make a confession, you need to give it to the authorities right away. I can't help you with that, and if you persist, I'm going to call the police."

"You'll be sorry if you don't come with me, Ms. Jacobs." Gordon's voice became more gravel than whine.

A shiver pulsed through Desi's middle. How did he find out where she was staying?

"Mr. Gordon, I'm going to call the police. If you don't leave right now, you'll be arrested."

This man was either genuinely off his rocker or insanely clever and dangerous. She reached for the handset and the instrument rang. Desi jumped.

Tony sorted through papers while the receptionist at the Boston end put him through to Hajimoto. The familiar voice came on.

"Haj, Tony here. I hope you've pulled a rabbit out of the hat on Romlin. We need something fresh."

The man gave his rolling chuckle. "You must have been reading my mind when you called. First off, he's not a real minister. At least not an ordained one like he claims. He never went to the school he says he graduated from, but he does have a real license to marry and bury — easy enough to come by these days. And his real name is Arnold Bletch, son of an undertaker from Scranton, Ohio."

"No wonder the guy changed his name." Tony doodled a downward spiral on his pad. "Or is this another case of a dead man with a fictitious identity?"

"Nope. Bletch never died. He just disappeared, and no one cared because both of his folks were dead, and the family wasn't close. I've been on the phone with a second cousin who says he's not surprised Arnold got into a religious racket. As a kid, he was a choirboy with a silver tongue — literal choirboy, but with a scam artist's heart." Haj snorted a laugh. "He talked some lonely old lady into leaving him her estate. After she died, he took the money, left town, and was never seen or heard from again."

"And no one in his hometown recognized him when he went on television?"

"He changed more than his name. The cousin told me his own mother wouldn't recognize him."

"So far you've given me plenty of shady history, but nothing outright illegal."

"Sorry, boss. I can't tell you what's not there. If the news media gets wind Romlin's lying about his past, the scandal will shut down his ministry, but it won't put him in prison."

"Fax me everything you've got anyway." If only he could tell Haj to fax the information to the nearest network TV station or major newspaper. "Keep digging. If we can prove improper use of ministry donations, that *will* put him in prison."

"Like diverting big bucks to construct a

secret compound in the desert?"

"Or if some of the money embezzled from the company or profits from pirating ended up in Inner Witness coffers. Someone's got their fingers in a lot of pies, and tons of dough is disappearing. Oh, and a new wrinkle's come up that links GC with meth distribution. Drug money propping up a media ministry? That'd put Romlin in the slammer and bury the key."

Haj whistled low and long. "Polanski's got Slidell looking into the source of Inner Witness money. I can hardly wait for the results."

Tony let out a short laugh. "Guess I'm obsolete before I'm gone more than a day."

"Not hardly. Get back as soon as you can. Things aren't . . ." A heavy breath came over the line. "It feels weird around here. You know, without Ben and now you out of the office."

Tony exhaled through his nose. "I know what you mean." He heard a female voice in the background. "That Polanski? Put her on."

"Sure. See ya soon."

Tony heard Haj yell to Polanski. A few seconds passed.

"Hey, boss-man," she said. "How's Albuquerque treating you? Desiree all right?"

"Albuquerque's good. Des was 100 percent Des when I talked to her this morning. She bounces back like a Super Ball and is already off on the next crusade. I think she'll be back in your neck of the woods today. A crisis with Max Webb's husband."

"You think we need to put more protection on the Webb family than a retired agent?"

"Stevo's more than I'd wish on King Kong. Besides, who do we have to spare? The threat is vague and from an unreliable source that may be out of the picture." Too bad he couldn't get his hands on Cheama to demonstrate the proper way to carry out a threat.

"You okay?"

Tony unclenched his fists. "Fine."

"Riiiight. Well, I don't mind admitting that we're a little shaky around here. It'll be good when you get back."

"You know how to make a guy feel needed even when his fill-in has everything under control." He tried a laugh, but it came out a grunt.

"They release the body tomorrow. The funeral should be in a few days. You going?"

"Wouldn't miss it."

"The rest of us feel the same way."

"Tell them to put in for vacation when we

have a firm date. I'll sign off and pass it up the line. I doubt we'll hear any squawking."

"And if we do?"

"I'll squawk back."

They ended the call, and Tony surveyed the disorganized information on the table. He glanced around at the almost empty bulletin boards that circled the room. Time to organize, try different patterns, see what jelled, what didn't. The answers had to be lying in front of him.

All he had to do was put the right questions to the data.

Desi took a deep breath and answered the phone. "Hello?"

"Des?"

"Max! Are you ever a sound for sore ears."

"Sorry I didn't call you back sooner, but it's been a horrendous night. I just got home. Dean is going to live. He's without a spleen and has a few broken bones, but he's going to make it. Do you hear that? And do you know something else? I love the man. Despite everything. I'm going to stick by him. The kids and I are going to visit him on the next family day, and —"

"Slow down, Max. Come up for air."

Max's laugh rang with a freedom Desi hadn't heard in a long time. "You think I'm crazy, but this is right for me, Des. No family curse is gonna get *my* marriage!"

"I've got goose bumps hearing the confidence in your voice." She glanced at the closed and locked hotel room door. "I'm dealing with a situation at the moment. Hold on. I need to look out my peephole and see if a certain pest has vamoosed."

Desi laid the receiver down and tiptoed to the door. The hallway was empty, but she sure wasn't going out until she called Tony. He'd go ballistic. Max first, though.

She went back to the phone. "I'm happy for your sake that Dean's going to pull through."

"But not for his?" Her tone darkened. "He's sorry about everything, you know. He wants to see you. We talked about it last night when they let me see him. Will you go?"

Desi gritted her teeth. "I don't know if I'm ready for that, Max." Cement encased Desi's heart. Helping a terrorist kidnap her was a tall order to be sorry for. An even taller one to forgive.

"But you'll think about it?"

"I will. Can we change the subject now?"

"Are you all right? What was the problem at your door?"

"No problem. Just a nuisance." Desi sat

down on the bed. "I was going to come home, but if it's okay with you, I'll stay in Albuquerque another day. Call it curiosity, but now I've got to see how a certain situation involving my unwanted visitor comes out."

"No need for you to rush back. Things are good here. Or rather, they're getting better than they've been for a while."

"Did you make any progress on locating the Holy City?"

"Are you sure Little Missy Sunshine, that Hope girl, wasn't leading you astray? I spent a whole afternoon making phone calls to contractors, plumbers, and building supply places, as well as checking public records like permits and such. No hint of odd building projects going on with Inner Witness Ministries or Hamilton Gordon."

"They're not building anything?" Desi's stomach clenched. Did that big-eyed innocent at the Santa Fe headquarters mislead her?

"The ministry completed a new warehouse and office a few months ago. And Gordon just built himself a sprawling ranch-style mansion on a little oasis west of Albuquerque. Both recent, legitimate, well-documented projects."

"But I saw a picture of a ground-breaking

ceremony in the desert and a detailed model that was *not* a ranch."

"I don't know what you saw at that ministry hole-in-the-wall. That office is closed by the way. All mention erased from the Net. But —"

"Doesn't it seem strange that the address I visited suddenly goes poof off the grid?"

"Maybe. Maybe not." Max's voice sharpened into a close approximation of Desi's sixth-grade teacher when she didn't want to continue on a dead subject. "The timing might have coincided with a planned closure. What did they need the space for anymore?"

Desi let out a long breath. "Okay, Max. You have a point." Too bad she didn't buy the point. She opened her mouth to argue then closed it. Max had shut down on her. The poor woman was on overload. Besides, she'd done everything Desi asked of her. "You get some rest; spend time with your kids. Take as much vacation as you need."

Max let out a loud yawn. "Thank goodness for my mom and Steve. They took the kids out for brunch, and then they're going to the park so I can catch a few z's."

"Hit the hay, Max."

"Just a sec. One more thing. A personal note on Gordon that turned up in my snooping around. He's not a well man. The medication he's taking for chronic colitis has given him a disease called Cushing's syndrome. Causes weight gain, particularly in the stomach, face, and neck, and a mottled, reddish complexion."

"That's Gordon."

"Don't know what that information has to do with anything, but it was interestin'."

Desi pictured Gordon's moon cheeks wet with tears outside her door. "I'd feel sorry for him if he didn't scare me so much." She said good-bye then punched in Tony's number. The phone went right to voice mail.

"Hi, hon," she told the recorder. "I had a scary visit from Hamilton Gordon a few minutes ago. I wouldn't let him in, and I think he's gone now, but he wanted me to go with him to talk to you. He sounded desperate. You might want to find him as soon as possible if he doesn't show up there." She cleared her throat. "From a talk with Max, it looks like I might have been wrong about the secret compound in the desert. She can't find a trace, and that woman's too good to miss a thing. Oh, and Dean's going to make it." Desi let out a strangled noise. "That's great, of course, but it's just that . . . oh, never mind. I'm going shopping at the mall for a few clothes and plan to stick around Albuquerque for one more day. See you later."

All right, what next? Do safe things that will make a certain FBI agent turn cartwheels. First of all, stay out of the investigation. Check. Done that. She sent the man to Tony so he could handle the situation his way. Big star on the report card. And she let him know right away what had happened. Bonus points. Not her fault she had to do it via voice mail.

Now for traveling precautions. Desi called a cab, then hotel security for an escort out of the building. A paunchy guard showed up at her door, ill-hidden smirk on his face.

"Hamilton Gordon is stalking you, miss?" He cocked a fuzzy eyebrow at her in the elevator. "He's as harmless as they come. A real do-gooder, as they say. If he's taken an interest, maybe you should just talk to him. Let him down gently."

She answered with a level stare. The man cleared his throat and looked away.

A few minutes later, Desi climbed into the cab and settled back against the seat cushion. Tony should be ecstatic. Now she was labeled a loony or a bimbo by hotel staff. Out on the road, she swiveled her head this way and that, watching traffic. The cabdriver must've thought she had a tic. No one appeared to be following them, at least not in the expensive type of transportation that would haul a man like Gordon.

The coolness of the mall entrance welcomed her inside. She stopped at the directory, gaze taking in her surroundings. A dusky-skinned family chattered in Spanish as they wandered up the hall. An elderly couple shared a bench. A cluster of teenage girls giggled past. No Jabba the Hutt. Tension faded. By now, Gordon must have connected with Tony.

Macy's, here I come.

A power-shopping hour and a half later, she had two changes of clothing, personal items, the makeup basics, and a cell phone. She'd even picked out a striking pair of genuine turquoise earrings. After all, if a gal visited the Southwest, she needed to acquire some local color. Wearing comfortable capris, a bright top, and new sandals, she left the department store swinging her bags.

Near one of the exits, she called for another cab and waited. That group of teenage girls she'd seen earlier stopped in front of her, debating whether to go for ice cream or a swim. The swim had won out — with, from what she overheard, the possibility of attracting "hot" guys — when the yellow car pulled up.

Smiling, she walked out of the mall. Her burned skin tingled as she stepped away from the shade of the building. She turned her face up to the sun. *Thank You, God, that I'm alive to enjoy this new day. Wherever Karen is, Lord, comfort her and send deliverance . . . though it looks like I'm not meant to find her.*

Someone tapped her shoulder. She turned — and gasped.

A huge figure blocked the light.

Tony inched around the room, surveying his handiwork on the bulletin boards. Lab reports, crime scene photos, witness statements, pictures of suspects alive, dead, or missing — Karen Webb, Hamilton Gordon, Bill Winston aka Bernard Walker, Leon "Tank" Bender, Pete Cheama, and a file photo of the presumed dead gigolo whose fingerprints had shown up on the meth package recovered from Cheama's truck. And then there were pictures of victims. Tony stared into Ben Erickson's blue eyes. The guy always looked like he was carrying around a funny secret he couldn't wait to tell the world.

Tony moved on to a photo of the dead guard from the museum. An electric jolt shot through him. He grabbed the picture of the guard and compared it to the picture of the gigolo on the suspect board. A resemblance too clear to ignore. The guy must've handled the meth package prior to the museum robbery, because he was dead for real before Cheama was run off the road. Chances were good that all the crooks worked together loading and unloading shipments, and Leon, being such a genius, didn't wipe the package down well enough before planting it in Cheama's pickup.

Tony dug through papers and found the statement from the guard after he came to in the hospital. No holes in the man's story, but he should have been looked at closer as a suspect . . . except all eyes were on the missing Karen Webb. Maybe the thieves snatched Karen to keep attention off the guard. And the fact that the man died later from his staged injury wasn't planned.

Finally, something that made sense. Almost.

How did the guard get the thumbprint and the voice code to gain access to the computer control room? Tony grinned and tapped the photo of the guy's suave mug. By acting true to form, that's how.

Tony called the museum and asked to speak to the administrator. The man came on with a gruff hello.

"Mr. Spellman. This is Anthony Lucano with the FBI. I need to ask you a question."

"Go ahead." The voice was cool, cautious.

"The guard that died. Who in your facility was he dating?"

Long pause. "I have no idea. Why would you think — ?"

"Is someone around who might have that information?"

"Are you people still trying to pin this on one of my employees? The poor man is dead. What could he —"

"We're trying to find the truth, Mr. Spellman. If he wasn't romantically involved with any of your other staff, then we've hit another dead end. But I need to know."

Spellman huffed. "My secretary. She stays up on that sort of thing. I'll ask her." A soft thunk said the phone had landed on the desk. "Hannah, could you come in here, please?" The voice was distant, followed by sounds of movement. "The FBI is on the phone. They want to know who was dating the security guard."

Silence.

Then a woman shrieked and burst into tears. "I'm so sorry . . . I never thought . . . I didn't mean . . . he was going to marry meeeee . . ." The voice fell away into blubbering.

Spellman breathed hard in Tony's ear. "You heard?"

"I did. Detain her, and I'll send someone over to pick her up."

"Will do." The man's voice was strangled. "Hannah, how *could* you —"

The connection broke.

Tony hung his head. Sad deal for everyone. He made the call to send a squad car to collect Mr. Spellman's secretary. In hindsight, a logical suspect — the person with limitless access to her boss's dictation tapes and a high probability of finding out the code words. Grab a print from Spellman's coffee cup, and the boyfriend could open the door to whoever hacked the computer and inserted the virus. People did the most awful things for what they thought was love. And to have her lover die . . .

The woman must have been ready to crack for days. Just needed the right question to break the dam.

But his loose ends weren't quite tied up. A big question remained.

While the plant of a "dead" crook at the museum tied Gordon to the theft, the act made no sense. Why steal artifacts worth thousands when you're running a pirating operation and embezzling scheme worth millions? There had to be a purpose for those artifacts more valuable to Gordon than money.

Desi said she'd formed a wild theory at the museum, but she hadn't told him what it was, and he'd forgotten to ask Ortiz this morning. With everything else going on, he'd given Desi's speculation low priority. He should know better. She might be waltzing around the country with the key to all three intertwined cases in that gorgeous head of hers.

He pulled out his cell. She called and he missed it? Must have been while he was on the phone. He played her message and a frozen fist rammed his gut. The ice shattered before a blast of fury that shook him.

Ham Gordon was after Desiree, and she was out shopping minus a chaperone.

Desi stared up into moist hazel eyes, surprisingly similar in shade to hers.

Gordon kneaded puffy hands together. "I mean you no harm, Ms. Jacobs. Please believe me. I'm not a strong man . . . or a well one. Help me to do what I must."

"Why me, Mr. Gordon?"

A tremor shook the man's jowls. "Did your father ever talk about how the Yakovs, a brother and sister, came to America from Lithuania in 1920?"

"What do you know about that, and why do you care?" Alarms pinged in Desi's mind.

"Did Hiram explain to you that the siblings changed their name to Jacobs when they entered the United States in New York?"

Desi didn't answer.

Gordon licked his lips. "Amelia Yakov — or Jacobs, as she became — married Albert Gordon and moved west, while Anton stayed on the East Coast."

A noose tightened around Desi's middle. This conversation was *not* going the direction this man suggested. She shook her head.

Gordon nodded. "We are distant cousins, my dear. From the research done by my personal assistant, you may be my closest relative. And I yours." He lifted his arms in a shrug. "If a medical condition didn't make me obese, you might even detect a family resemblance."

A pit opened in Desi's stomach. "Should I fall all over myself and hug you?" Desi hugged herself instead, packages rustling. "You're suspected of multiple criminal acts, and you know you're guilty."

Gordon hung his head. "I was guilty once upon a time, but the blood has washed me clean. I'm not guilty of what they wish to accuse me of now." He lifted his round face and stared into her eyes. "You were kind to me at the party and at the DC airport when Agent Lucano was rude and hostile. I would crave your presence while I tell him whatever I know that might help him find out who's responsible for siphoning money from my company."

The man blinked fast, wetness filling crevasses in his cheeks.

Pity stirred in Desi's heart. *Yellow light, Des. Don't give Tony an opening to say you're a soft touch again.* One stranded-in-the-desert experience was enough. "I've got a cab waiting for me, Mr. Gordon." She motioned toward the vehicle idling at the curb. The frowning driver waved for her to get in.

Gordon nodded. "If it would make you feel safer, you could follow my limousine to the FBI headquarters. Is that an acceptable arrangement?"

Desi studied Gordon's face. Mottled complexion, dull eyes, and drooping stance confirmed an unwell man. But was he an honest sick person or a decrepit crook? "Can I call Tony and tell him we're on our way?"

"Please do." Lines of tension melted from his face.

Desi's breath caught. If one pared away excess flesh, a hint of her father peeped at her in the line of a strong jaw and the way dark brows slashed across a bold forehead. Or maybe she saw those things because he had suggested the relationship. She swallowed against a tight throat. "Let's go then." She turned toward the cab.

Gordon moved forward, reaching for her door. Desi shrank away. Thunder cracked, and the rear passenger window exploded. Desi's scream overlapped the driver's. Gordon staggered backward and sat down hard on the sidewalk, eyes and mouth round *O*s. A sharp pain drew Desi's gaze downward.

Oh, bother! A widening red stain marred her new shirt.

EIGHTEEN

Tony jammed the number of the Albuquerque PD into the keypad of the landline phone. The dispatcher came on, but Tony interrupted her spiel.

"This is Supervisory Special Agent Anthony Lucano requesting a patrol car stop by the Coronado Center Mall and page Ms. Desiree Jacobs. There may be a situation developing —"

"Cars are already at the scene. A shot was fired. One casualty."

Tony's heart stalled. "Male or female?"

"Female."

A dark film rose in front of his eyes. "Condition and identity?" Who asked that sensible question? He made himself drag in a breath, clench and unclench numb fingers.

"Unknown and unknown."

His heart mule-kicked his ribs. "I'm on my way to the scene."

"Ten-four. I'll notify —"

Tony slapped the phone into its cradle and ran. Brain jammed into business-only, he rounded up a car and driver. Outside, sunlight gleamed against dry tarmac, but the vehicle moved like sludge through spotty traffic. He tuned the radio to the police frequency.

Lots of meaningless chatter — a fender-bender, a high-speed chase on I-25, a call for backup on a possible robbery in progress. Silence on the mall shooting. Necessary personnel must already be on-site. They wouldn't do any extra jabbering and no mention of a victim's name. Too many people had scanners.

Just another crime scene. Keep a tight rein on speculation. *Desiree! I can't lose you!*

Two-hundred-sixty-two heartbeats later, the car turned into the mall parking lot. The driver honed in on the emergency vehicles. Tony leaped out before the car came to a stop.

He strode between an ambulance and an APD crime lab van. A female figure lay on the canopy-shaded sidewalk with a man in a dark uniform crouched over her . . . poking . . . prodding. Not the way an emergency response person handled a live victim. Dread slammed Tony to a halt. He sucked in air tainted with a flavor like a scorched frying pan — the taste of his own terror.

Who died? He had to know. Even if the truth killed something inside him, not knowing was worse.

He ducked under the crime scene tape. A police officer moved toward him, scowling. Tony flashed his credentials. The officer nodded and went back to watching the perimeter.

Tony took a step toward the dimness. Then another and another, gaze fixed on the slender, limp body haloed by a pool of inky liquid.

"Tony?"

The voice whipped his head around. He squinted at the woman running toward him. Someone else lumbered in her wake.

"Look out, Des!" He vaulted the yellow tape, snatched her around the waist, and hustled her to the far side of the lab van. She squirmed in his arms. Warm. *Alive!* He pressed her against the side of the vehicle.

She shook her head. "What in the world —"

He silenced her with two fingers against her lips. "Gordon's following you. Stay here. I'll take care of this." He swept the area with his gaze. No one else nearby. Everyone intent on the crime scene. He moved to the front of the van, patting the empty spot where his holster should be. Gordon came on. Tony flexed his hands. Stupid time to be without a weapon. He could halt the slimy pachyderm before he got another millimeter closer to Desiree, but now he'd have to —

A hand grabbed his sleeve. He stared down into furious hazel eyes. Didn't the woman have a grain of common sense? "Get back, Des. Now!"

Desi stepped away and glared up at him. "Hold your horses, Wyatt Earp. He's my cousin." She jerked her head at Gordon, who stopped and looked from one to the other of them. "At least I think he is. Maybe." A trembly smile crumpled into tears. "Oh, Tony!" She flung herself at him and buried her nose in his tie. "That poor t-teenager was killed."

Gordon lifted baseball plate hands. "I haven't told the police, but the bullet was meant for me." He grimaced. "I came to give you cart blanche to tear my offices apart in order to find whoever is destroying Gordon Corp. Yesterday I discovered that money is missing." The man slumped, staring at the pavement.

"Ham isn't well," Desi wiped her eyes. "We should find him a place to rest."

Tony stared at her. All of a sudden it's long lost cousin Ham? "You'd better tell me water flows uphill, Des, because I'll believe that before I buy you being related to this lowlife."

Gordon stiffened. "My personal assistant assures me it is so. He's brilliant at research. Took him mere minutes this morning to find out where Desiree was staying."

Desi went pale and clapped a hand over her mouth.

Tony stepped into Gordon's space, so close they breathed each other's air. "Invasion of privacy is nothing to brag about. And you'll excuse me if I need more than the word of a Gordon Corp employee about your relationship to Desiree. You don't hire the salt of the earth." His jaw muscles knotted. "One of your truckers shot and killed a member of my squad two days ago. You remember Bill Winston? One of the pet crooks you keep in your kennel? You signed off on his hiring papers. *You* are going down for the murder."

The whites showed around Gordon's eyes. "Oh, dear Lamb of God, help me." The man staggered over to the van and collapsed against it, swaying and moaning. "Not my signature. He signs *for* me. I trusted . . . Why didn't my Inner Witness tell me? Why didn't I know?" The last word stretched out into a howl, like a wounded wolf.

The guy was sick all right. Sick in the head.

"Tony, don't you get it?" Desi touched his sleeve. "It's Mayburn."

"Who?" He kept a corner of his eye on Gordon.

"Ham's administrative assistant. It's been him all along. Hope told me Mayburn has a finger on the pulse of everything to do with Ham's business."

Eerie warmth breathed over Tony's skin. Like a crack had opened in the earth and released a puff of smoke from hell.

Desi squeezed his arms. "It makes perfect sense. We both know Ham's been caught up in Inner Witness. What an opportunity for a 'brilliant' employee to step forward and do what he likes with the company."

Tony looked at the miserable mound of flesh hunched against the vehicle. The guy was guilty of something, and he was going to prove it. No way Gordon didn't know what his most valued employee was up to. But maybe this Mayburn *was* the mastermind. The bootlegging operation would take razor-sharp organization. Gordon was so far gone in the cult he didn't have two thoughts to rub together about anything else.

Tony's gut did a dive. As much as he hated to admit it, Desi's conclusion added up.

He'd had Gordon so big in his sights that he missed the evil hidden in the man's shadow. Everyone at the Bureau had, and today another innocent had paid for their tunnel vision. His gaze went to Desiree. A dark splotch on her shirt caught his eye, and his breath hitched. "You're hurt."

She looked down and touched the spot. "A pebble of flying glass hit me. Just a scratch, but it did ruin one of the two shirts I have to my name." She shook her head, dark hair bouncing. "Unimportant."

Tony touched her hair and gazed past her shoulder to the crime scene. His fingers fisted in the softness.

"Ouch!"

Tony jerked his hand away and jammed it into his pocket. "You couldn't sit tight and wait until someone could escort you? Did you even call hotel security? What were you thinking? You scared another decade off my life, Des."

Her chin came up. "I seem to have that gift. So tell me, please, what part of this —" she waved over the area — "is my fault?"

Tony choked on furious words. *She* was mad at *him?* "No one said anything about fault, but you need to think before —"

"Now I'm an airhead? You have no idea what I did to satisfy your concept of *safety* for me. But nothing will ever be enough, will it?" She swiped some of that beautiful mane behind one ear. A turquoise earring gleamed at him. He'd never seen that one before.

He pointed at it. "A guy like Gordon knocks on your door, and you go shopping?" The heads of bystanders and a uniformed officer turned their direction. He lowered his voice. "What am I supposed to think? Would it have been too hard to call the APD and have a squad car take you to my office? You should have been in protective custody until Gordon was rounded up."

She turned toward the van and nodded at the big man slumped on the pavement with his head in his hands. "Turns out he was pretty dangerous."

"Whoever fired that fatal shot was."

Pain and horror filled her eyes.

His mouth filled with apology, but he stuffed the words down. She needed to realize once and for all that some mad dog could snuff out her flame and not give it a second thought.

Her nostrils flared. "Seems to me your precious case is solved. Don't waste time worrying about me. I'm going back to my hotel and booking a flight for home." She turned and marched away.

Tony strode after her. "Ms. Jacobs!"

She jerked to a halt, spine rigid, head high.

Tony grasped her arm. "I'm detaining you as a material witness. Gordon, too." Tony motioned to his driver, and the vehicle cruised up. He opened the rear door; Desi glared at him.

"Don't look at me that way. This one isn't used for transporting prisoners." She sniffed and folded herself inside. Tony looked in at the driver. "Take her to the office, make her comfortable in a private room, and don't — whatever you do — let her out of your sight. I'll be along with Gordon in a patrol car."

He watched the vehicle drive away. Desi didn't look back. Hollow-chested, he turned to Hamilton Gordon. Maybe the man wasn't behind the bootlegging operation, but he had a lot of questions to answer . . . and a lot to answer for.

Tony pulled out his cell phone and dialed Ortiz. She answered with a curt hello.

"Your talk with Tank not going well?"

She snorted. "The guy has the vocabulary of an ape and half the IQ. He kept moaning, 'I'm a dead man.' I think he means it'd be for real if he talks. We wasted our time. Now Rhoades and I are chugging a gallon of coffee with the precinct captain and going over *again* what the PD has on Snake

Bonney's bikers. Maybe there are more living dead in the bunch."

Tony took a step toward Gordon, who was pulling himself to his feet. "Haul Tank back into interrogation and mention the name Chris Mayburn. You may end up with a talking ape. As soon as he spills enough for a warrant, round up a small army and go arrest Mayburn and his friends at Gordon Corp. He's our miracle worker and no doubt operating under a manufactured identity like the rest of them."

"And you discovered this how?"

"I'll tell you at the office. I'm coming in with Hamilton Gordon."

Ortiz groaned. "Don't tell me you strayed off the reservation."

"Long story. Another dead body." And a wounded relationship with the most fascinating, frustrating woman in the world.

". . . the most annoying, frustrating man in the world!" Desi muttered as she paced the little room. It had a small sofa, even a TV. Off, of course. Who could think about watching the idiot box when she needed to throttle somebody? Preferably somebody with dark hair that refused to lie flat and killer brown eyes that could x-ray lead.

Maybe she should conk him over the head

and drag him off to a cave in the middle of nowhere. At least they could get to know one another without any bad guys disrupting their lives. Desi stifled a grin at the mental picture of her petite self trying to drag the big lug anywhere.

Sighing, she plopped onto the sofa and looked at the wall clock. She'd been here over an hour. A small table held the nibbled remains of a ham sandwich beside an empty orange soda can. She sent a sideways look toward the closed door. Should she make a break for it? Yeah, right. Dollars to doughnuts that fresh-faced agent who'd driven her here would be lurking in the hall.

Why was *she* under guard? She hadn't done anything. Not like the last time she sat alone in a room at an FBI office building. But that was before she and Tony had made a twosome. Now he'd stuck her in this cubicle and hadn't the courtesy to let her know what was going on.

She got up and resumed pacing. He could be raiding Gordon Corp right now, confronting armed felons masquerading as truck drivers, or throwing out a search grid for a desperate and dangerous Chris Mayburn. A picture zapped across her mind of yawning gun muzzles spurting bullets and a tall figure crumpling. It had happened to

Ben. It could —

Stop it!

And he was worried about her. So not fair.

The door opened, and Tony stepped inside, his attention glued to papers in his hand. He left the door open. Mr. Fresh Face in the hallway flashed a smile and wandered off. Maybe she should fix him up with Hope of the Perky Ponytail. They'd make a cute couple.

She cleared her throat and glared at the source of her irritation.

Tony looked up, gaze sober but gentle. "Hey, sweetheart. Everyone treating you right?"

"If by everyone you mean my bodyguard-slash-jailer, yes." She motioned toward the food on the table.

"Good." He lowered the papers to his side. "Preliminary report from the mall shooting indicates that either you or Gordon was the target, and the young woman who was killed happened to step in the way. By the time the projectile reached the taxi, where it shattered a window, it had been deflected through her body. Otherwise, one of you . . ."

Desi plunked onto the sofa and ran her hands over her face. "Way to make me feel like two cents."

"The teenager's death wasn't your fault. Gordon's unhealthy fixation on you put everyone around him at risk. And that's not your fault either."

"Then why do I feel like it is?"

"Normal reaction from a caring human being. Maybe it'll help to know that the shooter's in custody."

"That was some fast FBI footwork."

Tony shook his head. "Not us. The guy wasn't a pro hitter. Got rattled in the getaway and broke a few traffic laws. The APD chased him on I-25, but didn't connect him to the shooting until he pitched the gun out of the car before hitting a light pole. Just another half-witted crook given a new life by this Mayburn character."

Desi clasped her hands together. "What about Mayburn? With the failed shooting, he's not just going to sit and wait to be arrested. He —"

Tony held up a hand. "Tank confirmed that Mayburn gave him the new identity and hired him to haul illegal goods. That gave us all we needed to send a team out to round up Mayburn and any of the other suspected truck drivers. I should get a report anytime."

"You didn't go with them?"

"Can't." He sat down beside her. "I'm on

restricted duty until a highbrow committee back in Boston reviews my psych status and the incident reports on the shooting there."

"And you didn't think to tell me this?"

"There hasn't been a whole lot of time for heart-to-hearts."

Heat crawled up Desi's face. Little wonder they hadn't communicated when their one private moment could have benefited from supervision. "We do need to talk."

"I know."

She peered up at him.

The corners of his mouth lifted. "Truce?"

"I want a lot more than that."

"Me, too. But first, I want your help. The Bureau needs you."

A giddy thrill shot through her. "How'd *that* miracle happen?"

Tony gave a slight chuckle. "Gordon won't talk to us without you there. Are you in?"

Desi jumped up. "Lead the way. I have questions for the man myself."

"Bureau business first." Tony towered over her, smiling.

"Deal." She stuck out her hand. He pulled it to his lips and kissed the back. Sparklers ignited in Desi's middle. She yanked her hand away. "You don't fight fair, mister."

He motioned her out of the room. "What's

that old saying? Something about 'all's fair'?"

A minute later, they settled at a table in a claustrophobic interview room. Gordon was already there, the scent of expensive cologne mingling with the smell of common sweat.

"Hello, Ham." Desi nodded to him.

His mottled skin flushed. "I've been much trouble to you, my dear, when I intended to be a blessing. My Inner Witness has told me for some time that we are destined to be one."

A cold finger touched Desi's spine. How did she respond to the outrageous statement?

"What do you mean by that, Mr. Gordon?" Tony's voice was steady, but Desi read the storm brewing in the lowered brow.

"Oh, nothing improper, I assure you." Gordon's gaze darted from one to the other. "Business. I'm not well, as I've said, and I wanted to connect with family. Imagine my delight to discover that my nearest relative is an astute businesswoman I could entrust with my life's work."

Desi rubbed her hands on her capris. "Ham, I'm not interested in inheriting your business. I know nothing about the meat packing industry."

Gordon's head bobbed. "Quite so. And

that would not have been a problem, except now . . ." The smile went away. "With no Chris to show you the ropes, I'll have to delay my retirement and teach you myself."

"Ham, I —"

Tony motioned her to silence. Desi bit her lip as he leaned toward Gordon. "You're talking about retiring, not dying."

Gordon nodded. "I wish to devote myself to the deeper mysteries of the Inner Witness. Reverend Romlin is certain I will find my healing if I remove all distractions from my life." His gaze was childlike.

Tony opened a file on the table. "Were you aware, Mr. Gordon, that Archer Romlin isn't the Reverend's name? In fact —" Tony flipped a page — "his credentials are less impressive than what he's led his followers to believe."

"I am aware of my minister's humble origins. A few adjustments on his résumé to gain credibility when he was starting out can be forgiven in light of the greater good. He wanted to set the record straight some time ago, but I urged him to leave matters as they were."

"So you're content to follow a liar."

Gordon's chins jerked. "He has spoken the truth to me. What he is to others is not my affair. It doesn't become the great-grandson of one of Al Capone's enforcers to judge anyone else." The words rolled from his lips with the rumble of an oncoming train. "Did you tell the whole truth on your application to the FBI, or did you shade your story to help your chances?"

Desi looked at Tony. He stiffened, and pallor crept over the tanned planes of his face. "The people who need to know are aware of everything."

"You understand my point then." The chair creaked as Gordon leaned back.

Desi sat frozen. *The people who need to know.* Didn't she need to know? So many compartments of himself this man hid from her. She'd asked him about his family tree point blank in the cab in DC, and he'd changed the subject to Max's problems. On purpose. She could see that now. Wasn't that a lot like lying? Would he ever let her in? Could she even consider settling down with someone who didn't trust her with the worst as well as the best?

And what business did Hamilton Gordon have telling tales? She glared at him. This distant relation presumed too much. "Mr. Gordon, where's the secret compound you're building in the desert? Is Karen Webb there? Her family needs her back."

His eyes widened.

"That's right. We know about Sanctuary."

He wiped his mouth with his palm, like a man brushing away a bad taste. "You refer to my new home west of Albuquerque. Please come for a visit, but I'm afraid you won't find a woman by that name." His forehead crinkled. "No, I'm certain I don't employ a Karen Webb."

Tony slapped the file shut. "And you had nothing to do with the theft of Anasazi artifacts at the Albuquerque Museum?"

Gordon returned an owlish stare. "Why would you think I did?"

"Because the inside man on the job was one of those dead crooks resurrected by your right-hand man, Chris Mayburn."

The big man lowered his gaze. "I know nothing about hiring criminals as employees."

"Gordon." The word radiated threat. "Go home. You're not to leave the state or go any farther from town than your private residence. We'll be speaking to you again. You're not going to skate scot-free on this."

The big man flowed out of his seat. "My home and offices are open to your investigators. I'm sure you'll find evidence to help bring my assistant to justice." He dipped his head. "If you will excuse me, I need time to commune with the Lamb. This has all been . . . a shock." His gaze found Desi, and unease prickled across her skin. "I'm sure my little announcement of our relationship was also — er, disorienting. When you get used to the idea, please come visit me. We have much to discuss." He nodded to her, then to Tony, and headed for the door.

"Ham, wait!" She leaped up. "This is going to sound crazier than anything yet today. And Tony doesn't even know about it. Ortiz does, but she said —" She glanced at Tony, who stood with a puzzled notch in his brow. "Oh, well. I've got to get this out, so here goes." She turned her attention back to Gordon. "Were you aware of the purpose of the stolen artifacts? That the Anasazi may have practiced ritual cannibalism much the same as the ancient Aztecs did? Inner Witness is all about relating to the Almighty through the body and blood. I thought maybe . . . Well, it occurred to me . . ." Both men stared at her like she'd just landed from Jupiter. She sat down and scrunched into herself. "You're right. I'm nuts."

A chuckle rolled from Gordon's ample belly. "Not at all. You're a victim of a persistent legend about the ancestors of the Pueblo people." He shrugged. "Gives the tourists a thrill. Rest at ease, my dear, I'm on a restricted diet. Aside from a bite of mutton each day during the sacrament, I don't even eat the meat packed at my own company." He opened the door, and the agent stationed outside escorted him away.

Tony frowned down at her. "You all right?"

If only she could crawl back in bed and sleep without dreams. The day had gone on too long. She rubbed her eyes. "You can add embarrassment to frustration about Karen and grief about the girl who died today. No, I'm not all right." She forced herself to stand, limbs heavy. "And you. What am I supposed to do? How should I feel? You did it again — shut me out. It's a pattern that doesn't change."

His lips thinned. "You hold a bad seed in my ancestry against me? I didn't think you were that shallow."

White heat swept through her. "*I'm* not the shallow one, Lucano." She poked him in the chest. "This isn't about who your relatives are. It's about you trusting me with yourself."

"I didn't think you'd be interested in such a minor detail."

"It's not minor to you. I saw your face. In your mind it's huge, like a blemish in the middle of your spotless reputation, and you deliberately chose to hide it from me."

Tony flushed and looked away.

"I'm thrilled when I can tell you something about me you don't already know, but I know next to nothing about you. Why is that?"

She waited. He didn't answer. "You've let the secretive FBI mentality take over your personal life. Or maybe you became an agent because it suits your need to keep to yourself. Closeness with another human being is a two-way street. We can't get anywhere until you let me in, but that's your call." Desi stepped to the doorway. "If you want me, you'll have to stop hiding the man, Anthony Lucano, behind the badge. See you back in Boston . . . when you're ready."

She walked away down the hall. No footsteps hurried to catch up with her. Her heart wept.

He was letting her go.

NINETEEN

Seated at the conference room table, Tony got on the phone to the ASAC in Boston.

"Cooke here."

"Lucano."

"You got good news for me?"

"The job's done."

Deep chuckle. "That's what I like to hear. Can you find your own way home, or do we have to come get you?"

Very funny. "Any news on Ben's funeral?"

"Just a sec." Paper rustling. "Set for day after tomorrow." Cooke rattled off the details.

"I'd like to take leave until after the service. And my squad wants it as a personal day."

Heavy silence. What was up with that? Tony went still.

"No problem on the personal day for your squad," Cooke said. "But you've got a box the size of Africa waiting in your office. Stuff for that reorganization committee. And less than two weeks to absorb it all before the first meeting in DC. Not a good time to put your feet up."

"Relaxation wasn't what I had on my mind."

Another dose of silence, followed by a burst of pent-up breath. "I ought to order you back here as of yesterday, but I'd better see your ugly mug bright and early the day after the funeral. You're going to be busy round the clock."

"No problem." Big problem. His personal life was imploding, and he needed time to fix it.

"Give me the bare bones of what happened with the Gordon case. I presume you have him in custody. With that potential cult scenario, the Director's had his eye on the situation."

"Gordon's not under arrest. Yet. Depends on what the agents swarming his home and office find. We have his administrative assistant in custody. He was calling himself Chris Mayburn, but it turns out that's not his real name. Surprise. Surprise. He's a loose cannon from a West Coast mob that got busted up six years ago. Their computer guru. Warrants on him are still hot. Another Most Wanted suspect bites the dust."

"Excellent. But don't let up on Gordon."

"For sure. He's as crooked as a hound's hind leg."

"Any more on that secret compound?"

"Looks like that was smoke and mirrors."

"Looks like?"

Tony stood up and stretched his legs. "There's no proof it exists, except for what Desi was told at the Inner Witness Ministries office. That building is empty now, swept clean. We're looking for the young lady Ms. Jacobs talked to."

"What do *you* think?"

"Desiree Jacobs is a reliable witness, but her statement is only as good as the information she was given. Her source may not have been credible."

"Good. The director will be happy. And Lucano, get this." Cooke laughed. "You know how I joke about putting Jacobs on the payroll? Turns out that's a done deal."

"What?"

"Her name's gone to the top of the list of consultants for art and antiquities theft cases."

"That's where it belongs." How could he get it removed?

"Too right."

Tony hung up and stared at the wall. He'd bought himself a couple of days. What did he want to do with them?

He could let her go. Maybe he should. They could both cut their losses, and find someone else. She could anyway. No point in him looking any more if Desiree Jacobs slipped away from him. His mom would kill him for losing her, but he'd been dead meat in her sights before. She'd forgive him. At least he'd have her linguine to look forward to on Sundays.

A video played in his mind. Himself in his sixties . . .

Paunchy, gray, he bends over to plant a kiss on his eightysomething mother's wrinkled cheek while she rocks on the front porch. He sits down in the other rocker, picks up a newspaper, and buries his nose. A flock of red-hatted women flutter up the walk and whisk his mother away, laughing and jabbering. He stays behind. Alone. No demands or expectations. He can keep himself to himself. Just the way he wants it.

Then why does he wish his heart would quit beating?

Not much to pack. Desi surveyed her hotel room after taking a shower and changing into her other new outfit — jeans and a sleeveless blouse. She grabbed the blood-stained top off the bed and tossed it in the trash. No reminders of this day, thank you very much. From the dresser, she picked up the Macy's bag containing her personal items and makeup and then slung her purse over her shoulder.

Maybe she should call Max and let her know she was on the way back to Boston. No, her friend wouldn't be awake yet. And what would she say? *Hi, Max, I'm on my way home. Your niece is still missing, and no one has a clue where she is. Plus, her dad's dead. Oh, and I just broke up with Tony. So glad you're getting together with your art thief husband and your mom's dating Oscar the Grouch on steroids.*

Desi dropped her bags and sank onto the easy chair in the corner. *Whoa!* That was so ugly she ought to slap herself. Her lip quivered. No crying. She had to be at the airport in half an hour, and the last thing she needed was second looks from strangers ogling her red eyes and splotchy face. If anyone glanced at her sideways, she'd turn into a puddle in public.

Suck it up, Des. Go home and get to work. At least you have that much.

Yeah, but what did a career mean with no one to share her life?

Shut up, Des!

She rose and snatched up her things. A

loud knock sounded at the door, and she tensed. Gordon again? Cousin or no cousin, his elevator didn't go all the way to the top. Careful not to let the shopping bag rattle, she settled it on the bed and padded to the door. She peered through the peephole, gasped, and stepped back.

A stranger in black. He was turned sideways, looking up the hall with his hands in his pockets. Mayburn? No, this man in black was tall, but too solidly built for Ham Gordon's beanpole assistant. Desi took another peek and blinked. Tony! Dressed in boots, jeans, and a black leather jacket like he was going to a motorcycle rally?

She fumbled with the locks on the door and poked her head out. "What in the world?"

He looked down at her. Something lurked in the backs of his eyes. Uncertainty? Fear? So not Tony.

The expression reminded her of the neighbor boy who stood on her doorstep one day, shifting from foot to foot. Tony's nervous equivalent was the hands in the pockets. The young man's mother had ordered him to confess that he broke her garage window with his baseball. The sincere but bumbling apology was kind of cute and endearing. She sent the boy away with a smile on his freckled face.

But the problem between Tony and her was a tougher fix than replacing a broken pane of glass.

"Can I come in?" He nodded toward the half-closed door.

Desi moved back. "Just for a minute. I need to head for the airport."

Tony stepped inside. "I'll give you a lift. If you decide you still want to go." He cleared his throat. "I rented a cycle and thought you might like to drive up to Santa Fe with me, maybe visit that Georgia O'Keeffe museum. She's your favorite Southwestern artist, right?" A hand jingled change in his pockets. He looked at his boot-clad feet then back up at her, a desperate courage in the whiteness around his mouth.

Don't soften, Des. She picked up the bag from the bed. "Don't you have to work?"

"I took a couple days leave. Give that committee a chance to flex its muscles and get me back up to speed. Can't miss the funeral anyway."

"When is it?"

"Day after tomorrow. Will you go with me?"

Desi groaned and plopped down on the edge of the mattress. "You know how to push the right buttons. Of course, I'll go."

"And the motorcycle ride?"

"Since when are you a biker?"

He shrugged. Too bad that shiny black jacket looked so good on him. "When I was in high school I got my hands on a worn out Ducati. Fixed it up with baling wire and duct tape. Rode it through college — starving student transportation. But I sold it when I got into Quantico. See?" He attempted a smile. "Something new to know about me."

She didn't smile back. A few bones tossed her way just weren't enough.

He frowned. "But this ride's not for me. It's something I wanted to . . . share with you. I'm trying, Des." He glanced at the ceiling then back down at her. "Ben lived and breathed bikes. The ride's for him."

"Oh, my." The flood waiting to happen overflowed. She ran to the bathroom, tasting salt. Slamming the door, she dove for the tissues.

Tony's heart double-timed. A quarter in his pocket bit his palm. *Good going, Lucano. You made her cry.* He shouldn't have tried to see her — push her — so soon after she nailed his hide to the wall. But no way could he let her walk out of his life. He'd rather swear off Sox games.

Man, he was pitiful. He scrubbed a hand through his hair.

So what now? How would that wise woman who raised him advise him to handle this situation? Go in after her? Wait out here? Probably he should do whatever came least natural.

He eyed the door, the same feeling in his bones as when he faced an armed suspect. He was going in. *Move, feet!* They didn't. He sat down on a chair and lowered his head. Not only pitiful, a coward, too. *Lord, You've got to help me here. I'm a cornered man.*

Desi sat on the toilet lid and dabbed at her eyes. So much for her makeup job. Not that anyone would notice if she wore makeup while flying down the road on a motorcycle.

Wait just a red-hot second. She couldn't give in and go with him. But Georgia O'Keeffe. *Don't be a sucker for a bribe, girl.* But riding a cycle with Tony. Hadn't she known that would be fun when she was stuck with her arms around Snake? *Get a grip, woman.* A little fun now. A whole lot of heartache later on. But this was a memorial ride, and he wanted to take it with her. Maybe there was hope for the guy. Sure, there was hope for anyone.

Oh, she was hopeless.

She stood up and threw her tissue away. Oh, yeah, bloodshot eyes, blotchy skin. She ran cool water on a cloth and finished washing away her makeup. At least she didn't look like a malaria victim anymore. Just pale and tired. But she knew what she had to do.

Did she have the courage?

The bathroom door opened, and Tony jerked his head up.

Desi marched out, white-faced, jaw set. His stomach dropped, and he stood to receive his sentence.

She glared at him. "Where's my helmet?"

He squelched a whoop, but a grin slid past his guard. "Down at the front desk with mine."

"Let me call the airline and cancel my ticket." She made her call and then walked over to him. "No promises. Understand?"

"Sure." *Yep, promises. Lots of them. And the first one is that I'm not letting you go, lady.* He opened the door.

In the elevator, she ran a hand down his jacket sleeve. "No bugs. Must be new."

"There's a smaller one like it waiting with your helmet."

Her face lit. Good thing the salesman at

the motorcycle shop didn't know he would have paid twice what he did to make her smile.

They collected their gear, and he held the jacket while she slipped it on. At least the salesman knew the right size for the general dimensions Tony gave him. He smoothed down the collar. Maybe a quick little neck-nuzzle. Nope, better bide his time.

She looked up at him and grinned, and Tony's insides puddled. Decked out in her leathers, Desi turned biker chick into a class act. *His* class act, if only he could get her convinced of that once and for all.

"Our steed awaits." Tearing his gaze from hers, he led the way out of the lobby.

She laughed. "Corny but cute."

Tony held the door for her, and she tugged at his jacket lapel on her way past.

"Niiice steed." Desi's gaze devoured the Harley Road King he'd rented for an arm and a leg.

"Let's go." He straddled the seat and nodded over his shoulder.

She put on her helmet, but stood her ground. "I take it since we're headed for Santa Fe that the Gordon Corp menace has been defused."

"A woman after my own heart. Cautious." Tony chuckled. "Mayburn's on ice, and all but a few of the truckers have been rounded up. Those'll be scattered to the winds by now, but every law enforcement agency in the country is looking for them."

"And you don't think you need to be in on the chase?"

He met her level stare. "I'm right where I want to be."

"You're such a smooth talker . . . when you want to be." She slid onto the seat behind him and wrapped her arms around his waist. "Let's see what this pavement burner can do."

"You got it, darlin'." He revved the engine, and the smooth snarl sent them onto the street.

Oh, my.

How right she'd been.

Riding a motorcycle with Tony gave a whole new dimension to fun. The stark but beautiful New Mexico countryside whizzed past. No-man's-land, wild and free. The wind plucked at their clothes and whistled past helmeted ears, sometimes stealing their breath. No conversation. Just the feel of Tony's muscles as he guided the big bike north on two-lane back roads. Way more interesting than the interstate.

An odd claustrophobia crept over her as

they reentered civilization. The bike drew stares from motorists and pedestrians as they wound through the streets of quaint Santa Fe. At last they stopped in front of a pair of joined adobe buildings. The sign read *Georgia O'Keeffe Museum.*

Tony handed her off the bike.

She shook out one leg then the other. "Not used to that mode of transportation."

He stood and swept off his helmet. Love what that thing did to his hair. Made him all bad boy Marlon Brando. Her fingers itched to comb through the pesky waves he hated. She hid her hands behind her back.

"You going to walk in with that thing on?" He grinned at her.

She unsnapped her helmet and handed it to him.

He patted the bike's handlebar. "Should get one of these. Maybe we could ride often."

Desi bit back the "yes" that tried to come out and turned toward the museum, but not before she saw his face settle into planes of disappointment. Maybe this trip was a bad idea. She needed time to think, and here she was letting him lead her in a direction they might not be able to go.

They went inside and left their helmets at the front desk while they toured the exhibits.

The sweeping lines and stark splendor of the art stroked her with calming fingers. Tony's hand found hers, and she didn't pull away.

"I like that one." He pointed to the Black Mesa landscape. "Can we see if they have a print in the gift shop? I could hang it in my living room."

An hour later they arrived at the gift shop. Closing time breathed down their necks, so they split up to look for the scene Tony wanted. Desi hummed as she browsed, her gaze often distracted from the prints to the live male who dominated the room. The woman behind the counter seemed to have the same problem. *Put your eyes back in your head, lady. This one's taken.*

What was she thinking? *Put your eyes back in* your *head, Des.*

She looked at the next print and froze. Where had she seen this one before? Ah, yes, the original hung in the Albuquerque museum. Maybe she should buy this one for herself. Bold colors. Trademark flowing lines. The desertscape sucked attention straight to the dark doorways of the cliff dwellings in the background. The scene looked familiar. She'd seen this cliff somewhere other than in Georgia's painting.

Little ants crawled across her scalp. A

photograph from the Inner Witness office popped up in her memory. Reverend Romlin and Ham Gordon shaking hands over a ground-breaking ceremony, a picture that was now missing, along with everything else in the abandoned office.

"Tony?" Her voice quivered.

He joined her. "You found it?"

"Not your landscape. The location of Sanctuary." She pointed. "All we have to do is research where this painting was done." She explained about the ground-breaking photograph.

Tony frowned. "The photo could have been taken at the location of Gordon's new home."

"He'd never be allowed property within view of an ancient dwelling site. Georgia, on the other hand, didn't find her inspiration along the beaten path. This place might not even be on any map, but the directions to it could be in historical archives on the artist."

"Okay, we'll follow up."

He believed her. She'd almost stopped believing herself.

He snapped his fingers. "How about we buzz back to Albuquerque. We can get a researcher on it. One of our people that specializes in that sort of thing will get results faster than either of us. Besides, the wait will give us a chance to go out for dinner. Someplace nice."

Desi looked down at her clothes. "Not too nice. This is all I have to wear."

He laughed and brushed fingertips down her cheek. Desi looked away. The man was getting to her without half trying. *Where's your backbone, Des?*

"We can fix the wardrobe tomorrow." He spread his arms. "I offer myself a willing sacrifice on the shopping altar."

Just call me jellyfish. "I'll hold you to that." She tottered away, smiling.

Outside the building, she turned and gripped the open edges of his jacket. "Wouldn't it be wonderful if Sanctuary was found . . . with a live-and-well Karen? Jo and Brent think she was still okay a couple of days ago when Jo's car went missing."

Tony frowned and looked at his watch. "Guess I can tell you now. Ortiz should have had enough time to inform Mrs. Cheama." He breathed deep and let the air out. "Karen didn't take her mother's car. Tank confessed to the theft, as well as running Pete Cheama off the road."

"But where did he get the keys to Jo's car? And what about the blood drops?"

"He hot-wired it. Said Mayburn told him

to grab the vehicle in order to stir up the hunt for Karen, take eyes off their operation. He doesn't know where she is, or even if Mayburn had anything to do with her disappearance. The blood at Jo's is Tank's. He cut himself jimmying the car door open. We still don't know who left blood evidence at the museum."

One step forward, two steps back. *Aaak!* Desi whirled and marched toward the motorcycle.

Tony's hand on her shoulder stopped her, and his dark gaze searched her face. "You mad at me for not telling you sooner."

Her hand covered his. "No, hon. Jo deserved to know first. It's not confidential things about your job that bug me. It's . . . well, let's not ride that old mule again. Okay? Our steed awaits." She spread her hands toward the gleaming Harley.

"Let me call in first. Get someone started on the hunt for your mystery location."

Tony finished a brief conversation and folded his phone away, but didn't put on his helmet. "I want to tell you something that I've never discussed with anyone except my mother. Ever."

"I'm listening." Desi went still on the inside.

"You were right about that Capone thing

bugging me. Not because I'm ashamed. Because I'm angry about what that man's choice did to my family line. What it's still doing. My great-grandfather wasn't an ordinary kneecap breaker. He spearheaded the infamous St. Valentine's Day massacre. He and several other wise guys riddled a group of unarmed men from a rival mob with over 150 bullets. Great-granddad enjoyed his job."

Desi shivered.

Tony frowned. "Remember what I said about a single choice impacting generations? Maybe unleashing spiritual forces?"

She nodded.

"I have shirttail cousins still in the mob. They can't see any other way to live."

Desi shook her head. "Now I don't have to feel bad about being related to Ham Gordon."

He flashed a smile then sobered again. "My grandfather walked away from the lifestyle when he was barely past puberty. The mob relatives cast him off like he was a traitor to some sacred cause. But he made a life in a little town in Iowa and became a pharmacist."

"Good for him! That must be where you get your determination and integrity from."

"Not everything worked out great. There's

another branch of the Lucanos that has always been honest. Stick straight. They didn't welcome granddad back onto the narrow path. Wouldn't have anything to do with him or his children. As large as our family is, my mom and me — and my dad when he was alive — have never been welcome among them." He looked away from her, lips compressed. "It's like we're tainted forever in their eyes."

"Oh, Tony." She put her arms around him. "That's got to hurt."

He pulled her close. "My mom's been praying up a storm and holding out olive branches. We're starting to see a thaw, but . . ." He shook his head.

"But what?" She looked up at him.

"I'm not sure I want to know the people who thought they were too good for us. My dad might be alive today if he hadn't felt driven to prove something. He specialized in going after mobsters, and a Chinese mafioso killed him. Almost killed me, too. Seems like the mob — or the spiritual forces behind organized crime — meant to get us one way or another." He met her gaze. "Does that sound out in left field?"

"Not a bit. When evils sinks its teeth into people, it doesn't like to let go. We'd never break away without God on our side. This

Romlin character prattles about the body and blood, but there's nothing in it unless it has the power to move us from the kingdom of darkness into the kingdom of light."

Tony nodded. "I know that's why I'm still here, but I think family attitudes play a key role one way or another. The clean-living Lucanos left us out in the cold when they should have rallied around us. Should I forget that and play old-home week with the self-righteous bunch?"

Desi touched his cheek. "But staying aloof from your relatives will perpetuate the problem into another generation."

"Knowing that doesn't change how I feel."

"I hear you." She wrinkled her nose. "But sometimes we have to rise above our feelings and do what's right until the emotions line up with the actions." She gasped. "Oh, *nuts!*"

"Nuts?"

"This means I have to go see Dean. If I'm going to tell you to forgive and change the cycle of destruction, I have to do the same thing."

Tony chuckled. "Then I guess if you can, I can. Let's get back to Albuquerque and see if we can bust the devil's chops some more by finding a missing woman."

"You're on." Desi climbed on the bike

behind Tony and hugged his waist. "Thanks."

She didn't need to explain what she was thanking him for. She heard his understanding in the gruff "Welcome" right before the cycle roared to life.

Out on the narrow county highway, a road less traveled, Desi laid her head against Tony's broad back and watched the scenery fly by. Warm contentment flowed from deep within.

What a marvelous creation You thought up, Lord. And if Karen's no longer part of it, I trust that Your mercy brought her back on the right path in the end. All I ask now is that You grant closure to the family she left behind. In Your Son's name.

The blast of an air horn brought her head up. Tony's back stiffened. Their heads swiveled in tandem. The grinning grill of a monster semi roared down on them. A hundred feet, maybe less. Closing fast. Beneath her, the bike leaped forward, tires screeching on the pavement.

She gripped Tony tighter and looked back again. Tons of flame-red metal whooshed toward them as if they were stalled on the highway. Seventy-five feet. Less. A dark windshield hid the driver. The air horn wailed again, sending shivers to Desi's core.

The cycle's engine screamed. Tony leaned forward, helmeted head almost to the handlebars. Desi pressed close. His heart beat hard against her hands locked around his chest. Hers drummed in echo. *God, help us.*

Wind tore at the strands of hair that poked from beneath her helmet. Speed pressed her cheeks against her teeth and fluttered her lips. Her eyes watered from windburn, despite her visor. But Tony was taking the brunt. His big, gloved hands held steady on the throttle. The bike clung to the highway around one curve, another, speed increasing.

Engine heat radiated onto her legs, then her back. Her back!

She glanced behind. Metal teeth snarled at her from an enraged giant that filled her vision. The creature breathed hot coals from its belly onto her neck.

The bike wobbled. Desi screamed and looked forward. A second semi shimmered toward them from the opposite direction, a metallic blue rocket.

Muscles gathered in Tony's back. Desi clung.

They swept into another curve, but the cycle held straight and went airborne as it left the pavement. Her stomach curled around her backbone. The tires hit the packed desert sand, telegraphing protests from her tailbone. The rear wheel dug in and threw a cloud of powder and sun-browned grasses. Sage smell clogged her nostrils. Desi choked, grit stung her cheeks, and they surged ahead. Waffling. Slowing. No, gaining speed.

To her left, the blue semi plowed toward them through a stand of yucca, flinging spiky leaves and branches before its gaping maw.

A rise loomed ahead. The cycle labored to climb in the clinging sand. The tires bit bedrock and the bike flew forward, topped the rise, plunged down. A cluster of rocks grabbed the front wheel. The rear end whipped into the air. Desi flew, somersaulting in midflight.

Bright pain splintered through her body, and the light winked out.

Twenty

A tunnel opened far away, and Desi saw light. Was she supposed to walk toward it? Isn't that what some people said about life after death? She blinked. Wait a second. Do people blink after they die? And their mouths sure wouldn't taste like they'd eaten dirt for breakfast.

She turned her head and disturbed angry bruises up and down her body. Not dead then. But where? All was dark except for the patch of light she lay in. The small hole that admitted the beam opened in a stone ceiling. She patted the surface beneath her. More stone. A cave?

"You're awake." The female voice came from a place behind where her head rested.

Desi sat up, ignoring the protest of stiff muscles. Her head whirled. She closed her eyes and swallowed. Gradually, her mind cleared. She opened her eyes, grateful when the room stayed steady.

On a stone ledge sat a woman in a white robe. An angel come to carry her to glory?

The woman rose and stepped into the light, robe swishing. The garment was little more than a long sack. Dirty bare toes peeped beneath it. Her dark hair hung lank and uncombed around her shoulders, but rose to a widow's peak at the forehead.

"Karen." Desi breathed the name. "We found you."

"You shouldn't have looked." Karen squatted beside her, hugging her legs to her chest, robe puddled around her. "Who are you and why would you care?"

"Desiree Jacobs." Desi touched the girl's knee. "Your Aunt Max's best friend."

Karen's dark eyes widened. "The one who captured a terrorist? *That* Desiree Jacobs?"

"At the time it seemed the other way around, but I guess it's how things end up that counts."

The girl rocked back and forth. "Things haven't ended well now. Not the way I intended. I wanted to protect them, but I'm here, and nothing's been fixed."

"What are you talking about?"

"Adam. Brent. My mom. Are they all right?"

"They're fine, but they miss you. Did you run away, or were you kidnapped?"

The girl licked cracked lips. "Both."

"But —"

Karen gripped her arm hard enough to hurt. "Can you get us out of here?"

Desi looked around. "Where's here?"

The young woman's gaze roamed around the twilit walls that became more visible with every passing moment. A second source of light came from a rectangular doorway behind her. "An Anasazi cliff dwelling. It's in a blind canyon closed off by a rock slide. I haven't been able to find a way out. But someone like you —"

"Where's Tony?" Desi turned her head in every direction. The bare room had grown light enough to see, but no one else occupied the space.

Karen stood. "You mean the dude they put down in the kiva hole? Can't get to him, but he sounds like he might be bad hurt."

Desi leaped up, and pain flashed up her leg. She staggered and cried out. Karen stopped her from toppling with an arm around her shoulder. Desi leaned into the robed woman. "Show me." She jerked her chin toward the door.

Desi hobbled behind Karen onto a wide ledge overlooking a narrow valley between sheer sandstone cliffs. She squinted against the sunlight. Morning, but not early because the sun didn't reach this gouge in the earth until it was well up.

"Come on." Karen motioned her toward a set of hand and foot holds carved into the wall. She climbed down the six feet or so to the valley floor.

Favoring her leg, Desi followed. At least the ankle wasn't broken. Karen picked up a fat clay jar from a rock. The pot had several small spouts with tiny openings. She put a spout to her lips and guzzled, then thrust the jar at Desi. "You're supposed to have some."

Stop for a drink or find Tony? She pushed the container away. "Tony first. He might need it more than we do."

Karen led across sparse, yellowed vegetation, around a nest of boulders, and across a patch of stone to an earth-covered mound about twenty feet in diameter. "He's down there."

Desiree knelt at the edge of the kiva and gazed into the pit through a crack in dirt-covered wooden slats that were little more than sticks.

"Tony?" Desi's heart throbbed with the silence that answered. She looked up at Karen, who stood with slumped shoulders and dangling arms. Desi stood and grasped Karen's shoulders. The girl was thinner than the photo she'd seen, and from her pinched face, no doubt dehydrated. "How deep is the pit? Can we use the ladder?"

"Wouldn't even reach halfway." She brushed a lock of hair out of one dull eye.

"Who put him down there, and how did they do it?"

"Lowered him with ropes, but they took them with them when they left."

"You keep saying 'they'? Who did this?"

Karen blinked at her. "The one with the bandage on his hand and the one that flies. They keep coming here looking for something, but they don't find it. Makes 'em mad."

"Looking for what?"

Karen made a squiggle in the sand with her big toe. "Don't know."

Desi crossed her arms. "You're holding back on me, Karen. You've got to know more than you're saying."

Her nostrils flared, and the vagueness receded from her face. "You have no idea what's planned. They've given me my robe of sacrifice." She spread her garment. Her mouth slackened, and she looked up at the sky. "They'll come for us later."

Desi groaned. The woman hadn't gone dim-witted — she was drugged. "What's in the drinking pot?"

Karen's shoulders rippled. "Water. Not the stuff that drips out of the wall back in the cave. Tastes awful." She made a face. "The good stuff. What they give me."

"Quit drinking the good stuff. The bad stuff is better for you."

Karen squinted at her and comprehension flickered. "Okay."

A low moan floated up from the kiva pit. Desi's breath caught. "We're going to get down there, and you're going to help me. Take me to the bitter water."

Karen put a finger to her lips. "They don't know about the spring."

Desi leaned close. "It'll be our secret."

Karen headed toward the farther cliff on tiptoe. Whatever was in that joy juice had to be potent and fast acting. Desi followed the dipsy-doodle leader around an outcropping in the striated sandstone. They stopped at a hand-width fissure tucked into a wrinkle in the cliff face.

"Here we are." Karen giggled like a flower child. "Clever, huh?"

"If you're a gecko or a snake." Some of those critters could be in there. Desi shuddered and stepped back.

"Oh, come on, 'fraidy-cat." She walked forward and disappeared into the cliff.

"Hey!" Desi moved ahead and passed

through into cool dimness. She looked back. Optical illusion. The fold in the wall disguised an opening that more than accommodated a slender female. Clever, indeed. No wonder their captors hadn't found this place.

Ahead, Desi spotted a glimmer of light, but no Karen.

"In here." The young woman's voice pulled Desi forward.

Forty cautious steps downward and at a right angle brought her to the edge of a spacious grotto. Sunlight poured down from a larger hole than the one in the cliff dwelling where she woke up. A steady *plink, plink* echoed softly. Desi crunched across sparkling grit toward a small pool that formed at the base of a natural spout of stone that jutted from the wall at the height of her head. As she watched, a bead of water formed, fattened, stretched, and released. *Plink.*

Water from a rock. Moses would be as green as the stripes on the wall.

Stripes on the wall? Desi looked closer. She ran a finger along the greenish tint, then the bluish layer. Finally, two plus two added up the way it should. All this booga-booga about a cult compound in the desert — just a smoke screen for the oldest motivator for crime in the book.

She turned and found Karen kneeling at the pool's edge. The young woman dipped a hand, brought it to her lips, and grimaced. "Nasty. Tastes like copper."

"Because it has a high copper content. Reason aplenty for some greedy creepazoid to want a secret base in the desert so he can look for what you've found. If this is high-grade ore, the Pueblo Santa Rita operation will look like chump change. And if it's not on res land, whoever stakes the claim is lousy, stinkin' rich."

Karen stared at her with huge eyes. "You mean I've found something important?"

"Girl, you buy up this patch of sand in the middle of who-knows-where, and Adam's college fund will leave the latest Trump baby's in the shade."

Karen stood, robe fisted in her hands. "I never thought I could do anything great."

"Depends on how you define great. For me that's getting Tony out of a pit."

The girl's face blanked then brightened. "Yeah, him." She bit her lip. "I'm sorry. I want to help, but I can't seem to . . ." She pressed her palms to her temples.

"Stay here. Drink some of this water, but don't guzzle a gallon, or you'll risk copper poisoning. Come find me when your head clears. I'm going to look around for some way to get at Tony."

Desi retraced her steps. When she emerged from the crevice, she looked back and shook her head. Amazing! Less than two feet from the opening, and it looked like nothing more than a crack in the sandstone. Her heart sank. If Karen had made this well-hidden discovery, she'd scoured the canyon for a way out. And if the young woman's days of searching hadn't found an escape, what made her think she could reach Tony in the pit, much less succeed in leaving this canyon where Karen had failed.

Her gaze swept the cliff line then halted above a tumble of boulders. What was that? She crossed the open space to the mound of rock. She wasn't dreaming. Etched into the cliff face were shallow grooves at even intervals. Manmade, but old and weathered in a way that would take a long time in this dry climate. She followed the grooves upward as far as she could make them out. An ancient Anasazi ladder. Useless now.

Gladness gripped her. Why wasn't she disappointed?

A picture came to her mind, and her heart tripped over itself. She clung to the side of the Tate Art Gallery building, fingers and toes jammed into too tight spaces. She smelled the brick. Tasted the desperation. Then the sensation of falling. Her stomach lurched.

She clutched her middle and plopped down on a boulder. Another shot at wall-climbing would be tempting God. Big no-no.

That was good, because she wouldn't do it. Couldn't walk through that horror again.

Tony jerked awake, and his body howled a protest. A long groan left his lips. Had a herd of elephants trampled him? He opened his eyes to darkness striped with slivers of light that pierced a covering above him. Where was he? What happened?

His mind scrambled to remember. He saw desert landscape fly past. A hill, rocks, and then a screech of twisting metal. Motorcycle crash. Very messy.

Des! Where was she?

"Desiree?" No answer. The sound of his voice communicated enclosed space.

The air was dry, stale, and hot. He smelled his own sweat. Tiny legs crawled across the skin of his wrist. Millipede. He yanked the arm away, and pain raked through him. Dislocated right shoulder for sure. What else?

Breathing hurt. He ran his left hand up

and down his torso. No blood beneath the shredded motorcycle jacket. He tried light pressure. "Aaaah!" He lay panting. A couple busted ribs. Maybe other things wrong on the inside. His gut burned.

That left his legs. He bent a knee and pulled one leg up, then the other. Both of them good to go, if only the rest of him would go with. Just the thought of moving his upper body hurt.

"Tony?" The voice filtered down from above.

His heart leaped, and pain shot through his rib cage. "Des?" The word came out a gasp. "You all right?"

"Better now that I hear your voice, but hon, I can't get to you. You're down in a kiva pit. I've searched this whole canyon, and there's nothing —"

"Canyon? Take it easy, and tell me where we are."

"I don't know." Her voice went thin. "A blind canyon in the desert. No way out except up. There are a few Anasazi dwellings in the cliff face, but this wasn't a major settlement."

She sounded discouraged, not at all Desiree. "Are we at the site of that O'Keeffe painting?"

"No, but if snatching us is part of Ham

Gordon's cult fantasies, we could be near it."

He grunted. "Makes sense Gordon's behind this. He's still on the loose, and I knew he was dirty."

"That and just plain nuts."

"No argument here, darlin'. So if there's no way out but up, maybe they get in by helicopter."

"Fits with what Karen told me."

"Karen? She's here?" Tony struggled onto one elbow, ribs screeching. A drop of sweat from his forehead stung his eye. "I'm going to . . . *groan* . . . stand up. See how close I am to the top of the hole."

"It's twelve feet down if it's an inch."

"Can you remove some of the covering?"

"I can try." The words were listless. "But I think you're stuck."

What was with her? His Desi never said never. He heard digging and grunting. Dirt splatted his jacket. He edged away and came up against a wall. Above, a patch of light grew. Careful maneuvering brought his body into a sitting position against the side of the kiva. Desi was right. Climbing out of this thing wasn't an option. Even if he could reach the lip, which he couldn't even with a running leap, he was capable of neither the leap nor pulling himself out.

"That's good, Des. You can stop."

Her face appeared in the opening. "I could lower myself over the edge, and then jump the rest of the way. I want to hold you." She cleared her throat. "I mean, I want you to hold me."

"Nothing I'd like better, sweetheart, but you don't need to be trapped down here, too."

"What's the difference between being trapped down there or up here?"

Des, snap out of this. "Up there maybe you can find a way to escape and go for help."

Her head disappeared. No sound, and then a little sob.

"Des, talk to me."

"I found a place the Anasazi used to climb in and out." Her shadow covered the opening, but he couldn't see her. "They must have been little like me, small feet and hands. But it's impossible. The finger- and toeholds have weathered. Maybe they're even crumbling. Besides, I have a sore ankle."

So that was it. She felt guilty for not being superwoman. "It's okay, hon. If you say it's impossible, it is. I trust your judgment."

"You do?" Her face reappeared. "You could've fooled me."

Now there was his fierce Desi.

She scowled down at him. "I didn't dare tell you why my toe was sore when you picked me up for the White House bash, because you would've had a fit. I was doing a human fly on the side of a skyscraper. Not on purpose. It just happened, and there I was — in a situation with no Tony to save me. Just me and God, and He got me through in time for our date. How's that for divine protection?"

The burn in Tony's middle heated up. "How am I supposed to respond to that? You're up there. I'm down here. And why are you telling me now?"

The spunk drained from her face. "I just wanted you to know that I could get through situations without . . . Never mind. Stay here. I need to think."

Stay here? Where did she think he'd go? "Des?" Silence. The hole showed nothing but sky.

Hissing through gritted teeth, Tony worked himself to his feet. He swayed and steadied himself against the wall with his good arm. His injured arm dangled, aching.

She was gone, stuck with life-and-death issues bigger than she was. The cruds who put them in here could arrive at any moment, and he couldn't help her.

■ ■ ■ ■

Some cat burglar *she* was!

Desi stared up at the cliff face, heart fluttering. Each gouged-out hand- and toehold mocked her. *Foolish Anglo,* ancient voices taunted. *You cannot go where we went. We were agile. Our feet had wings. Our fingers the strength of talons.*

Desi climbed the rock pile that led to the base of the cliff-ladder. She fitted her hands in the highest holds she could reach. Lifted a foot and put it in the crevice. Then the other foot, ignoring her complaining ankle. Her cheek pressed against the warm rock. She could do this. She must.

Up a notch. Hand. Hand. Foot. Foot. Hand up, but slipping on grit. The arm flopped down, and she cried out as she fell and lay crumpled against a boulder, breathing in, out, staring straight ahead. Something stared back at her.

Not something — someone! The eyeholes of a skull gaped at her.

Desi screamed and scrambled back until she hit a rock. She swallowed her heart back into her chest. Whoever that dead person had been, the bleached remains couldn't hurt her. She crawled back to the cracked and grinning skull. No other bones lay where she could see. Scavengers must have carried them off, leaving this testimony of a climber who never made it.

And she couldn't make the climb either. Foolish to try. Darkness swelled inside her. She hugged her knees as Karen had done on their first meeting. May as well dress her in a robe of sacrifice, too.

"I give up." She put her head in her hands.

Hurting and nauseous, Tony slid down the wall of the ancient kiva. He cradled his injured arm between his bent legs and his chest.

God, You leave me no choice. I give her into Your hands.

"Pssst. You awake down there?"

Tony looked up to see a woman looking down at him, face framed by long dark hair.

"You're Karen Webb. Lots of people are looking for you. Me included."

"Because you're a friend of Desiree Jacobs?"

"No, because I'm an FBI agent."

"Really? Cool." She looked to both sides, then back at him. "I want to confess."

Tony's chuckle turned into a moan. "Be my guest."

"I took a bunch of Anasazi artifacts and

hid them."

Tony's heart sank. Desi was going to be disappointed, not to mention family members devastated. He stretched out a leg. "I'm surprised. I'd pretty much decided you weren't in on the museum theft. Did you also club your accomplice a little too hard on the head?"

"What? No way! I didn't take the things from the *museum*. I stole them from Hamilton Gordon, and he was hopping mad. Couldn't do what he wanted with them."

"You're using past tense. Did he get the items back?"

Heavy sigh. "Last night when he brought you two in, he said they'd found 'his property.' " She snorted. "Like he's got a drop of Pueblo blood!" She hung her head. "I'm not surprised he found the stuff though. I didn't have much time to stash them. Pretty worthless, huh?"

"I'd call it courageous but a little misguided — like someone else I know." He shifted his arm into a less painful position. "Fill in the blanks for me. Gordon robbed the museum —"

"Not Gordon. He had someone do it for him. I doubt he even knew how it was done."

"All right, he took custody of the goods

after someone else stole them. Then you grabbed the artifacts from him where and when?"

"The day after the theft. If I let Gordon keep the things from the museum, he meant to do something bad to someone innocent . . . like Adam." She stopped and bit her lip. "But if not Adam, someone else pure and fresh. I had to stop him. So after Adam went down for his afternoon nap, I watched until I saw Brent's car coming toward the house, and then I ran out the back door into the alley and took off in our old rattletrap Honda. Drove up to Gordon's new estate. He welcomed me in as a fellow believer, and I whipped out this pistol my daddy gave me when I was a teenager, grabbed the Anasazi stuff, and hopscotched off into the desert. Thought I could make it to friends of my father's and disappear for a while. But then my car broke down, and Gordon's dudes caught me, and here I am."

"But they didn't catch you before you hid the goods."

"Right."

"And why did you do all this instead of reporting Gordon to the police."

"Who would believe me? Some crazy is going to kill and eat people using an ancient

Indian ritual? Nope. But I knew right away who took the stuff and why. And it was my fault. I had to fix it."

A piece of the dirt roof came loose and hit the floor near Tony's foot. He coughed and wished he hadn't. "How was it your fault?"

The girl stared down at him. "Guess I'd better get it off my chest. It's not like anyone else is ever going to know. We're due to be the main course of a sacred meal."

"I wouldn't bet on that Karen. We have the Lord Jesus Christ on our side."

"The Lamb of God? He's what got Gordon thinking about taking the body and blood to the next level. I figure he's on Gordon's side."

Tony shook his head. "Not the empty fantasy Gordon made up. The real Jesus, the One you believed in when you married Brent and had Adam."

Karen gave a strangled noise, and her head disappeared. The sound of running feet faded.

Way to go, Lucano. Chase her off just when the conversation is getting interesting.

Heat settled over him like an unwelcome blanket. Reality faded, and he drifted in a fog filled with pain and dread.

Dirt plopped onto his head. He sneezed

and cried out, red haze filtering through his brain.

"Sorry."

Karen. Tony's eyes popped open. She stared down at him with a tear-streaked face.

"Desiree needs you. She's sitting in the sun with her head in her lap. What do we do? She can get us out of here. I know it."

"Your Inner Witness tell you that?"

"Forget about that stuff. I think . . ." She let out a breath. "I think I quit believing when I found out what Hope did with the information I gave her. Now I don't know what I believe. Jesus wouldn't want me back anyway."

"Don't be too sure about that. What did you tell Hope?"

She sighed. "The ditz came to visit me two days before the theft. Hadn't seen her in a couple of weeks. We never hit it off, but there she was all sisterhood on me. Guess I was lonely, so I let her in. She cooed and gushed all over Adam. Kept calling him the perfect little lamb. The way she said it spooked me. That and the brochure she left about healing sacraments helped me put two and two together after I heard about the theft.

"At the time, I didn't understand why her

interest in Adam bugged me. But then she changed the subject and told me a bunch of confidential stuff about her job with the ministry. Made me jealous. The Reverend Romlin trusted her with *everything,* and this bigwig CEO Ham Gordon had an Inner Circle going, and she was in it. All I got to know at the museum was where the keys were to the display cases."

"And you think that information helped the thieves get the artifacts?"

She lifted her chin. "It did."

"I've got news for you, Karen. A computer virus disabled the alarm system, but the case that held the artifacts was smashed, not unlocked. They never touched the keys."

The woman's mouth dropped open. "So I didn't help them get the artifacts?"

"Nope. But you shouldn't have tried to handle the problem on your own."

"I had to. This *voice* kept telling me it was my fault, and I had to make it right."

"Any time you're driven, not led, the voice isn't God's."

"But I left my baby, my husband . . ." She made strangled noises, shaking her long mane from side to side. "All for nothing."

"Don't run off on me again."

Karen stopped shaking her head, but she didn't look at him.

"We've got to help Desi. I want you to tell her something for me."

She peeked at him between the curtain of her hair.

Tony made himself smile. Then he gave her his message for Desiree, some of the hardest words he'd spoken in his life.

A shadow fell across Desi, and she looked up. Karen had sand in her hair and dirty tear streaks down her cheeks, but her gaze was clear. A little copper water did the trick.

The young woman wavered a smile. "I came from Tony. He gave me some things to think about."

Not just water. A stiff dose of Lucano practicality. Good for him. She looked away across the sterile valley. "You made your peace with Jesus?"

"Not yet, but I think I will." She crouched to Desi's level, her Pueblo features dominating the Anglo green eyes. "He told me to tell you something."

"I'm listening."

"He said to say it just this way, so act like this is him talking." She closed her eyes. "Tony says, 'I thought all the scary things that happened to you these past few days were to teach you to live more cautiously, but now I see they were to teach me that

I'm not your protector. God is. Whatever He tells you to do, do it. You'll be fine.' "
She opened her eyes. "That mean anything to you?"

Electricity washed through Desiree. Shackles she hadn't known were there melted like ice on a sun-baked stone. Maybe she hadn't missed God's leading the past few days. Maybe there was still a purpose. She stretched out her legs and stood up. Lifting one arm and then the other, she reached toward the pale heavens. Every muscle tingled.

"I'm terrified, Lord, and You know I don't want to do this. Can't do it alone. So if I've messed up, and I'm not hearing You right, I'll die. So what? At least I give my life trying to help Tony and Karen, not on some crazy man's altar." She lowered her arms.

Karen stared at her with eyes as big as silver dollars.

Desi smiled. "Let's go get some of that bitter water. I need a drink before I climb a cliff."

TWENTY-ONE

Ten feet up, Desi paused. She puffed from her mouth like a woman in labor doing Lamaze. Only ninety more feet. Keep going. Her ankle ached, but the hand- and toeholds were sturdy. A little deeper would have been nice. Maybe they'd get better higher up. Maybe not.

Don't think about that.

She moved up like a human spider on the wall. Thank goodness there was no wind. Another pause. Don't look down. Not up either. A small laugh passed her lips. The look on Karen's face when she said she was going to climb the cliff belonged in a museum. A few more puffs, and she went on. Sweat soaked her skin, her clothes. She blinked moisture from her eyes. Was she halfway yet?

Don't ask, just keep going.

A little more. The sun baked her back, stronger now than when she was at the bottom of the canyon. Another step up. She had to be — oops! A hand slipped. She smacked it back onto the cliff and grabbed. The dismal truth crept upon her consciousness. The holds were getting smaller, along with her strength. The muscles in her calves trembled.

Puffing air, she studied the cliff face. Up and to the left a piece of rock jutted. Narrow, but no more narrow than the ledge she'd conquered at the Tate Building. If she could reach it, she could rest. If the lip would hold her weight.

Almost there. Got to go higher. Her hand reached for the hold. Not there. Panic grabbed her throat. Gurgling, she pressed herself against the rock wall. *Try again, girl.* Systematically, she probed the cliff for the depression. Her eyes widened. Nothing. She inched her chin up and rolled her eyes skyward, searching for the top of the cliff. Close, but not close enough. Twenty feet might as well be two thousand. Her holds had run out.

She fixed her gaze on the ledge. No way to reach it except to lunge sideways and grasp the edge. And if she succeeded in pulling herself onto the perch, she was trapped, because going down wasn't an option.

Lord, You ask us to take the next step we can see and leave the rest to You. Here goes.

Her muscles gathered, released. Airborne. Her fingers curled around the edge of the outcropping. One hand slipped. She brought it back. Grabbed. Now she dangled eighty feet in the air over a pile of unforgiving rock eager to break her and drink her blood.

Yuck! Get that image out of your mind, Des.

An odd fact intruded on her awareness. The place where she gripped the ledge was curved inward, a tailor-made handhold.

Do a pull-up now.

She'd done thousands in her little lifetime. She strained. Her body drew up toward the ledge. She stuck a bent leg out to give herself leverage against the cliff wall.

There!

She sprawled full-length on a narrow table of stone, breathing and laughing. So what if she had no idea where to go next.

A cheer wafted up from below. Muscles quivering, Desi peered over the edge and waved. The dark-haired woman waved back and then took off toward the kiva. At least Tony would get the news that she was alive, even though she'd failed her assignment.

Desi got to her knees on the ledge and looked around. She made the climb, but what was the point? Too bad she didn't have a rope. She could attach it to the thumb of rock jutting on the far side of the ledge and let herself down. That outcropping was worn in a way that suggested ropes had been used on it before.

She sighed and examined the cliff face above her. As she'd thought, no hand- or toeholds. They petered out at the level of her perch. Why did the Anasazi make the gouges at all? An ancient practical joke? If so, it was a dangerous one.

She just prayed it wasn't fatal as well.

The sun hurt her eyes, and she looked down at the cliff face near her thighs. Something glittered inside the rock. *Inside?* Desi looked closer and found a crevice no wider than a fist about a foot above the place where the ledge pushed out from the cliff. A spark flashed again. Desi swallowed. Should she reach inside? Who knew what scaly critter might be in there?

Curiosity killed the cat, and it could be the death of Desiree Jacobs, because the force was impossible to resist. Okay, just put a couple of fingers in there, and see if she could reach the shiny object without disturbing any rock-dwelling denizens. Holding her breath, she probed and brushed something hard that moved with a small scrape. She jerked her hand out of the hole.

Quit being silly! What she'd touched wasn't alive. She reached in, grabbed the object, and pulled it out. A necklace. The long gold chain dangled from her fingers. The links were thick and heavy, and on the end swayed a large, round medallion studded with green stones. This was no Anasazi work or even Pueblo. Pure Spanish and old, too — a relic from the days when the Spaniards of Mexico dominated the region.

Desi looked toward the ground. Had this necklace belonged to whoever died at the base of the cliff? Made tragic sense. Maybe the person, either a woman or a boy, judging from the size of the skull, made the climb, but when she got up here, she realized the same thing Desi did. This was no way out, and there was no way down. Rather than face a slow death under the merciless sun, perhaps that person jumped, leaving behind this testimony of who she was.

Desi slid the necklace back into the crevice. The creeps who'd be dropping by soon didn't need to get their grubby hands on it. But if she got out of this mess alive, she'd come back to investigate. A piece like this had a history, and so did the person who'd owned it.

Desi stood and surveyed the canyon. How could she find this place again if she needed to? From here she could see the entire canyon. At one end, it narrowed into a closed point. On the other end, an earthquake or other natural disaster had collapsed a cliff wall into an impassable barrier.

Her gaze traced the ridgeline opposite. A red stain like someone had tossed the contents of a giant paint can splashed the cliff at her eye level. The stain rose into the air on a monolith of rock jabbing high above the rest of the canyon face. The way the red finger pointed, it wouldn't be visible from the floor of the canyon, but it would be from the air. A perfect landmark. No chance of their captors mislaying them. They could be here anytime.

Desi sighed and sat down, dangling her legs over the edge of the rock lip. She could only wait for rescue by the bad guys. How ironic was that?

That crazy-wonderful woman made it to a safe spot! If anything other than his legs were working, Tony would have danced. He laughed instead, and even that was too much. Man, he was a wreck. But a happy wreck.

All they could do now was wait for Gordon and company. He didn't expect mercy, but he wouldn't give any either. A strong set of legs was better than nothing, and let him anywhere near a gun . . . Ham Gordon better watch out.

Whump! Whump! Whump! The deep tone began as a vibration and grew.

Helicopter. Tony's heart beat in time with the rotors.

The wait was over.

The chopper's thunder shook the ledge under Desi's legs. A pale blue whirlybird lowered toward her. The gale wind of its rotors pressed her back against the cliff wall. She lifted an arm to protect her face, but peered above her elbow to watch the approach. The helicopter hovered level with her perch. She met the gaze of the passenger seated next to the pilot. Not Gordon. Reverend Archer Romlin. The preacher's slack-jawed stare mirrored her own.

Desi snapped her mouth shut. Why was she surprised? The guy was a shyster. And he'd approved of Ham Gordon's construction project in the wilderness. Goodness, he was even planning on setting up his own harem full of little Hopes. No doubt he was the one prospecting out here for copper.

Why shouldn't he be a full accomplice in this too-weird combination of greed and insanity? But he was a *minister,* for crying out loud. Guess there was something in people that expected a shred of decency out of someone who professed spiritual leadership.

The chopper rose, and a rope ladder fell toward her. Desi stood and reached for the rungs. All aboard who're going aboard. Like she had a choice.

Desi reached the open rear door, and male hands pulled her inside. One of the palms was wrapped in a dirty bandage that had probably started out white. She came face-to-face with a muscle-bound goon that had coyote breath and stained teeth. One of the truckers who ran them off the road yesterday? He shoved her into a seat, drew up the ladder, and slammed the door. The goon took the seat next to her and pulled a rifle onto his lap.

She glanced at the bandaged hand. "Been in any interesting museums lately?"

He stared at her, face blank. Probably couldn't hear over the din of the descending helicopter. They bumped onto the canyon floor, and the roar faded as the rotors slowed.

Romlin turned toward her. "Desiree Jacobs, I presume." He chuckled. "Who else might we expect to find camped out on a cliff-side aerie?"

The melodious voice flowed over Desi, and her heart rate gentled. She looked away from his silver gaze. Hypnotic man. No wonder people followed him.

He chuckled again. "Now we'll have Jack and George collect the other members of our party and be on our way. You and I can wait here." The muzzle of a handgun pointed toward her from Romlin's white fingers.

The pilot and the goon climbed out.

"How do they plan to get Tony out of that pit? He can hardly move."

"Don't worry." A scrape came from the pilot's side of the helicopter. "I believe that was George detaching the telescoping aluminum ladder. The federal agent will climb unless he wishes to perish of dehydration in that hole."

Heat flared in Desi's chest. "Maybe he'd prefer that over what you and Hamilton Gordon have planned."

Romlin shook his head. "Not me. Ham's developed his own outlandish theology. I don't understand how he got his notions from what I preach." The man shrugged. "But I make allowances for such a generous donor." Romlin flashed even white teeth.

This guy was greed personified. Wonder what *allowances* he'd make for news of the copper deposit right under his nose? Desi pressed her lips together. He wouldn't find out from her that his dream had been found. Let him go away as empty as Francisco Coronado in his quest for the Seven Cities of Cibola. That misguided search led to centuries of Spanish oppression over the Pueblo people. News of a copper find on unclaimed land surrounded by reservations would unleash a feeding frenzy among the rich and influential. Enough to endanger what land the tribes had. Karen better have enough wits about her to keep her mouth shut, too.

Out the front windshield, Desi saw the lanky pilot coming toward them herding a white-robed Karen, who picked her way with bare feet among the spiny vegetation.

"The Indian girl is quite striking," Romlin said. "Cleaned up a bit —"

"Keep your lecherous thoughts to yourself, you disgusting worm."

Romlin tut-tutted. "Name-calling doesn't become a Christian. You *are* one of those true believers, aren't you?" He cocked a brow at her.

"If Jesus called the scribes and Pharisees

snakes, naming a deceiver like you among those belly crawlers strikes me as right on target."

His eyes slitted, and the gun poked toward her. "You have a disturbing mouth."

Desi gripped the edges of her seat with sweaty palms. "So I've been told."

"Well, keep it shut." He turned his head. "Ah, here comes our last passenger."

"Tony." The name breathed between her lips.

He moved like a man treading on egg-shells. His left arm crossed his chest and clamped his right to his body. Behind him, Mr. Goon gave him a shove. Tony staggered and went to his knees, head thrown back in a silent scream.

Desi cried out and lunged forward. A gun barrel in the face forced her back into her seat.

The passenger door opened, and Karen climbed in behind Desi. Seconds later, Tony filled the doorway. A moan escaped as he crawled inside and took the seat beside her.

The goon with the gun took the last seat, right behind Tony, and the pilot started the engine. They climbed out of the canyon into a cloudless sky. The helicopter skimmed close to the earth, and small wildlife scattered before them. A short time later, the chopper took an abrupt turn around a butte, dropped, hovered, and then settled next to a bright orange bulldozer. The huge machine looked as out of place as a cactus in a rainforest.

The doors of cliff dwellings gaped in the face of the butte, just like in the O'Keeffe painting, but where was Sanctuary? Nothing in the landscape resembled the model she saw in Santa Fe . . . except for the humongous mound of earth ahead of them. The granddaddy of all kivas, and from the ribbon of smoke rising from a small chimney, it was occupied. No wonder Max hadn't found evidence of a clandestine construction project if this was all there was to Sanctuary.

Romlin got out, as well as the pilot, who also lugged an impressive firearm. Goon shoved Karen out ahead of him, and then hopped to the ground. The young woman shot Desi a frightened look between strands of hair whipped by the slowing rotors. Desi tried a smile, but managed only a frown and shake of the head. Romlin motioned her out with his gun. She stepped down and turned to help Tony, if they'd let her.

He staggered from his seat in a crouch, and then fell forward between the pilot and passenger seat, just missing the front panel.

He writhed, groaning.

"Get him out of there!" The pilot almost screeched the command. "Those are touchy instruments."

Romlin grabbed Desi's upper arm, and his gun pressed against her temple. "Mr. Lucano, I suggest you disembark before this pistol accidentally discharges."

"I'll be . . . right with you." Tony levered himself up using the front passenger seat and came out through the forward door.

They all headed for the kiva, Romlin gripping Desi's arm.

"Crude structure." He shook his head. "Did you know that roof is nothing but crisscrossed logs and dirt, and we have to climb across it to get inside?"

"Thank you for the Pueblo culture lesson."

"I told you to keep quiet." His fingers dug into her flesh.

Desi stifled a cry. Strong for such a pipsqueak. The man couldn't be over five feet five, a few inches taller than she.

They passed a fat metal pipe sticking out of the ground. Ventilation shaft? Beyond the pipe, a pair of those beehive-shaped adobe ovens squatted. Heat emanated from them.

At the kiva, wooden rungs made hand- and footholds for climbing to the apex of the mound. Karen and her guard went first and disappeared through the open hatch at the top. Romlin motioned for Tony to go next.

Tony took a step forward and winced. "Hope you've got all day, because I'm not moving too fast." Sweat beaded his forehead.

Desi's heart twisted. "Let me help him."

"Sure you can help." Romlin wrenched her arm, and she yelped. "Move along, Lucano. Ms. Jacobs will let you know if you're not progressing fast enough."

Tony's stare could have incinerated stone. Then he turned and began the climb.

The sun baked down on Desi's head as they waited. Romlin growled something nasty under his breath, and his hold tightened.

"Twist my arm again —" she glared at him — "and I'll mash my heel onto those pretty Gucci loafers on your dainty little feet."

The pseudopreacher's mouth flopped open. His face went red, and he flung her at the kiva. "You next. Shove Lucano down the hole if you have to."

Desi climbed. No opportunity to make a run for it with a pair of guns trained at her back. "You're doing fine, hon," she told Tony. "Just a little farther."

Her answer was a pain-filled grunt. She hurt just watching him. He reached the apex and slowly descended into the opening at the top. When his head disappeared, Desi followed down a sturdy ladder. The air cooled as she descended. Twenty rungs. This was one deep hole in the sandbox. Finally, her feet touched bottom.

She edged toward Tony. Mr. Goon eyed them, cradling his gun. Romlin and the pilot reached bottom, and the pilot jabbed his gun at Tony, making him back away from her. She moved to go with him, but Romlin stepped between them. She glared at him. "Where's Karen?"

He grinned. "You'll join her in a moment." He walked away. Her gaze followed him to a door in the curved wall. He entered and closed it behind him.

Desi looked around. Four fat wooden pillars supported a roof of logs spaced at regular intervals. The gaps were filled in with shaved poles chinked with adobe. At the base of each pillar lay a long stone slab, and toward the head of each, a deep gouge in one side of the rock led to a cavernous clay bowl on the floor. Chills snaked through Desi's middle.

For catching the blood from the severed jugular of the sacrifice.

Twenty-Two

Don't think. Look at other things. Tony has a plan. He won't let . . . Desi gulped and tore her gaze from the altars.

Lamps flickered at intervals on the wall. A continuous bench ringed the perimeter, and on the bench, many red-robed figures sat silent. They passed a clay jar from one to another and sipped. The air smelled of earth and vaguely of rot.

Cloth rustled, and a huge figure flowed toward her. Jabba the Hutt in a red gown.

Hamilton Gordon beamed. "Welcome, my dear. I'm so happy this moment has come. The other young lady has gone to be prepared. The acolytes will escort you to join her."

A pair of women appeared beside her. One of them was built like a linebacker. Desi took a second look at the other one. "Hope?"

The ponytail was gone, and the woman's

unbound blond hair draped her shoulders. She smiled, perfect white teeth gleaming. "Isn't this exciting? Such an honor for you." The two women tugged Desi toward another door she hadn't noticed before.

"But —" She looked back over her shoulder.

Tony took a stride in her direction. "Wait just one —" Goon jabbed him in the side with the gun. Tony gasped and subsided.

Gordon lumbered over to him. "You will not disrupt the service. To you the honor of sacrifice has not been given. We had hoped you would be the ram for our sacrament, but your injuries have disqualified you, and we've found another. Watch in silence and learn. Perhaps you will become enlightened." He nodded toward the armed men. "Bind the unbeliever and put him with the other. And get those guns out of here. This place is for reverence, not violence."

Desi's gaze sought and found Tony's. Then she was pushed inside the antechamber, and the door separated them. In the center of the rectangular anteroom sat a pair of large metal tubs filled with steamy water. A soft coo turned her attention to the far end of the chamber.

Karen, eyes glassy, held a baby. Though she was clearly drugged, a smile lit her face.

"It's Adam. I never thought I'd see him again."

Desi glared at the red-robed women. "How did you get the baby? What have you done with Max and her family?"

"Who's Max?" Hope moved between her and Karen. "We found the little lamb at home, just as Ham's Inner Witness said." She glanced toward the mother cuddling her child and then beamed at Desi. "So perfect." The young woman stepped away and offered Karen the water jar.

"Don't drink any more of that." Desi charged forward, but the linebacker tackled her, and they hit the dirt. Ms. Linebacker twisted one arm behind Desi's back and rested a knee on her wrist. Hot spikes radiated up to Desi's shoulder, and her hand began to go numb.

"Be calm." Linebacker's voice was as dainty as her build was sturdy. She lifted Desi to her feet like she were no more than a puppet. "Drink!" She thrust a jar at her. Under her glare, Desi took the ceramic pot and sipped. The flavor on her tongue was wonderful, fruity.

"Swallow!" Linebacker stepped toward her.

Desi let the drops slide down her throat. Probably not enough to turn her gaga, but the moisture whetted her appetite for more. It had been a dry day.

"You will bathe now." Linebacker motioned toward the tubs.

Nursing a stiff shoulder, Desi disrobed and eased into the water. Linebacker nodded approval. Karen slipped into the other tub with Adam. "Mommy's glad to see you." She leaned him back on the water, supporting his head, and tickled his bare belly. Adam burbled and kicked, splashing water onto Karen's chin. She laughed and lifted him and kissed his fat tummy.

Desi's heart filled with a strange ache. A wholesome envy, if such a thing were possible.

Hope handed Desi a cake of pink soap. Desi put her palm over the bar and curled her fingers around the cult member's hand. "Do you have any idea what you're doing?"

The young woman canted her head, eyes wide and innocent. No, not innocent. Vague. This one was on the joy juice, too. Desi glanced at Linebacker. Not that one.

Hope pulled her hand away. "There's nothing to fear. You'll be blessed above all others in heaven because you gave your health and vigor to us who remain behind."

"Wash," Linebacker said.

Desi scowled, but drew the soap over the

dirt and bruises that covered her skin. The warm water mellowed her weary bones and muscles. More hot water poured into the tub caressed her abrasions. Her body went slack, and her head began to go woozy. No way could she take another drink out of that water pot. The stuff was too potent.

"Relax." Hope's voice tickled her ear from behind. The woman massaged Desi's scalp with warm oil. Linebacker put the jar to Desi's lips. She took in a mouthful, then sank her chin into the bathwater and released the toxic moisture her dry throat ached to swallow.

The bath ended too soon. Reprieve over. She got out and was given a soft towel. She dried herself in slow, dreamy movements. Was she convincing as a drugged person? Too bad only part of it was an act. She *had* to clear her head.

Desi took in deep breaths, while Hope rubbed more oil into her hands, her feet, her face and neck, then gave her a white robe. Not as soft as the towels, but it covered her everywhere except where the oil glistened on her skin.

Karen stood beside her, face slack, dressed the same as Desi. Hope placed a naked sleeping baby into Karen's arms and gave her another drink. Linebacker came to Desi and lifted the pot to her lips. She let the cool moisture enter her mouth, but held it there. When the red-robed women went to the door, Desi wiped her lips with her sleeve and spit the water onto it.

They were led out into the round room. A spicy odor came from incense burning on a small table that now sat in the center of the room under the ladder. Other items sat on the table — the knives missing from the museum and the ceremonial bowl used for drinking the blood of the slain sacrifice. Desi's mouth lost what moisture remained.

"Our lambs are lovely, aren't they?" Hamilton Gordon drew Desi and Karen with the baby to the center of the room. Others in red robes swirled around them, touching, smiling, congratulating. Mostly women. Few young. Some with ravages of illness on their faces.

Desi backed away, shaking her head. "Wait one minute. What do you get out of this?"

The Red Robes stared at her, eyes unfocused.

Gordon took her hands. "Haven't you understood? We lead half-lives here on earth. A physical debility keeps us from wholeness. Even young Hope. She just found out her leukemia is back. But you —" he squeezed her hands — "are the picture of vitality." He leaned closer. "I had meant for you to handle my business affairs, but Reverend Romlin convinced me that this is the proper course for our relationship. You do see the beauty, the symmetry? I told you we would become one, and when we do, I shall receive health, and you will achieve glory unspeakable."

Desi's stomach churned.

Gordon turned toward his motley congregation. "Did you know that this morning my dear cousin proved herself by the ancient ways and is doubly worthy of honor?" Heads shook. "The Reverend tells me she climbed the initiation ladder. He found her on the exalted perch."

"Initiation ladder? I was trying to get out of the canyon."

Gordon chuckled. "The ladder was never intended as a way out. When the Ancient Ones made the grooves in the rock face, the canyon was open. Where was the need? No, the ladder tested the courage of young warriors, but you were supposed to bring a rope to let yourself down. Good thing we had a helicopter." He beamed.

"I'm supposed to say thank you?" She gazed around, bile rising. "You think drinking the blood and eating the flesh of another mere mortal will get you anything but a murder conviction? You don't need to partake of any body and blood except the Spirit of the Lord Je—"

"I don't believe our lamb is properly prepared." Romlin stepped into the room from the other chamber. He wore a black robe with a white stole. Very ministerial. His silver gaze glittered. "If it does not stop using its mouth as I instructed it some time ago, it will regret the consequences to someone it cares about."

A goon followed Romlin, shoving Tony ahead of him. Tony's hands were behind his back and one shoulder drooped. White edged his compressed lips. Then the pilot came out pulling another bound man, this one dressed in a white robe. Desi's eyes widened. Brent!

"Karen!" The young man struggled against his captor, and the pilot slugged him in the mouth. He reeled, but kept his feet. Blood trickled down his chin and stained his robe. Bruises already marred one side of Brent's face.

Gordon spluttered. "Reverend Romlin, I must protest this abuse of our ram."

Everyone ignored him.

Brent stared at his wife. Karen stared back. She mouthed his name and then looked at her feet, face pale, clutching Adam to her chest.

Desi narrowed her eyes at Romlin. “Why did you grab Brent? What have you done with Max and her family?”

The Reverend lifted white brows. “I don’t know any Max.”

“This fake preacher —” Brent jerked his chin at Romlin — “and his bully boys pounced on me and Adam this afternoon as soon as we got home from the airport. With my name cleared, I flew out last night to get the little guy and came back today.”

Romlin smiled. “That sums the matter up well. We brought the baby’s father here to fulfill Ham’s need for a sacrificial ram. However, Mr. Webb has been uncooperative about taking his medicine, which makes this whole matter more unpleasant for him.”

Brent’s eyes went bleak. “I thought Adam would be safe after we heard . . . well, you know.” He nodded at his drooping wife.

Desi’s heart ached. Pete was reported dead, and Karen had no idea. But what did it matter if none of them got out of here alive? Karen would never be found. Brent and the baby would disappear — little Adam’s life cut off before he ever had a chance to live. Pete Cheama’s family *would* be destroyed, just like he dreamed. And Max and Jo would live in agony, never knowing what happened to any of them.

Fury choked Desi. "In the name of Jesus, no!"

Everyone turned to stare at her. The color washed from Romlin's face. Gordon staggered backward, mouth agape.

Tony smiled. "You go, babe."

Romlin growled, spittle showing at the edges of his mouth. "Let's get this done. Now!" He strode to the central table where the knives lay.

"But *Archer.*" Gordon's whine grated Desi's raw nerves "This is supposed to be a solemn celebration. Not rushed. We don't want to diminish the efficacy of the sacrament."

"Sit. Down."

At the snarled command, Gordon sniffled, backed away, and sat on the bench.

Romlin's gaze traveled the room. "Sit. All of you." The other Red Robes found places.

The Reverend closed his eyes and took deep breaths. His face settled into a mask of calm. "That's better." He opened his eyes and shook himself, as if emerging from a bad dream. His stare bored in on Desi. Karen cowered against her, and the baby whimpered in his sleep.

Romlin picked up a knife, then looked toward the room where he had changed clothes. "Mayburn, help Jack and George bind the sacrifices to the altars."

Gordon's lanky assistant stepped out of the anteroom, and Tony jerked.

"What the — ? You're behind bars."

Gordon leaped up. "What are you doing here? Haven't you caused enough trouble?"

Mayburn pushed his glasses up on his nose. "Bail, my friends. My true boss —" he nodded at Romlin — "is a wealthy man."

Gordon spluttered. "Reverend Romlin, what have you to do with this . . . this thief! He embezzled money from Gordon Corp. He —"

"Obtained the sacred instruments." Romlin lifted the knife in his hand. "Didn't he deserve extra compensation?"

Gordon's jowls trembled. "I don't know. It doesn't seem . . ."

"All is well." The Reverend held out the drinking pot, a saccharine smile twisting his features. "Regain your inner peace, and prepare yourself for the ceremony."

Gordon took the jar. "Yes, of course. You have your eye on the important thing, as usual." He gulped from the container.

Romlin guided the big man toward a spot on the bench.

Tony glared at Mayburn. "You and Romlin don't believe any of this, but you're going along for kicks? You're sicker than I thought."

Mayburn's cold smile stretched his lips. "I've seen a lot, but never watched anyone eaten. Besides —" his voice dropped to a whisper Desi had to strain to hear — "Gordon's going to sign a check for 2 million dollars to Inner Witness Ministries after the ceremony's over. Then we bulldoze this place with everyone inside, and no one ever knows what happened to any of you."

Romlin hustled up and turned savage eyes on his hired help. "Be quiet, or you can stay down here, too."

Mayburn paled and faded into the shadows.

Nostrils flaring, the Reverend turned toward the waiting Red Robes and lifted his arms. "Are you ready to receive the Feast of the Lamb, a sacrament of healing for your flesh and exaltation of the spirit?"

The Red Robes answered as one. "We are!"

"Hold it a second!" Everyone looked at Tony. "A last request. Romlin, whatever your beliefs, or *lack* of them, you're licensed to perform marriages." He turned his gaze on Desi. "Will you marry me, sweetheart?"

Desi's heart stuck in her throat, and heat zinged to her toes. Better than any drug.

"You *want* to marry me? I wondered . . . I mean, I didn't know . . ." Joy sang in her veins. She could be dead meat — literally — in a few minutes, but right now she wanted to dance.

Tony smiled. "I've always wanted to marry you. I was waiting to ask until I thought you'd say yes. Guess this is my last chance to find out."

"You drive me nuts sometimes, Lucano, but I can't imagine a future without you. Yes, I'll marry you. Only —" she looked at a gaping Romlin, and her joy dimmed — "he's lower than a rat's toenail. I don't want him performing the ceremony."

Romlin moved forward, knife in hand. "Good, because I'm not going to."

Gordon cleared his throat and rose, blinking glazed eyes. "Reverend Romlin, you are a minister able to perform all manner of sacred rites." He nodded toward Desi. "As she is prepared to give her all to us, the least we can do is grant her happiness in her last earthly moments. Any less would dishonor the Feast."

Romlin uttered a crude word under his breath. "As you wish, Ham." He made a tiny bow toward the big contributor, then scowled at Desi and Tony. "But it's going to be the quickest wedding in history."

Desi glared back. "I don't want —"

"It's okay, hon," Tony said. "We watched *The African Queen* together a couple weeks ago. Remember? Humphrey Bogart and Katherine Hepburn didn't mind that a Nazi navy captain performed their ceremony."

"You paid attention? I thought you slept through half of it in my dad's easy chair."

"I didn't miss the ending." He sent her a lopsided grin.

Desi expelled a long breath. "Okay, you've got yourself a wife, Mr. Lucano."

Tony stepped up beside her, and no one stopped him. "I'm honored, Mrs. Lucano-to-be."

Desi motioned Karen to come forward. "You can be my bridesmaid." The woman edged toward her, bewildered comprehension dawning on her face. Tony nodded toward Brent. He hurried to stand beside his wife, battered face fixed on her and the baby. He said her name. She looked down, biting her lip, but her body swayed toward him.

Archer Romlin glowered and ground out the words. "Dearly beloved —"

"Could you put down the weapon while you marry us?" Desi pointed to his hand.

Romlin flushed, but laid the knife on the table. He jerked his chin at Desi. "Not another word from you except *I do.*" He turned a glare on Tony. "It's tempting to let you both live so you have to live with *her.*" He started the ceremony again.

The words were devoid of warmth or originality, but Tony gazed into her face like the hosts of heaven were their guests, and the Lord Himself performed their union. Desi's heart did more amazing acrobatics than when she clung for dear life to the Tate Gallery wall. Her smile hurt wonderfully.

Tony's "I do" held more conviction than an umpire making a call at a Sox game. Oh, boy, she was even starting to *think* like him.

Her turn now, but her throat closed up. "I do." The words squeaked out.

"You may kiss the bride," Romlin snarled.

Tony stared down at her, hands trapped behind his back, eyes sad and strong. She went up on her bare toes. He leaned toward her. Their lips touched, held, sealed.

People began to cough. Odd reaction. Weeping would be good. More coughing. An acrid stench permeated the room and grew stronger.

Desi pulled away from Tony. Water poured from her eyes. She coughed. His chest heaved, and he wheezed a moan.

"The . . . cavalry." He choked. "Knife. Untie."

She stared around, but could see little from the haze filling the room and the tears clouding her vision. Hacking, she headed for a dark blob she thought was the table. Her toe found the leg. She gritted her teeth and groped around the top. Yes, here. Her hands closed on the knife. Ouch! Wrong end. She found Tony and did her best to slice his bonds without slicing him.

A stampede toward the ladder began.

"Brent! Where are you?"

"Here." The voice came from nearby.

She grabbed him and cut his ropes. "Take . . . Karen and Adam."

"I've got them . . . and I'm . . . not letting go." The little huddle of coughing bodies disappeared into the murk.

A deep rumble began outside the kiva. The ground shook. Dirt fell.

"Mrs. Lucano?" Tony's voice carried over the bedlam.

She couldn't find him in the murk. Bodies bumped her and thrust her into the wall. The roar grew louder. Daylight poured down as the roof hatch opened and people poured out. Visibility improved, but the roar became an earsplitting din.

Desi edged around the kiva wall. Her foot hit something soft. She knelt and found a body, breathing but unconscious. Someone trampled in the stampede to get out.

Dark-suited figures in face masks clambered into the kiva. A pair of them grabbed a staggering figure, who gave another hoarse call. "Mrs. Lucano!"

"Help! Over here." Desi went into a coughing fit.

Several of the masks headed her direction. The air continued to clear, but the burning in Desi's lungs went on. Her eyes streamed tears.

Dark figures reached her. One tapped her on the shoulder and pointed toward the ladder. The other two hefted the unconscious person. Desi darted for fresh air. She reached the bottom of the ladder as one of the rescuers pushed Tony out the opening. Desi followed. That husband of hers wasn't going to get far without her by his side.

Her head popped out into glaring sunlight and pristine desert air. She lunged out the hole, then tumbled and rolled down the side of the kiva onto the hot sand. Spitting grit, she sat up.

Mirage! She had to be seeing things. Desi wiped her eyes. Holy cow!

FBI SWAT swarmed the grounds in their labeled flak jackets, and the Air Force circled in helicopters. Law enforcement ATVs surrounded the kiva. A man she recognized as Officer Swamp Eyes of the APD snapped cuffs on the hand-bandaged goon. And there was Sergeant Seciwa of the tribal police in hot pursuit of a fleeing Archer Romlin.

Oooh! Great tackle!

What about her husband and her friends? There!

Karen and Brent clung together, kissing each other's faces and clutching a wailing Adam between them. Poor little guy, that tear gas had to be hard on him. Desi's heart expanded, and tears came that had nothing to do with toxic fumes. A family with a chance for a new start.

But where was *her* new start?

Desi stood, brushed off her robe, and scanned the area. A handcuffed Hamilton Gordon was led away, blubbering, along with other red-robed figures and a pasty-faced Chris Mayburn. Men in masks emerged from the kiva, carrying a limp Hope between them. Still no Tony.

A helicopter touched down nearby, and Agent Ortiz hopped out. She waved at Desi and approached. A second figure leaped from the aircraft, red hair flying as she raced toward her daughter and family. They pulled Jo into the group hug.

Desi's chest filled. If she got any happier,

she'd pop.

Agent Ortiz stopped in front of her. "Great to see you made it through another tight spot."

"Where did all the cavalry come from? And how did Jo get in on it?"

Ortiz smiled toward the family group swaying in each other's arms. "We took Jo into protective custody after Brent and Adam disappeared. Looked like someone was after the whole family. Then our researcher figured out the location of the O'Keeffe painting around the same time as this distress signal started blipping out of the desert from the same spot. Fair bet, we'd find you two and maybe the other missing people. When Jo got wind we were ready to move in, she wasn't about to be left behind."

Desi chuckled. "I suppose not. She'd probably have grown wings and flown out here on her own. But what's this about a distress signal?"

"From that helicopter." Ortiz pointed toward Romlin's chopper next to the bulldozer.

"Ohhhh." Desi pictured Tony falling between the front seats almost into the control panel. Close enough to flip a switch. Clever man. But where was he?

"Oh, Mrs. Lucanoooo."

Tony!

"Got to go." Desi waved to Ortiz and darted around the kiva, wheezing as her lungs drained of burning chemical. A man was being carried on a stretcher toward a waiting helicopter.

She ran up to the EMTs. "That's my husband. I'm riding along." She took Tony's good hand — the other was strapped to his side. "Pretty smart, triggering that emergency signal."

Tony winked. "The chopper transmitted our location the whole time we were down in the kiva. Good thing you took your time preparing to be sacrificed."

"Ewww! And we had a wedding ceremony."

His face sobered. "Ah, honey, I wish we were married for real."

"What? Stop this gurney!"

The EMTs continued toward the chopper.

Tony nodded to them. "Do as she says."

"Sir, you need —"

Tony shot them a look, and the technicians stepped back, frowning.

He sighed. "You didn't think about it yet?"

Desi shook her head. Think of what?

"Romlin had a license, but we didn't."

She lowered her head. They weren't married. Her heart fell. "So the marriage proposal was to buy time? That was some dirty trick, Lucano."

"Don't take it like that, sweetheart." He squeezed her hand.

She snatched it away.

"Des, the *proposal* was 110 percent sincere. Just the ceremony was bogus. We can fix that anytime you're ready. And this time we'll do it right."

She studied him. "You weren't making fun by calling me Mrs. Lucano?"

He shook his head. "I love the sound of those words."

"You do want to marry me?"

"I'd cross my heart, but it would hurt too much." He chuckled. "Ah, that did hurt. To paraphrase the most beautiful, outrageous woman I know: You drive me nuts sometimes, Jacobs, but I can't imagine a future without you."

Desi glared at the EMTs. "Let's get this man some medical attention. He has to be able to drop down on one knee with a ring in his hand."

"Des." Tony groaned. "Quit making me laugh. You're killing me here."

"Not hardly, Lucano." She followed his stretcher into the helicopter. "I sentence you to ancient age with me. Just a couple of old codgers rocking on the porch."

"I can live with that."

TWENTY-THREE

The rental car left a trail of dust in its wake as Desi drove up the gravel road toward the country church in rural Minnesota. Ripe brown cornfields alternated with plowed black earth as far as the eye could see.

Tony sat beside her, stiff against the seat. "We're cutting it close, but I'm glad we made it at all."

"We're walking wonders, sweetheart. And seeing Karen back with her family . . ." Desi shook her head, tears pricking her eyes the way they'd done off and on for the last twenty-four hours.

"I'm with you, babe. Being an FBI agent isn't all about the seamy side. Sometimes we get moments like those."

Desi pulled a face. "I can't say I'm thrilled that the Bureau found a document at Gordon's house granting me power of attorney. That's going to be one monster of a mess, especially with him headed for an asylum."

She glanced at her passenger. "And I got an opinion from HJ Securities' legal department. They say that nuts or not, since I'm Ham's closest relative, the paper will probably stand up in court."

Tony shrugged and winced. "You don't have to take the job. The document isn't fully executed until you sign it."

"I'll sign. Family needs to look after each other — even family you wish you didn't have. Besides, I can't stand the thought of any more goofball stuff going on with this man's affairs. There's too much power in that much money. I'll put most of the tasks on my legal department."

"Like you're having them look into purchasing a piece of the desert, mineral rights and all? What about Karen? Doesn't she want a slice of the pie?"

"Doesn't even want to know what she knows. She found her treasure — or rediscovered it. We've agreed to keep our mouths shut. I've got my treasure, too." She fluttered her lashes at him.

He smirked, and they both laughed — though his was more of a wheeze as he clutched his ribs.

They came to the church, and Desi pulled into an almost full parking lot on the far side of the building. She stepped onto gravel and waited for Tony to ease out of the passenger side. Stubborn man wouldn't let anyone help him. Except for his tie. She had to do that this morning.

She joined him as they crunched between cars toward the front walk of the white clapboard church. A square steeple rose tall against a deep blue sky.

Desi took Tony's good arm. "This is so Norman Rockwell. I love it."

He nodded. "Suits Ben. He was so wholesome he put milk and cookies to shame."

"Wait a minute, sweetheart." Desi tugged Tony's sleeve.

He stopped, and she adjusted the lay of his tie and smoothed the knot at his neck.

"You do that great."

"Fix ties?"

"The wife thing."

"Practicing." She frowned. The pinched look at the corners of his lips said he was in pain. "You should have worn your sling."

"Negative, babe. This is about Ben today. I'm not inviting attention to myself."

"Well, don't try any heroics. The minute you need to lie down, we're out of here. The doctor about hog-tied you to the bed when you said you were leaving the hospital without at least an overnight stay. That bruised liver is nothing to fool around with."

"Gotcha, Mom."

Desi narrowed her eyes. "Now I'm your mother? Not hardly. And when we have kids, please remember I'm still not your mother. There's one person you should call mom, and she deserves a medal for putting up with you."

Tony chuckled and winced. "When I called her last night, she said the same thing about you." He shook his head. "You ladies have a mutual admiration society going, so I can see I'm in for it."

"Poor baby." Desi gave the tie a last pat. She went up on tiptoe and kissed his cheek. Well, that was her intention, but he turned his head quicker than thought and caught her on the mouth. A shiver ran through her that had nothing to do with the fall breeze.

He grinned. The lout knew the effect he had on her. She should mess up his hair for fun.

Tony tugged her toward the steps. "Let's go say good-bye to Ben."

In the small foyer, a man in a clerical collar greeted them. "I'm Pastor Bob."

Desi looked up into eyes as kind as the Minnesota prairie was long. "Desiree Jacobs." She shook his hand. Calloused palms. A man who did manual labor as well as spiritual.

Tony offered his left hand. "Anthony Lucano. Ben's supervisor."

Pastor Bob smiled. "I guessed that much. The rest of your squad is here. They've saved you a place toward the front." The man looked at his watch. "We'll start in five minutes."

Desi and Tony moved toward the casket that sat outside the sanctuary doors. A dark-skirted mortuary attendant had begun to close the lid, but she put it back up when she saw them approach. She ducked her head and stepped back.

"They did a good job with him." Tony's voice was hoarse. "Got that 'I can't wait to share a big joke' look spot-on."

Desi didn't answer, just let him squeeze her hand until the bones creaked. She heard a ragged breath fill his lungs, and then he moved with her into the sanctuary. The church was full, and ushers were setting up folding chairs in the back. She and Tony went up the aisle. A break in the heads in one pew led them to the Boston delegation. Hajimoto, Polanski, and Slidell looked up and nodded. No smiles. Tony stood aside, and Desi took the spot beside Valerie Polanski. Tony settled in with the caution of a man twice his age.

The service was solemn and liturgical, but

Pastor Bob's glow of quiet joy made it anything but dry. Tony made a choked noise when the pastor spoke of Ben's personal faith, and Desi looked at him. But the light in his eyes told her all she needed to know. That was a happy sound. Then came a time of reminiscing by family and friends. A sister got up, a brother-in-law, a cousin. Every story brought a ripple of laughter.

Desi glanced up at Tony. The shadows had left his face, and he was smiling. *Thank you, Ben, even now you make him lighten up.*

The pastor called for any more testimonies. Tony eased to his feet. He walked to the front, gaze roaming the congregation. Desi's heart swelled for the peace she read on his face. He turned his attention to Ben's parents on the front pew.

"I'm Tony Lucano, Ben's supervisor with the FBI. I only knew your son a few months, but I'll never forget him. He was an outstanding agent and a good man. We can get a little intense around the office sometimes."

A snicker came from the pew full of agents. Desi covered her mouth and looked down.

"Yes, I know that's an understatement," Tony continued. "And if my squad will please remember their manners, I'll get to the point."

More chuckles, and not just from the agents.

A smile played around Tony's mouth. "Ben knew how to put life into perspective for us. We'd be out on a case, all of us strung tight as piano wire, but he'd say something off the wall, and we'd quit stressing and just do our job."

Ben's mother's head began to nod.

Tony took a step toward the family section. "But I never knew until this moment that he had faith in Jesus Christ. We didn't talk about spiritual things, and when he was killed I . . . well, I blamed myself for neglecting something so vital. This service has been a great comfort to me." He nodded at the pastor, who inclined his head. "But that doesn't mean I haven't learned a lesson about talking important things over with people who matter."

His warm gaze settled on Desi, and her heart melted. She reached for a tissue from her purse.

"That last day . . ." Tony cleared his throat. "That last day, Ben's actions saved my life at the cost of his own. There's a passage of Scripture that says there's no greater love than a man giving his life for another. I wanted you to know —"

"My uncle was a *hero!*" A boy not much

taller than the pew leaped up. "That's what I tell everybody at school."

His parents shushed him and tugged at him to sit down.

Tony motioned the boy forward. "Let him come here."

The kid trotted up to Tony, face bright. No mistaking that this boy was related to Ben, and in more than just the hair color and profile that Desi could see from where she sat. From the few times she'd socialized with the squad, she caught on fast that the towheaded Minnesotan didn't have a shy bone in his body.

Tony offered his hand, and the young man shook it. "You can tell anyone you want that your uncle was a hero."

"Will you be my supervisor when I'm an FBI agent?"

"More likely the director," Polanski stage-whispered.

Tony glared at her. She grinned back.

Ah, Tony, you've got your hands full with this squad. A laugh froze in Desi's throat. She'd let herself forget that Tony was on the fast track upward. He wouldn't be in Boston forever. What did that mean to her? To their relationship?

Boston was her home. She'd lived in that city her whole life. Every memory with her father was there. And the center of her business. Could she give up HJ Securities? Walk away from the legacy Daddy died to give her? The church walls shrank in on her.

But she loved Tony, wanted a future with him, a family.

Her pulse roared in her ears. Words passed over and around her. As if from a distance, she felt Tony settle in beside her again. More words; then the service was over. Desi stood beside Tony, forced her face into neutral, and shuffled out with the group.

Tony took her hand, brow puckered, as they walked across the lawn to the little cemetery at the rear of the church. "What's up?"

She shook her head at his whisper and kept her eyes on the canopied grave site. Her feet halted.

Tony hissed and stopped with her.

Desi looked up at him. "I'm sorry. That was an abrupt stop. It's just that . . ."

"You're thinking about your father's funeral."

"And other things."

"We can leave."

She shook her head. "No, I think the family would like a chance to talk to you over lunch. I'll be fine."

They went on, Tony hovering close like

she was the wounded one. She edged away from him when they stopped with the crowd. A little space to think, that's all she needed.

Pastor Bob began the committal service. Ben's mother hunched over a white handkerchief, and his father kept an arm around her. Next to Desi, the husky agent Hajimoto shifted and bumped her, forcing her to move closer to Tony. She glanced up at him. He stood stiff, chin like a rock. He hurt, but in a way bed rest couldn't help. Behind her, Slidell whispered to someone, Polanski probably, "You buy that next life stuff?" The woman hushed him.

Desi looked down at the thick grass. Dell might be light on social skills, but at least he was asking questions. He might find his answers a lot easier than she was going to find hers.

Forget thinking. Just be here — now — with Tony. She squared her shoulders and tuned in to Pastor Bob.

He finished a reading and closed his prayer book. "We'll miss Ben, and that's why we grieve, but not as those who have no hope." The kind eyes traveled the crowd, and then settled on the immediate family. "If Ben had been asked about it, I doubt he would have chosen to go at the time and in the way he did, but I'll never forget what he said when he announced to the church that he was leaving the family farm and heading for Quantico to become an FBI agent. We were so proud of him that day and still are today."

Ben's mother's head came up, and the pastor smiled at her. "Ben said, 'I've got a whole trunkful of memories to pack up and take with me. So this move isn't about leaving my world behind. It's about stepping into a new one.' That's what Ben did last week. But he won't come home to visit. We'll go to him, and you'd better believe he'll have an eternal stockpile of jokes to keep us from taking ourselves too seriously."

A cool breeze whispered around Desi, and tree leaves tinted with gold rustled together. The air smelled of rich soil. A beautiful place Ben had called home, but he left for a higher calling.

You're talking to me, aren't You, Lord?

She touched Tony's arm. He slid it around her waist and pulled her close. She wasn't married to Boston, but she would be married to this man who made her heart trip over itself like a lovesick duck with two left feet. The move would be a wrench when the time came. And as a wife, hopefully someday a mother, her role with HJ Securities would change . . . eventually. But it wasn't etched in stone that the company had to be headquartered in Boston. The headquarters could go wherever the head went.

Too simple. Too obvious. Which is why she hadn't seen the path in front of her feet.

And there was something else she needed to do. She hadn't called Max yet to let her know what she'd decided about visiting Dean in prison.

The service ended and people dispersed, quietly talking, toward the church for lunch in the basement. Desi stayed where she was. Tony questioned her with his eyes. She smiled and pulled out her cell phone. She punched in Max's number.

"Hey, girlfriend," she said when Max answered.

"Hey, yourself. When are you comin' home so I can squeeze the stuffin' out of you for all you did for my family?"

"Tony and I'll be back in Boston tomorrow. Before then, would you do me a favor?"

"Girl, I'll lie down across a mud puddle and let you use me as a bridge. What's up?"

"Tell Dean I'm coming to visit him."

"Oh, Des." Max started to cry. "You have no idea how much that will help."

"It'll help me, too. Gotta go now. A certain FBI agent has this gooey look on his face." She put the phone away.

"*Gooey* look?" His eyebrows climbed toward his hairline.

"Yeah, like you might kind of like me or something."

"Woman, you're delusional." He tickled her under the chin. "Guess I'll have to try harder to show you how I feel."

"Oh, yeah, and how would you go about that?"

"How about I start by keeping my word?"

"What promise is that?"

He grinned. "I hereby place myself on the shopping altar, so we can look for that rock to put on your finger. I want the world to know that Desiree Jacobs is all mine. The future Mrs. Lucano."

Desi took his arm, and they strolled toward the church building. "How far in the future would that event be, Mr. Lucano?"

"Not one second longer than it takes you to put together a wedding that'll make your father shout in glory."

She couldn't hold back the grin. "Shouldn't take long, hon. I'm a Jacobs, remember? We get things done."

"Amen to that, sweetheart." Tony chuckled, winced, then leaned in to cover her lips with his.

Dear Reader,

Storytelling is an ancient art common to every culture and time period. Stories have unmatched ability to touch the human spirit for good or ill, to convey truth or spread deception. Have you ever been moved or changed by a well-told tale? Why do some stories stick with us longer than others? Do they touch on something so integral to our nature that we cannot forget them?

Jesus knew the power of story. In fact, Scripture says He didn't speak to people without using stories to convey His meaning.

In the *aha!* moments of writing *Reluctant Runaway,* I broke new ground in my understanding of the basics of faith and the battle for the human soul in the unseen realm. Plus, I understood afresh the unique claim of Christianity: that God Himself became a man, the Christ. Not simply a good person or a wise teacher or a miracle-working prophet, as some belief systems claim, but fully human and fully God. Then He willingly paid the ultimate price to purchase mankind out of slavery to sin and Satan. Without the understanding that Jesus is the Christ, there is no salvation. Christianity is that simple and that mind-boggling, and there is no alternate method to approach God, except through His own redeeming sacrifice.

I'm delighted that you joined Desi and Tony for their second outing in the To Catch a Thief series. I hope their adventure offered thrills and entertainment. More than that, I hope you take away fresh insights that will enrich your life. Their next adventure, *Reluctant Smuggler,* takes Desi and Tony south of the border in pursuit of thieves and killers involved in a deadly antiquities-for-drugs scheme.

I love to hear from readers. E-mail me at jnelson@jillelizabethnelson.com or visit me online at www.jillelizabethnelson.com. My Stealth and Wealth page features a contest for a signed copy of *Reluctant Runaway,* and my contact page gives you an opportunity to sign up for my newsletter.

Jill
www.jillelizabethnelson.com

READER'S GUIDE

1. Desi and Tony have jobs that carry them into danger. Tony struggles to balance his need to know that Desi is safe with his admiration for her just the way she is. Do you think this is a common conflict for people in a relationship with those who have high-risk careers, such as police officers, firefighters, or soldiers? Have you ever felt anxiety about your spouse because of a job? What coping skills would be of help in such a situation? Is this anxiety higher for men in relationships with women who have high-risk careers? Why or why not?
2. Communication is a critical factor in a healthy relationship. Desi feels shut out when Tony shies away from personal subjects. Is her feeling justified? Why does Tony prefer not to talk about himself? Should we always expect our loved ones to tell us everything? Or are there times

when a matter should remain private? If so, how do we know when silence is a good thing? Think of examples on either side of the communication issue, and share your experiences.

3. Desi fears that Tony's career will take him away from her. In this fast-paced world, both men and women often work outside the home — sometimes by economic necessity, sometimes by choice. How can Christian couples balance the demands of the job with the needs of their families? What are *your* priorities in regard to faith, family, and work? How did you arrive at those priorities, and how well do you live by them?

4. Do you believe that unseen spiritual forces affect our lives and the lives of those in our families as a result of our attitudes and actions? Why or why not? If yes, how should Christians go about breaking the power of evil forces that would invade their lives and the lives of loved ones? Read Ephesians 6:10–12, and discuss what these verses have to say about this issue.

5. Karen Webb is a new Christian, a true

believer. Is it easy for the young in the Lord to get sucked off track before they become established in their faith? How can more mature believers nurture and protect babes in Christ?

6. More and more often, mental illness is found to have a biological and treatable cause — as in the case of postpartum depression like Karen had. How can the church educate itself to deal with often misunderstood mental and emotional conditions with compassion, wisdom, and grace?

7. Max says her sister Jo has tried lots of "faddy spiritualities." Desi answers that Jo is an example of a person who is always learning but never coming to know the truth. Read 2 Timothy 3:7. What does this mean? Do you know anyone like Jo? Brainstorm strategies for reaching this type of person.

8. What is the difference between a cult and a religion? Which definition does Reverend Archer Romlin's movement fit the best, or does it contain elements of both? A religion implies a degree of acceptance and respectability, which a cult does not have.

Does Romlin deliberately capitalize on similarities to Christianity in order to lend credibility to his brand of toxic faith? Romlin's movement has a public face masking a sinister private inner circle. Which definition does the private inner circle fit?

9. Pete Cheama credits his tribal beliefs with "saving" him and regards Christianity as an evil system forced on his people. Why might he have come to that conclusion? How can Christians answer those who see Christianity as either harmful or just another option among many?

10. Snake Bonney and his motorcycle gang live in blatant sin and rebellion. They have no illusions about themselves as either respectable or righteous. Would Jesus go to Snake's house for supper? How can we as individuals and as church bodies reach out to the Snake Bonneys of the world and show them God as He is, not as religious legalism has portrayed Him?

11. Chris Mayburn operates like his "real boss," Archer Romlin — public respectability, private corruption. What motive do they share? What further motive does

Mayburn voice for going along with the ritual in the kiva? Are there people who enjoy evil for its own sake? What makes people this way, or do they choose this path? Have you ever had to deal with someone like this? How did you do so?

12. Desperation drives people to justify doing the unthinkable. What "theology" does Hamilton Gordon concoct to make it right and even noble to kill and eat human flesh? Does this approach bear any resemblance to the mindset that glorifies suicide bombing? What is a Christian's response to such ideologies?

13. What does the Bible teach about the consequences of pivotal choices on our lives and future generations? Give Scripture verses and biblical examples. Discuss the choice that Max makes, which negates the "family curse" in her life. Do you think this choice will carry down positively in future generations? Would her choice necessarily be the right one for everybody in a similar situation? Why or why not? What choices do Desi and Tony make in the scene outside the Georgia O'Keeffe Museum in order to stop evil from wreaking more havoc in the new generation they

hope to start together? Have you ever felt as though your family bore a "family curse"? How has God helped you to overcome that struggle?

ABOUT THE AUTHOR

Jill Elizabeth Nelson takes art seriously — when she's not having fun with it, that is. The To Catch a Thief series combines her love of the written word with her love of other art forms. She's thrilled if the adventures that spill from her imagination can raise awareness about art theft — deemed "a looming criminal enterprise" by the FBI. Jill and her husband, Doug, have four children and live in Minnesota.

The employees of Thorndike Press hope you have enjoyed this Large Print book. All our Thorndike, Wheeler, and Kennebec Large Print titles are designed for easy reading, and all our books are made to last. Other Thorndike Press Large Print books are available at your library, through selected bookstores, or directly from us.

For information about titles, please call:

(800) 223-1244

or visit our Web site at:

http://gale.cengage.com/thorndike

To share your comments, please write:

Publisher
Thorndike Press
295 Kennedy Memorial Drive
Waterville, ME 04901

P
LP

C.P.C. REGIONAL LIBRARY
3 4208 20235 4709